K. D. CAPENER

HIDDEN
BY
THESE
WALLS

Copyright © 2025 by K. D. Capener

All rights reserved. No part of this publication may be reproduced, distributed, or transmitted in any form or by any means, including photocopying, recording, or other electronic or mechanical methods, without the prior written permission of the publisher, except as permitted by U.S. copyright law. For permission requests, contact authorkdcapener@gmail.com.

Published by Brampton Crescent Books, Layton, Utah, USA

Cover design by Getcovers

ISBN 979-8-9994484-1-5 (paperback)

Library of Congress Control Number: 2025917254

Dear Reader,

Please be advised that this novel contains instances of abuse and alcohol use that can be disturbing. The story was written with the intention of bringing awareness, not to trigger. Life is hard, and facing our trials with courage, no matter what they may be, is a challenge we all face. No matter what you're up against, please remember there is always hope. Hope for a better future, hope for healing, hope in the humanity of others. There is always someone you can turn to, always someone you can trust. It might be a family member, a teacher, a coach, a neighbor, a co-worker, a school counselor, or a friend. For any who may find themselves in a situation like Libby's, there are resources listed in the back of the book.

K. D. C.

For Danny,
who encouraged me all the way.
You're my favorite.

1
Thursday, March 3, 1988
Late that night

The sleep I craved remained far from my grasp. Slipping into that unconscious state was the only thing that could help me forget this entire dreadful evening. But every time my eyes closed, the terrifying scene played on repeat. Mom's eyes had flashed fire before she came at me, pushing, punching, chasing, screaming. It was yet another episode of "Don't Do Anything Mom Won't Like."

You'd think by now I would have learned not to push my luck with her. How could I get out of this mess I'd created? I sighed and stared at the shadows in my tiny bedroom. A hint of moonlight shone through the flimsy, outdated curtains on my window, illuminating the Duran Duran poster on my closet door. The red block numbers of the alarm clock on my dresser informed me I'd been in bed for an hour, crying, stewing, and completely stressing out.

At least I knew Anna and Edie were safe. I'd taught them what to do when conflict raged in the house: Go straight to the shed out back and stay there until all was quiet. I'd heard the scrape of the shed door on the sidewalk and the faint click of the back door when they came back inside. I knew they'd tiptoed upstairs in slow motion to their bedroom, careful not to wake Mom.

The girls would have stayed warm in the shed even though the temperature had dropped today, leaving the air feeling much more like the frosty Indiana winter we'd left behind than the spring we were anticipating. A couple years ago, when Mom's escalating tirades had necessitated an escape plan for my sisters, I'd placed several old blankets in the shed for cold nights like this. I'm sure if I checked tomorrow, I'd find the blankets piled in a heap in the back corner where the girls huddled together, waiting for the calm after the storm.

The TV was still on in the living room, blaring random conversations intertwined with music. If Mom couldn't hear it, that meant she'd passed out on the couch after downing her "feel-better drink," as she'd named it for my sisters. More and more, Mom claimed she needed to drink, always blaming it on someone or something that upset her. Tonight, that was me. The real reason she drank was a mystery to me. It was one of many things about my mother I didn't understand. Like why she erupted over every little thing and why she hid in her bedroom for hours on end.

I rubbed my hand over my aching ribs glad I'd had the sense to stow some aspirin in my backpack for times like this. I hated sleeping on my back, but there was no choice tonight. I'd be sore at school tomorrow, that's for sure, but hopefully there'd be no bruises to cover up. The thought of school reminded me that tomorrow was Friday, and while most people were excited about that, I had become conditioned to hate the last day of the school week. Maybe if I ever had weekend plans with friends, parties to attend, games or dances at school, I'd love it. But for now, Fridays were a jail sentence, two days of confinement doing the same old boring things I always did: cooking, cleaning, laundry, and of course, walking on eggshells around Mom, trying not to set her off.

The room felt chilly, so I pulled the faded pink quilt up under my chin. Grandma had made it for me when I was four years old, and it was showing its age. For a second, I smelled roses and glimpsed a thick, dark ponytail being tossed over the shoulder of a smiling, middle-aged woman. The memory slipped away as quickly as it came. What would our lives look like now if Grandma was still alive? Would we still be living in this house with her or would Mom and I have moved out when Mom married Nolan? Nolan. Although my sisters had regular contact with their father, I never got to see him, so why think of him? I shook my head, frustrated by the speculation that didn't matter anyway. Sometimes though, I missed Nolan as much as I missed Grandma. My memories of both were happy ones. Too bad it hadn't lasted.

Tears clouded my already dim vision, and a lone teardrop rolled toward my ear. I thought I was all cried out. Apparently not. It wasn't rare for me to have a pity party after a conflict with Mom, but only in a safe place like my bed. Another tear dropped as I pondered the deep hole I'd dug for myself. I don't know what I'd been thinking at the store. I knew applying for the job wasn't a good idea, but the thought of having some freedom, some say in my life, had propelled me forward. For once, I acted on what *I* wanted. I told myself Mom would be happy about the job, just because I wanted it to be that way. Instead, she painfully reminded me I wasn't the one in control. But now I'd been hired, and I desperately wanted to keep the job. I had one day to convince Mom to let me at least try it out. That required some solid arguments, so it was essential I come up with something, and fast.

2
Tuesday, March 1, 1988
Two days earlier

I had just finished drying the last of the dinner plates when Mom walked in the back door. She tossed her purse on the table and lowered herself into one of the cheap metal chairs that surrounded the Formica-topped table. The vinyl-covered cushion breathed a puff of protest from one of the many tears that riddled it.

"What's for dinner?"

"I made pancakes and eggs tonight. I have a lot of homework, and it was quick to make." Besides the fact that breakfast for dinner was my sisters' favorite. "Your plate is in the fridge."

Mom stared blankly at me. "Well?"

Several responses popped into my head, but since none were likely to be received well, I bit my tongue and retrieved Mom's plate and the syrup out of the fridge. I set the syrup next to Mom's elbows where she'd propped them with her head dropped into her hands. I warmed her dinner in the microwave, grateful Mom had finally splurged on one. I think she'd just gotten tired of eating cold dinners, but it benefited the whole family.

"How was your day?" I asked.

"I'm tired, Libby. I'd rather not talk about it right now."

Okay then. I resisted the urge to roll my eyes.

I snagged a fork from the nearest drawer and when the microwave beeped, I placed the warm meal on the table. Mom lifted her head and shook her bangs back into place.

"Where are the girls?"

"They're upstairs cleaning their room. I told them they had to do it before they could watch *Who's the Boss?* tonight. And just so you know, we're getting low on milk and eggs."

Mom groaned and grabbed her purse. She lifted out her wallet with the embroidered flower cover and handed me a five-dollar bill. "Be quick about it."

Ah crap. I should have kept my mouth shut. So much for getting right to my homework. I shoved the money in my pocket and stalked through the living room to the front door. Yanking my denim jacket off the coatrack, I glanced at my watch. Just after six o'clock. If I hurried, I could be back before it got dark.

I lifted the collar of my jacket and shut the front door behind me, giving it an extra tug to make sure it closed tight. It had been hanging a little crooked lately. Probably needed the hinges tightened. Dusk had settled in and with it came cooler temperatures. The breeze had an icy edge to it that sent a shiver down my back. It felt like rain was coming.

I kept a quick pace as I walked down the street, my mind on the essay I needed to write for my World Civilizations class. It wasn't due until next Friday, but I wanted to finish it early. I hated procrastinating. I passed Buckley Park, where the towering trees blocked what little sunlight was left. A young mother pushed her whining toddler in a stroller, away from the playground. Little League games had just finished for the day, and families gathered their belongings and headed to the parking lot.

At the end of the next block, I turned the corner and saw the welcoming lights of Pop's Market shining up ahead. The sign on the roof displayed the store name in red block letters. In fancy script below the name, it pronounced Pop's as Buckley's choice for over 40 years. My mom's choice was usually SaveMart, because it was closer to her work and a little less expensive than Pop's. But Pop's was closer, so it worked in a pinch. As I neared the glass doors, a flash of red caught my eye. A "Help Wanted" sign read: Part-time Stocker. Apply Within!

Ooh, to have my own spending money! Mom always complained about how much it cost to feed and clothe us. A job would also get me out of this boring rut of a life I led. I pondered what Mom might say if I told her I got a job. *Ha! Who are you kidding, Libby?* Chances were high she wouldn't take it well. But now the idea had wiggled its way into my head, and I couldn't stop thinking about it. I wasn't used to making decisions like this for myself. Was it worth making Mom upset?

Business was pretty slow tonight. I bypassed the candy aisle and headed to the dairy section at the back. A young mother bounced her drooling baby in one arm, while she held a red basket in the other. She gave me a tired smile.

I grabbed the eggs and milk while the idea tumbled around in my head. Did I dare apply? I felt capable enough. An exhilarating tickle of freedom filled my chest, and I made up my mind. I'd ask for an application. I just needed to summon up enough courage.

At the register, the middle-aged cashier, whose name tag said "Rosie," wore a serious expression. Her lips lifted in a tight smile that I guessed was supposed to be welcoming. She rang me up while I fidgeted and I handed her the crumpled bill. She handed me my change and the receipt without even looking at me. "Have a nice day."

"Wait." I took a deep breath.

Rosie's eyebrows raised slightly behind her oversized glasses. "Yes?"

"Um...I want to apply for the stocker position." I pocketed the change and grabbed the sack.

"You'll have to ask over there." Rosie pointed in the direction of the customer service desk, then turned her attention to the elderly man standing next in line.

I took a deep breath. *Come on, Libby. You can do this. It's not that hard.*

My heart pounded in protest against my ribs.

Mom's not going to like this. But... you can't change anything if you don't try! My thoughts played tug-of-war. Negative. Positive. Back and forth.

No one was at the front desk, so I glanced back at Rosie and waited. This was nuts. I was nuts. Rosie finished her transaction and looked my way.

"Jerri must be in the back. I'll call her up."

I nodded, my hands clenching the paper sack. Rosie picked up the black phone receiver next to the register and pressed a few buttons. I couldn't hear what she said.

My stomach rolled, like when I had to give a presentation at school. My shirt was damp with sweat. *I'll count to twenty. Then I'm out of here.*

Just as I got to seventeen, a tall woman with braided, dirty blonde hair came to the desk. She had crinkly, happy eyes and she walked with a slight limp. "Hi, I'm Jerri. What can I help you with?"

The words practically fell out of my mouth. "I want to apply for the job." I pointed at the sign on the door.

Jerri's eyes widened. "How old are you? You have to be at least sixteen."

"Oh, I turned sixteen in the fall," I said. Did I look younger than that to her?

"Alrighty," she said after a short pause. "The job is about fifteen hours a week. I'm flexible on the time of day it's done. I just can't keep stocking. I'm getting behind on my own job since Rudy quit."

She ducked behind the desk, then stood with an application and a pen in hand. She seemed curious about me for some reason, and I felt her eyes on me as I wrote in my name, date of birth and address. No past employment, so that section stayed empty. I signed my name and pushed the application across the counter.

Jerri's green eyes scanned over it. "Libby Curtis?" Her eyebrows furrowed and she looked me up and down. I didn't understand her reaction to my name, but before I could really think about it, she blinked, then smiled.

"Can you come for an interview on Thursday? Say, 3:30?"

"Sure. School gets out at three."

"Great!" Jerri said, with a wide smile. "My cousin, Linda, will do the interview. She's the big boss."

I nodded my thanks and left the store. My house was six blocks away, so I had plenty of time to think about what I'd just done. I felt a little nauseated. How was I going to tell Mom? Would she even allow me to work? Maybe I could keep it a secret. But no, that wouldn't work. Anna might be able to keep quiet, but there's no way Edie could. My mom worked until six each day. If I wasn't home every day after school to babysit my sisters, Edie was bound to let it slip. Then again, I could have my own money. And some independence. My thoughts bounced around like a ping-pong ball. I was so engrossed in my dilemma, I barely registered that I'd made it to the park.

"Hey, Libby!"

Startled, I turned to see a familiar long-legged boy with a mop of blond hair waving me over to a nearby willow tree that was rippling in the cool breeze. He sat on the grass, tying his shoe, a baseball and mitt beside him. I grinned and hurried over. "Hey, Jake!"

"Whatcha doing?" Jake's smile revealed a mouthful of braces. He grabbed his ball and mitt and stood.

"Oh, my mom sent me to Pop's for a couple things." I held out the bag and he peeked inside.

"Well, nothing exciting there," he said.

"No room in the budget for gummy worms and ice cream. You know that."

Jake's smile wavered. "Yeah. I was just kidding."

"You won't believe what I just did," I said, bouncing on my toes.

"You bought eggs and milk."

I rolled my eyes and shook my head.

"For real, though? No idea. You tell me." He tossed the baseball up and caught it.

I leaned close and whispered, "I applied for a job. I have an interview on Thursday."

"No way! Your mom let you apply for a job?" Jake's mouth dropped open.

"Well...she doesn't know...not yet. I'm crossing my fingers it will be okay."

"Really, Libby?" Jake shook his head, and his hair fell in his eyes. He brushed it aside. "You think she's suddenly going to let you choose for yourself?"

"Oh, come on Jake," I said, my voice hard. "You're the one who's always telling me to fight back, to stand up for myself, to call the cops on her. I finally did *something* and you think it's a bad idea? Give me a break!" I turned toward the sidewalk.

"Libby." Jake reached out and caught my arm. "When I say those things, it's out of frustration for your situation. But I don't know if they're actually good ideas. We both know she'll get back at you somehow."

"Well, it's done now." My spirits deflated like a balloon, and I was nervous again. Jake's words had forced me back to reality. "I won't say anything to her unless I get the job, which isn't likely anyway since I have zero work experience." I didn't like the way my voice wobbled.

"Hey, I'm sorry." Jake squeezed my arm where his hand still rested. "I know I shouldn't dash your hopes." He pulled me back around to face him. "If you do get the job, let me know if you want me there when you break the news to your mom." Jake's smile returned and his eyes focused on something in the distance. "Shawn is coming to pick me up." He gestured with his head toward a rusty Toyota pick-up truck rattling towards us.

"Alright, I need to hurry anyway. My mom's probably timing how long I've been gone. Say hi to Shawn for me."

"See ya at school tomorrow," Jake said with a backwards wave.

I knew Mom's eyes were glued to the clock right now, so I jogged off in the opposite direction. I didn't need her mad at me for something like taking too long at the store. I still couldn't believe I'd even asked for the application, let alone filled it out and turned it in. I flip-flopped between scenarios. One where Mom was happy I'd have my own money and one where she screamed in my face as she hit me. I sighed and crossed my fingers. I needed all the luck I could get.

3
Thursday, March 3, 1988

The bell rang, signaling the end of fifth period. Startled, I dropped my pencil on the floor. I'd been so spaced out; I didn't realize class was even close to being over. My mind was preoccupied over the interview this afternoon. I snatched up my pencil and books and headed toward the door. Thank goodness it was lunch time.

"Don't forget! Reflection essays on our poetry unit are due tomorrow!" Miss Lane's voice rose above the chatter. "Late work will not be accepted!"

I jogged down the stairs and turned the corner. High school hallways were like a game of dodgeball, only the objective was to dodge all the students coming my way. Although I could be klutzy at times, I skirted past everyone today. My locker was in the science hall, and after getting stuck behind some turtlelike seniors, I finally made it there. I spun the numbers of my combination and swung open the grey door. Kirk Cameron smiled at me from a magazine-sized poster while I shoved my books inside and grabbed my sack lunch. I took a peek in the small mirror under Kirk's photo. My chestnut bangs still looked in place, thanks to a cloud of hairspray this morning. I pushed my long hair over my shoulders and peered closely at my hazel eyes. They looked a little red – a side effect of not getting much sleep. I'd been too nervous about the interview to sleep well. A nap sure sounded good right now.

Jake appeared beside me and shook the locker door, making it rattle. My face bounced around in the mirror.

"You look fine," he said, flipping a section of my hair up with his finger.

"Jake! Knock it off!" I swatted his hand away.

"Aren't you hungry? Let's go!"

Jake slammed the locker door when I stepped back. He had a sack lunch in his hand too, only his looked much fuller than mine.

"Too bad it's raining today. We could have eaten outside." Jake pointed at my denim skirt and checkered blouse. "You're all dressed up today."

"You just now noticed? Did you forget I have the interview after school?"

Jake cracked a smile. "Nah, I remember. You're still going through with it then?"

"Yeah, I'm trying to be brave, but I'm so nervous," I said. "I can't even concentrate in class. I'll be glad when it's over."

We walked into the cafeteria where the volume was always set to one level: LOUD. One of my teachers claimed it had the decibel level of a concert. Our table still had a couple of seats open, so we headed that way. Getting there required careful maneuvering around students walking out of the hot lunch line carrying their meat loaf, potatoes and rolls. Yum. I'd love to trade someone my cold lunch for a hot meal. I pulled out a chair and plopped down. Jake took the empty chair across the table. I waved a silent hello to our friends and tuned in to their conversation about a recently released movie. I hadn't seen it and probably wouldn't, so I just listened. Besides, I was starving.

As I sunk my teeth into my peanut butter and jelly sandwich, all conversation was drowned out by the music of Poison's *Nothin' but a Good Time* blaring from somewhere near the windows. Curious, we turned to see two senior boys holding the ends of a boom box high in the air. They were dressed identically: Guess jeans, Nikes, and Buckley High red and white letterman jackets. A third boy, with model-like good looks and the same jacket, pulled a petite blonde out of her seat. Her mouth gaped open while her friends laughed and whistled. Model Letterman pulled a pink rose from behind his back and presented it to the girl, then he leaned in close and spoke to her. The music was way too loud to hear his words, but the girl's smile lit up her face, and she nodded. Her friends clapped and whistled.

The music stopped abruptly, and all was silent. One of the jocks holding the boom box had turned off the cassette seconds before Mr. Demhoff, the assistant principal, reached them.

"Nothing to see here!" our bespectacled administrator bellowed, addressing the entire cafeteria. But that didn't stop anyone from watching as he confiscated the offending cassette player, much to the chagrin of the popular kids. Several students approached Mr. Demhoff. One even tried to take the boom box out of his hands. I wasn't close enough to hear their argument, but the three athletes looked annoyed. The blonde girl, on the other hand, still smiled like she'd won the lottery.

"Looks like someone just got asked to the prom," Holly said.

"She probably gets asked to every dance," Nicole said, frowning.

"Probably so," Holly agreed. "I can't wait for that to happen to me."

"It will. Once you make the dance team, you'll be sitting with the popular kids at lunch too." Although her words were optimistic, Nicole's eyes looked sad behind her glasses.

I didn't say anything. Nicole had a point. Holly was tall and thin with dark red hair and a long, narrow face that had never seen much acne. She had been dancing since elementary school, and despite her long legs, she'd never been clumsy, tripping over herself like I was prone to do. Holly's brown eyes were huge and her makeup perfect.

Once the braces came off her teeth, there would be no flaws that I could see. She'd looked like she belonged at the popular table.

Nicole was almost a complete opposite, at least physically. Her height was average, just like her weight and her bushy brown hair. She had a birthmark on her forehead that she was self-conscious about, so she kept it covered by bangs. Her teeth were slightly crooked. She was like me, in that she wasn't comfortable being the center of attention, whereas Holly loved the spotlight.

It was surprising, given they were such opposites, that Holly and Nicole had remained best friends. Ever since elementary school, when proximity determines who kids usually play with, they had been inseparable. I lucked out in a middle school art class, when Nicole sat on one side of me, and Holly on the other. To communicate during class, they pretty much had to include me. Besides Jake, they were my closest friends, although I rarely saw them outside of school. Mom didn't let me get together with friends very often. Well, more like never.

Nicole couldn't pull her eyes away from the popular kids. I knew we'd never be sitting at that table when we were seniors. But it was likely Jake and Shawn would join Holly there. The boys both played on the JV baseball team, so if they made varsity, their popularity status would skyrocket. The thought of us not being together made me a little sad too. I don't know what Jake saw in my expression as I lifted my gaze from my lunch to his ice-blue eyes, but his next words surprised me.

"Libby, do you think your mom would let you go to the prom with me?"

All movement at our table ceased. My face felt hot, and I realized Jake had mistaken my look. He must have thought I was sad because I didn't have a date to the prom. Five sets of eyes stared at me, waiting for my response. Was he serious? I mean, this was Jake. He loved to joke around. Was he trying to embarrass me? Because it was working.

"Um, well, probably not, but thanks for asking, Jake." I looked down and focused on my sandwich. After a second, I raised my head and snuck a peek at my best friend. He smirked and his eyes twinkled as if we had just shared a private joke. Ugh, why was he such a tease? I wanted to smack him.

"Your mom won't let you go?" Holly's voice rose and her eyes pierced mine. "Why not?"

I glanced at Jake. He should have known better than to bring up my mother.

"It's just that my mom is strict, that's all," I said. "You guys know that."

Jake raised his eyebrows and stared at me. I knew he was thinking about my job interview. If my mom was as strict as that, would she really let me get a job? I stifled a groan. I was the biggest idiot. He'd tried to warn me, and I hadn't listened. I was getting into some sticky territory.

"Gosh, I'm glad my parents aren't that strict," Holly said. "If someone asked me to the prom, my mom would be so excited!" Her red curls bounced, and her face lit up.

"Well, Jake, it looks like Holly needs a date to the prom." It was my turn to smirk. It felt satisfying to put him on the defensive. Too bad he didn't respond how I expected.

"Good to know!" He grinned at Holly. Her cheeks reddened slightly, and she returned the smile. Yep, I really was an idiot. If Jake went to the prom with someone like Holly, he'd never ask someone like me again. I felt sweaty and hot. I had to get out of here.

I gathered my garbage, waved a quick goodbye and headed for the cafeteria doors. Behind me, I heard Nicole yell, "Wait up, Libby!" I knew I'd just made myself look jealous. Whatever. I had much bigger problems to worry about right now. Holly and Nicole placed their lunch trays in the kitchen window. Jake and Shawn stayed at the table, laughing about something. Probably me.

The rest of the day was spent in P.E. and World Civilizations classes. We were stuck inside for P.E. because of the rain. I wasn't complaining though, because it meant we got to play basketball, my favorite sport. Holly and Nicole were both in my class, so we teamed up against three other girls and clobbered them. The game distracted me from worrying about the interview.

Coach Barnes' whistle shrilled. "Class is over! I'll see you tomorrow!"

"Good job, team!" Nicole gave Holly and me high fives.

"I don't know why you aren't on the basketball team, Libby!" Holly puffed. She wiped her sweaty forehead with the bottom of her Buckley High Bears tee shirt. "I can barely keep up with you!"

"Thanks, but I just play for fun." The truth was I loved the game and would have given anything to be on a team, but my mom had shot down that idea back in the seventh grade. I hadn't brought it up again. Once my mom said "no," I usually just accepted it. Not happily though. More like the wind had been taken from my sails and I was stuck in the doldrums. If I got hired for this job, I was really going to have to stand my ground and that terrified me.

Mr. Wilkes' monotone voice droned on and on in World Civilizations. My eyes were on the board, but my mind was elsewhere. I tapped my pencil on my leg in time to the songs playing in my head. Then I thought through possible interview questions I might be asked. Why do you want to work here? What skills do you have? What would you do if...(fill in the blank)? I conjured up such scenarios like someone shoplifting, or the freezers breaking down and ice cream melting all over the floor. Some were more ridiculous than others, but all possibilities.

At one point during his lecture, Mr. Wilkes smacked the blackboard for emphasis and half the class jumped. "Wake up people! I see several students not taking notes!"

I forced the interview out of my mind and focused on notetaking for the last twenty minutes of class. When the bell rang, I scooped my textbook and binder and reached the door before anyone else. At my locker, I loaded up my backpack, pulled on my jacket and grabbed my umbrella. I hurried to the front doors and had my umbrella ready to pop open the second I got through the door. I hoped I wouldn't be soaking wet by the time I reached Pop's.

I paused at the doorway to pull on my hood and got jostled from behind.

"Geez, move!" snarled a short, shaggy-haired boy. He shot me a glare and veered around me. I stuck my tongue out at his back. Jerk.

"Hey, Libby." Jake appeared out of the crowd, a little winded, like he'd been running. "I'm glad I caught you. Do you want a ride to Pop's?"

"Oh, for sure!" I said. We exited the school and Jake jogged ahead, then peered back to see if I was following. He let the rain wet his hair as if it didn't bother him at all. Not me. I huddled under my umbrella and felt the cool air tickle my face. A breeze was blowing the rain, so I angled the umbrella to keep my face and hair dry. I watched the rain splash around my feet and only looked up occasionally to make sure I was headed in the right direction. There was too much water on the ground to run. I would have soaked my nylons and flats and been a shivering mess by the time I reached the car, so I took it slow and steady. My careful steps were almost pointless because some of my fellow students made a run for it and splashed my legs with icy drops of water anyway.

The front parking lot was the smallest of the school's two lots, so I made it to Jake's sister's white Ford Escort in about thirty seconds. Jake was already inside with the engine running. He reached across the passenger seat and opened the passenger door from the inside. I hopped in and placed my backpack on the floor in front of me.

"Why are you driving Emily's car?"

"On the news, the weatherman said it would rain most of the day. I knew you had to walk to Pop's, so I asked Em if I could drive today."

"Aw, that was nice of you, but didn't she have classes at the J. C.?" The J. C. was what all the locals called the junior college in Millsburg.

"Yeah, but she called Peter. He said he could take her as long as she could get a ride home after work. So, I'm probably that ride."

"Gotcha." Emily was in her first year of college and had started dating Peter around Christmastime. They had graduated from Buckley High together, but apparently never knew the other existed until taking a freshman English class together.

"What time is the interview?" Jake glanced at me while he waited to make a left turn out of the parking lot.

"Three-thirty." I blew a puff of air at my bangs and rubbed the back of my neck.

"Are you having second thoughts?"

"Nope," I lied. Of course I was having second thoughts, but I couldn't tell him that or he would try to convince me not to go through with it.

"You'll be rad!" Jake pulled onto the road and flipped the wipers on high speed. The back-and-forth rhythm had me mesmerized for a moment.

"Well, my stomach doesn't feel rad!" It was doing somersaults, and I was beginning to feel sick. "What if I really do get the job and then have to face my mother?"

"Just be confident," Jake said. "Interview first, then worry about your mom."

I nodded, then narrowed my eyes and fixed him with a sidelong stare.

"What? Why are you looking at me like that?"

"Why did you ask me about the prom at lunch today?"

"Is this a trick question?" Jake laughed.

"Well, that's what I wondered when you asked me that in front of everyone. Were you being serious?"

"What do you think?" Jake clicked on the blinker to change lanes and looked over his left shoulder. Pop's was just ahead.

"Well, I didn't know if you truly wanted to ask me to the prom or if you just wanted to emphasize how strict my mother can be." I shifted in the seat to face Jake.

"Maybe both." Jake shrugged and pulled into the Pop's parking lot.

"Okay." I decided to let it go. Jake might be a tease and a pain sometimes, but I was glad to know his words were not intentionally trying to hurt or embarrass me.

Jake switched off the ignition and looked at his watch. "Looks like you still have fifteen minutes."

We stayed in the car and talked about Jake's weekend plans. I knew he was trying to distract me, but every few minutes, I had to take a deep breath to calm the butterflies in my stomach. I pulled a small mirror out of my backpack and checked my hair and makeup.

At 3:25, I said, "Well, here goes!" I tried to smile, but it felt more like a grimace. Jake wished me luck and said he'd wait to drive me home. I hopped out into the rain with my trusty umbrella.

The mat by the doors was soaking wet. When I closed my umbrella, some of the water droplets landed on my skirt and I ran my hand over them. The bright lights were welcoming, and an old Beach Boys song played softly in the background. There were two open check-out lanes being manned by a husky, college-aged guy with a mullet and what looked like his twin sister, minus the mullet. A couple of young moms chatted while they waited in line. I saw Rosie at the customer service desk looking through a magazine, her glasses perched on the tip of her nose. She looked up as I approached and removed her glasses which hung from a silver chain around her neck. Her face held no emotion, and I wondered if it was difficult to learn how to keep a blank expression.

"I'm here for an interview with Linda," I said.

Rosie nodded. "Alright. I'll take you to her office." She left her perch and beckoned for me to follow. My palms felt sweaty, so I focused my attention on Rosie. She wore a white polo and high-waisted tan slacks. Her frizzy hair had more gray in it than I noticed the other day. She led me to a small hallway at the side of the store. To the left were the restrooms and to the right were two closed doors. The first door had a sign designating it as the employee lounge. The second door said, "Office." Rosie knocked twice and walked in.

The first thing I noticed was the smell of pizza; the second was how cramped the room felt. Two desks sat facing each other. Behind the nearest one sat two dark gray filing cabinets. One drawer was slightly open as if someone had only halfheartedly tried to close it. The first desk was tidy with a file tray on one corner and a picture of a dark-haired man with a German Shepherd in a gold frame on the opposite corner. The nameplate in the middle identified the desk as belonging to Jerri Argus.

The second desk was messy, with scattered papers lying over the top of it. I saw a file tray there too, but it was much fuller than Jerri's. Several small picture frames lined the opposite side. A half-full bottle of Coke stood in the center of the desk, condensation bubbling on the glass. A beautiful woman looked up from the papers she'd been perusing and smiled.

"She's here for the interview," Rosie said, then closed the door behind her as she left. Linda stood and extended her hand to me, introducing herself. My palms were still damp, so I didn't really want to shake her hand. I hesitated, then clasped her hand anyway. "Hi, I'm Libby." My words came out softer than I intended. If Linda noticed my clammy hand, she gave no indication.

Linda held no resemblance to Jerri, but her eyes twinkled in the same way. Her makeup was perfect for her coloring: soft pink lipstick on her lips and blue eye shadow that emphasized her steel blue eyes. She wore her dirty-blond hair in a bun on the crown of her head, a bit of gray showing at her temples. I felt her size me up the same way I did her. It made me glad I'd dressed up for this. I forced my hands to stay at my sides, instead of wringing them like I was tempted to do.

"Let me get you a chair." Linda opened a large closet at the back of the room and produced a metal folding chair from within. She pulled it open and gestured for me to sit down.

"So, you're Libby." Linda rifled through the papers on her desk. I recognized my handwriting on the application she pulled out of the mess. She scanned it, then looked up at me.

"Is this the first job you've ever applied for?"

"Yes, I just barely turned sixteen," I said.

"So, why do you want to work at Pop's?" she asked.

"Um, I'd like to make my own money, you know, for clothes and things." My voice trailed off. Gosh, I sounded so lame. I wanted to close my eyes and disappear, but I settled for taking a deep breath. "And this seems like a nice place to work."

Linda smiled. "Just relax, Libby. I won't bite." She launched into the job duties and expectations before she asked, "Does that sound like something you'd like to do?"

"Yes," I said. The tension in my stomach eased a bit.

"It's hard work, but I think you'll find most of the employees are great to work with, so it can be fun. We want everyone to be happy here." Linda uncovered her calendar, then continued. "Since you're in school, your hours would be from 3:30-5:30 Monday, Tuesday and Wednesday, 3:30-6:00 on Thursdays and Fridays, plus four hours on Saturdays. The Saturday shift can be worked anytime as long as you work the entire four hours all at once."

"That sounds great!" I said. Would Mom think it was great, though? Anxiety clawed at my stomach.

"Good! Would you be able to start on Saturday? Around noon?" Linda didn't seem to pick up on my inner turmoil.

"So, I got the job then?" Had she really only asked me one interview question? That didn't seem right.

Linda chuckled. "Yes, I feel good about you even though you have no other work experience. But everyone has to start somewhere. Now, about Saturday?"

Holy cow! I had just been hired for my first real job! "Sure, noon on Saturday!" I said.

Linda listed off the paperwork items I needed to bring with me. She handed me a typed list of all the store employees and their phone numbers. I counted ten others.

"Now, let's get you a couple shirts." She opened the same closet that had stored my chair and pulled down a box. "I don't know if you've noticed, but at Pop's we wear red, white or black polos." She gestured to her own black shirt. "I'll give you two shirts. What colors would you like?"

I didn't care. I was still trying to process the fact I'd gotten a job. "Anything you have in a medium is fine."

Linda searched through the box and pulled out a red shirt and a black shirt. I stood and she shook my hand again. "It's great to have you on the Pop's team. We'll see you on Saturday."

As I opened the office door to leave, she said, "Oh, I forgot to mention that Jerri will be your direct supervisor. She'll train you for a few days until you have a grasp of your responsibilities."

"Okay, great!" I couldn't stop smiling. "Thank you so much!"

I walked out of the office, past the restrooms and candy aisle to the front doors. The same two checkers were still working, and Rosie was mopping up a trail of water from the doors to the service desk. I waved to her and hurried out the door. Jake had moved the car to a closer parking spot, so I didn't even have to put up my umbrella.

He seemed surprised to see me. "That was quick!" He placed the biology book he'd been reading on the back seat.

"Yep, it was short and sweet!"

"So, you got it then?"

"You're looking at the newest Pop's employee!" I gave a little bow.

Jake fist pumped the air. "I knew you'd get it! But now...your mom."

I sighed. I honestly hadn't thought I'd get the job. Not really. I dropped my face into my hands and thought for a bit. Jake was right. How would I bring this up to Mom? No answers came; I only heard the rain as it pelted the car windows.

Jake broke the silence. "If you want me to come over when you tell her, I will."

I grimaced and shook my head. "Thanks, Jake, but I got myself into this, so I'll deal with it." It wasn't Jake's problem. I didn't want him to face Mom's wrath too.

The rain kept a steady beat as we drove the few blocks to my house. Its faded gray wood siding seemed to blend right in with the cloudy sky. The house looked sad, like it needed some love. Some basic upkeep would make a huge difference. But Mom didn't pay much attention to that sort of thing. Jake pulled into the gravel driveway and stopped close to the house.

"I think you should tell her today," he said. "It will be worse if you wait until the last minute to tell her."

I groaned. "You know, five minutes ago I was so excited. Now, I'm just stressed out."

I pulled the house key out of my backpack while Jake gave me a quick pep talk. "Thanks for the ride, Jake."

I got to the front door just as my sisters, huddled together under a pink and white polka-dotted umbrella, started up the sidewalk on their way home from school. Both girls had their hands on the umbrella shaft. Anna tugged it over her head and body, then Edie pulled it her way. Their giggles told me they were enjoying their game. The girls walked the five blocks to school and back each day. Anna was a responsible fourth grader who kept a good eye on our second-grade sister.

"Hurry, girls!" I called. The girls' careful steps became a run, the tug-of-war over the umbrella forgotten. We hustled inside and dropped our wet umbrellas and bags by the coat rack. Once our wet coats were hung up, I hugged them both.

"How was school?" I asked.

For the next fifteen minutes, the girls regaled me with stories from their day, including one about Edie's teacher, Miss Jansen, who had tripped coming into the school and broken the heel off one of her shoes.

"She had to go barefoot all day! And it was cold." Edie's green eyes always sparkled when she had a story to tell.

I told the girls to start on their homework then moved on to making dinner. Edie groaned, but Anna obediently got her math assignment out of her backpack and plopped down at the kitchen table with her pencil and eraser handy.

"All I have to do is study my spelling words for the test tomorrow," Edie said. She handed me the list so I could quiz her. She waited with her pencil and paper, while I thumbed through Mom's Betty Crocker cookbook searching for something I could cook. It had to be something nicer than our usual weekday dinners. If I cooked something new and different, maybe it would put Mom in a good mood before I broke the news about the job.

I gathered ingredients for creamy potato soup as I read Edie's words to her. When she finished writing the tenth word, she jumped up from the table, bumping it as she ran away.

"Hey, watch out!" Anna cried. She scowled as she erased the errant marks on her paper.

I looked over Edie's paper. "Edie!" I called. "Come back! You need to try two of these again."

A door slammed upstairs. I glanced at Anna and shrugged, not really surprised. Edie consistently tried to get out of doing things she didn't like, homework and housework being top of the list.

I made the soup with shaking hands. Each tick of the clock brought me closer to having to spill my guts to Mom and I dreaded it. I peeked over my shoulder at Anna. She had finished her math and had pulled a chapter book out of her backpack to read. I walked over to take a closer look.

"Hey, I read *Tales of a Fourth Grade Nothing* when I was younger. It's funny."

Anna smiled. Of my sisters, she and I were more alike. She was more serious and reliable than Edie. She was also the shy one, the one who took everything hard. Edie was impetuous and wild and had the craziest fashion sense I'd ever seen. She didn't care if her clothes matched, or her hair was combed. She cared more about playing and avoiding responsibility than anything.

I mixed up a batch of cornbread to go with the potato soup and slid it into the oven. If I was lucky, we'd have enough leftovers for a couple days. A break from cooking would be nice.

I decided Anna should know about my job before I told Mom about it later. If a showdown and fireworks were going to be our after-dinner entertainment, she needed fair warning. I plopped down in Edie's vacated chair.

"Anna, I have to tell you something."

She lifted her eyes from the book and sniffed. She looked toward the stove top where the soup simmered.

"That smells good. What is it?"

"It's a new recipe. Creamy Potato Soup." I waited until she looked at me. I told her all about the "Help Wanted" sign at Pops, the application and interview. With each new detail, Anna's dark eyes grew larger.

"Mom doesn't know yet?"

I shook my head. "I have to tell her tonight."

I didn't expect her eyes to fill with tears, but they did. Her typically rosy cheeks reddened even further.

"No, Libby!" Anna's voice rose like the shrill whistle of a kettle. "She's gonna be so mad at you!"

I stood and grabbed my sister's hands and pulled her toward me until I had my arms wrapped around her.

"Shh, I know." I rubbed my hand over her soft dark hair.

"Why, Libby?" Anna choked out the words.

"I guess I'm just tired of never getting to do anything," I explained. "I'm growing up and I need to experience things like a first job. I know it's hard for you to understand." I stroked her tear-stained face. "You know, if I can make some money, I won't have to ask Mom for new clothes for me or you and Edie."

Anna nodded and wiped her eyes. I cupped her face and said, "You know what to do if she goes crazy." It was a statement, not a question, a reminder of our plan for escaping volatile situations.

Anna nodded again and whispered, "I love you, Libby."

"Love you too." I squeezed her tight. It wasn't fair we'd learned to be so wary of Mom's reaction to things, that it caused such anxiety. I felt bad I would be the cause of the problem tonight.

I turned off the burner under the soup and pulled the bread from the oven.

"Let's go change into our warm, comfy clothes," I said.

Anna stuffed her homework and book into her backpack and dropped it by the front door on her way up the stairs.

"Tell Edie to change, too," I said as I headed to my room. If the cold shed was where the girls ended up tonight, warm clothes were essential.

I traded my skirt and blouse for sweatpants and a sweatshirt, and silently thanked whoever had invented them. When I called for the girls, Edie ran in dressed like me. Her eyes were huge, so Anna must have broken the news. Anna followed, rubbing her reddened cheeks.

"Listen. We're going to have a nice dinner, and nobody will mention anything about the job. I'll tell Mom after we're finished cleaning up and you're watching *Who's the Boss?* But you know what to do if she loses her temper. It's wet and cold out there tonight, so if you can grab your shoes or coat before going out, do it."

I hugged both girls and glanced at my reflection in the mirror on the wall. I looked worried, but there was no going back now.

4
Thursday, March 3, 1988
Later that evening

I had my English essay finished by the time Mom walked in late from work. She seemed to be in a decent mood and even expressed how much she liked the soup. I could tell my sisters were happy she seemed fairly even-keeled, although Anna's eyes kept flicking toward mine. My stomach was turning somersaults by the time the dishes were washed and the kitchen cleaned. I was afraid what little dinner I'd managed to get down wasn't going to stay there.

The girls were lying on the floor watching TV when I came into the living room. Mom sat in the corner of the couch, her legs pulled up beside her.

"Libby, it's cold in here. Grab me a blanket, will you?" She gestured toward Grandma's old trunk across the room. I pulled out her favorite green and tan blanket that Grandma had crocheted and handed it to her.

I sat in the worn recliner rocker next to the trunk. My hands were sweaty and shaking, so I stuck them underneath my legs. My heart beat furiously as I stared, unseeing, at the television screen.

Come on, Libby! Just do it. Waiting just makes it worse!

I was afraid of Mom's reaction but that wasn't anything new. I was always afraid. I counted to ten, swallowed hard and cleared my throat. "Mom, I need to talk to you."

Mom shifted her gaze from the TV to me, her mouth pursed. Out of the corner of my eye, I saw that Anna had immediately picked up on my words. She must have been waiting for me to speak. Without waiting a second, she grabbed Edie's hand and walked into the kitchen.

"Gee, Libby, why so serious? Did you fail a test or something?" Mom was always sarcastic when it came to my efforts in school. She often made fun of the fact that my grades were good, and that I cared enough to keep it that way. Most parents would be happy about that, but Mom never liked school much, so she didn't care like I did.

I shook my head, and the words fell from my mouth in a rush. "No...I got a job, and I start on Saturday." I didn't dare look at her. The couch springs squeaked as Mom shifted. Then silence.

I lifted my head, just to where I could peek at her. She stared at me, disbelief written on her face. Oh boy. That had gotten her attention.

"You did what?" she whispered through clenched teeth.

My pulse raced and I trembled all over. My typical reaction to Mom's anger.

"Um...I saw a 'Help Wanted' sign at Pop's on Tuesday when you sent me for milk and eggs. It's just a stocking position." My voice shook, but I forged on. "It's only fifteen hours a week. A couple hours every day after school and four hours on Saturdays." I desperately tried to remember what else I'd rehearsed in my mind as I visualized the conversation.

"I do not remember giving you permission to get a job!" Mom's voice rose and she sat upright on the edge of the couch, like a tiger ready to pounce on its prey.

Be brave, Libby!

I was trying so hard to keep my courage, but it was draining faster than batteries in a flashlight left on all night. I pressed on, but my shaking voice betrayed me.

"It was a split-second decision. I thought it would be good to make some spending money. You know, for clothes and makeup and stuff." I realized I'd said the wrong thing when Mom bolted off the couch and stood above me.

Quick as lightning, she yanked my hair until my neck tilted all the way back and my face looked straight up into hers. My scalp burned, but I tried to ignore the pain. Mom's green eyes glowed with fury.

"You thought that, huh? Do I not do a good job providing for you?" she sneered and tightened her grip on my hair.

"You do, Mom," I gasped. "I'm sorry!" Tears threatened and I fought to keep them from falling.

"Don't you start crying!" she yelled. Crying always seemed to aggravate her whenever we had a conflict. "I do not want you working when you should be here watching your sisters after school!" Her tone was harsh. "Did you forget about that?"

Mom grabbed my jaw in her right hand. "Your job is to babysit, keep the house clean and cook dinner for your sisters!"

For my sisters? Funny how she always benefited from those same dinners. I shut my eyes to avoid hers.

"Look at me!" she screamed. I didn't want to do it, but in a burst of self-preservation, I fixed my eyes on hers and a traitorous tear leaked out.

"Stop crying!" Mom growled. She yanked on my hair again and slapped my face. White-hot pain seared my cheek. I could no longer keep the tears from falling and I broke out in sobs. My face stung and my scalp burned.

"I did not give you permission to get a job!" She was repeating herself, as if I hadn't already gotten the gist of her displeasure.

My own voice was almost unrecognizable. "I just thought the extra money would help. I'd be able to buy things for the girls and myself and wouldn't have to ask you for it." I stumbled over my words as I choked them out. Plus, that sense of independence was so enticing.

Mom released her grasp and relief flooded through me. For a second, I thought she was finished, then she pulled me up from the rocker. Being the exact same height, she looked directly into my eyes as if she'd just realized something.

"You already had an interview?" She wrapped her hand around my upper arm. I nodded, tears streaming down my face.

"You little..." she called me an ugly name and pushed me into the wall. I almost choked on my own spit as I gasped in pain. I tried to take a breath as she repeatedly pummeled my ribs. Leaning over, I tried unsuccessfully to curl myself up to avoid the blows. My gasps set off a coughing fit.

"When are you supposed to start?" Mom yelled.

"On, on...Saturday," I breathed out the words between sobs.

"You will *not* start on Saturday!" Each syllable was pronounced with another hit to my ribs. I could barely breathe. Why hadn't I listened to Jake? I should just tell Mom I'd call Pop's and turn down the job. But the more she hit me, the angrier I became.

"Stop it!" I screamed. I jerked away and ran toward the stairs. From the corner of my eye, I saw my sisters crying as they stood next to the kitchen table. Why hadn't they left? I flung my arm in the direction of the back door, so they would go. At my signal, they turned and ran outside. I didn't hear the door slam, so they must have remembered not to call attention to themselves.

Mom was hot on my tail. "Libby!" she bellowed, "I am not done with you!"

I took the stairs two at a time. I didn't stop running until I entered my bedroom. I tried to slam the door, but she was too close. She pushed back on my door with a growl. I ran to my bed and flung myself on top of it. My ragged breaths hurt clear down to my belly.

Enraged, Mom slapped my back. My hands gripped the sides of my pillow as I sobbed into it. Why did she freak out like this?

"Turn over!" she demanded. "Look at me!"

I slowly turned and gazed at her through clouded eyes. Much of her shoulder-length permed hair she'd been wearing pulled back had come out of the clip and created a curly, clown-like frizz around her face. She still had on the purple blouse and black slacks that she'd worn to work that day. Her face was red, and her breaths huffed out in quick bursts. Her fists rested on her hips, elbows out. The perfect picture of over-the-top rage.

I felt extremely vulnerable lying face up while she hovered there. My back and face stung from the slaps and my ribs ached. But the worst pain I felt was in my heart. I didn't know why she seemed to hate me so much, and although I was used to it, it still hurt that she treated me this way.

Of course, anytime Mom got angry with me or my sisters, it was always our fault, never hers. There were times we didn't even know why she was so angry. It seemed to come out of nowhere, like a furious funnel cloud. The problem was its destructive path cut right through her children.

Mom's eyes shot daggers into mine. "You don't make the decisions around here, Libby. Got it? If I wanted you to get a job, I would have said so!"

I knew it was dangerous to say anything right now, but I couldn't help myself. "But I'm sixteen now. A lot of kids get jobs when they turn sixteen. When do I get to make decisions for myself?" I sounded bitter to my own ears.

Mom's response was quiet but fierce. "When you're eighteen and you no longer live here!"

"That's two years away!" I whispered. My tears had stopped, but everything hurt.

"Well, then in two years!" Mom's smirk was triumphant. Ah, victory, what she aimed for in every confrontation.

I detested that look. A flash of loathing jolted through me. I was so sick of being her puppet, her Cinderella. Everything I did had to be directed by her, or she wasn't happy. I had no choice but to comply or this was the result. I sat up quickly, ignoring the ache in my side.

Startled, Mom took a step backwards.

"I'm sick of this!" I yelled. "I'm sick of being treated like a child. And I'm sick of taking care of everything around here!"

Mom's glare hardened and she put her face right up to mine. "Shut your mouth! Unless you want to be grounded!"

Grounded from what? I didn't have any extracurricular activities, so...? I was suddenly so tired. I fell back on the bed and turned toward the wall. I had majorly lost that battle, but I wasn't ready to give in. I could be stubborn too.

Mom interrupted my thoughts. "We're done here. I don't want to see you the rest of the night! I need a drink."

Of course she did. She needed a drink to relax, to enjoy herself, or whenever she couldn't cope and wanted to forget her horrible life. It had been that way since Grandma died. After Grandma's funeral, Mom spent a lot of time in her room. Mrs. Judd, an older woman who lived across the street, came over every day. Mrs. Judd must have made the meals because I rarely saw Mom. She was either at work or in her room. When she stayed in her room, sometimes she drank. Mrs. Judd would pick up her cans and usher me out of Mom's bedroom when I followed her in. I remember asking her once, "Is Mommy dead?" She patted my hands and said, "No, she's just sick right now." I think Mrs. Judd helped my mom work through her grief and eventually she started being a little more present. Occasionally she lost her temper with me, but for the most part, I felt like things were okay.

It wasn't long afterwards that Mom met Nolan. Mom married Nolan Rigby when I was five years old. I remember being the flower girl at their wedding. Even though I couldn't remember details, I remember how happy I felt when Nolan gave me a toss in the air after he and Mom took their vows. His laughter mingled with mine as he hugged me and Mom. That was my strongest memory from their wedding day.

I remember Nolan moving into Grandma's house with us. He worked construction and Mom worked part-time at a bank. It was a happy time for all of us. We went on picnics, played together in the backyard and at the park. Then late one night, I was awakened by Mom's raised voice and Nolan's placating tones coming from their bedroom below mine. After a few minutes, Mom quieted down, and I went back to sleep.

The day Mom told me that she was going to have a baby, Nolan was all smiles. He kept saying, "I can't believe it! I'm going to be a dad and you'll be a big sister!" Then he tickled me while I rolled on the floor, laughing.

I didn't really understand what the whole baby thing entailed until Mom and Nolan brought home a little bundle wrapped in a yellow blanket. I remember thinking that Anna had the teeniest toes and nose. I was thrilled by her, except when she cried. Mom became grouchy in her tired state and took it out on me and Nolan. She was short-tempered and would banish me to my room for the least bit of typical six-year-old behavior. Toward Nolan she was like the weather, sunny and happy one day, stormy the next. There was a weird tension in the house that even I could feel.

When Anna got moved upstairs into a crib, I learned to hear her cries. I was quick to hop out of bed to retrieve her pacifier. Sometimes, I fell asleep on the floor next to her crib. I thought by helping with Anna, my mom could rest more, and she would be her normal self again.

Time went on in that same pattern for a while. Anna was at the age where she toddled around and got into everything. One night at dinner, Mom announced she was pregnant again. She seemed excited about it, but Nolan, who'd been so happy the first time around, was strangely silent at the announcement. I was feeding Anna in her highchair and except for her babbling, it was dead quiet. The idea of a new brother or sister was okay with me, but the look on Nolan's face confused me. His deep brown eyes looked sad as he whispered, "This is terrible timing."

From the arguments between Nolan and Mom, I soon realized that Nolan had recently been laid off from his job, so he was worried about money and providing for the family. Mom became even crankier with the stress of needing to work full-time again. That's when I began to witness her abusing Nolan. She would scream at him, then use her hands as weapons in any way she could. He generally held off her blows with not much physical damage done because he was stocky and strong. Whenever Mom started yelling at him after her workday, he scooted Anna and me upstairs to my bedroom. His deep voice rose above Mom's many times, but it didn't sound menacing, so I was never afraid of him. I wasn't even afraid of Mom at that point. I just hated it when she yelled. The yelling always made Anna cry, and I had to comfort her.

My fear of Mom set in after Edie was born. Often, Mom raised her voice in anger at me, or Anna, or even Edie. Mrs. Judd came over occasionally to help Mom with housework or to play with me and Anna. Even when Mrs. Judd was here, Mom would sometimes yell at us.

I guess Nolan finally had enough of Mom's outbursts and physical aggression and filed for divorce. I knew things were not okay when he moved out of the house. He stayed in Buckley for a year before he moved to Florida to start a new job after Mom got custody of us. When Nolan left, I was almost ten years old. Anna was almost four and Edie was two. I took care of them more than Mom did. I learned how to cook, clean, and do the laundry. I had to in order to survive.

The only time we saw Nolan after that was in the summers. He would take Anna and Edie for a few weeks to his new home, but I wasn't allowed to go. Mom said he wasn't *my* father, so ,she refused to let him take me too. He always gave me a big hug and said, "Hang in there, kiddo" before leaving with my sisters. Now that my sisters were older, Mom put them on a plane to Florida, and I hadn't seen or talked to Nolan in a few years.

I'm sure he'd be interested in knowing how my mom treated us. The problem was I didn't know how to contact him and the distance from Indiana to Florida was too far to go looking for him. But I had longed to tell Nolan what Mom was doing for a while. I felt sure he could alter our home life dramatically. I pictured him throwing open the front door and in a big, booming voice announce he was taking his girls away from this life of abuse. I hoped that I would magically become his girl too. I mean, he was really the only dad I'd ever known.

The only other option would be to find my Uncle Paul, my mom's brother. I hadn't seen him in years either, but I felt like he might come to our rescue. I wasn't sure if he still lived in Columbus, Ohio, but the drive to Columbus was only a few hours and I could take a bus and get there before Mom even knew I was gone.

I rubbed my face and moaned. Why was I even thinking about these things? I couldn't just run off and tattle on Mom. She'd drilled it into our heads so many times. Our home life wasn't anyone else's business, and we were never to breathe a word about it, or we'd be sorry. I'd always been afraid to find out what that meant.

Hopelessness gnawed at my insides. In two years, I would graduate from high school and leave home, and the next victims of

Mom's abuse would be my sisters. I couldn't let that happen. I needed someone's help.

5
Friday, March 4, 1988

My radio alarm went off at seven, waking me from a restless sleep. I rolled over to stop *Tears for Fears* from proclaiming that "everybody wants to rule the world," but the movement made me gasp. I rubbed my ribs. Why did they hurt so much?

My eyes popped open as I recalled the events of the previous night. I moved a little slower as I touched the alarm clock with my fingertips. Ugh. I did not want to get out of bed. I gave myself an extra two minutes before I gingerly sat up to assess the damage.

I pressed my fingers to my ribs, face, the back of my neck, and my head. My ribs hurt the most. Maybe a warm shower would help.

I grabbed some clothes and left my room. I paused and stared at my sisters' door. I didn't want to wake them yet, but I needed to see that they were okay. I took a quick peek inside. Anna and Edie were curled up next to each other in the double bed they shared, still sound asleep. I felt like crawling into bed next to them and giving them a squeeze, but knowing my ribs couldn't take it, I resisted the urge.

In the bathroom, I peeled off my sweatshirt and caught a glimpse of my ribs in the mirror. Red, blue and purple bruises were like a neon sign on my pale skin. Well, wasn't that just great? I'd have to wear a tank top under my shirt and keep it on in P.E. so no one would see the bruises while I changed clothes. My face had a few small scratches from mom's fingernails but other than that, there was no other visible evidence of last night's indoor storm. I heaved a sigh, staring into my hazel eyes in the mirror. They were puffy from crying and my dark hair was a mess.

I eased into the shower and although the water hurt my ribs at first, by the time I finished, I felt a little better. I went through my morning routine of applying makeup and styling my hair. Then I woke the girls.

Anna threw her arms around my neck. "Libby! Are you okay?"

"Yeah, I'm fine. Don't you worry."

Anna pulled her head back and studied my face. "I don't believe you."

"I'm alright!" I nuzzled my face close to hers. "I promise."

I made breakfast for the girls and threw together some lunches for us. Mom wasn't up but that was normal. We rarely saw her before school. I was more than happy not to see her after last night. At some point during the night, the TV had been turned off, but just like I'd thought, there were some empty beer bottles by the couch. I gathered them up and put them in the garbage can. I made sure the girls had their homework in their backpacks, then I left Anna in charge and took off. I never worried if she was responsible enough to watch the clock and leave for school on time. She was used to the routine.

I was glad the rain had stopped, and the sun was peeking out of the clouds. As grim as last night felt, just seeing the sun lightened my mood. Maybe it could also give me courage to move forward with some kind of plan to get help.

When I got to school, I stowed my backpack in my locker and set out to find Jake. Students streamed through the doors, some barely awake, others energetic. I turned down the math hall, where Jake had his locker. A small crowd was gathered outside a popular teacher's classroom. The students laughed and playfully pushed each other around. I veered to the opposite side of the hall to avoid them, craning my neck to see if Jake was nearby. Yep, I could see that blond halo shining ahead of me. He was talking to someone.

Suddenly, I stopped. Jake was leaning his shoulder against his locker and smiling down at a girl. Not just any girl, but Holly. That really wasn't anything to get worked up over, but for some reason, I felt a tightness in my chest and my pulse quickened. There was something in his posture, the tilt of his head and the way he was laser-focused on her that made me feel...what? Jealous? I didn't really know.

Holly was her usual radiant self, flashing her beautiful smile. She swayed a little as she and Jake laughed together. Did this have something to do with the prom question at lunch? I hesitated, not sure I should interrupt. I was an island in the hall, students parting around me like the flow of a river.

Knock it off, Libby! So what if Jake and Holly chat? Friends do that.

I strolled over, as if I hadn't just been studying them. "What's up?" I sing-songed, looking from one to the other. Jake shifted his stance to include me in his circle and casually threw his arm over my shoulders. Holly turned her mega-watt smile to me. "Not much."

"Am I interrupting something?" My eyes bounced from Jake to Holly and back.

"Nope, nothing that can't wait," Jake replied.

"Okay, I was hoping to talk with you about something, Jake." My gaze shifted to Holly.

"Got it." She winked at me. "See you in math, Libby. Talk to you later, Jake." She flashed a quick peace sign and took off down the hall.

"Thanks!" I called after her retreating form. Holly threw me a wave over her shoulder. I watched her red curls disappear into the crowd.

Jake dropped his arm from my shoulders and faced me. "What happened with your mom? I wanted to call, but I didn't think you could really say anything if I did."

"No, don't call! Don't ever call," I reminded him.

"So?" he prompted. "What did she say?"

For a second, I felt like lying, just so I wouldn't have to hear "I told you so." But I wasn't sure Jake would believe me anyway. I wasn't a good liar.

"Well, it wasn't great," I admitted. "She said I had no right to apply for a job without her permission. Then she said I can't work. She got offended that I would want my own spending money. She thought I was implying she doesn't take good enough care of us." I shook my head at the irony.

Jake's icy-blue eyes bore into mine and he scoffed. "Everything is always about control with her." He lowered his voice to a whisper. "Did she hit you?"

I responded with a tiny nod.

Jake huffed out an angry breath at the same time his nostrils flared and his jaw clenched. He leaned his head against the locker door. I was jostled by a group of boys who came up behind me. Jake grabbed my hand and pulled me across the hall into an alcove by the staircase.

"Where?" he demanded.

Again, I didn't respond verbally. I waved my hand over my torso. In truth, I felt if I vocalized my injuries, my "I'm fine" façade might crumble, so I kept quiet.

"Bruises?" he asked.

"Mm-hmm."

"Did she say anything to you this morning?"

Before I could reply, the bell rang. Jake scowled. He seemed flustered by the lack of time we had to continue the conversation.

"I never saw her this morning. Pretty sure she's got a hangover though." I watched some of the cowboy crowd hurry by and stepped away from Jake. "I've got to get to class."

Jake reached out and grabbed my arm. I looked up at him, forehead creased. I knew he wanted answers, but I couldn't be late to Spanish class. Señor Flores assigned extra work when one was tardy.

"Let's eat outside at lunch. Just you and me. Meet me at the bench by the storage shed?"

"Sure," I said. I would see Jake in my biology and home-economics classes later, but neither class was conducive to an important conversation. The bench he'd chosen for our talk was well hidden and there was no real reason for anyone to go down there and disrupt us. We had never figured out why a bench beside the sports shed was necessary. But since it was nicer outside today, a lot of kids would head to the benches near the trees or the back courtyard. So, a bench by the equipment storage? Perfect.

I GOT OUT OF ENGLISH a little late because Miss Lane updated each student individually on their current grade in the class. Since my desk was in the last row, I was the last to talk with her.

As soon as I heard my grade was an A and Miss Lane praised my latest essay, I hurried to my locker and got my lunch. Instead of moving with the flow of students headed toward the cafeteria, I squeezed through the crowd until I reached the side doors. It had warmed up outside and birds filled the air with music. Just as I'd predicted, several students already occupied the benches under the tall trees. It took a couple minutes to walk past the tennis courts and along the fence around the football field and track to the storage shed. Behind the shed, I found Jake munching on Cheetos and drinking a soda.

He raised his eyebrows. "Thought you weren't coming." He swallowed and wiped his hand over his mouth.

"So, what's the plan then?" he asked.

"The plan?" I'd been expecting more questions about my confrontation with Mom.

"Yeah, the plan. What are you going to do about the job?"

"Oh...I still want the job, and I don't want to give in to her. I'm sick of her deciding everything for me, so I'll have to talk to her again. I just hope she'll be calmer next time."

Jake rolled his eyes and opened his mouth to interrupt, but I cut him off.

"I'll know more after I talk to my boss, Jerri, this afternoon."

"What does he have to do with it?" Jake asked.

"Jerri is a woman," I clarified. "I'm going to ask if the girls can come to the store after school every day and hang out in the staff break room while I work. If Jerri says it's okay, then what could my mom complain about? I'd be taking care of the biggest concern she has."

I pulled out my sandwich and took a big bite. For a few minutes, I concentrated only on my food. I didn't want to look at Jake. I was afraid he would see right through me. I may have sounded sure of myself, but inside I was a frightened mess. But having a plan helped me focus on something besides my fear.

Jake crunched into an apple as he considered my words. "What if Jerri won't let them come?"

I shrugged. "I'll have to convince her somehow. I need this job, Jake. I need the money so I can find my uncle."

"What are you talking about?" Jake's brow furrowed.

"I'm sick of being my mom's punching bag! I'm only two years away from turning eighteen and graduating. What happens when I leave home? All I can think is that Anna and Edie will replace me in that role because right now, I'm the one who takes the brunt of my mom's anger." I shook my head. "I refuse to put them in that position. I have to find a family member to help get my sisters away from my mom!" I slapped the bench. "I can't find Nolan as easily because he's in Florida. Although he would be the most ideal person."

Jake looked confused.

"What? What don't you understand?" My temper was beginning to flare. "This is important!" I slapped the bench again.

"Libby, I know it's important," Jake said. "I really do, but can't you just call your uncle?"

"Not without a phone number."

"Well, how do you plan on finding him?"

"A bus." I waited for a response, but Jake was quiet.

For the next few minutes, neither of us spoke, so I finished my sandwich and drink. A glance at my watch told me we had ten minutes left of lunchtime.

"So, the plan is to earn money for a bus ticket to find him? You find him, you tell him that your mom abuses you and ask him to rescue you and your sisters?" Jake's voice was calm, but his eyes sparked with intensity.

"Yes, so working and earning money is critical to that plan. Except, there's one thing you need to add in there." I stared at him, serious.

"What's that?"

"I was hoping you'd go with me to find Uncle Paul." From the look of surprise on Jake's face, he hadn't expected that. I let the words hang in the air for a moment.

"As far as I know, he lives in Columbus, Ohio. I could work until I have enough for bus fare for both of us. When we get there, we can use the phone book to find him. I'm sure there's more than one Paul Curtis in that city, so we'll call them all. But we'll have to leave at night, so my mom doesn't realize I've gone."

Jake looked as uncertain as I felt. But I wasn't brave enough to do this without him.

"I'm scared, Jake. That's why I want you to come with me."

Jake ran his hands through his hair. "It's crazy that you even have to come up with a plan like this," he said, "but I'll help you if you think it's the only way."

"It is the only way!" My hands hit the bench again.

Jake looked at his watch. "Better finish eating. Lunch is almost over." He propped his head in his hands and stared at the football field while I ate.

I didn't speak until we were walking back up the sidewalk. "Do you remember when you first saw my mom hit me?"

"How could I forget that? I was shocked. I had no idea what to do."

Jake had come over to my house when we were in seventh grade to work on a term project for our English class. We'd already been friends for a couple years so when we got to choose our own partner for the project, our eyes zeroed in on each other and with a smile and a nod, we sealed the deal. We had already researched the report part of the project at school. For the second part of the project, we had to create a diorama of our favorite scene from *The Outsiders* by S.E. Hinton. We wanted to recreate the scene where the church caught fire and Johnny and Ponyboy saved the children inside.

We'd gone to my house to find some supplies from the shed. My grandma's craft things had been boxed away and placed there after she died and occasionally my sisters and I used the supplies for art projects.

Jake and I had brought a couple of boxes inside to look through. When my mom came around the corner from the kitchen to the living room, she tripped over one of the boxes and fell. She was already in a bad mood, but that sent her over the edge. She swore, scrambled to her feet and slapped me across the cheek. The sting of the slap brought tears to my eyes and my embarrassment brought even more.

My mom hadn't seen Jake sitting in the rocker in the corner until he jumped off the seat, eyes wide and cheeks flushed. His shock was mirrored on my mom's face. She just blinked and stepped away from me. Jake bravely stood next to me and glared at my mom. I just stood there and cried. Mom told Jake to keep his mouth shut or he wouldn't be allowed near me again.

For a moment, I'd thought Jake was going to give my mom a piece of his mind, but he must have thought better of it. Later, I begged him to keep it a secret. He reluctantly agreed after a long discussion about what went on at my home. Jake had been my supporter and best friend ever since. Remembering all this as we walked back to the school building, I asked him to please support me again.

Jake gave me a hug and wished me luck with my mom. I knew him well enough to see the worry behind his smile. My own anxiety had settled on my shoulders like a heavy backpack. How could I bring up the job without Mom going ballistic again? I certainly didn't need more bruises, so if she came after me this time, I'd just leave the house. Would she dare come after me then?

6
Friday, March 4, 1988
Later that afternoon

I wanted to leave school immediately, but I kept getting stopped by people in the hall. First, Nicole invited me to go to the movies with her and some friends that night. I made up an excuse but thanked her for inviting me. Holly invited me to a party on Saturday night at her house to celebrate Shawn's birthday. I lied and told her I'd ask my mom. Jake caught me last. He wanted me to promise I'd call him after I talked to Jerri and Mom. I couldn't promise anything. I could only do that if Mom left the house.

Once I made it out of the building, I hightailed it to Pop's. Breathless, I approached the doors. The 'Help Wanted' sign had been removed and I hoped it wouldn't have to go right back up. I went straight to the customer service desk where a young woman in her twenties was wiping down the countertop. She had long, dark hair that was so thick, I wondered if it gave her headaches. Her badge said her name was Portia.

Portia looked up and smiled. "Can I help you?"

"Yes, I'd like to talk to Jerri," I said.

"Oh, I'm sorry. Jerri isn't in today." She looked down at a shift schedule. "She'll be in tomorrow from nine to five."

Crap. Now what was I supposed to do? My mind raced through my options.

"Can I help you with anything else?" Portia prompted.

I sighed. "No, I'll just talk to her tomorrow." Disappointed, I left the store and trudged home. The only option I had now was to try to reason with Mom. Ugh. I wasn't looking forward to that at all. My neck and shoulders felt tight, so I did what I always did when stress threatened to push me down. I thought of a song with a catchy rhythm and hummed the tune, tapping my legs to the beat of the drums. This time it was my favorite Duran Duran song.

Since there were leftovers for dinner, I didn't have to cook, so I started on the laundry. When Edie and Anna came home, I got them started on their homework, then vacuumed the house. I even had time to finish my homework before Mom came home. That rarely happened.

When she came in the back door after her shift, Mom looked awful. Her eyes were tired and every wrinkle on her face looked more pronounced. She didn't say anything to us except a whispered "Hi." As we ate dinner, I asked my sisters about school, their friends, what they wanted to do over the weekend, anything to keep the conversation light. Mom just ate in silence. Anna's eyes bounced back and forth between me and Mom. I shrugged. I wasn't going to ask Mom anything right now.

Finally, Anna asked in a quiet voice, "Mom, are you sick?"

Mom barely glanced up. "No, I'm fine." She picked up her glass and took a sip of water. Her hand shook as she set the glass down. "Actually, that's not true. I have a headache. I'm going to my room." She placed her dishes in the sink, then stopped at the fridge and pulled out a couple beers before heading to her room.

"Wow, another headache," I mumbled once the bedroom door closed.

"Yeah, she gets those a lot," Edie said.

"Two or three times a week," I agreed.

Anna's mouth fell open. "Do you think she's faking it?"

Did I? Kind of. It felt like another excuse to get drunk. But I couldn't say that to Anna.

"I don't know. Maybe."

I was worried Mom would hide in her room all night and I wouldn't have a chance to ask about the job. The countdown to my first shift was on and I caught myself checking the clock every few minutes while I cleaned up after dinner. At this rate, I'd end up in bed with my own headache. The girls planted themselves in front of the TV while I got the clean clothes out of the dryer. I folded them and thought about Nicole, Holly and Shawn at the movie together tonight. I knew Jake wasn't there because he had to babysit, so that made me feel a little better. I bit my lip, wishing I could have some fun instead of always being stuck at home. Sometimes just being in this house drove me bonkers. Another reason why the Pop's job was so important to me. A taste of something new, something different from this mundane routine was within reach. I just had to hold onto it.

I looked at the pile of Mom's clothes and wondered if it was a good time to approach her. I had the excuse of delivering her clothes to get me into her room. But she might be asleep.

Holding the stack of clothes, I placed my hand on the doorknob and heard a strange sound. Mom didn't have a TV or radio in her room, so what was it? I leaned my ear to the door. The jagged breathing, moans and muttering confused me. Then I knew. She wasn't just talking to herself. She was crying.

It would be a mistake to go in and catch her in that state. I knew, because it had happened years ago. Was this what Mom did every time she had a headache and closed herself in her room? Hmm. My curiosity was piqued, but there was no way to bring it up without her knowing I'd eavesdropped.

I decided to wait a few hours and try again. It was either that or wait until morning. But that was pushing it. I had nothing to do, so I joined Anna and Edie for some TV time.

When the girls got bored, I sent them upstairs to play for a while before bedtime. I sat on the couch, head in my hands, and tried to work up the courage to talk to Mom. I hesitated to wake her, but I also didn't want to have a sleepless night worrying about it.

I plodded down the hall toward Mom's room, my chest tight. Each step felt like I was marching to my execution. I listened at the door but heard nothing. I pushed the door open and let my eyes adjust as the light from the hall lit up one corner of the room. *Well, here goes nothing.* I nudged Mom's shoulder to wake her, then saw the two empty bottles lying on the bed next to her.

"Mom," I whispered. "I need to talk to you."

She moaned but opened her eyes a slit.

"I have an idea. It's about working at Pop's."

"Already said you can't work." Mom mumbled, her eyes closing again.

"But what if I promise to still take care of all the chores and cooking *and* take Anna and Edie with me to work?" I kept my voice low, soothing.

"What are you talking about, Libby?" Mom's breath smelled of alcohol and her eyes struggled to open.

"Well, there's a break room at Pop's where Anna and Edie could do their homework and read or watch TV while I work. They could come to the store after school, and they'd be taken care of. Isn't that what you were most worried about?"

Mom pressed her temples, and her forehead scrunched in wavy wrinkles. "They want you that bad? With two little girls tagging along? Doesn't make sense."

I heard the frustration in her voice and knew she wasn't far from losing it.

"Well, I thought I could go in for the shift tomorrow. While I'm there, I'll find out if it's okay. Then we'll know for sure."

I crossed my fingers and held my breath. Probably only ten seconds went by, but it felt like ten minutes. My stomach twisted. *Please, please, please agree!*

"Why...you want this job so bad?" Mom gritted her teeth. Her eyes narrowed like she was trying to solve a puzzle.

I ignored the question, not willing to give answers she wouldn't like. "Please, Mom, just let me try it out."

Mom's jaw clenched and I waited for the explosion. My breathing quickened as she stared at me for several seconds, then flopped back on her pillow with a huff. Her eyes closed again. I waited, ready to spring out of her way if she decided to come after me, but she just lay still. My eyes watered and I swallowed the lump in my throat. I guess that meant no.

I turned to leave, my hopes dashed, when she whispered, "If girls can't come, you quit."

I think that means I have a chance! Hallelujah!

I wanted to jump and cheer, but I didn't want to break the spell my mom must have been under. It was so rare for her to give in to anything. I prayed Jerri would agree to my proposal. Suddenly, I was excited for this weekend. I crossed my fingers that Pop's would soon become a safe place for me just like school. Anywhere but home.

7
Saturday, March 5, 1988

The sun was already shining through my curtains when I woke up. I let loose with a noisy yawn. Finally, a great night's sleep. I smiled, my mood matching the brightness of my room. I still barely believed Mom had agreed to let me go to work today. I knew she could change her mind at any time, so I was determined to hold her to her agreement. I hoped Jerri and Linda would agree to let my sisters hang around at the store every day. If not, I might find myself fired before I even started. It could be the shortest employment period in history.

Last night, I'd waited until Mom had fallen back to sleep before I called Jake. Even then, I only spoke in a whisper. Our only phone was a dark yellow push button type that hung on a wall in the kitchen, its color matching the tufts of wheat on the wallpaper. My grandma had grown up in Kansas and Mom said she hung that wallpaper because it reminded her of home. I dialed Jake's number, then held completely still except for running my finger over the nearest stalk of wheat. I was jumpy, afraid Mom would wake up and hear me.

The phone was picked up on the third ring, by Jake's younger brother, Tyler. His voice was garbled, like he'd just taken a big bite of food. I asked for Jake in a soft voice. He must have been nearby because it was only seconds before he was on the line.

"Jake!" I whispered. "It's Libby. My mom said yes!"

"Wait, what?" he asked. "Speak up."

I moved the volume of my whisper up a notch and repeated myself.

"No way!" Jake exclaimed. "How did that happen?"

I envisioned his astonished face and grinned. "I'll explain later. I just wanted to let you know."

After I hung up the phone, I went upstairs to my sister's room. Edie's face was sparkly from the play makeup Anna had applied to her face. Now Anna was having her turn being made up by Edie. I coughed to cover my laugh at Anna's clown-like appearance. Edie shot me a mischievous grin.

"Libby, doesn't Anna look rad? Like a movie star, right?"

"Mmm-hmm," I said. I walked behind Anna and faced Edie. I shook my head and drew my finger across my neck.

Edie's grin grew bigger. I wasn't sure why Anna had entrusted the little imp to make her look pretty.

I placed my hands on Anna's shoulders as I stood behind her. "Guess what? Mom said I could start the job at Pop's!"

Anna jumped out of her chair and faced me, her eyes wide. Unfortunately, Edie had been applying her lipstick and Anna's movement caused it to leave a bright red trail from her mouth to her ear. I chuckled and Edie sputtered and laughed.

"Really? I can't believe it!" Anna squealed. She threw her arms around me.

Edie grabbed Anna's arm and tried to force her back into the chair. Anna swatted her away like a pesky mosquito, her eyes still on me. "So, you start tomorrow?"

"Yep, at noon," I said. "But I still have to ask my supervisors if it's okay for you two to come hang out there every day after school. Cross your fingers they say yes."

Anna's brows shot up. I gave her a quick squeeze, spun her around and pressed her shoulders down until she was seated again.

Edie piped up, "Oh, I hope we can go to the store every day. Then I can get snacks!"

"Don't count on it, Edie," I warned. "You'd have to buy them."

I picked up a hand mirror from Anna's dresser and grinned at Edie. "Finish the makeover." I handed the mirror to Anna, then booked it to my bedroom.

Seconds later, Anna screamed, "Edie! You're dead meat!" Edie laughed hysterically while Anna issued threats. From the bumps and thumps, it sounded like a wrestling match had begun. I'd gone to bed after that feeling relieved and hopeful.

I stretched and got out of bed. Yikes! I was still sore. The right side of my rib cage hurt to touch. My bruises were slightly less purple in color, but they'd blended to look like one huge bruise on each side of my torso. It was the worst I'd seen in a long time. If I had to lift boxes at work, it might be painful. I gently stretched again to loosen my muscles.

The morning passed quickly while I helped my sisters clean out their closet, which was a disaster. Anna blamed Edie and Edie gladly took credit for the mess. I just shook my head and reminded them it was easier to clean a little at a time than all at once.

I waited until Mom got in the shower before I went into her bedroom to get the documents I needed for work. I slid my birth certificate and Social Security card out of a file and placed them in an empty school folder I found in my room. I didn't even see Mom until it was almost time to leave for work. I changed into my red Pop's polo and my athletic shoes and went to the kitchen to get an apple to eat on my walk to the store. Mom was hunched over the table, pen in hand as she studied some kind of paperwork. She looked up at the sound of the fridge door.

"I've never seen that shirt on you before."

"Well, it's the first time I've worn it," I rubbed the apple on my jeans and held it up to take a bite. "Gotta go!"

The sun was shining, but I knew the air was cool, so I grabbed my jacket from the coat rack. I shoved my arms through the sleeves and picked up the folder I'd placed on the floor by the girls' shoes. Mom followed me, confused.

"Where are you going?"

Was she for real? Did she not remember the conversation we had last night?

"To my new job." I smiled and opened the door. It protested with a squeal like a trapped mouse.

Before I could shut the door behind me, Mom caught it. What did she want? My skin prickled as I started down the steps.

"I already said you can't take the job!" Mom said to my back.

What? Was she losing it? I spun around, expecting to see anger, but she just looked baffled.

"No," I said. I backed down the last step onto the sidewalk. I was not going to let her stop me. "You changed your mind last night, as long as Edie and Anna can come to the store after school every day."

"What?" she asked softly.

I turned away, hoping the conversation was over. Let her figure it out. I heard the door close behind me and smiled.

"Wait!" Mom called.

My mouth drooped and I stopped but didn't turn around. I said a quick prayer in my head. *Please let me go! Please!*

I heard Mom's footsteps closing in, so I slowly faced her, wary.

"Did I *really* say that?" she looked at me with narrowed eyes, daring me to cross her.

"Yes, you did. The girls can tell you it's true." I was glad I'd told them about our conversation, but I felt a teeny bit sorry for Mom. How would it feel to not remember something that just happened the night before? Then again, it was her own actions that made her forget.

"So, the girls can come to the store every day then?" Mom folded her arms, ready to argue.

"I'm finding that out today," I reminded her. "I have to actually go in so I can ask them."

Mom scowled and said nothing. I took that as my signal to leave. I shoved my balled fists in my pockets and headed down the sidewalk. When I made it past the neighbor's yard, I blew out a breath I hadn't realized I was holding.

The warm sun on my face felt heavenly. The closer I got to Buckley Park, the louder the sounds of people enjoying the day became. Families picnicked, children chased balls and frisbees, and the swings on the playground were full. Their squeaks didn't quite drown out the sound of happy children. I wondered if Anna and Edie would end up there this afternoon.

When I got to the store, Rosie was manning the customer service desk again. Even her solemn face didn't put me off. I grinned and asked for Jerri as I bounced a little on my toes. Rosie must have heard I was starting today because she said, "You're early."

For some reason her response made me want to laugh, but I settled for a smile. "Well, better than late, I guess."

I wondered if she had experience with teenagers, because her eye roll was as big as the ones I saw every day at school. Still, she picked up the phone and called the office. "The newbie is here." She listened for a moment, then asked me if I had my paperwork. I held up my glittery purple folder.

Rosie confirmed that I had come prepared, then hung up and directed me to Jerri's office.

I thanked her, but she looked away. Whatever. Nothing was going to erase my good mood. I mean, it was a miracle I'd made it at all.

The first part of my shift was spent filling out paperwork in Jerri's office. Linda popped her head in and welcomed me to the team. Jerri handed me a packet of company policies and asked me to read over them at home. I wanted to ask about Edie and Anna, but it didn't feel like the right time. Honestly, I hesitated because I was afraid of the answer, but I still had my entire shift to bring it up.

When we finished in the office, Jerri gave me a tour of the store. I saw everything from the breakroom to the delivery bay to the refrigerated rooms in the back of the store. I met the two cashiers I'd seen the last time I'd come in. I was right – Robyn and Keith were siblings and they'd been working at the store since they were teens. We ended the tour in the back of the store next to some shelves of unopened boxes.

"This is the area you'll pull from to stock our canned foods and dry goods." She explained the system they used for keeping track of inventory and food expiration dates. It seemed straightforward enough. Once Jerri finished her instructions, it was time to begin. We each grabbed a dolly and loaded boxes of canned fruit on them. I stifled a groan as my ribs protested the weight of the boxes. The load felt very heavy and at one point I almost dropped the dolly. Mick, the balding middle-aged warehouse manager, offered to help. I thanked him but told him I'd better learn to do it myself. He told me the more I did it, the easier it would become.

As Jerri showed me how and where to place the cans of applesauce, peaches, pineapple, and fruit cocktail, we chatted and got to know each other. She talked about her husband and their fishing, hiking, and camping adventures. She told me they'd never had children, which she used to be sad about, but she said it gave her more time to dote on her nieces and nephews.

I thought about my Uncle Paul. How well did I know him? The truth was, not well at all. If I showed up on his doorstep and told him my story, would he believe me and be spurred to action? Or would he even care?

Stocking shelves on a busy Saturday afternoon meant we were sometimes in the way of shoppers. We had to work around them, which made filling the shelves go a little slower than I'd thought it would. The store was filled with sounds of squeaky shopping carts, crying babies, announcements about sales, and music playing over the intercom. I saw some classmates walk by, but I turned my head so they wouldn't see me.

After working side by side for a couple hours, I felt comfortable enough with Jerri to bring up my sisters. As I placed new cans of peaches behind the older ones, I told her that I had two younger sisters and explained that I had to watch them while my mom was at work. She didn't respond, so I pulled my head out of the shelf I was filling to look at her.

To my horror, there stood my mother, glaring at Jerri as if she wanted her to go up in flames. Jerri didn't flinch. She kept her professional mask in place.

"Hello, Donna," she said.

My eyes widened. Jerri knew my mother? And why was Mom here? Was she trying to get me fired? Whatever the reason, this was not an accidental encounter. I wrung my hands together and felt perspiration break out on my face and torso.

Mom took her eyes off Jerri, put her hands on her hips and glared at me. "Well, what did she say?" Mom asked, pointing at Jerri with her elbow.

Crap! I should have asked earlier. I blinked a few times and mumbled, "I was just about to ask her."

"Ask me what?" Jerri prompted. Her eyes flicked to me.

Mom folded her arms and smirked. Ugh, the expression I hated most.

Looking back at Jerri, I explained, "Since my mom works until six o'clock every day, and I watch my sisters after school, I was wondering if they could walk here after school and hang out in the break room until my shift is over." I suddenly realized that arrangement might be asking too much. Embarrassed for being so presumptuous, my cheeks flamed red.

Jerri studied my face, which embarrassed me even more. She turned to my mom, who wore her smirk like a gold medal.

"Are they well-behaved, Libby?" Jerri directed her question at me but continued to stare at my mom.

"Yeah, they are. Anna is quiet, studious. Edie's a bit feisty, but she'll behave here." I hoped with all my might that would prove to be true. I'd have to explain the consequences of misbehavior to her later if Jerri allowed them to come. I was eager for Jerri's approval of me and my work, but I was desperate for her permission to let my sisters come every day.

Jerri was silent for a long harrowing moment. Finally, she looked at me and said, "Then I don't see why not."

I released the breath I'd been holding into an audible sigh. Jerri was an angel.

"Oh, thank you so much!" I said.

Jerri turned back to Mom, whose mouth had dropped open. "If there's nothing else I can do for you, Donna, I've got to keep training Libby."

"Now you wait just a minute!" Mom argued. "She's my daughter and..."

"And she's on the clock right now, so we need to work." Jerri cut off her protest and gestured toward the stack of boxes.

Mom looked as if she didn't know whether to fight or retreat. Her eyes sparked with anger, but she said nothing. I chose to do what Jerri did, so I turned to the unopened boxes. I reached in my pocket for the box cutter and squatted down to slice open the next box. Jerri caught my eye as we both leaned over our boxes.

"Thank you," I mouthed. She just nodded.

I was startled when Mom blurted, "You just remember, Libby, if you don't keep up on your grades and do your chores and make dinner, you'll have to stop working here." I looked up to see her paste on a fake smile before she stalked away down the aisle. I watched until she was gone, then glanced at Jerri.

"I'm sorry, I shouldn't have just assumed I could bring the girls with me. I really appreciate it." I slid a few cans of pineapple slices onto the lowest shelf.

Jerri caught my wrist. Her face was serious. Had she changed her mind?

"Look, I'll have to run it by Linda, but as long as your sisters stay in the break room and don't cause any trouble, it shouldn't be a problem. Besides, I like you, Libby." Jerri's eyes had regained their familiar sparkle. "Things usually have a way of working themselves out."

My heart regained its normal rhythm, and I marveled at my luck in meeting this woman. When the fruit was fully stocked, we took the dollies back to the warehouse. Jerri showed me the paperwork that I had to fill out for Mick, so he would know which foods to order in the correct quantities. I was introduced to two more cashiers, Pam and Nadine, who also sometimes manned the customer service desk.

My shift was almost over when I remembered to ask Jerri how she knew my mom. She scrunched up her nose like she smelled something rotten.

"We went to high school together. We were so-so friends, but your mom was kind of hard to like. It seems she hasn't changed much."

Jerri's frankness surprised me.

"Yeah, she's angry a lot. I don't really know why, though." I ducked my face and studied my shoes, embarrassed by the admission.

Jerri's lips pressed into a flat line. "She always did have a fiery temper. I remember she could be very bossy."

I wanted to ask more questions, but Jerri said my shift was over. She walked me back to the time clock and watched as I punched out. She thanked me for my hard work and told me she'd see me on Monday.

I exited the store into the busy parking lot and almost collided with a shopping cart being pushed by a white-haired lady who could barely see over the top of it. I scooted around her and smiled as she apologized. I rubbed my ribs, which felt painfully tender from moving heavy boxes around. I strolled home at a snail's pace, in no rush to get there, almost positive I'd be facing my mother's fiery temper again.

8
Saturday, March 5, 1988
Later that day

B uckley Park was even busier than it had been before work. Three boys around Anna's age were throwing a baseball around, the ball smacking their mitts with a satisfying thwack. A couple of pre-teen girls were trying unsuccessfully to keep a kite aloft. The jungle gym and tall slides were crawling with children eager to leave behind the confines of their homes after a long winter. Even though I was sore and tired, I made a detour through the park, wondering if Edie and Anna had come here to play today. Tiny lavender crocuses were pushing their way out of the soft ground in the beds surrounding the main path through the park.

I passed by the ball fields occupied by tee ball teams whose players were barely taller than the tee. The kids seemed to be doing whatever they wanted while their parents shouted encouragement from the stands. I thought it must be painful for them to watch their children make up their own rules while the coaches tried to provide instruction and correction. I laughed out loud as one gangly, freckle-faced boy ran the bases in the reverse order. The crowd got especially loud as they screamed at him to go the other way.

A few families were beginning to gather under a large, covered bowery. One of them had a bucket of fried chicken, the smell of which made my mouth water. Hunger gnawed at my belly. A quick peek at my watch told me I'd better get a move on. I'd dawdled long enough. It was time to face the dragon.

As I reached the corner of the park, I saw two girls basking in the sun. A familiar head of long, red hair was splayed out on a blanket. The shorter girl beside her wore glasses that had slid down her nose while she painted her toenails bright pink. Her dark hair was pulled back with a neon green scrunchie.

"Hey there!" I called and trotted toward them.

Nicole looked up and smiled, "Oh, hey Libby!"

I stopped at the blanket, where Holly opened one eye, saw it was me, and closed it again. "I'm enjoying this sunshine today," she said, waving her arm through the air.

"Whatcha doing?" Nicole paused her painting.

"I just got off work at Pop's. I'm headed home now."

"Did you like it?" Holly asked, as she rolled onto her side and squinted up at me.

"Yeah, I thought it was fun!" I wasn't embellishing my enthusiasm. I really did enjoy it.

Nicole replaced the lid on the bottle of nail polish. "It would have to be *very* fun for me to want to get a job!" She giggled.

"How much do you get paid?" Holly asked. Her hand shielded her eyes from the sun.

"Minimum wage," I replied. "$3.35 an hour." It was my first time getting paid for doing any kind of work, so it sounded like a lot to me.

Nicole snorted.

I was proud of the fact that I'd gotten hired and was getting paid, so I felt a bit defensive. "Well, that's $3.35 more an hour than you're making."

Holly laughed and covered her mouth. "Ooh, Nic, she just burned you!"

Nicole rolled her eyes. "Yeah, yeah, I hear you!" She paused, then addressed Holly. "You invited Libby over tonight, right?"

Nicole's question seemed to light a fire under Holly, and she pushed herself to a sitting position with her ankles crossed. "You have to come Libby! We're going to watch *Ferris Bueller's Day Off* and have cake and ice cream for Shawn's birthday. We're starting at seven."

"Oh yeah, I'll ask when I get home," I lied. There was no way I'd be asking Mom, not after what just happened at the store. "And, speaking of home, I've got to get going."

With a promise to call Holly if I could come over later, I trotted back to the main path. I thought about my first day on the job. I felt proud when talking to my friends about it. But now I had to make sure I didn't do anything to upset Mom so she wouldn't forbid me to work. I did not want to lose this feeling of independence. It was new for me, and I liked it.

The house looked deserted when I reached it, but Mom's car was parked on the gravel drive. I was surprised Anna and Edie weren't playing outside on such a nice day. I wondered if Mom was still angry about the store confrontation. I wasn't too happy with her for embarrassing me, but it could have been much worse.

Not wanting to call attention to myself, I eased the front door open, but I forgot about the new squeak. My sisters sat on the living room floor playing Chinese Checkers. When they heard the squeaky door, they jumped up from the game.

"Libby!" They both ran at me and nearly knocked me over.

I laughed. "Alright, alright! Let me in the house please!" I tickled them and they let go of me. I hung up my jacket while they parked themselves on the brown shag carpet again. Mom must have heard the commotion because when I turned around, she'd appeared from the back of the house. Her arms were folded, and she was scowling. Inwardly I sighed, and my heart thumped faster. Not this again! I didn't want to argue with her anymore. It seemed she was always angry about something.

But Mom didn't say a word. She just stood there glowering. My good spirits crashed to the floor.

"Look how many jumps I got!" yelled Edie. I glanced over to see her eyes filled with glee. Anna was a good sport, congratulating Edie on her successful turn.

"How do you line it all up so perfectly like that?" Anna asked.

Edie shrugged, but the look on her face said she was up to something. Anna didn't seem to notice. I looked back at Mom, who had also been distracted by my sisters.

"I'm going to my room to do my homework," I said. I started up the stairs, but Mom said, "Libby, stop right there!"

I paused on the third step. Since Mom was around the corner from the staircase, she couldn't see me, but my sisters could. Hearing Mom's tone, they froze like statues. I tilted my head in the direction of the front door. Anna knew what I meant right away.

"Edie, let's go play outside for a while. We can finish this game later." She jumped off the floor and grabbed Edie's arm, half-dragging her across the living room. Edie smacked at Anna's hand. "Stop it, Anna!"

"You two!" Mom bellowed. "Knock it off unless you want to be punished!" Edie frowned and plugged her ears.

"Come on!" Anna whined, still pulling on Edie. Edie must have realized she didn't have much choice, so she ran to the front door and flung it open.

"Fine! I'm going now!" She stuck her tongue out at Anna and then glared at Mom before spinning around and throwing herself out the door. She was on the verge of a temper tantrum. Anna followed and slammed the door behind her. Mom mumbled something I couldn't hear as she came into view.

"Libby, go sit down." Mom pointed at the couch. Her scowl said she meant business.

This was so unfair. I felt like I'd just gotten caught breaking the law. All for walking into the house. Well, that and the store confrontation.

I did as Mom demanded, my hands shaking slightly. I sat down and shoved them under my thighs, feeling the fuzzy fabric of the couch under my knuckles. "What's going on?"

"You know exactly what's going on!" Mom snarled as she stood over me. "You tricked me last night into letting you keep that stupid job! Then I go to check on you only to find you being buddy-buddy with one of my former friends."

What? That wasn't what happened last night. She was crazy! I shook my head. "I didn't trick you!" I pulled my hands out from under me and balled them into fists.

"Yes, you did! You got me to say you could work only after I'd been drinking."

I shook my head back and forth. This was ridiculous. The heat of my own temper began to flare. "No, I asked last night because I was supposed to start the job today." I didn't add that it wasn't *my* fault Mom chose to drink last night.

Mom gritted her teeth, then grabbed my wrist and dug her fingernails into the underside of my arm. I gasped and tried to yank my arm away. She dug in harder, so I let my arm go limp. Mom's jaw hardened as she flung my arm down.

"Wimp!" She leaned close to my face and breathed out a threat. "There's more where that came from if you lie to me!"

I rubbed my arm and drew my head back, so her face wasn't so close. I just wanted to go to my room.

Mom folded her arms, her jaw clenched. "So, what did you and Jerri talk about?"

I rehearsed the responsibilities and procedures my job position required. "Jerri just taught me how to do all that."

"What did she say about me?"

My forehead creased. Why was that such a big deal? "Jerri said she knew you in high school. That was about it." No way was I going to tell her what Jerri actually thought of her.

"And she didn't say why we aren't friends now?"

I shook my head. "We really only talked about work stuff."

"Well, you're lucky, you know," Mom spat. "I could've dragged you right out of that store if I'd wanted to." Her face once again loomed inches away from mine. I tightened my balled-up hands.

Oh, I knew she'd wanted to drag me out of Pop's. I had Jerri to thank for preventing that from happening. Mom had seemed hesitant to act against me in Jerri's presence for some reason. That was something to explore in the future.

"I find it hard to believe that the store would want two little girls hanging around there every day," Mom went on.

I just shrugged. I knew Mom was shocked Jerri had agreed to that. I'm sure she thought it would be a deal-breaker, the one thing that could prevent me from keeping the job. But Jerri had come through for me, even though she didn't really know me and without having ever met my sisters. I owed her for sure. Mom and I continued our staredown. She looked so old, hard lines etched in her face.

"Can I go now?" I asked. "I have homework to do."

Mom hesitated, then stepped back and flicked her hand, dismissing me. Inside, I sighed in relief. I raced up the stairs to my room and shut the door behind me. I went to the window to search for Anna and Edie. My window faced the backyard, so I figured they'd be there.

I pulled the worn curtain aside. Sure enough, there they were, on the sidewalk, playing hopscotch. The grid had been drawn in wobbly pink chalk lines, with blue numbers marking the squares. I watched as Anna tossed a rock down the grid, then hopped through the course, pausing to pick up her rock. Edie sat alongside the sidewalk with a bored expression. She mindlessly pulled tufts of grass from the lawn, then piled them up by hopscotch square number three.

I opened my window and called down to them. I said everything was fine and suggested they ask to play in the park where they could enjoy the nice weather and find some of their friends. Edie immediately jumped up and grabbed Anna's hand.

I left the window open while I sprawled on my bed and worked on my geometry problems. I didn't understand the new concept very well, so the assignment took a while to complete. When I was finally finished, I slammed the book and stretched my tense muscles. The time on the clock surprised me. It was later than I thought. Why hadn't I been called for dinner yet? Mom always made dinner on the weekends.

The house was quiet when I ran downstairs, looking for the rest of the family. No one was in the living room or the kitchen. There was also no sign of a hot meal either. Weird. I peeked into the laundry room. Nobody. That left Mom's bedroom, where the door was closed. There was no answer when I knocked, which probably meant she was asleep. Without making a sound, I opened the door. The room was tidy, no clothes littering the floor today. The double bed with its frilly cream bedspread took up one side of the room. A large brown dresser with a mirror attached took up another wall. On top of the dresser sat a stack of envelopes, a letter opener and a small, framed picture of Grandma. I stepped into the room and picked up the photo. I hadn't looked at it in a long time. Grandma's smile showed no teeth. She had more of a placating expression than one of happiness. Gosh, I missed her. I set the picture back on the dresser. Maybe everyone was outside.

The backyard was deserted. I even checked the shed. Next, the side yard, then around the house to the front yard. Mom sat on the porch step, her elbows propped on her knees. Her chin rested on her hands as she stared at the street. I couldn't discern her mood, but she didn't look angry.

"Hey, I was looking for everyone. Where are the girls?"

Mom's eyes flicked in my direction for a split second, then went back to watching the street. "They went to the park for a bit, but here they come now." She pointed down the road. "You sure took long enough on your homework," she said, as if I purposely couldn't figure out my math problems.

"It's geometry," I replied. "It's tricky." I knew I sounded defensive, but I was irritated she thought I should race right through it.

My stomach growled, reminding me I hadn't eaten since that apple before work. "When is dinner?"

Mom's jaw tightened. "Whenever you make it." Her tone was icy. *Wait. What?*

Mom must have seen the confusion on my face because she said in a slightly sing-song voice, "It's your responsibility."

"But...I don't cook on the weekends."

Mom's eyes were flinty, and her voice like steel. "Well, that was before you took that job. So, it just became your responsibility." She raised her eyebrows, triumphant.

My mouth dropped open. "But that's not fair!"

"You know the girls are going to be hungry." Mom pointed at my sisters, who had almost made it to the yard.

I jerked back, stunned. I already cooked all the meals Monday through Friday. But I knew what she was doing. She wanted me to have so many responsibilities that I wouldn't have time for the job. She wanted me to fail so I'd have to quit working.

A silent scream echoed through my brain. My fists clenched tight, and I took a deep breath, willing myself to be calm. Mom was waiting for a reaction, and I didn't want to give her the satisfaction.

"Fine, I'll start it now." It took much effort to keep my voice steady, when all I felt like doing was crying my eyes out. I didn't have long to dwell on it before I got hugged from behind by a pair of little arms.

"Libby! You should have gone to the park with us," Edie exclaimed. "Mikey's dad was making the merry-go-round spin so fast!"

"Yeah, it was so fun!" Anna agreed.

I pried Edie's arms from my waist and tousled her hair. "Sorry. Homework had to be done."

"What's for dinner?" Edie asked Mom.

Mom's smirk was back. "Libby just became our full-time cook. You'll have to ask her."

The glint in her eye made me sick to my stomach. I couldn't take it anymore. Ignoring everyone, I stomped to the backyard. I didn't realize Anna had run after me until I stopped by the tree stump next to the shed. She didn't say anything, just gave me a searching look. I was angrier than I'd been in a long time, and I kicked the stump over and over until my toes began to protest.

Anna pulled at my arm, but I barely noticed she was there. Hot tears dripped down my face as I plopped onto the stump, bent forward and dropped my face to my lap. After a minute or so, I realized Anna was patting the back of my head. She didn't say anything, just kept patting. Eventually, my tears stopped and when I lifted my head and wiped my hand under my nose, she whispered, "Why does Mom make you do everything?"

I shrugged. I'd been asking myself that quite often lately.

"It isn't fair!" she said.

I nodded, not trusting my voice to give a response.

"I have an idea," she said. "You could teach me to cook. That way I can help you, especially if you're really busy."

Gosh, I loved this girl! She was always so sweet. I took a deep, shuddery breath and grabbed her into a hug. "Okay then, let's get started."

We plodded up the back steps and went inside. Mom and Edie must have still been on the front steps, because there were no lights on and the house was getting dark. I flipped on the kitchen light and opened a couple of cabinets, trying to figure out a last-minute meal. My eyes landed on a box of macaroni and cheese. That would work. I pulled it off the shelf and handed it to Anna.

"Is this okay with you?"

"Yum, I love mac and cheese!"

Anna's enthusiasm made the corners of my lips lift. "It's super easy to make. I'll let you read the instructions and try it. I'll help you when you need it."

We washed our hands and Anna read the box and began gathering supplies. She filled the pot with water, too much at first, then set it on the stove, adjusting the gas flame underneath. She opened the box and pulled out the cheese powder packet. I watched Anna out of the corner of my eye while I gathered the rest of our dinner: a can of corn, a can of black-eyed peas and bread to make garlic toast. It certainly wasn't a special meal, but it seemed special to me because my sister was there helping me.

Mom wasn't going to be happy with mac and cheese, but I wasn't a fan of being the chef every single day, so I guess we were even. I heaved a deep sigh and Anna glanced at me.

"I'm fine," I said. As fine as I could be after working hard all day. I had hoped to relax a bit, but I couldn't be that lucky, right?

Anna waited for the noodles to cook while I made the toast and heated the side dishes. I helped Anna drain the pasta and as she added the powder mix, butter and milk, we heard the front door squeak open. I glanced at the clock. It was six-forty. I wondered what

Mom and Edie had been doing outside while they waited for dinner to be made.

Edie made her usual noisy entrance. She dropped her shoes with a thud and yelled, "I'm here!" She came into the kitchen, took a look around and whined, "I'm hungry! Isn't it ready yet?"

I bit my lip, so I wouldn't snap at her. "You could help by filling the water glasses."

Edie stuck her bottom lip out in a pout. "I don't want to."

Anna jumped in before I could. "Well, we won't be ready until you do that."

Edie grumbled but started the task. Score another point for Anna.

Mom wandered in and leaned against the fridge. She looked at the food. "Macaroni and cheese is disgusting."

"Sorry." I shrugged and glanced at Anna. Her shoulders had fallen, and her smile sagged. *Gee, thanks, Mom! Way to put down Anna's first dinner-making attempt!* I nudged Anna and gave her a wink.

Anna set the table while I brought over the steaming food. No one said anything as we dished up. I took a big bite of the noodles and praised my sister. "Oh, yum! Good job, Anna!" She beamed and Mom shook her head, annoyed.

Edie began a long commentary about the park, the competition with her friend to see who could swing the highest, and the little boy who had fallen off the see-saw. I certainly didn't feel like talking, so I was glad she rambled on and on.

As I cleared the table, Mom announced that she needed to run to K-Mart to get some light bulbs and cleaning supplies. She left her dishes on the table and took the store list off the fridge door. I acknowledged her with a nod, then watched as she lifted her purse from the coatrack and left out the front door.

"Thanks for helping with dinner, Anna." I put my arm around her shoulder and gave her a squeeze. She helped finish dinner clean-up, then I suggested we all play a game. I thought about calling Holly to let her know I couldn't come to the party, but I didn't feel like answering any questions.

The three of us sat cross-legged on the living room floor around the game Edie had chosen, *Hi-Ho Cherry-O*. We played it three times, each of us taking a win by having the most cherries in our basket. Anna wanted to play *Clue* next. It was her favorite game, but since Edie wasn't great at figuring out the suspect, weapon and room where the crime was committed, she whined, "I don't like that game!"

"Too bad," I said. "We played your game three times, so you get to play ours too."

Edie moaned, "But it's too hard."

"Look, if you can't be a good sport, you can do chores instead."

Anna and I shared a smile while Edie flopped to the floor. Finally, she sat up and folded her arms, a frown on her face. "Okay, fine!"

I couldn't help but laugh and we started the game. I figured out the solution, but could tell Anna was close, so I let her beat me to it. After we picked up the game, I looked at my watch. It was eight-fifteen. Mom had been gone a long time for just picking up lightbulbs and cleaning products.

I told the girls my pick was *Twister* and they both squealed, "Yes, yes, yes!"

We were in the middle of our third round when the front door opened, and Mom walked in. Edie was positioned in an awkward backbend. Anna's arms stretched under Edie and my feet were spread four dots apart, with one arm over Edie. I had just flicked the spinner with my free arm and called out, "Left foot blue!" We shrieked and laughed as we tried to maneuver around each other without falling over.

"What is all the commotion?" Mom yelled. All three of us froze. We didn't dare move a muscle. Mom's expression was full of rage. "I could hear you all screaming when I got out of the car!"

Edie squealed, "I'm going to fall!" She toppled over, dragging me and Anna with her. Anna shrieked and I groaned as she trapped my leg underneath her and my sore ribs got bumped.

"Ow!" I moaned and tried to pull out my pinned leg.

Suddenly Anna seemed to fly off me. I heard her cry out as some part of her body connected with the coffee table. I couldn't tell what had happened because I was facing the other direction, but Edie screamed, "Leave her alone!"

I rolled over and saw Mom drag Anna to the couch. She shoved her down and smacked her face. Anna burst into tears, her eyes filled with terror. She clamped her hands over her face and leaned onto her legs. Edie pulled at Mom from behind and Mom turned toward her.

"Stop!" I yelled. I started to rise from the floor when Mom kicked my already bruised ribs. The blow took my breath away and I fell back to the ground, desperately trying to suck air into my lungs. I watched, helpless, as Mom pushed Edie down. Edie began to cry, but she jumped up and fought back, wildly flinging her arms at Mom. Mom grabbed her arms and held them. Edie managed to get her foot on Mom's leg and pushed. By that time, I had risen, holding onto my side. I took two steps toward Mom. She saw me coming and released Edie.

"I want it quiet out here!" she roared. She picked up the K-Mart bag she'd dropped in her haste to shut us up. She held the bag close to her chest, but I had already seen the contents. There were no cleaning supplies, just lightbulbs and beer. Two of the cans were empty and slightly crushed. That explained why she'd taken so long to run the errand. She'd probably sat in the parking lot and downed the beer before driving home.

Disgusted, I glared at her back as she carried the bag into her bedroom and slammed the door. Anna had curled herself into a ball on the couch. Her cries were muffled by the sofa cushions, but her back shuddered violently. Edie sat against the wall, tears on her furious face. She took my outstretched hand, and I pulled her up. I inspected her face and kissed her forehead. We moved to the couch where Edie sat on one end, and I sat on the other. Gently rubbing Anna's back, I whispered, "It will be okay." I repeated it over and over, wishing that saying the words would make it true.

Gradually, Anna's sobs subsided, and I lifted her, so she was sitting next to me. I wrapped my arms around both of my sisters. Tears threatened as we embraced. I was their protector, but tonight I had failed them. I couldn't keep doing this alone. We needed someone's help.

We sat without speaking for close to ten minutes, then I whispered, "Get your pajamas on and brush your teeth. Bring your pillows and blankets to my room and we'll have a sleepover." Edie popped up and I added, "A very quiet sleepover!"

The girls headed upstairs while I picked up the *Twister* mat, folded it and placed it in the game box. I stacked the games we'd played back on the bookshelf in the corner. I locked the doors and turned out the lights and hauled myself upstairs, exhausted from the long day.

The girls dragged their blankets to my bedroom and quickly arranged everything so we all could sleep together on the floor. In the bathroom, I inspected my injuries again. I stared at my reflection in the mirror and promised I would get us out of this mess. Later, as an extra precaution before crawling into the blankets on the floor, I pushed my dresser against the door. I didn't want Mom to come in during the night.

The girls were ready to discuss what had just happened as we cuddled together. I tried without success to answer Edie's questions about Mom's behavior. It wasn't long before the girls drifted off to sleep. I lay there, too many unpleasant scenes replaying through my mind. Instead of dwelling on them for long, I made plans, discarded plans, then tried again. Eventually, my eyes closed, and I gave in to my fatigue.

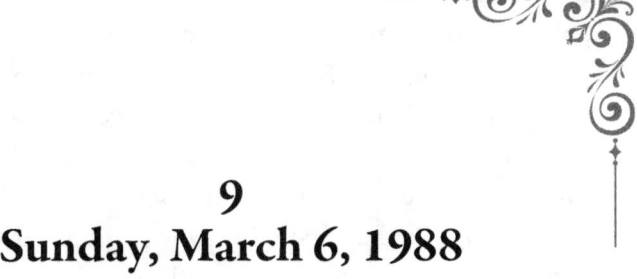

9
Sunday, March 6, 1988

Saturday's events left my sisters and I physically, mentally, and emotionally exhausted, so despite sleeping on the hard floor, we slept in Sunday morning. Even once we were awake, we stayed snuggled together for a while, not wanting to face another day at home with Mom.

Lucky for us, Mom stayed in her room most of the day. To pass the time, I did some reading. The girls watched TV, but tired of it quickly.

"I'm so bored, Libby," Edie said. She pulled at my shirt while I read.

"Go do something else then," I said, refusing to be distracted from my fictional world.

"I don't know what to do though," Edie whined.

I flipped the book closed but kept my finger inside to mark my place. "Look, Edie, what are you gonna do at Pop's every afternoon if you're bored? Because you'll be there every day for a couple of hours."

"I don't know." Edie flopped onto my lap.

"Well, then, let's talk about it now." I let the book close and set it down. "This is what you'll do. First, homework –"

Edie groaned. Anna rolled off her belly and sat up, listening.

"—that Anna will help you with if you need it."

Anna's brow furrowed. "I will?"

I sighed. It was better we were having this conversation now than at Pop's tomorrow. "Yes, Anna, I'm sorry. Just do the best you can." I looked at Edie again. "Then you'll need to read or color or watch TV. But you *must* follow the rules, or you won't be allowed to come with me. Got it?"

Edie looked wary. "What are the rules?"

I held up a finger. "Number one. You have to stay in the breakroom." Two fingers. "Homework gets done before anything else." Three fingers. "No fighting. You have to listen to Anna." Four fingers. "Do not bother any of the employees. Oh, and number five would be to come straight to Pop's after school."

Once both girls agreed, I sent them off to gather crayons and coloring books to put in their backpacks for after school.

Anna and I made a chicken pot pie from a Bisquick recipe along with baked potatoes for dinner. Anna was a fast learner and seemed to enjoy cooking. When I complimented her on the food, she smiled. When dinner was ready, Mom shuffled out of her room looking disheveled. She ignored us and ate with her head propped in her hand the entire meal. No one talked much. Anna seemed jumpy and she shoveled her food down, the first to finish and be excused. Mom finished next and without a word, went directly back to her bedroom leaving Edie and me at the table. I was more relieved than anything. No explosions at dinner usually meant a calm evening.

As I packed our lunches for school on Sunday evening, I realized again that we were running low on food. We were almost out of milk, and the cupboards and fridge were looking empty. Mom really needed to go shopping, but I feared telling her.

Only the thought of not having enough food for my sister's lunches made me swallow my fear. Holding Mom's stack of clothes that were still in the laundry room, I knocked on her bedroom door and waited for a response. I put my ear to the door, but heard nothing, so I knocked again, louder the second time. I heard Mom groan. Then, "What do you want?"

I opened the door but didn't enter. The room was pitch black and it took a second for my eyes to adjust. Mom was lying in bed with a washcloth draped over her eyes and forehead.

"Here's your clean laundry." I walked to her dresser and set the clothes next to Grandma's photo.

"Okay," she mumbled and rolled over in my direction. I hesitated, not wanting to make her angry again.

"Um, we're running low on food."

Mom didn't respond. I repeated my words, even though I was more nervous to repeat it than to say it the first time.

"I heard you, Libby. Make me a list. I'll go tomorrow after work." Mom's voice was weak.

"Are you alright?" I asked.

Mom huffed. "Would you please just go? And make the girls be quiet." Whatever the girls were doing upstairs was creating a lot of noise.

"Yeah, okay. I'll leave the list on the table."

I made a very long list, including some snacks the girls liked. Mom would veto buying them if she couldn't afford them, but it didn't hurt to try. Packing my Pop's polo into my backpack made me smile. I couldn't wait to get back to the store. Mondays made me happy anyway because I got out of the house. So, tomorrow was like getting the extra credit problem on a math test correct. A happy bonus. I crossed my fingers the girls would behave themselves at the store, that Linda would agree they could continue to come to Pop's, and that I would stay caught up in school with all my new responsibilities.

10
Monday, March 7, 1988

Anticipation put a smile on my face as I walked out the door for school. If I hadn't been excited about my new job, the chill in the air would have ruined my mood. Mother Nature did this every spring. Cold rainy days were followed by a quick warm-up, lulling us into believing the cold days were over, only to drop us back into cooler temperatures. The sky was a dull gray, the kind that refused to let in any sunlight. I shivered.

My mind wandered back to the sleepover I'd had with my sisters. Anna had asked with that serious tone of hers, "Libby, what's wrong with Mom?" I told her I didn't know, which was mostly the truth. I'd been too mad at the time, so I purposely pushed the question out of my head, not wanting to waste time thinking about someone who seemed to care so little for us. But I kept hearing Anna's sweet voice asking me again and again. Now it was my turn to wonder.

I didn't understand Mom's behavior or her increased rage. True, she'd been abusive toward me in the past when she was angry, but those episodes used to be a little more sporadic. They occurred more like every couple of weeks. Lately they'd come every couple of days. What was making her so bitter? And why did she think it was okay to hurt her children?

When I was younger, I thought that since Mom was sometimes mean and violent, all moms acted the same way. As each year brought more maturity, knowledge, and experience, I realized how wrong

I'd been. Mom needed counseling, but I knew she'd never agree to it. She had never once apologized for her actions, always putting the blame on us. So, no matter *what* was wrong with her, it was imperative someone step in. I was scared though, because Mom had often threatened us to never say anything to anyone. "What happens in our family is our business and no one else's!" she yelled for the first time a couple of years ago. Her next fit of rage brought the full threat, "If you ever say anything about me, I'll make you pay!"

The malice in her eyes made me believe her. I had no desire to cross my mother. I *had* to earn the money to get me and Jake to Columbus to find Uncle Paul, although it was going to take all the courage I could muster. Once we decided on the date to leave, it had to be done fast, because if Mom found us before we found Paul...well... I shuddered at the thought.

The long honk of a car horn startled me out of my worry. I'd almost stepped into the path of a rusty, blue VW Bug that was turning into the school parking lot. The driver's window came down and a ruddy-faced boy stuck his head out, "Hey, watch where you're going!"

"Sorry!" Sheesh, I was going to get hit if I didn't pay more attention. A high school parking lot wasn't exactly the safest place to walk.

I admired the old, red brick building which made a U-shape around the front parking lot. The main entrance sat under an oversized clock which was evenly lined up with the second story windows. A courtyard with benches and trees extended out from the main doors. It had a welcoming vibe but the only thing it was missing was a dormitory. Then I could live at school instead of at home. My daydreams were filled with ideas like that.

Several students congregated outside, while many more poured through the entrance. I had no desire to stay outside in the cold, so I headed indoors. The small commons area was packed with students, and I had to dart through them in an erratic path. I wanted to find Jake so I could fill him in on all that had happened over the weekend.

I passed the oversized trophy case that was bursting at the seams and headed to Jake's locker. He wasn't there, so I wandered through the halls searching for his white-blond hair. When the bell rang, I shrugged and gave up. Either he was late or absent.

Later, when I walked into second period biology, Jake was seated at his desk next to mine. I hoped it was a lab day, so I'd have more freedom to talk to him, but Mrs. Zeigler lectured all period while we took notes. I only managed to ask Jake where he'd been earlier. He pulled out his cheek with his thumb and finger, letting them go with a squelching sound. "Dentist," he responded. "Got a cavity filled. Can't feel my face."

I got lucky in home-ec though. It was a cooking day, and we were making mint brownies from scratch. Jake and I worked in a group with two boys, Boyd and Scott, who had no desire to learn to cook. So Jake and I always cooked while they did the clean-up. They always managed to look like they were participating when Mrs. Fielding walked by. It was fine by me because then Jake and I could chat.

We gathered our ingredients and headed to the yellow kitchen to start on the recipe. The yellow kitchen was surrounded by six other kitchens, each in a different color. Cooking days were always a little chaotic and noisy. Once the brownies were in the oven and the mint icing was mixed, I whispered to Jake, "My weekend was rough."

Jake's eyes darted to Scott and Boyd who were at the sink washing dishes. Then he looked at me, his eyes cloudy. "What happened?"

I filled him in about my mom confronting me at work, whispering so I wouldn't be overheard. Jake's eyes widened, "Oh, wow! I'm actually a little shocked."

"I know. But Jerri helped me out. I totally owe her." Then I told him about Saturday night when Mom came home after drinking and hit my sisters and me. "We were just playing a game, but the noise must have bothered her, because she went berserk!"

"What?!" Jake exploded, his face red.

"Shh!" I glanced around, but all the kitchen groups were being so loud no one had noticed. Boyd and Scott put the dishes away while Jake and I leaned against the far cupboards.

"I don't know how you put up with it, Libby!" Jake pounded his fist on the bright countertop. "Is this the first time she's hurt your sisters?"

"No. It's usually just me, but she's getting worse. That's why it's so important to find my uncle. Someone needs to know."

"Well, *I* already know!" Jake's jaw tightened. "I could go to the school counselor and tell her about it right now, and it could all be over!"

"But my mom will just deny it, Jake. Then she'd find a way to get back at you. I don't want that. I just think a relative would be a better option. As soon as I make enough money for two bus tickets and food, we're going to find my uncle."

Jake sighed. "How long will it take to earn the money?"

I did some calculations in my head. "A few weeks at least."

"Maybe I just need to witness her in action again," Jake suggested. "I mean, I'm not a little kid anymore and I'm not afraid of her!"

I shook my head. The buzzer sounded on the oven. Jake grabbed an oven mitt and pulled out the brownies. He took them to an oversized refrigerator across the room to cool before we iced them. When he returned, he whispered, "It could work!"

"No, it won't!" I answered fiercely. "I'm afraid you might go after her if you saw her hit me. Then who would be in trouble, huh?"

"Who's in trouble?" Boyd peered around Jake. "Is Mrs. F. onto us?"

"No." I shook my head. "No one is in trouble."

I gave Jake a warning look. When the brownies were cool, we iced them, then split them between the four of us. The boys immediately began eating theirs, but I was saving mine for my sisters.

"Oh, these taste awesome! I'm glad we have such a good cook in our group." Scott wiggled his eyebrows at me.

Well, I'd had years of practice, but he didn't know that.

At lunch, Nicole sat between me and Holly. The boys stood in line for sandwiches and fries. Holly peered at me. "We missed you at the party on Saturday."

I wondered if that was really true. "I'm sorry. My mom wasn't in a good mood, so I didn't dare ask about going." I looked down at my sandwich, avoiding her gaze.

"Yeah, Jake told us your mom doesn't let you go out much," Holly said.

I bit back a response as Jake and Shawn, along with a few of their athlete buddies, filled in the seats across the table. Holly was still watching me.

"He's right. When I was in junior high, it made me so mad I snuck out once, but I got caught. Trust me, there are worse things than missing a party." Sheesh! Why did I add that bit at the end?

I felt a bit unsteady with the attention, so I tuned in to the boys' conversation. It was all about a car race they'd watched over the weekend. I had zero interest in car racing, but I pasted a smile on my face and acted like I did.

After lunch, Holly, Nicole and I walked to the locker room for P.E. Nicole told us a story about the boy she currently had a crush on. He had messed up the pot he'd spun in ceramics, so he'd taken the flopped over lump of clay to the kiln and told the teacher it was a paperweight. I laughed as I pulled my gym clothes out of my bag and laid them on the bench. Nicole took off around the corner to her locker.

I unbuttoned my blouse and slipped it off my shoulders. I hung it on the hook in the locker before I turned to pull on my gym shirt.

Holly's gasp startled me, and I glanced at her. She was staring at me as if I'd grown another head.

"What?" I asked. "What's wrong?"

She pointed her finger at my torso. "What's that?"

I looked down and realized my mistake. Two large yellow bruises and two smaller blue ones were visible on my rib cage. I'd forgotten to wear a tank top! I snatched my shirt off the bench and pulled it over my head, covering the evidence of my mom's actions.

"It's nothing, really." I frantically searched my mind for an explanation.

"Did you fall?" Holly took a step toward me, her eyes piercing mine. "Or did someone do that to you?"

I looked away. Long ago, I'd learned to cover my bruises with makeup or clothing, and I'd always been careful to keep them hidden. How had I gotten so careless? I could tell Holly I'd fallen down the stairs or into a wall, but what if it happened again? I didn't know how to respond. My stomach was a knotted ball. No words came, so I just shook my head.

Lucky for me, there was enough distraction from all the other girls changing their clothes. So much talking, laughing and teasing swirled around me, it gave an excuse to keep quiet. The chaos was compounded by slamming locker doors. We only had five minutes to change before roll call in the gym, so everyone had to hurry.

I finished tying my gym shorts and saw that Holly was almost ready for class. She sat tying her sneakers, but her eyes were on me. I felt my face flush from the scrutiny. Once my shoes were tied, I looked at my friend. "Yeah, I fell."

Holly raised her eyebrows and searched my eyes. "How?"

I averted my eyes again and automatically began walking toward the door of the gym. I felt her join me. "The stairs."

Holly exhaled a loud huff, grabbed my elbow and steered me toward the bathroom stalls.

"Hey!" I exclaimed. "What are you doing?"

Because she was so tall and standing so close to me, I was forced to tilt my head to look into her face. Smooth, sun-kissed skin dotted with freckles covered her perfect features. Holly leaned back a bit and folded her arms. "I don't believe you."

For what seemed like an eternity, we stared at each other, neither willing to venture further into the topic. Nicole saw us locked in a standoff and yelled from the gym door, "Hey, you two! Hurry, you'll be late!"

Holly waved her off. "In a minute."

Nicole held her hands out in question, then walked out the door.

"We *are* going to be late," I said, my heart racing.

"I don't believe that you fell," Holly said, her eyes shooting darts into mine. I shifted uncomfortably and looked down. I knew I looked guilty because I felt guilty. Guilty and frightened. I felt hot all over, and a headache was forming behind my eyes. I pressed my fingers against the bridge of my nose and closed my eyes. The gym door slammed for the last time as all the girl's voices drifted away. I heard Coach Barnes whistle, then call the class to take their designated spots in their squads. The air felt heavy and warm and a voice in my head screamed, "Run away!" After years of keeping so many secrets, it was all going to come out. My eyes filled with tears, and I gazed through them at my reflection in the mirror. I looked tired. Tired and broken.

Holly stood beside me, her arm now around my shoulders, her eyes locked onto mine in the mirror. When she spoke, it was in a whisper. "Did your mom do it?"

As the realization hit me that my secret had been discovered, I sobbed. I felt like I was drowning, like a huge weight threatened to pull me under. Mom's threats echoed through my head. Holly threw her arms around me and held me close while I cried. When my tears slowed, she eased back, and I could see the questions in her eyes. Her voice was soft when she asked, "Was this a one-time thing, or an all-the-time thing?"

I sniffled and Holly grabbed a handful of toilet paper for me. I wiped my nose and looked her in the eyes. "It's been going on for years."

Holly closed her eyes and dropped her head. Before she could respond, I hurried on. "You can't tell anyone! No one can know! If she finds out I told you, it will only make things worse for us." I didn't mean to include my sisters, but it slipped out in my haste to demand secrecy.

"Please promise me you won't tell anyone!" I begged.

I watched as Holly's emotions played out on her face: hesitancy, pity, anger, and understanding. When she spoke, I was surprised by her question. "Does Jake know?"

Holly knew we were close. She must have realized on some level that we shared this secret together. I nodded. "He saw something happen a long time ago. He's kept it secret ever since."

Holly hugged me again and helped me clean my face where my mascara had run down. "Okay, Libby," she conceded. "I won't tell anyone...for now. But I'm afraid for you. What if your mom does something worse? I'll never forgive myself for keeping it quiet. You understand that, right?"

"Yeah, I do, but I *am* working on it, I swear," my voice trembling as I spoke. "Please trust me."

The gym door slammed open, hitting the brick wall behind it. Holly and I both jumped, then startled again when Coach Barnes appeared around the corner. Her eyes were fiery and her cheeks red. She stared at us and her features softened. She must have noticed my red-rimmed eyes and Holly's worried expression. "Girls, is everything okay?"

We both nodded and she beckoned us forward. "Then let's go now."

I glanced at Holly, and she nodded before we followed Coach Barnes into the gym.

I WAS SO RELIEVED WHEN school was over, I practically ran to Pop's. What had started as a promising first day of the school week had somehow gone downhill in gym class. Nicole had been curious, darting glances between Holly and me. I finally just ignored both of them and played basketball with some girls from my English class.

I gave myself a little pep talk as I changed into my work polo in the restroom. *Forget about it all for now. Concentrate on your job. You can think about it later.*

After I clocked in, Jerri gave me my assignment for the day. I grabbed my box cutter and filled my dolly with boxes of snack crackers and chips. Jerri helped me get going and then left me on my own because the customer service desk was so busy. The snacks were much lighter than canned goods, so the work would move faster today. The most difficult part was working around shoppers and trying to stay out of their way.

I was about fifteen minutes into the job when my sisters came into the store. Jerri called me to the customer service desk so I could take them to the break room. I showed them where the restroom was, then settled them at a table. I reminded them to finish their homework first, including reading time, then they could watch TV or draw or color. Edie whined that she was hungry. I remembered the brownies from school that I had placed in my lunch bag. Her frown changed to a smile when I pulled them from my backpack and handed them over.

As I pulled chips from the shelves, I noticed some Pringles that were almost expired. I didn't know what the store did with food that didn't get sold before the sell-by date. When Jerri came to check on me, I asked her if I could take a couple cans. She agreed, so I ran them to my backpack to take home. I was pleasantly surprised to see that my sisters' homework was almost completed. I high-fived the girls and got back to work.

Linda came down the aisle to greet me. Her hair sat in a bun on top of her head that wobbled when she walked. Her eyes sparkled like she'd just been given a gift. She asked if I had any questions. I had only one. "Did Jerri talk to you about my sisters?"

"She mentioned it. As long as your sisters aren't causing problems or keeping you from doing your job, I'm fine with it."

Awesome! Maybe this day was looking up. Even Rosie greeted me as she walked past me to the breakroom. I hoped Edie and Anna wouldn't bother her. Rosie didn't seem to have much patience.

As I worked, I tapped my fingers and hummed along to the music playing on the loudspeaker. I'd just replaced a large section of the shelves with new bags of pretzels and was cleaning up empty boxes when Jake materialized beside me.

"Whoa! You scared me!" I jumped back.

"Libby!" Jake's eyes were intense and the vein in his temple bulged. "I talked to Holly after school."

I sighed and shook my head.

Jake looked down the aisle past me, then over his shoulder. He lowered his voice to a whisper. "Will you get in trouble if I'm talking to you?"

"I don't know," I whispered back. "Probably not, as long as I keep working. So, what did Holly say?"

"She told me she saw the bruises on your ribs and figured out that it was your mom who did it. At first, I thought she was just guessing and wanted me to confirm her suspicions. When she told me you had panicked, then begged her not to tell anyone, I knew she wasn't just fishing for answers. Anyway, I wanted to make sure you were alright."

I sliced the tape on the bottom of an empty box and popped it down. I thought "panicked" was a nice way for Holly to say that I'd been a teary mess. I realized Jake was waiting for a response, although I really didn't know what to say. "Yeah, dummy me forgot to wear a tank top under my shirt today to cover the bruises." For some reason that made me blush, so I hurried on. "So, now two of you know. I'm sure Nicole will figure it out soon enough. She knows something is up. And I'm okay, I guess, but I was scared out of my mind at the time."

"Well, I'm kind of glad Holly knows," Jake said, then seeing my startled face, quickly added, "I mean, it's just more witnesses against your mom when you're ready to tell an adult."

I spotted Linda and Rosie coming down the aisle again, so I quickly pulled a bag of Doritos from the shelf and handed them to a bewildered Jake. "I heard this flavor is delicious! I'm sure you'll like them." Then I turned away from him to pop down my last box.

"Do you need a ride home? When is your shift over?"

I saw Linda's sneakers stop by my last box. She answered for me. "Libby has five minutes left, then she can go." She and Rosie continued down the aisle, then Linda turned back. "By the way, Libby, your sisters are darling. They've been very well-behaved."

"Oh good!" I breathed a sigh of relief. "Thank you."

I wondered how many times Linda checked on them if she knew they'd been so well-behaved. I turned to Jake. "Let me get rid of these boxes and clock out. I can meet you at the front."

Jake nodded, then placed the chips I'd given him back on the shelf.

"No, Jake," I teased. "You have to buy the chips."

I laughed at his dumbfounded expression and shoved him toward the cashiers.

I was glad Jake had offered to drive us home. I was worn out and I still had to make dinner and do my homework. But I'd told my mom I could handle it, so that's what I would do. It would only take a paycheck or two before I could go to Ohio to find Paul. That was the goal to keep in mind, especially when I was exhausted.

11
Thursday, March 17, 1988

I finished my biology vocabulary assignment and moved on to the Punnett square worksheet our substitute teacher had handed out. Mrs. Zeigler was sick, so she'd left a bunch of busy work for us. I found our genetics unit to be quite interesting. For some crazy reason, I understood everything we'd learned, so I actually enjoyed the busy work.

Despite the sub's repeated instructions not to talk, the classroom buzzed with chatter. The sub looked perplexed. She was definitely out of her element. After repeating her instructions again, she gave up and plopped down in the teacher's chair. She pushed her bifocals up on her nose and buried her face in a novel, ignoring everyone.

Jake and I were probably the only ones in the room not chatting. Not because we were strict rule-followers, but because I was a little irritated at him and embarrassed at myself. I could feel the tension between us, but I didn't know how to fix it. My pride had been hurt and honestly, I was jealous. Hence the embarrassment.

Jake had come to my locker earlier, just as I'd arrived at school and was putting my things away. He startled me by tugging on a lock of my hair from behind. I jumped and looked over my shoulder.

"Oh, hey, Jake. What's up?" I pulled a binder and textbook off the shelf.

"I have to tell you something."

Curious, I turned and gave him my full attention. His white-blond hair was wet or gelled, I couldn't tell which, and his cheeks were flushed. He grabbed the top of the locker door and moved it back and forth.

"I asked Holly to the prom last night, so I need your opinion on some things if you could help me."

"Wait, what?" I felt my own cheeks flush as I replayed his words in my head. He asked Holly to the prom? My skin prickled and a stabbing pain shot through my chest. I turned back to my locker and fished around in my backpack, trying to hide my reaction. Holly was my friend, but that didn't mean I wanted Jake to take her to the prom. All I felt was envy, and it made me uncomfortable. Then again, why did it matter so much if we were all friends?

"So, will you help me?" Jake asked again, sounding hesitant.

"What do you need my help with?" My voice sounded sharp and cranky.

"Wait, are you mad?" Jake placed his hand on my shoulder and leaned closer to look at my face. I couldn't let him see my jealousy. I turned away, my long hair flicking him in the face.

"Just go, Jake. I'll see you later in class." I yanked on the locker door and Jake released it. I slammed the door and walked away, not even glancing back. It took me a while to calm down but once I did, I was immediately appalled by my reaction. There was no way Jake could miss the fact that I was jealous. So, when he sat down next to me in biology, I stared awkwardly at the front of my textbook. He didn't say anything while we waited for class to begin, but I felt him watching me.

As I finished my third Punnett square, Jake whispered, "What's bugging you, Libby?"

I sighed. "Nothing. I'm fine."

"Are you mad that I asked Holly to the prom?"

Ugh. He totally knew. But I didn't want to admit it.

"My first choice was you, Libby," he said, "but you said your mom won't let you go."

He was right. I had said that. And it was the truth. I ducked my head and let my hair fall as a curtain between us. My cheeks felt hot again, but this time for another reason. He said I was his first choice! I blinked a few times, then dared to look at my best friend. His face was scrunched in concern.

"I'm sorry. I guess I didn't know what to think."

Jake grinned. "I think you're just—"

"—Ready to help!" I blurted. "What do you need me to do?"

Jake started to laugh, then covered it with a cough. His eyes twinkled and I braced myself for the teasing to come. Instead, he said, "I thought you could help me pick out the corsage. My mom offered to help, but I'd rather have your opinion, since you know Holly better."

"Okay, I can do that." We discussed when to visit the only florist in town and where to look for a tie as we finished our assignment. Then I changed the subject to something else we needed to discuss.

"I get paid today! My first paycheck!" I smiled and rubbed my hands together.

"Do you think it will be enough to cover bus tickets?"

"Not sure. We'll see."

I was fairly certain I wouldn't have enough money yet. Jake had called the bus station in Millsburg last week to find out the price of tickets to Columbus and to get the full schedule. He told me that tickets were $30 each round trip. I knew it was a buck and a half to go from Buckley to Millsburg, plus we needed money for food. I figured as soon as I had $80 or $90, we'd be ready to go. I was nervous about the whole idea of taking such a bold step, but I had to do it for my sisters' sake.

I SLAMMED THE FRONT door behind me as I walked into the house after work. The girls and I had trudged home after my shift at Pop's. All the way home, Anna told me how annoying Edie had been at the store.

"She kept changing the TV channel even though I wanted it on something else! And before that, she wrinkled up her paper instead of writing her spelling words!"

"Did she stop?" I sighed, giving Edie the evil eye.

"After, like, for-ev-er!" Anna emphasized each syllable.

I spent the remainder of the walk home lecturing Edie about her behavior and my expectations. She argued and sassed me.

"Edie," I fumed, "I can't work at Pop's if you can't behave yourself!"

Once inside, Edie dropped her backpack on the floor and threw herself dramatically onto the couch.

"Edie," I warned, "you're going to make it so I can't work there. I'm not kidding!"

"I don't care!" she mumbled into the couch cushion.

I hung up my jacket, then pulled Edie up. "You get to do the dishes tonight."

"No!" Edie screamed. "I don't want to!"

"I don't care." I was tired and didn't want to put up with her antics. I had to get dinner started or Mom would pitch a fit too. I was glad that last weekend, I'd planned menus for the week. It sure saved me time after work if I already knew what to cook.

I breaded pork chops and fried them while Anna whipped up instant mashed potatoes and boiled some frozen mixed vegetables. We were almost finished when Mom walked in the back door. I took a deep breath, hoping she was in a decent mood. Last night, Anna and I had discussed how we could help Mom be in a better mood when she got home each night so our evenings could be more peaceful.

I gave Anna a nod. She dried her hands on a paper towel while I took the dinner plates out of the cabinet. I turned my head slightly so I could watch out the corner of my eye. Mom was pulling out a chair at the kitchen table when Anna reached her and said, "Hi, Mom!" She threw her arms around Mom's waist. At first, Mom stiffened, then she patted Anna's hair.

"Hi, Anna," she whispered.

I called Edie for dinner, but she didn't respond, so I asked Anna to get her. I set the food on the table. Mom's eyes were glazed over, and she seemed to stare straight through me.

Anna and Edie ran downstairs sounding like a herd of elephants. As they sat down at the table, Mom snapped out of her trance.

"Do you have to be so noisy?"

"Sorry, Mom. We were trying to hurry," Anna said.

Edie looked at the mixed vegetables and whined, "I hate peas, and carrots, and beans!"

I glared at her. I'd had enough of her behavior today. Anna and I were trying to create a calm environment, but Edie was going to ruin it.

Edie glared back at me. "Mom, Libby said I have to do the dishes tonight, but I'm not doing it!"

I scooped some potatoes onto my plate and passed the bowl to Anna. I avoided looking at Mom, who was sure to ask for an explanation. I was hungry and focused on my food. Mom must have felt the same because she just sighed and shook her head.

"Mom! Tell Libby I don't have to do it!" Edie picked up her fork and banged it on her plate.

"Stop it!" Mom scolded, reaching for Edie's fork. Edie snatched it away before Mom could nab it.

"Edie!" Mom half-stood and yanked the fork from her fingers. Edie swiped her arm at Mom and almost knocked over her glass.

"Eat your dinner!" Mom growled, her eyes flashing. So much for creating a calm environment.

"You took my fork!" Edie yelled.

"Use a spoon," Mom snapped.

Edie crossed her arms and glowered at me. The rest of us ate in silence. I didn't know why Edie was so ornery today.

Mom broke the silence. "So, why does Edie have to wash the dishes?"

"She wasn't behaving at Pop's today." I didn't provide any details. Mom could think what she wanted. I was worn out. I just wanted to eat, do my homework, and go to bed.

"Pop's," Mom scoffed.

I had no idea what she meant by that, but I wasn't going to take the bait. I cut my pork chop into small pieces.

Edie kicked my leg under the table. It didn't hurt but it startled me. I narrowed my eyes at her. She finally picked up her pork chop with her fingers and took a bite. Then she scooped up some potatoes with her fingers. I stared at her, then realized that Mom and Anna were also staring. Edie had always loved an audience, so I looked away, refusing to give her one any longer. I cleared my dishes from the table and took them to the sink.

My movement must have broken the spell because Anna followed me and Mom asked, "Why is this kitchen such a mess?"

Was she kidding? I'd just made dinner. Cleanup always came after.

Mom continued, "The living room looks like a mess too."

What was she talking about? I'd straightened it up before school this morning. Edie had left her Colorforms out and Anna's blanket had been lying on the floor. While the girls ate breakfast, I had tidied up.

Edie cheered, "Ha-ha, now you're in trouble too, Libby!"

I ignored her and turned on the light in the living room. The carpet was littered with paper and coloring books. A box of crayons had been emptied onto the coffee table. Edie must have made the mess while Anna and I made dinner because it sure wasn't there when we got home. My back had been to the living room while I ate, but when I got up, Mom had a clear view into the room.

"Edie made this mess!" I called to Mom.

"Well, what about the mess in your bedroom?" she called back. "Did Edie make that mess too?"

I clamped my lips against the retort I knew better than to say. Mom smirked and Edie looked downright gleeful. "I've had a lot of homework. I'll clean my room on Saturday. But I'm not cleaning the mess that Edie just made."

"You'll do it if I tell you to do it!" Mom said.

"She can clean it herself!" My patience was running on empty. It wasn't fair that I'd already cleaned the living room this morning and Edie had just messed it up for revenge.

Mom pushed back her chair and stood.

Oh, crap! Here we go again!

I stalked to the sink and snatched up the dishcloth and wrung it out so I could wipe down the countertops. I felt Mom behind me.

Just clean, Libby! Ignore her!

As I swiped the cloth over the countertop, Mom gripped my upper arm and tried to turn me around. I resisted and switched the cloth to my left hand, then continued wiping the ugly gold Formica.

"I do not like your sassiness!" Mom said, tightening her grip on my arm. My face flushed and I felt my heart rate amp up. I was so sick of confrontations.

Anna piped up. "The living room was clean this morning. Edie just made the mess to get Libby in trouble."

I heard a chair scoot against the linoleum, then scampering feet.

"Edie!" Anna yelled. "Come back!"

More running feet and then thumping on the stairs. Of course, she'd run away while Mom was occupied with me. Edie wasn't stupid, but I was equally ticked off at Mom.

"Turn around now!" Mom demanded. Too tired to argue, I obeyed. I kept my gaze on the tufted wheat wallpaper. It was so quiet, the faint ticking of the clock above the back door reminded me of a time bomb. Mom's fingers pinched my face. "I told you that you can only work at Pop's if you stay on top of your responsibilities." Each word was a staccato.

"I'm doing my best." I made sure not to sound whiny, although her fingernails penetrated my skin, and it stung.

"Hmm, are you? Because if this is your best, you'd better step it up!" Mom released her hold on my face.

"I said I'll clean my room on Saturday, but I have homework first!" I knew I was headed down a slippery slope with my fierce response but I just couldn't help it. I was sick of doing everything for everyone, and trying to do it perfectly too.

I saw Mom's hand coming a second before I felt the slap. My face burned and so did my temper. I glared into her green eyes. For a second, I thought she was finished, but I saw her hand twitch, so I spun back to face the counter.

"You will show me respect!" Mom screamed into my ear. I cringed at the volume and tilted my head away. I was physically trapped with her right behind me and unless I could push her back, I was stuck.

"Turn around!" Mom screeched. She pulled at my shoulders, but still I resisted. I shook my head back and forth. Hot tears threatened to spill out of my eyes, blurring my vision. I hated this so much. Why wouldn't she leave me alone?

Mom gave up on my shoulders and I relaxed. Then to my horror, her hands encircled my neck and squeezed. She muttered something I didn't understand.

Oh no! Please not this! This couldn't be happening!

I clawed at her hands with both of mine. If I could've screamed, I would have. Mom was speaking, but I couldn't focus on the words. I was too busy trying to get her hands off my throat, where the pressure of her hands was relentless. I felt the burn and simultaneous ache and I craved air like nothing I'd ever craved before. My fingers pried at Mom's, and I wiggled my body in an attempt to push her away. Little pinpricks of light distorted my vision. I felt lightheaded.

"Stop it! Please stop it! Mom!"

At first, I thought it was just Anna screaming, but as the plea was repeated, I heard Edie too. Suddenly, my neck was free, and I lay my torso across the Formica, inhaling precious air. My throat ached like when I'd tried as a youngster to break through the arms of my classmates as we played Red Rover but was clotheslined instead. As I took another deep gulp of air and coughed it out, I stood up and saw Anna and Edie yanking on my mother's arms. They were both crying. I blinked and tears fell. Another big gulp of air burned my throat.

Edie shouted, "I'm sorry! I'll be good at the store! It's not Libby's fault! Don't hurt her!" She backed away, crying.

Mom pushed Anna away. "Go to your room!" Her face was red, but that's all I saw before I wiped my eyes and held shaking hands over them.

Anna's voice cracked with emotion. "Edie is cleaning up the living room. It's all fine." She repeated those three words several times. All I could think was, *no, it isn't!* It would never be fine until we got away from Mom.

I pushed myself off the counter, then dared to look at Mom. She stood in the middle of the kitchen wringing her hands, her expression was one of shock. She looked uneasy as she glanced at Anna, who cowered by the table. She seemed unsure of her next move.

Finally, she cleared her throat and said, "This is your final warning, Libby. Keep up in the things you said you would, or your job is finished."

I nodded and managed to croak out, "Fine. I have homework."

I took out my frustrations on the stairs as I stomped up them. Edie caught up to me halfway up and grabbed my hand. I looked at her tear-streaked face but said nothing until we walked into my bedroom. A scrambling sound behind us meant Anna had followed. I looked into Edie's eyes. "Do you see what happens when we don't cooperate and help each other?"

Edie's expression was sad, her eyebrows pressed together. She bit her lip and nodded. I hugged the girls in a tight circle and whispered, "I love you." They repeated the sentiment back and I sent them off to their room holding hands. The click of the latch when they closed my door was like a gunshot. As much as I wanted to curl up on my bed and cry, I had work to do. I pulled my math book out of my backpack and an envelope floated onto the carpet. I'd forgotten all about it. I tore it open and stared at my paycheck. $80.42. I blinked. That amount was enough to make the journey to Columbus. Judging by what Mom had done to me tonight, we needed to go sooner than later. The best night to go would be on a Sunday because Mom wouldn't realize I was missing until at least Monday afternoon. I would tell Anna and Edie that I had to leave very early for school, that way they wouldn't know I'd left town either.

Now I had to run it by Jake.

12
Friday, March 18, 1988

"It's got to be this Sunday, Jake," I protested. I angled in my seat to look at him as he drove. He'd borrowed his sister's car again so he could pick up a job application from the roller-skating rink in Millsburg after he dropped me off at work.

"Look, I'm just not sure if we've really got all the details figured out. Or if we have enough money." Jake shook his head and flipped on the turn signal.

"It's not that complicated," I argued. "We buy bus tickets for the last bus of the night. We get to Columbus late. We sleep for a while at the bus station. We find a pay phone with a phone book and start calling every Paul Curtis in the city. We find my uncle and explain why we're calling. We ask for his help, then buy bus tickets back to Buckley. If it all goes smoothly, we make it back home in less than 24 hours."

Jake maneuvered the car into a parking spot at Pop's. "But what if we don't? What then? Our parents will call the police, and it will be bad for both of us. The only way it wouldn't be bad is if we tell them the real reason we left. But you don't want to do that." Jake pushed his fingers through his hair, revealing his creased forehead. The vein in his temple throbbed.

I closed my eyes and sighed. Yes, going to the police was an option, but my fear had always been that they wouldn't believe me.

Then what would Mom do to me? Her threats alone were enough to keep me from telling the police. I felt tears welling up.

"Jake, please," I begged. "Please let's try. I'm not brave enough to do this without you, and you may have a job soon and be too busy working, And the prom is coming, and..." I sniffled and a tear rolled down my cheek. Frustrated, I brushed it away.

We sat unmoving, each lost in our own thoughts. The car's engine purred softly. I glanced at my watch. I still had to change before my shift started. I hadn't wanted to use it as leverage, but if I showed Jake my new injuries, he'd likely be convinced.

I rubbed my temples and said, "I didn't want to tell you, but this is what my mom did to me last night."

Jake jerked his head toward me. I took a deep breath and pulled down the collar on my turtleneck to reveal the red marks left by my mom's fingers.

"What the....?!" Jake gasped, his eyes like saucers. "She choked you?" The volume of his voice doubled. He reached over and touched my neck, then pulled away as if burned.

"Sorry! Does it hurt?" His face was pale.

I shrugged. "A little, I guess. It hurts to swallow more than anything."

Jake's fist hit the steering wheel hard. He hit it twice more as he spewed curses on my mom. "She's going to kill you one of these days!"

I swallowed down my emotions. I couldn't go into work looking like a crybaby.

"Didn't anyone see your neck in gym class? Like Holly? Or Nic?"

"Well, I actually faked a stomachache, so I spent the entire period lying on the cot in the nurse's office."

Jake sighed and rubbed his hand over his face. "Okay, Libby. I'm worried this might not be as easy as you think, but I'll go with you."

"Oh, thank you, Jake!" I grabbed him into an awkward hug. "I have a plan. We can meet on the trail from the pond to the library around 9:15 Sunday night and go from there." The bus stop was by the library. Although it was about a mile walk from my house, it was longer for Jake, but it was the only option.

As I walked into the store, I reminded myself of the plan to keep my neck covered once I changed into my polo. First, button it all the way to the top. Second, since my hair was long, I'd curled it today to make it bigger. That way it hung closer to my neck. I didn't know if it would be enough to keep my coworkers from noticing, but I couldn't exactly walk around with a scarf tied around my neck. Talk about drawing attention.

I was almost to the breakroom when Jerri intercepted me.

"Good afternoon, Libby!" She pointed in the direction of the bakery. "You'll be working with me today. We have a project to do. Just be ready to be tempted by goodies all afternoon."

I smiled at her enthusiasm and changed my shirt. I fluffed my hair around my neck and face. If I moved carefully, I'd probably be alright. Swinging the restroom door open, I was surprised to bump into Rosie, who was on her way in. She laughed and apologized. Since starting my job, I discovered Rosie didn't always wear a stone face. She had thawed a bit recently. Jerri said Rosie distrusted all teenagers, but since I had proved to be a reliable worker, she had relaxed. Still, that was the first time I'd heard her laugh. I rushed off to clock in and find Jerri. Milt barked that I was two minutes late. I rolled my eyes and headed to the bakery.

The project Jerri had mentioned turned out to be rearranging the entire layout of the bakery product displays. It involved moving shelving, tables and racks around, along with repositioning some of the products. Jerri explained that Linda had visited a few grocery stores when she'd gone to a conference last week in Chicago. She'd come back with some ideas to make sections of the store more accessible and appealing. This was one such project. I was excited to help with the sweet smelling, freshly baked goods. It was a nice change from dealing with cans, boxes and bags like I usually did.

Since I'd started at the store, Jerri and I worked together at least twice a week. I felt closer to her in that short amount of time than I did any other adult I knew. She had a contagious laugh, and I was comfortable around her. We talked about school, music, friends and her travels. I told her I hadn't yet figured out college or career plans, while she told me about her struggle with infertility and the car accident that had left her with a slight limp from fracturing her tibia, fibula and ankle. Conversing with Jerri was so easy.

We were making good time on the bakery project when Jerri handed me a package of cookies that was a day past it's sell-by date and said my sisters could have it.

"Oh, thank you. They'll love this!" I said.

In the breakroom, I found both girls at a table with pencils, paper and open textbooks in front of them.

"Libby!" Anna jumped up and hugged me.

I returned the hug and tousled Edie's hair. "Looks like you're working hard."

"Just like you," Edie peeked up at me. Anna must have reminded her to be on her best behavior.

"Are those for us?" Edie pointed to the box of cookies.

"They're only for girls who are getting their homework finished. But they have raisins!" I warned.

"I don't care!" Edie sat up straight. "I'll just spit them out."

I chuckled and handed them the box. "You can each have one and we'll take the rest home for later. Deal?"

"Deal," they agreed.

I returned to Jerri's side just as she was starting to pull rolls off a rack. I grabbed each bag, piling them on the table as she handed them to me. Suddenly she stopped and squinted at me.

"What happened to you?" She gestured to my neck.

"Oh, this? It's nothing." I touched the marks. "I accidentally burned myself with the curling iron." I didn't like lying to Jerri, but it couldn't be avoided. Lie or face Mom's wrath? Definitely lie.

Jerri scrunched her face in thought. I could see the wheels turning. She opened her mouth, then shut it again. The scrutiny made my stomach clench.

"So, how's your mom been lately?" she asked.

I looked away. "Fine. Same as always."

"Is she still upset about you working here?"

"A bit," I admitted.

"So, you said she gets angry often." Jerri continued to probe.

"Yeah." I really did not want to talk about this. Jerri was getting too close to my secrets. "That's just the way she is."

"Well, I could never figure out why your dad liked her so much." Jerri shook her head, then moved behind the rack to push it to the opposite wall.

Her words put the brakes on my work. For a second, I couldn't breathe.

"You know my dad?" I exclaimed too loud, almost dropping the rolls I held.

Jerri peeked around the rack. "Well, yes." She drew out the yes. "He was a friend of mine."

I sucked in a deep breath. I couldn't believe it. Jerri knew my father! No one had ever mentioned knowing him before.

"What's his name?" I leaned forward, hungry for information.

Jerri peered at me through the rack, her expression confused. "Don't you know his name?"

"No, my mom has never talked about him." By this time, I was next to her, my hands clasped in a beggar's pose.

"She never told you anything?" Jerri's eyes expanded.

"No, my birth certificate doesn't even list a father."

Indecision stole across Jerri's face. "Um, maybe you'd better ask your mom about this."

"Please tell me, Jerri! I won't tell my mom you told me," I promised.

"Oh, wow!" Jerri rubbed her temples with her thumb and middle finger. "I don't want your mom to be upset if she finds out I told you."

"But, don't you think I have the right to know?"

"Well, yes, but it probably isn't my place to say." Her voice trailed away as she saw my frown. She bit her bottom lip and clicked her tongue, thinking. "Okay, I'll tell you about your father if you promise not to tell your mom that you heard it from me." She emphasized her words with a slash of her hand.

"I promise." I mimed zipping my lips. My heart was racing. I wanted to jump up and down but forced my body to stay still.

"Your dad's name is Dennis Fletcher," Jerri said. She shook her head and asked, "You've really never known that?"

"Dennis Fletcher," I repeated. "No, I've never heard it before. Dennis Fletcher. So, my name should be Libby Fletcher." It sounded strange on my lips. "He's not still in Buckley, is he?" I knew I sounded overeager, but this discovery was such a shock. All these years I'd known nothing, but one comment from Jerri changed everything.

"No, he left Buckley years ago," Jerri said.

"Before I was born? Or after?" For some reason, I felt an urgent need to know everything. If my father had left before my birth, maybe he never knew about me. But if he left after my birth, maybe he just didn't care.

Jerri finished sliding a stack of doughnut boxes onto the central table and glanced up at me. I held two bread loaves tightly.

"Careful, Libby. You're smashing the bread."

Jerri took the loaves from me, placed them on the stack of doughnuts, then grabbed my hands. She seemed to recognize the significance of my question.

"He left before you were born, but he knew your mom was pregnant. She was angry with him for not being ready to commit to her."

I felt as if I'd been punched in the gut. I pulled one of my hands away and placed it on my stomach. Physical blows were almost easier to take than emotional ones like this that hurt deep in my mind and heart.

"Do you know what happened?" I asked, my voice trembling.

"Not exactly." Jerri scanned the list on her clipboard, making another check mark. "I do know your mom treated Denny like garbage. When they started dating, right after high school graduation, it was a shock to me. He put up with a lot from her. Although," she paused and thought for a bit, "sometimes I'd see them together and they looked happy. Then other times they both looked miserable. I would hear some things through mutual friends, but because your mom was so jealous, none of us gals could even be Denny's friend anymore. My guess is he put up with her control and jealousy for long enough that he just couldn't take it anymore."

"So, he just left, even with a baby coming?"

"Well, they were both young and immature. I don't think Denny was ready to be a father." Jerri looked apologetic. "He joined the military and a few years later, he..."

Jerri froze and looked away.

"He what?"

Jerri shook her head, her forehead creased. "Libby, it's not really my place to tell you this." Her voice was soft, almost pleading.

"Tell me what?" I knew I sounded whiny, but I didn't understand why she didn't finish the story. What was so bad she couldn't tell me?

I held my breath and watched as Jerri's lips pressed into a flat line. Her sigh was heavy. "Libby, your dad was killed in a helicopter crash during a military training." She reached out her hand and gently rubbed my shoulder.

I felt a rush of emotion in my chest. I couldn't even pinpoint what I was feeling. Sorrow? Remorse? Betrayal? Anger? All I knew was I felt like crying, throwing up, and screaming all at once. A combination pizza of emotions. Only, it tasted terrible, and I wanted my money back.

"Are you alright, hon?" Jerri asked, her eyes filled with tenderness.

I shook my head, and tears welled up for the second time today. Jerri pulled me into a hug. I don't know how long we stood there, me breathing hard with my thoughts rushing a hundred miles an hour while Jerri rubbed my back. My trance was broken by the PA system as Rosie called for Jerri to come to the customer service desk.

Jerri pulled away and wiped my tears. "Will you be okay?" Her typically sparkly eyes looked downcast. "Why don't you go take a break?"

I walked woodenly with Jerri to the front of the store, wiping my tears so no one else would see me cry. She nudged me toward the restroom.

"I'll check on you in a few minutes," she promised.

I pushed open the restroom door, happy the room was empty. I stared in the mirror, sniffling. I gazed at each of my features like I'd done a thousand times before: nose, lips, forehead from Mom, wide-set hazel eyes, pointy chin, oval-shaped face and dimple had to be from Dad. Focusing on the features that came from my father now held so much angst.

Jerri burst through the door, making me jerk. She handed me some tissues and instructed me to "fix my face." She rubbed my arm while I did, her touch reassuring.

"I'm sorry, Libby. I really am. You know, I guessed who you were the first time I met you, but I had no idea you've been kept in the dark all this time. It really burns me up that Donna withheld that information from you!"

I said nothing, rubbing the tissues under my eyes one last time.

"We do need to finish in the bakery. A customer complained that she couldn't find *anything*, so Linda is coming to check our progress." She gave me a little nudge.

"Wait!" I cried.

Jerri raised her eyebrows. I snatched up her hands.

"Why do you think my mom never told me about my father?"

Jerri's mouth drooped. "I don't know, Libby. That's something you'll have to take up with her."

13
Sunday, March 20, 1988

I shivered and shoved my hands deeper into the pockets of my jean jacket. I wished I'd thought to wear my coat instead. I'd planned every other detail of this night, but I forgot that Indiana nights could still be so cold in the spring. I guess I'd had more important details on my mind. It wouldn't be long before we'd be at the bus stop, then on a bus. I could warm up then.

I had packed my backpack with a change of clothes, my toothbrush and comb, the cash from my paycheck, and sandwiches and apples for Jake and me. I even remembered a flashlight for walking in the dark, and had exchanged a ten-dollar bill at Pop's for quarters for the phone calls we'd be making to locate Uncle Paul. I hoped it would be enough. I couldn't imagine more than forty Paul Curtises in Columbus, but maybe the city was much bigger than I thought.

Silver Street was deserted and quiet as I made my way toward the pond. The only sound was the occasional scuff of my shoes on the sidewalk. The last glimmer of daylight peeked through the trees to the west, creating a faint glow around them. The air, although chilly, felt heavy, so I hoped it wouldn't rain. I hadn't thought about bringing an umbrella.

The sidewalk abruptly ended, and I stumbled slightly at the drop onto the dirt path. The remaining light gradually disappeared, leaving eerie shadows across the fields to the east. There were no buildings on this road; it was strictly for access to the pond or the trail that cut through the woods. The trail led to the newer part of town where the library, hotel and SaveMart were located.

I'd been walking fast, trying to put distance between me and home, but I slowed as I glanced at my watch with the glow-in-the-dark hands. I'd been antsy, so I left early, afraid of anything stopping me from meeting Jake. I'd told Edie and Anna I had to go to school early in the morning to retake a test, so I wouldn't see them then. I set the alarm on Anna's Kermit the Frog clock she rarely used, hoping the girls would get up when it went off. Then I sat on the edge of my bed, staring at the clock, fidgety and anxious. To me, the hardest part was making sure I got out of the house without being seen or heard. I had originally planned on leaving through the back door, but I got scared to cut through the kitchen knowing that Mom's bedroom door was right down the hall.

When it was time to leave, I'd tiptoed down the stairs with my heart pounding and silently removed my jacket from the coat stand. When I eased the door open, there was no squeak. Yesterday, I had greased the hinges when my sisters and I came through the door after taking a walk. I didn't know what to use exactly, so I'd melted a little Crisco and rubbed in on the hinges. After two applications, the squeak was gone.

I could barely see ahead of me now, so I stopped and pulled the flashlight from my pack. Switching it on illuminated the dirt clearing that everyone in town used as a parking lot when they visited the pond. It was a popular place in the summer for swimmers, rowboats, and canoes. It was large enough to accommodate several boats, which was good, because on summer weekends, the pond was the place to be.

My footsteps were soft as I kicked up dust crossing the clearing. I was almost to the trail. Jake would be coming from the south, which meant he had to walk through the woods most of the way. Keeping my eyes on the ground, I realized I'd made it to the trail. Even with the flashlight, walking into the blackness of the woods frightened me. I didn't like the feeling that something was lurking in the trees, and yet, I couldn't turn off my imagination. I didn't really want to go further, but I swallowed hard and took a deep breath. I held it like I was jumping into a pool, although this felt more dangerous.

If Jake and I were caught...well, I didn't want to think about the consequences. I didn't want to see him punished, but my punishment would be much more harsh, possibly even deadly. I shuddered at the thought. *Stop focusing on the negative, Libby! Just focus on the goal.* I gritted my teeth and plunged into the woods. My flashlight felt inadequate, but at least I wouldn't trip and fall.

I reached the intersection of the two trails and shone my light down the path to the south. No Jake yet. I looked at the time again. I was five minutes early. I had no desire to wait here for that long in the dark, but I probably needed to save my batteries for when I was walking. I switched off the flashlight. The silence suddenly seemed loud.

I was cold, so I bounced up and down on my toes while I waited. In truth, I couldn't believe I'd made it this far. I prayed we could find my uncle. Then I prayed we wouldn't get caught. Jake probably had a higher chance of that than I did since I never saw Mom on weekday mornings. I hoped he'd thought of a good cover.

I cupped my hands over my mouth and breathed warm air into them. Jake had better hurry. We couldn't miss the bus since it was the last one of the night.

A twig snapped to my right, and I gasped, frozen to my spot. A slight scuffling followed. I flipped on the flashlight and shone it in the direction of the sound. The leaves on a nearby bush danced, but nothing appeared, and it was silent again. Just an animal. Relief washed over me, but I couldn't bring myself to turn the flashlight off again. Another peek at my watch told me Jake was three minutes late. My nerves couldn't take this much longer.

"Come on, Jake," I fretted. "Where are you?" I paced back and forth, more worried with each step. I directed my light down the south trail. Soon, there were pounding footsteps, and a flash of blond hair appeared. Jake jogged toward me, his flashlight glow blending with mine.

"Sorry, Libby." He leaned over, hands on his knees, panting.

"Did you run the whole way?" I pulled a leaf from his hair, then realized he had no coat, and more importantly, no backpack.

"Where's your coat? And your backpack?"

Jake stood and held his empty hands out. His eyes looked sad. "Libby, I can't leave. I can't just take off and secretly go to Columbus. I thought I could do it, but I can't."

I gasped and took a step back. Jake's hands fell to his sides. My left hand flew to my face, while my right hand squeezed the flashlight hard.

"Oh, no, no, no!" I muttered, stunned. This had to be a bad dream. "You can't be serious!" I shook my head back and forth. My stomach felt like a rock and my legs shook.

"I'm really sorry, Libby!" Jake's eyes pleaded with me to understand.

As reality sunk in, I saw my plan go down in flames. Agitated, I grabbed a fistful of Jake's tee shirt.

"No, Jake! You can't back out! You promised!" I burst into tears.

Jake pulled my hand from his shirt. "I know, Libby. I just didn't think it all the way through. If my parents were to find out, I'd probably get kicked off the baseball team. They would ground me forever! And what if we couldn't find your uncle anyway? What then?"

I snatched my hand away. I had to get out of here or I was going to scream. Jake reached out to me again, but I stepped back. I couldn't even think straight. All I knew was I had to get away from Jake.

I turned back the way I'd come and broke into a run, aware enough of the dark to shine the light ahead of me. My breathing was ragged, and my lungs were on fire, but I dared not stop. In my haste, I tripped and dropped the light. I scrambled to pick it up before it rolled off the path. Jake called for me to come back, but I tuned him out and ran as fast as my shaking legs could carry me. The light bobbed up and down, but managed to stay on the path, leading me out and away from the oppressive forest. When I reached the clearing, I slogged along, sobbing loudly. There was no one out here to hear me, so what did it matter?

My tears soon turned to anger: anger at the situation, anger at my mom, but mostly anger at Jake. I stomped and kicked and screamed. If I couldn't get my best friend to help me, who would? And best friend? Yeah, right! Some best friend he was!

My tantrum soon gave way to weariness. I was out of ideas. I was exhausted and hopeless. Frustrated, I swiped at my tears and gazed up at the sky. The moon had appeared through the clouds, and I stared up at it as I moped down Silver Street.

"What do I do now?" I addressed the moon. A chorus of barking dogs was the only reply. I asked again, knowing I wouldn't receive an answer. There was nothing to be done. No one could save me and my sisters from my mom. I'd just have to accept it and do my best to deflect any physical harm aimed at them.

I reached my house, which was completely dark. I hadn't left the porchlight on when I left for fear of being seen.

"It wasn't supposed to happen this way!" I muttered.

I walked in and closed the door softly behind me, securing the latch. Once in my room, I threw myself on the bed. My backpack dropped to the floor and the coins inside jingled. I froze, afraid Mom would hear me from her room below. I took off my jacket, dropped it on the backpack and pulled back the bedcovers, rolling underneath. I stared around the darkened room and wondered what tomorrow would bring. I reached over to my alarm clock and switched it on. Back to being the responsible Libby. No more stupid plans. Stupid plans and best friends messed everything up.

14
Friday, March 25, 1988

It had been five days since the abandoned plan to find my uncle. School had been practically unbearable with Jake breathing apologies down my neck every time I turned around. I finally told him to leave me alone and when I was ready to talk to him, I would. Of course, Holly and Nicole knew something was going on because I hadn't eaten lunch with them all week. I wondered if Jake would tell them what happened, but so far, it seemed he hadn't. I'd been eating lunch on the bench by the equipment shed. The weather had been cool, but I didn't care. I came to school, stuck to my own business, went to work, did my homework, cooked, cleaned, and took care of Edie and Anna. I missed talking to Jake, but I couldn't bring myself to forgive him yet and I had no idea when I would. Life felt heavy right now. Even Jerri noticed the change in my demeanor. She asked if I was okay a few times, then dropped the subject when I didn't say anything more than "I'm fine."

To make matters worse, Mom had been on a rampage this week. She raged at me and my lack of something every day. Twice she'd pulled my hair and once she kicked my legs while I cleared the table. The kick made me fall and break the plate I'd been holding. She fumed about her boss and called him names. For someone who usually quietly seethed until her temper boiled over, she'd been extremely vocal this week. She brought home beer every night and didn't hide it in the back of the fridge anymore. The cans sat front and center on the top shelf. Edie thought it was a new brand of soda and had wanted to try one, so I told her what it really was. She promptly labeled it "disgusting" and asked Mom why she drank something that was bad for her. Mom clenched her teeth and told her to mind her own business.

Jake must have gotten frustrated with my lack of response to his apologies, so he'd written me a note explaining why he felt he couldn't go to Columbus. It was everything he told me in the woods. Maybe he thought if he repeated it, I'd understand. But I was still hurt, so I crumpled up the note and dropped it in the garbage can when I got to work.

I was worn out and actually looking forward to the coming week, which was Spring Break. Even though I'd be stuck at home, I intended to catch up on some rest. As long as Mom was at work most of the day, it would be fine. At least at home I could avoid Jake.

Yawning, I carried the last of my empty boxes outside to the dumpster. I'd worked in the back all afternoon. Pop's was having a huge sale next week, so I'd been too busy to check on Anna and Edie today. Edie had faithfully finished her homework each day, and I heaped on the praise. She always seemed more excited to tell me what she watched on TV afterwards though. *Diff'rent Strokes* and *The Facts of Life* were awesome, according to her.

I washed my hands off and clocked out. As I pushed the swinging doors open, I heard shouting from the direction of the bakery. I spied Portia and Linda running in that direction. Several customers peeked around the endcaps, searching for the source of the commotion. What was going on?

I walked through the dairy and meat sections and down the bread aisle. The first thing I saw when I reached the bakery was two long legs in sweatpants and two large feet clad in loafers sticking out from under the cookie table. Three employees squatted on the floor beside the man lying on the ground. Linda held one of his wrists, checking his pulse. I scurried over, not wanting to get in the way, but still curious. A bit of grey hair on an otherwise bald head told me the customer was an older gentleman. A black fedora lay several feet away where it had presumably landed when he had fallen. I wondered if he'd fainted or had a heart attack. The faint sound of emergency sirens signaled it was okay to continue on, that all would be fine, so some of the onlookers moved away to finish their shopping.

The volume of the sirens increased, and I remembered my sisters. I didn't want them to leave the breakroom to investigate. I raced back across the store, dodging customers and carts. I almost collided with Rosie who was headed to the front doors, most likely to direct the paramedics to the old guy in the bakery.

I threw open the breakroom door and Edie jumped up from the floor.

"I thought you were never coming! I'm hungry," she complained. She turned off the TV and grabbed her jacket.

"What's going on out there?" Anna asked. With the door open, the blare of the sirens and a honking horn were all we could hear.

"There's an emergency in the store," I said. "An old guy fell or had a heart attack or something."

"I want to see!" Edie pulled on her backpack and scooted out the door.

"Get your things," I directed Anna. "I'll take you to the bakery to see what's going on." I scanned the room, making sure the girls had cleaned everything up.

The paramedics rolled a gurney through the front doors as we emerged from the employee area. I led the girls to the bakery along the back aisle so we wouldn't be in their way. We stood off to the side and watched the paramedics check the man's pulse and look into his eyes. I had never seen paramedics at work before. In fact, I'd never witnessed any kind of emergency response. Once the man was lifted onto the gurney, he was wheeled to the ambulance. We followed behind and watched until it pulled away. I looked at my watch. *Crap!* We were going to be late getting home. We'd been so absorbed in the unusual incident, I hadn't realized how much time had passed. There was no way I would have dinner on the table in time.

"Girls!" I cried. "We have to hurry home as fast as we can!" I sprinted inside to retrieve my own backpack and jacket. I grasped my sisters' hands, and we rushed home as fast as we could without running. I *really, really* did not want to upset my mom. Maybe she would be late too. It happened occasionally, so I could hope. Once we turned onto our street, Edie lagged behind. I tugged on her hand.

"Keep moving! We're almost there!"

"Um, Libby?" Anna pulled on my other hand. She pointed silently down the road.

"What are you...?" My voice trailed off as I noticed what she'd already seen. Mom's car sat by the side of the house. Either she hadn't gone to work today, or she was early getting home. A sense of dread prickled down my spine, and my pulse quickened.

"Oh no!" I yanked the girls to a stop, then lurched forward again. "What is she doing home?"

"Are we gonna be in trouble 'cause we're late?" Anna asked, her hand tightening around mine.

"I sure hope not." I didn't want to worry them, but I was definitely worried. "Let's be quiet and calm when we walk in, okay?"

When we got to the front steps. I put my finger to my lips and turned the key in the lock. All three of us squeezed in together. Anna and Edie set their bags on the floor without a sound, while I put mine on the stairs to take up later. I gave them a thumbs up. So far, so good.

Edie went upstairs while Anna and I tiptoed into the kitchen. I switched on the light, then jumped at the sight of my mom leaning against the back door. Her frown was deep, and her arms were folded across her chest. Her eyes singed mine with their fire. Anna yelped, then pressed herself against me. My hands trembled as I hugged her close.

"Where have you been?" Mom snarled, her voice sounding like she'd swallowed gravel.

"At work." My voice shook and I edged closer to the fridge. "Why are you home?"

"Um, let's see..." Mom's tone was sarcastic. "Because I live here?"

"You're just early, that's all," I stammered. I was afraid to turn my back on her after what happened a couple weeks ago, but I needed to get the cookbook in the cupboard behind me so we could start dinner. I tilted Anna's chin up and pointed to the cupboard behind me. She nodded and reached for the cupboard door.

I waited for Mom to do or say something. But waiting for the fireworks to begin jangled my nerves. Finally, Mom pushed off the back door and came within two feet of me. I reached behind me and pushed Anna closer to the stove.

"You. Are. Late. Dinner should have already been on the table," Mom fumed.

I knew she was goading me, so I bit my tongue. I just stood there, my heart pounding. The closer Mom got to me, the more anxious I became. Especially after the choking incident. I tried not to think about how frightened I'd been.

"Explain yourself!" Mom screeched. Anna jumped and dropped the frying pan she was pulling out of the cabinet. It fell to the floor with a crash. She looked at me, panic in her eyes.

Mom's scream made my ears ring. I probably had about two seconds before she hit me, so I answered right away, the words falling from my lips double speed.

"I'm sorry we're late. There was an emergency at the store. The ambulance had to come for some old guy who fell, so we were late leaving."

"Is that true, Anna?" Mom's gaze dropped to my sister, who sat on the floor beside the dropped pan. I knew she was trying to make herself as small as possible, to hide in plain sight.

"Yes, we watched the ambulance take him away." Anna replied, her voice soft and shaky.

I stared at Mom, not wanting to move, but anxious to do something besides square off with her. She had ten seconds before I got to work. I counted silently, keeping the same pace as when we played hide-and-seek. Mom hadn't moved by the time I reached eight. I heard Edie bound down the stairs before I saw her. Mom's attention turned to her third daughter as Edie pranced into the room. She glanced around and asked, "When is dinner?"

"I really don't know, since your sister hasn't made it yet. She's still standing here doing nothing." Mom smirked.

"Probably 'cause you're bugging her!" Edie said. "Besides, why didn't you just make it? You were here first!"

It was as if everything moved in slow motion but still seemed to happen all at once. Mom's fingers curled around Edie's arm, and I lunged toward Mom and snagged the back of her shirt in my fists. I pulled on Mom while she pulled on Edie and Edie tried to free herself. Mom yelled profanities and Edie squealed and kicked at Mom's shin. She made contact and Mom released her. Edie ran out of the kitchen without looking back. I still had Mom's shirt in my hand, so I quickly dropped it and backed away. Mom was like a grenade. Dangerous, but only lethal once the pin was pulled. Edie had pulled the pin, and now the potential for harm had increased exponentially.

Mom whipped around and faced me. "I bet *you're* wondering why I didn't make dinner, right?" Her eyes were dark and hard.

I shook my head, not wanting to risk saying the wrong thing. I held my shaking hands behind my back, so Mom wouldn't notice them.

"Do you know why I'm already home?" Mom asked.

Is this a trick question? No matter what I said, I'd be in trouble. "Not my business," I muttered.

"True. But I'm going to tell you anyway." Mom reached into the fridge and pulled out a can of beer. Popping the top, she said, "I just got fired!" She looked back and forth from me to Anna, her scowl deepening.

Alarmed, I glanced at Anna. Her face reflected my shock. I wondered what Mom had done to bring that upon her. I didn't have to wait long to find out.

"Are you curious why?" Mom's syrupy sweet tone was at odds with the irritation on her face.

Well, yeah. Although I could probably guess. Mom's expression shifted from annoyance to anger.

"It's that idiot Marvin Keller! He claims I wasn't pulling my weight, that I was always late for work. Not true, by the way! Then he said I had made 'sloppy mistakes' with two of our accounts." She took a gulp of beer. "He's had it out for me since I've been there."

Now I knew she was lying. Mom had worked for Mr. Keller since I was young. He was soft-spoken and kind. I hadn't seen him in a few years, but if Mom treated people at work like she did at home, I could easily guess who was at fault.

The Christmas after Mom and Nolan had divorced, my heart was broken that Nolan was gone. Mr. Keller and his wife, who worked in our school cafeteria, had stopped by the house with gifts and treats. Mr. Keller had a long mustache that I couldn't stop staring at and a Christmas tie with Rudolph and his bright red nose all lit up on it. Mrs. Keller read us a Christmas story while we ate Christmas cookies. I remember a wave of loneliness washing over me when they left that evening. But Mr. Keller and his wife were both generous people and they returned for a few Christmases after that like it was their new tradition.

Mom continued her ranting. "He said I wasn't paying attention to the numbers, but I was!" She raised her fist and shook it.

I had no idea what she meant, nor did I want to know. If Mom was as lazy at work as she was here, I would have fired her too. Plus, at home, she was rude and demanding, selfish and abusive. Any of those things at work would have been grounds for termination.

"What are you going to do?" I asked. My biggest worry was the income. No income meant no food, no anything.

"Are you stupid, Libby?! What do you think I'm going to do? I'll have to find a new job since I have you three brats to support!"

Something in the way she said it, and the look of disgust on her face made me snap. Heat rushed into my face, and I heard the surge of blood in my ears. Before I could stop myself, I opened my big mouth.

"Well, you chose to have us, so why are you complaining?" My voice was hard and flat. As soon as the words left my mouth, I wished I could suck them back in.

Mom's jaw dropped. She rushed forward and pushed me up against the cabinets. Anna jumped off the floor and ran out of the kitchen.

I refused to look at Mom, so I was surprised when a hot liquid hit my face. It took me a second to realize she had spit on me. I held my breath and stared at the opposite wall.

Mom grabbed my ear and dug her nails in as she twisted it. It hurt, but I wasn't moving. "You think I *chose* to have you, Libby? I *chose* to have Anna and Edie. I didn't choose to have you!"

Her words startled me, and my eyes flicked to hers. "What?" I mumbled.

Mom's laugh sounded so cynical. "I got pregnant with you accidentally. Your father didn't want to get married, so I didn't want to keep you. But he refused to let me get rid of you and he went to your grandmother to tell her I was pregnant before I could do anything about it. Of course, she was on his side, and she said she would raise you if I didn't want to. That's why we lived here with her! So *she* could raise you! Then she died and that left you and me."

Hot tears formed in my eyes. It made so much sense. She was always after me, always punishing me, always hitting me. My sisters only faced that kind of treatment occasionally. She was getting back at me because I'd been born. I didn't know what she hated more, me or the fact that she had to raise me.

I struggled to move, to get away from her, but she had my arms pinned by my side. I pushed and squirmed. Tears clouded my vision, but nothing clouded the secret she'd just spilled. It played on repeat through my mind. How could a mother be so cold? So hateful to her own child? She blamed me for something that wasn't my fault. She was truly sick.

"Everyone always leaves, you know that? Everyone! First, my father when I was Anna's age, then Denny, then your grandma, then Nolan!" Mom's words didn't really register. I just wanted space between us so I could breathe. The harder I pushed against her, the harder she pushed back. Then with a grunt, she screamed, "You want to go? Then go!"

She yanked on my arm, pulling me halfway across the kitchen. I teetered, off balance and she got behind me. With a heave, she pushed me hard. Momentum carried me forward and I fell right next to the table. My hands hit the ground and kept me from smacking my head on the chair, but a burning hot pain seared through my left wrist. I screamed and rolled into a ball, clutching my injured arm. I writhed around on the floor, gasping for air, taking no notice of anything except the pain. Mom tried to pull me up from the floor, but I pushed her away with my good arm.

"Stop screaming!" she demanded. She reached for my injured wrist. I jerked away.

"I think you broke my wrist!"

Mom's face went pale, then the angry sneer returned. "I didn't break anything! You're the one who fell! Quit overreacting!"

"I need to go to the hospital!" I showed her my wrist, which was already swelling. I tried to move it, but that just elicited more burning pain.

"You don't need a hospital, you big baby!" Mom threw her arms into the air. "I'll go get a bandage from K-Mart. You'll be fine!"

"Well, if you don't take me to a doctor, I'll call someone who will! I'll tell them exactly what you did!" I didn't know if I was being brave or idiotic. I knew any retaliation would be worse than an injured wrist.

At my words, Mom recoiled. Several emotions danced across her face, and she finally settled on resignation. But I could see the anger simmering in her eyes.

"Fine. Get up. I'll go tell your sisters we're leaving."

Five minutes later, we were all on our way to the ER, which was forty minutes away. Anna and Edie wanted to know how I got hurt. I glanced at Mom and could tell by her look that I'd better stay silent. I wondered how I was supposed to explain my injury at the hospital. I obviously couldn't tell the truth there either. The rest of the ride was quiet except for my moans. I held ice on my wrist trying to calm the fierce ache. My sisters complained that they were starving, and I realized I was too. But I had my aching wrist to keep my mind off my rumbling stomach.

Mom spied a McDonald's and got in line at the drive-through. She ordered burgers and fries for all of us, then pulled into a parking space to eat. I had to do everything one-handed, but I still managed to wolf it all down quickly. When we pulled into the hospital parking lot, Anna and Edie hopped out to throw away our garbage and Mom took the opportunity to tell me what to say to the doctors.

"Tell them you fell on the stairs. Remember what will happen to you if you say anything about me."

I knew full well what would happen if I crossed her tonight. My job was to lie and make it seem like we were a happy little family. Well, I'd been lying about my injuries for years and I could certainly do it again.

It felt like we sat in the waiting room for hours. When we walked in, we found that we were fourth in line to see a doctor. That really annoyed Mom. A Friday night spent with her kids at the ER wasn't her idea of a good time and yet, I was the one who really wished the doctors would hurry.

The first person to be called back was a bearded man with a blood-soaked rag around his arm. He told us he cut himself on a sharp rock while working in his yard. He was waiting to be stitched up. Then there was a straggly-haired woman in a gypsy dress who laid across two chairs with her head in her husband's lap. He rubbed her back while she moaned in pain. He glared at me through his thick bifocals when he caught me watching them. A pale young woman with long black hair wiped perspiration from her face as she bounced her legs up and down. I couldn't even guess why she was there.

My sisters quickly grew bored of the magazines and books that sat on the tables in the waiting room. Edie started whining about it until she saw Mom's face. Then she seemed to resign herself to waiting. She and Anna played *I Spy* until it was my turn to be seen.

When the plain-faced nurse called my name, Edie yelled, "Yay! Finally!" The nurse chuckled. She led me to a bed that was curtained off from other beds in the large room. She asked what happened to my wrist. I dutifully told her I had fallen on the stairs, and she wrote it on my chart and inspected my wrist. She prodded and pushed, sending jolts of pain through it. She ordered x-rays, which was no fun at all. I had to turn my arm and hand in different directions to get the entire view of my wrist. I was relieved when it was over.

We waited for another fifteen minutes in the curtained room. Edie wanted to touch everything, which made Mom even more grumpy. Anna repeatedly poked the curtain wall, sending ripples through it. A tall doctor wearing glasses and a stethoscope around his neck came in. He placed the x-rays by a light on the wall so we could see the bones. He pointed out a clean line at the bottom of my hand and said, "See that? You have what's called a distal radial fracture, or in other words, a broken wrist, which I'm sure you already knew." He grimaced and I nodded. He went on to explain that the break was right at the bottom of my arm bones, and it was commonly caused by a fall.

I glanced at Mom when he said that. Her eyes gleamed, satisfied my story jibed with what really happened. I mean, yes, I did fall, but it was because I was pushed, not because I was clumsy. He said I didn't need surgery, but I'd be in a cast for six weeks. Anna and Edie watched, fascinated by the casting procedure. The doctor wrapped my hand and forearm with various stretchy materials followed by wraps of wet Plaster of Paris. It was smoothed out by another wrap and left to dry. We all grew tired as we waited for the drying process. Edie had finally run out of energy, and she slumped back in her chair, her eyes sleepy. Anna sighed and yawned. Mom tapped her fingers on her purse and looked everywhere except at me. When the doctor checked the cast and said we could go, I stifled a yawn and thanked him. The nurse gave me instructions not to get the cast wet. I was to wrap it in plastic to shower or bathe. She set up an appointment for us to come back in six weeks and told me to take over-the-counter pain killers for any discomfort.

The ride home was quiet as both Anna and Edie fell asleep in the car. I sat between them in the back seat, Anna leaning against my left side while Edie leaned on the right. I closed my eyes and thought about the doctor's order to miss work tomorrow and possibly Monday too. He'd asked what my job entailed and when I explained, he warned me not to lift anything more than a couple of pounds with my left hand. It was too late to call Pop's tonight, but tomorrow morning I had to call in sick for two days. And now that Mom had lost her job, she would be home too. Spring Break with her at home was going to feel like an eternity. I planned on keeping to myself as much as possible.

I thought about the night's events and wondered for the hundredth time what I was going to do. Just keep my head down and stick it out until I turn eighteen? Look for Uncle Paul on my own? Call the cops next time? I recalled Mom's words from earlier, the ones I hadn't paid much attention to the first time. "Everyone always leaves..." She'd said her dad left when she was Anna's age. I'd never heard that before. Could that be why she was angry all the time? Because she felt abandoned by everyone? The way my head was spinning, I felt like I'd been sucked into a funnel cloud. Feelings of anger turned to pity, then to disgust, then guilt and finally back to anger.

Maybe Mom didn't know how to cope because she never learned how. Maybe if she'd told someone how she felt, they could have helped her. Maybe if she had gotten the help she needed when she was young, she would be a different person now, a different mother now. A horrifying thought dawned on me. I was doing the same thing as my mother! I needed help too, but I hadn't been willing to reach out for it by trusting others with information about what was happening at home. What would happen if I didn't open my mouth? We'd all continue to suffer and none of us, including Mom, would have the opportunity to heal. That wasn't what I wanted for myself, but especially not for my sisters. I needed to be brave if I didn't want to continue living this way. It was up to me. By the time we pulled into the gravel driveway I felt the gravity of my own choices.

I woke the girls, and they sleepily stumbled into the house. Mom tossed her purse onto the table, told me to get the girls to bed, then disappeared into the bathroom. Before she closed the door, she looked over her shoulder. "Oh, by the way, the hospital bill is probably going to be a lot, so you'll have to help pay for it."

I stopped, stunned. What? It was her fault I had to go to the hospital tonight anyway! The girls were already on their way upstairs, so I stomped up after them, knowing this was just another way for Mom to get back at me for being born. I snapped at the girls to brush their teeth, and we all crowded around the sink together. I was glad my left wrist was the one injured, since I needed my right for things like brushing my teeth and writing.

Changing my clothes was awkward in a cast. My wrist throbbed, but I tried to ignore it. I slid under the covers and fell back on the pillow. I pushed aside the thoughts of getting help for now and wondered where and how quickly Mom could find a new job. Anna needed some new clothes because her pants were too short. Maybe tomorrow I could pull out the boxes from the attic that contained my old clothing that was too small to fit me anymore. Usually Anna and Edie's "new" clothes were my hand-me-downs or from a sale at K-mart. That would have to do for now.

15
Saturday, March 26, 1988

Why did my arm feel so heavy? I lifted it and forced my eyes open just enough to take a peek. I stared at the white cast, confused. My tired brain took a few seconds to catch up. Then the events of last night flooded my mind. Why was this happening to me? I'd always tried to be a dutiful daughter, and yet here I was with an injury caused by mother because she got upset and couldn't control her anger. Trying to be good made no difference to her because she didn't even want me around. I'd always tried to be a good friend too and here I was on the outs with my best friend. A wave of loneliness washed over me as I thought about Jake. I guess being a good student was the only positive thing I had going for me right now. I shut my eyes again. I wasn't ready to deal with my day yet.

When I woke again, it was to the sound of Saturday morning cartoons. Edie must have blasted the volume when she turned them on. I waited to hear Mom yell at her to turn the TV down, but that didn't happen. Hmm. Weird.

I rolled out of bed careful not to bump my cast on anything and pulled my quilt up with one hand. The bed was messy, but I didn't care. In the hall, I saw the door to my sisters' room was wide open. I plodded downstairs, yawning. Edie and Anna were lying on the floor of the living room, their heads propped in their hands and their feet kicking back and forth as they stared at the TV. I walked over and turned the volume down to a reasonable level.

"Hey!" Edie protested. "I like it loud!"

"Yeah, well Mom doesn't," I reminded her.

"Well, Mom isn't here, so turn it back up!"

"She's not here?" I looked at Anna for confirmation.

"Nope, she's gone," she said before turning her attention back to Scooby-Doo.

I shuffled to the kitchen, then peeked down the hall toward Mom's room. Where would she be? She usually slept late on Saturdays. "Do you know where she went?" I asked. No response. "Did you eat breakfast yet?" I called again.

"No, we want pancakes!" Edie responded this time. Of course she answered when the question was about food. I shook my head.

"Sorry, not today. I have only one working hand, remember? We'll have cereal." I pulled a box of Cheerios from the cupboard and poured them into three bowls, then covered them in milk. "Come and get it!"

The clock told me it was too early to call Jerri. Pop's didn't open until 9:00, so I had to wait a while. I wasn't sure when Jerri's shift started, but I'd been planning to work at one o'clock today before I'd been hurt. The girls came for their cereal bowls and hurried back to their cartoons while I ate at the table and stared at my cast. Taking a shower was going to be tricky. After breakfast, I told the girls if they helped me wrap my arm in plastic so I could shower, I would let them write something on my cast. Edie jumped up to help, momentarily distracted from her cartoons.

Trying to keep the cast dry was almost pointless. By the time I finished my shower, I was frustrated. It took twice as long to get ready as it normally did. Six weeks of this was going to be a giant pain. I couldn't fix my hair very easily, so I combed it out and decided to let it air dry. No way was I putting on makeup either.

I found a marker in my room that the girls could use to sign my cast. When I came back downstairs, I saw that my sisters had moved to the couch and the cartoons still played on. Anna pointed to the kitchen. "Mom's home." I held out the marker and they took turns decorating the blank canvas. Edie just wrote her name, but Anna added a couple of flowers to the cast too.

In the kitchen, I found Mom at the table with a newspaper open in front of her. She marked the newspaper with her red pen. I waited, not wanting to interrupt.

"Why are you staring at me, Libby?" Mom asked.

"Just wondering what you're doing," I said. The only time I'd seen a newspaper in this house was when I'd needed one for a school assignment.

Mom cocked her head at me. Her eyes drifted to my cast, then flicked back to the paper. She didn't ask how I was or if my wrist hurt. I don't know why that hurt my feelings, but it did. I bit my lip and started to turn away, but she grumbled, "I have to find a new job, remember? This is where to find them."

"Are there very many?" I was curious and stepped closer. Mom lifted the paper so the part she was looking at was hidden.

"Don't worry about it. It's not your concern." She glared at me.

I rubbed my good hand over my eyes. Not my concern? Didn't this affect her kids too?

"I got groceries while I was out," she added.

Surprised, I opened the fridge. I was happy to see the purchases mostly filled it up. But front and center on the top shelf sat two six-packs of beer. Ugh. Well, that certainly helped it look full. I slammed the fridge door and stalked out of the room.

For the next couple hours, I helped my sisters sort through their clothes and try on some of my old ones from the hand-me-down box. I kept my eye on the time, so I could call Jerri. I had been debating with myself all morning about calling Jake. I really did miss talking to him and now that I had another Mom-inflicted injury, I knew he'd want to know about it. The problem was finding a time I could call. If Mom was here, there was no way. I certainly couldn't say, "Guess what happened to me?" without her disconnecting the call and yanking the phone away.

My wrist ached after helping my sisters, but Mom wanted the bathrooms cleaned. I held up my cast and said, "How am I supposed to do that?" She scowled and assigned Anna and Edie to clean them while I supervised. Edie pitched a fit until Mom told her she couldn't go to the park over spring break if she didn't do the job.

We finished at about 12:30 and the girls were hungry again, so they headed to the kitchen for lunch. I carried the cleaning supplies back to the cupboard in the laundry room. I had always hated this room because it was so cramped. There was barely enough room for a washer and dryer. The walls were stark white and undecorated. I pulled dry towels out of the dryer and into a basket to fold in another room. When I carried the basket through the kitchen on my way to the couch, Edie rushed at me.

"Libby, Mom bought Twinkies!" She held up the box.

Huh? Mom never bought anything like that. I briefly wondered if she felt guilty about what happened yesterday and was trying to make up for it.

"Well, you can't eat that until you have a real lunch first."

Edie placed the Twinkie box on her chair at the table as if claiming them. Anna looked up from spreading peanut butter on a slice of bread. "Hey, those don't all belong to you!"

"Well, I found 'em!"

"Come on, Edie, really? Those are for everyone," I said.

"Fine!" Edie grumbled. She placed the box back in the cupboard and pulled out a can of Spaghetti-Os. "I want this for lunch."

I resisted the urge to gag as I heated it up for her. Once the girls were at the table with their food, I picked up the phone to call Pop's.

The operator gave me the number for the store when I pressed zero. I wrote it on the edge of an ad that lay on the table. As I disconnected the call, Mom walked into the kitchen. Her hair was curled, and she'd put on makeup. Her jeans had been replaced by a black skirt and a white blouse with black polka dots that I'd never seen before.

"Where are you going?" Anna asked.

Mom picked up her purse and the newspaper. "I'm going to fill out job applications. I'm going to try four of them. The other three have to wait until Monday because they aren't open today. I don't know when I'll be back. I might go out to dinner with a friend."

Mom never gave us that much information about anything. And she was having dinner with a friend? I'd never known her to do that before. I didn't dare ask if this friend was a woman or a man. When no one spoke, Mom rushed out the back door, slamming it behind her.

"Okay then," I said. I already felt lighter with her gone. Now I might even be able to call Jake.

Anna giggled. "Was that really our mom?"

"Duh, Anna, who else would it be?" Edie made a funny face.

I laughed. Edie could be so literal sometimes. There hadn't been much to laugh at lately, so I relished the feeling. Anna laughed too and Edie looked at us like we were crazy.

I took some aspirin for my wrist pain, then called Pop's. I stretched the phone cord into the living room so I could hear over the girls' chattering.

"Hello, this is Pop's Market. How may I help you?" I recognized Rosie's voice.

"Hey Rosie, it's Libby," I said. I asked to talk to Jerri and within a few seconds, she picked up.

"This is Jerri." She sounded distracted.

"Jerri, it's Libby."

"Oh, hi, Libby. Are you coming in today?" I pictured her looking at the clock.

"I'm sorry, I should have called earlier," I apologized. "I broke my wrist yesterday and had to get a cast on it. The doctor told me not to go to work for a couple of days. He said I can come back on Tuesday." I felt nervous having to explain what happened.

"Oh, I'm sorry, Libby!" Jerri said. "You just take the time you need. What happened?"

I should have known she would ask, but the question caught me off guard. My heart started racing. "Oh, I just fell on the stairs."

There was a long pause before she asked, "Are you sure you're okay?"

"Yes, I'm fine. I'll be there on Tuesday."

"Let me know if you need anything," Jerri said. "Anything at all."

We hung up and I walked the phone back to the kitchen. The girls had finished their lunch. Anna cleaned the table off, while Edie grabbed two Twinkies out of the box. She grinned at me, and I shrugged. She took that as permission and ran off with Anna. I suggested they go outside to play, so they tugged their shoes on and tumbled out the door.

I took a deep breath. If I was going to call Jake, it was now or never. I punched in the numbers I'd memorized years ago. Since Jake worked at the roller rink now, I had no idea if he was even home.

"Hello?" a gruff voice answered. Jake's dad.

I asked to speak with Jake and sat on the kitchen floor, my back against the refrigerator. I pulled my knees up and waited. Jake's voice suddenly boomed across the line.

"Jake, it's me, Libby," I said softly as my feet tapped the floor.

"Libby!" Jake shouted. Wincing, I pulled the receiver away from my ear. "Ow, Jake, don't be so loud!"

"Sorry! You surprised me. I thought you were still mad at me."

"I was upset," I admitted. "But I miss you, and something else has happened, and I need my friend back." My voice choked on the last words. I fought back the tears, then told Jake how I ended up in the ER with a fractured wrist and that my mom had also lost her job. Jake interrupted with his questions until I finally told him to wait until I finished talking. He was quiet, but I knew he was antsy. I finished my story with the fact that I couldn't go back to work until Tuesday and the only reason I got to call him was because Mom had left the house.

"Geez, Libby, I can't believe this!" Jake sputtered. "I mean, I *do* believe you, it's just crazy! This has got to stop! Are you sure you're alright?"

I told him I was even though inside I didn't feel that way.

"Now I feel twice as guilty for bailing on you last week!" Jake sighed. "This wouldn't have happened if we'd just gone to Ohio."

"It's okay, Jake, I feel bad for putting that pressure on you. I'm just glad we're speaking again." I felt the weight of my emotions and a few tears leaked out of my eyes. With a shuddery breath I changed the subject. "Do you still need my help with the prom?" Even though I wished it was me going, I wasn't going to refuse to help my friend.

"Yeah, I'm going to the florist to order a corsage on Monday morning if you can come," he said. We talked for another ten minutes or so, comparing our schedules and making tentative plans. Tentative because it all depended on Mom's schedule too. If she was home on Monday morning, I wouldn't be going anywhere.

"Do you care if I tell Holly what happened to you? I mean the real story, not the cover story." Jake asked, his voice low.

I hesitated, unsure how I felt about that. Holly already knew about the abuse, so what was holding me back? I reminded myself that I had to open up to people if I wanted their help.

"How about I see if she can come to your house with me? Since your mom is gone right now? I could ask Nicole to come too." Jake waited for my response.

Unless someone had spilled the beans, Nicole didn't know about any of the abuse. Was I ready to let someone else in on the secret?

Jake sensed my reluctance. "Libby, you don't have to suffer in silence. We're your friends. Let us be there for you."

He made it sound so easy. I swallowed over the knot in my throat. "If you're coming, do it now. I don't know how long my mom will be gone."

"No problem," Jake said. His voice dropped. "I'm glad you called."

I felt better and worse after talking to Jake. What if my friends came over and Mom came home? A jolt of anger coursed through me. If this family didn't have so many secrets, I wouldn't have to fear having friends over. Wasn't I allowed to do normal things like that? Or were those boundaries set up by me and my fears, and not by my mom? I couldn't actually remember her saying I couldn't have friends come over. Maybe I just feared letting people see this part of my life. Maybe it was *my* fault. Either way I was working up a sweat worrying about this impending visit. I slumped against the wall but jerked forward when the back door opened.

Edie jumped through the doorway out of breath. "I'm thirsty!" While she filled her plastic Muppets cup with water, she asked if I would play frisbee with her. I smiled and held up my cast. "Not this time."

"Oh yeah," she replied, not even noticing that the cast was on my left wrist, my nondominant hand. I made myself a sandwich without too much trouble, then tried reading the mystery book from the school library. After reading the same page three times, I set the book aside and leaned over the back of the couch to look out the front window. My forehead pressed against the cool glass. Were they coming or not? My stomach twisted. I let the curtain fall and went back to the laundry room to fold the last load of clothes. The telephone rang as I walked by. "Hello?"

"Hey, is it still okay to come?" Jake asked.

"Yes, hurry," I said. I knew it was risky, but I needed to see my friends. I peeked at my sisters through the kitchen window. They had lined up little green army men along the sidewalk and were rolling marbles to knock them over. I hoped that would keep them occupied for a while.

When the doorbell rang, I was waiting by the front door. Jake had his hands on both sides of the door frame, his tall body blocking my view outside. He looked anxious. Before I could say anything, he moved forward and enveloped me in a hug. His shirt was soft and smelled clean. I buried my face in his chest. He held me for several seconds, then released me and moved to the side. "I'm sorry, Libby." He searched my eyes then smiled and gestured behind him. "I brought Holly and Nic."

I blushed as I thought about them observing our hug, but they just looked concerned. Holly gently held up my casted arm. "I need a marker so I can write my name."

I snatched my wrist back. "No! You can't. My mom will see it and wonder when I've seen my friends." I knew my voice sounded forceful, so I added softly, "You can sign it when we get back to school."

Holly nodded and gave me a quick hug. Nicole hopped through the door and gushed, "I'm so sorry you got hurt. Jake said you fell?"

I nodded, then glanced at Jake and Holly. Jake shook his head slightly and his hair fell forward into his eyes. I was a little surprised they hadn't already told Nicole what really happened.

Jake pushed his hair back and said, "You can fill us in."

I gestured to the couch. "Have a seat."

Jake plopped down in the middle with the girls on either side. I sat in the rocking chair, the gentle motion soothing my frayed nerves.

"Tell us what happened," Jake said.

Was I ready for this? Ready to share what really went on at my house much of the time? Mom's screaming threats echoed through my mind, and I considered the seriousness of her words. I gazed at Holly, her freckles standing out brightly across her nose and cheeks. In her dark eyes I saw a glimmer of pity. I didn't want pity. I just wanted to get away from my mom and her abuse. I rubbed my good hand through my hair and sighed.

"Okay, here goes." I squeezed my eyes shut for a second, then faced my friends. Holly leaned forward with her hands clasped in her lap, her red curls shifting forward too. Beside her, Jake's leg bounced up and down, something I knew he did when he was nervous. On the other hand, Nicole looked relaxed but sympathetic. Some of her bushy hair was pulled back in a neon pink scrunchie that matched her neon pink tee-shirt. Her earrings of pink and yellow triangles dangled almost to her shoulders.

I held up my cast. "This was not my fault. I only fell because my mom pushed me." Now all three friends leaned forward. Jake's jaw tightened and Holly pursed her lips, but Nicole blinked several times. I hurried on, "And this isn't the first time she's hurt me." There. I said it.

Nicole's mouth dropped open, and her blue eyes widened behind her glasses. "Wait a minute." She held up a finger. "Your mom abuses you?"

I inhaled slowly. "Yes. It's gone on for years, but it's getting worse and happening more often." I told the girls about my plan to find my uncle with Jake. "But that didn't work out."

Jake started to say something, then eased back at the shake of my head. I wasn't going to give details. That was between us.

Holly and Nicole looked at Jake for more information, but he repeated my words. "It just didn't work out."

"O-kaay," Nicole drew out the word, "So how long has Jake known about this? Did you know about this too, Holly?" She pointed at her best friend with a slightly accusatory look. "And why am I just now finding out?"

I put up a hand to stop Jake and Holly from answering.

"Jake has known for years. When we were younger, Jake was here working on a school project with me. My mom didn't see him, and she got mad at me for something, so she slapped me. She'd hit me plenty of times before that, but that was the first time anyone else witnessed it. She was shocked when she turned around and saw Jake there. I begged him not to tell anyone, and he didn't. I think my mom was afraid he would tell someone, so she was nicer to me for a while, but it didn't last long."

"You know, I wanted to tell my parents, and if I had you wouldn't be dealing with this now," Jake reminded me, pointing to my cast. I knew he was right, but I didn't want to admit it.

I looked at Nicole. "Remember that day in P.E. when Holly and I stayed in the locker room until Coach Barnes came to get us?"

She nodded as comprehension washed over her face.

"Holly saw bruises on my side here." I indicated my ribs. "I swore her to secrecy, but I told Jake that she knew."

Nicole tossed her head back and gave me an annoyed look.

"I'm sorry I didn't fill you in, Nic. I'm so scared my mom will find out that other people know what's going on. She's threatened me most of my life. She says she'll kill me if I tell."

"Kill you?" Nicole questioned. "But that's just an expression!"

"Not when it comes from her! You don't know what she's capable of!"

She pulled back, shocked at the ferocity in my voice. I hadn't exaggerated anything, but I understood it was hard for her to fathom.

The back door opened, and I jumped, my heart suddenly thrust into overdrive. I ran into the kitchen praying it wasn't Mom. Thank goodness it was just Edie and Anna. They begged me to make them some Kool-Aid and asked for a snack. I mixed the purple powder with sugar and water, hoping they would stay put and not wander into the living room. Anna plopped at my feet, claiming to be tired.

"Well, I'm not tired," Edie practically shouted. I wondered if she was as loud to her own ears as she was to mine.

"Shh," I warned as I handed them both a graham cracker. "Go back outside and if Mom gets home, come and tell me!"

They agreed and took their crackers outside. I briefly thought about locking the door behind them but left it alone and hoped Anna would remember to give me a heads-up.

I hurried back to the living room, thankful my friends had not alerted my sisters to their presence.

"You guys," I looked over my shoulder at the back door. "I'm sorry, but I'm afraid my mom is going to come home any minute. I'm really glad you came by."

"We'll think of some way to help you, Libby." Jake was adamant. Holly and Nicole agreed as they made their way to the front door.

"I appreciate that. Just remember this stays between us."

"But what if we need to enlist more help?" Jake stopped and raised his white-blond eyebrows at me.

I thought about it for two seconds. "Just ask me first." I knew we needed more help but trusting someone with the information was still going to be difficult for me.

The back door opened again. Once again, my heart went into panic mode. Anna's voice rang out, "Mom's back!"

My friends scrambled off the couch and scooted out the door. As I closed the front door, I saw Jake peering toward the gravel driveway. He knew where my mom parked her car. If he couldn't see it, that meant she had already pulled in all the way. He gave me a quick thumbs up and I closed the door with a sigh.

16
Tuesday, March 29, 1988

I growled at the clock. I had never known time to pass as slowly as it had the last two days. Usually I liked Spring Break, but that was because Mom was always at work, while Edie, Anna and I had the house to ourselves. Not this year. Mom being unemployed meant we were all stuck in the house together and it was driving me batty.

Mom had resumed her job search yesterday and she had a couple prospects but nothing definitive yet. When she was home, she either stayed in her bedroom or lounged on the couch in front of the TV. The girls wanted to watch the shows they usually watched at Pop's, but Mom told them to "take a hike" and monopolized the TV. She was uptight and edgy, so we did our best to avoid her. If we crossed paths, she issued commands: "Fix me a sandwich," "Turn down that music," "Sweep the floor," or my least favorite, "Bring me a beer."

The alcohol did nothing to help her mood. We hid in the shed Sunday night because she lost her temper with Edie for not picking up her toys. We hadn't waited around after the first dish went flying across the kitchen. Later that night, when we tiptoed back inside, I cleaned up the broken glass while the girls went to bed.

Yesterday, just to get out of the house, I took my sisters to the park for a couple hours. I took a book and read while the girls played on the playground with friends from school. Later, while Mom was job-hunting, I took them on a walk to the florist's shop to help

Jake choose flowers for a corsage. Jake offered us a ride home, but since Pop's was only a block away, we walked there afterwards, and I treated us all to a doughnut from the bakery. Edie kept a running commentary about the poor man who had the emergency: "Ooh, that's where the old man was lying on the floor," and "That's where the ambulance guys told everybody to get out of the way!" I smiled and shook my head. Two of my coworkers saw me and asked what happened to my wrist, so that was twice more I had to lie.

I was currently lying on my back on my bed, with my head hanging off the edge of the mattress. Even looking at it upside down, I knew the clock did not yet say 12:45, the time I needed to leave for work. I had improved a little at using my left hand, so I hoped work wouldn't be too difficult. I rolled off the bed and brushed my long brown hair into a ponytail that I secured with a red scrunchie to match my red work polo shirt. My bangs had been teased and sprayed earlier. I peered closely at my reflection. The few freckles that dotted my nose seemed darker today, a sure sign I'd had more sun on my face recently. I nearly collided with Anna when I left my room. She was out of breath from running up the stairs.

"Libby, Mom said to tell you she'll drop us off at Pop's in one hour. She found out she has a job interview at a dentist's office later."

"She does?" That was fast. They must have needed a receptionist right away. "Just remember to bring something to do and make sure Edie does too."

Anna nodded and ran downstairs ahead of me. I grabbed my things and opened the front door.

"Libby!" Mom called from the kitchen.

I rolled my eyes. What now?

"Yeah?" I leaned back against the battered door frame.

Mom walked into view, studying a paper in her hand. She glanced up at me. "I have an interview."

I smiled in response. "I heard. Good luck!" I really did want Mom to get a job quickly. I worried about the money, especially since Mom frequently mentioned what a drain us girls were on the finances. She needed employment, the sooner, the better, and I crossed my fingers for her.

I was halfway to work when Shawn drove by in his rattletrap truck and honked at me. I should have stuck out my thumb and hitched a ride with him. The air was chilly and by the time I got to work, I was cold. I needed sunshine for an activity I'd planned for my sisters. On Sunday, while searching for Edie's roller skates in the shed, I came across two packets of flower seeds that we'd apparently forgotten about. If we cleaned up the flower beds by the front porch and along the side of the house, we could plant some flowers together. Because of my cast, Edie and Anna would have to be the ones digging in the dirt, but they would probably love it.

I wondered how many people would ask about my wrist at work and how many times I would have to lie about what happened. I mean, I'd had to lie for years about other injuries, so I don't know why it bothered me so much to do it now. Maybe my conscience had reached its limit and couldn't take it anymore. But I couldn't just blab the truth to everyone that asked.

The parking lot at Pop's was almost full. I was always in school at this time every weekday, so I didn't know if that was typical or if it was because all the kids were on break this week.

As the doors slid open, I was struck by how loud it was inside. Registers dinged. The telephone rang. Babies cried. Oldies music played on the PA system which meant Linda was working today. I smiled despite the music choice. It was good to be back. I clocked in and found Jerri in her office. She greeted me with a hug.

"I've been worried about you!" she gushed, her eyes twinkling. "I'm so glad you're back." She took a minute to inspect my cast, then with a mischievous grin, asked if she could sign it. With a bright red marker she found in her desk drawer, she signed her name in swirly cursive, taking up as much space as possible. I laughed, impressed at the size of her name.

Jerri grabbed a clipboard and checklist off her desk and said we'd be working together in the baking aisle. Inwardly, I groaned. The baking aisle was always the messiest job. I knew I'd be covered in flour by the time my shift ended.

Jerri kept an upbeat chatter as we loaded up the products we needed to take to the floor. Jerri did most of the lifting because of my wrist, so it took a little longer than usual. I wanted to tell her the truth about what happened, but Mom's threats were embedded front and center in my mind. A shiver ran down my back. Jerri seemed oblivious to my inner turmoil.

She told me about the fishing trip she took with her husband on Sunday. "I don't think he really wanted me to go, but since his friend backed out, I won by default," she said with a chuckle. "Reed thinks I scare away all the fish because I talk too much. Anyway, I finally got so bored, I fell asleep. That was when he finally caught a few!" We both laughed. I loved Jerri. She was so real.

Jerri said I could stock the spices, and she would stock the flour and sugar because those were too heavy for me. Now I knew why she was working with me today. Once I'd gotten the hang of all my duties, she'd let me do it on my own and now because of my injury, she had to help me again.

"So, tell me more about how you hurt yourself." Jerri pointed at my wrist.

Even though I'd anticipated her question and practiced my lie earlier, I felt uncomfortable giving voice to it. The injury wasn't something I could hide, so people naturally wanted to know the story. I hated always having to cover up for my mom. Still, I hesitated.

"I was running on the stairs and slipped and fell. When I caught myself with my arms, I broke my wrist. It hurt so much. We went to the emergency room, and they put me in the cast."

"How long do you have the cast?"

"Six weeks. And my mom wasn't happy we had to go that far away for help. She isn't too happy about the bill that's coming either." I realized I was rambling and took a deep breath. *Stop talking! Don't say anything else!*

"Whoa, I think you might damage that garlic powder!" Jerri nodded toward my hand. She pried the bottle from the death grip I had on it. "Are you okay?"

I looked up and realized Jerri hadn't moved. She was studying me intently. Her bright blue eyes searched mine. She looked at my wrist and back into my eyes. Her next words surprised me.

"Is there something going on you're not telling me?" She pointed to my wrist.

Well, yeah, of course. But I couldn't bring myself to say it. I just couldn't. I wasn't sure what Jerri would do with the information. I looked away and picked up another spice bottle. "I don't know what you mean."

"Don't you?"

I half expected her to make me look at her like my mom did. But she moved back to the sugar section and began moving the five-pound bags around. Had she somehow caught on that my injuries were not caused by my own carelessness? What was I supposed to say now? She definitely suspected something.

I was glad the aisle filled up with shoppers because it became impossible for us to continue the conversation. From the tidbits of conversation going on around me, it sounded like several mothers and their children were planning to make cookies over spring break. The packages of chocolate chips were rapidly diminishing. Maybe I could grab a bag and do the same with my sisters this week. Mom didn't usually buy ingredients for treats, so I would buy some before I left today.

I pondered the way Jerri had looked at me and questioned the wrist injury. Did she know or was she just guessing? I liked her well enough, but did I trust her?

I leaned down to pick up more spices bottles and didn't see Jerri scoot over beside me. "So, did you really fall on the stairs?"

I flinched and dropped a bottle which then rolled across the aisle. Jerri picked it up, then stood in front of me, tossing her long braid over her shoulder. I focused my gaze on Jerri's long blond bangs, her nose, her ears, everywhere except her eyes. I frantically wondered what I should tell her. A lie or the truth? My pulse quickened and I felt dizzy.

"Libby, look at me," Jerri said.

My eyes flicked to hers. All I saw reflected there was kindness, and it made me want to cry.

"I'm your friend. If there's something going on, you can trust me."

I nodded. Those were the words I wanted to hear, but forcing myself to talk was easier said than done. My eyes blurred with tears.

"Why don't we finish this job and go have a chat in my office?" she suggested. Why couldn't I keep my emotions under control? They always seemed to betray me.

Jerri seemed to sense my reticence and gave my arms a squeeze. We got back to work stocking the shelves, neither of us speaking. My mind raced with the decision I faced: continue lying or trust Jerri and tell her the truth. When we finished the job, we gathered the empty boxes and carried them to the dumpster behind the store. I glanced at my watch. Edie and Anna had likely shown up an hour ago. I wanted to check the employee lounge on the way to Jerri's office.

The closer we got to Jerri's office, the more tense I became. I needed to downplay what was happening at home. Jerri said I could trust her, but what did that mean exactly? Trust her to keep my secret? Trust her to call the police? Trust her to...what? These thoughts spun through my mind like the merry-go-round at the park, faster and faster, until I felt I might puke.

I peeked in the breakroom. My sisters were both coloring with a shared box of crayons between them. A rerun of "The Brady Bunch" played on the TV screen in the corner. Rosie sat at the table, obviously on her break. Her feet were propped on the chair across from her. She held a steaming mug of tea and sipped it with her eyes closed. The girls heard the door open and glanced my way. I didn't want to disturb Rosie, so I held my finger to my lips and said, "Shh!" I gave them a wave and let the door close softly. Jerri stood waiting at her office door. "Linda is just heading to customer service."

Linda bustled out with a grin, her bright red lipstick looking a bit wet, as if she'd just applied it. She fished a stick of Big Red gum from the pocket of her apron.

"Libby! I'm so glad you are back!" She reached for my hand and lifted it so she could inspect the cast. "Ouch! I'm so sorry about your injury. Are you having any problems doing your work with this?"

I shook my head and told her that Jerri was helping me.

"Well, it looks like Jerri thought she could take all the room!" She indicated Jerri's bright red name on the cast. "Let me sign it real quick." She pulled a black pen from her apron and popped off the cap. She pulled me close and wrote her name in small letters in a circular fashion around my thumb.

"What are you doing?" Jerri asked.

Linda laughed. "Well in real life I'm the bigger one." She patted her butt and belly, "So, I'm just giving you the chance to be the big one for a while." She pointed to Jerri's name.

Jerri snorted and pushed her playfully. "Time to go now!" She pointed down the hall. Linda grinned again and headed toward the store floor. Jerri beckoned me into the office. Instead of pulling a chair from the closet for me, she brought Linda's more comfortable chair around by her desk.

"Alrighty," she said, "talk to me."

I wiped my sweating hands on my legs and concentrated on keeping my legs still. I kept my face blank and shrugged. "I don't know what to say."

Jerri pursed her lips and locked her eyes onto mine. "Okay, how about I ask questions, and you give me honest answers." She gave me a no-nonsense look.

I barely blinked, but Mom's repeated words twirled around my brain. *Don't say anything! Keep your mouth shut or you'll pay!* I wanted to scream back at her. *Shut up! Leave me alone!*

"But first, let me tell you what I think." Jerri propped her elbows on the desk and interlocked her fingers as she gazed at me.

I shrugged again. She seemed confident she knew something. I narrowed my eyes and waited.

"When your mom came in the store on your first day, you were shaking, and she was just so...angry. Whenever I ask anything about your home life, you clam up and avoid the subject, but today you said your mom wasn't happy she had to take you to the ER or about the hospital bill. What kind of parent gets mad that their child got injured? I would think she'd be concerned more than anything." She pointed at my wrist. "So, did you really fall down the stairs or was that something that was done to you?"

I dropped my head and stared at my legs. Had it been that easy to figure out? My legs bounced a little of their own accord. My heart pounded against my ribs, the pressure inside needing a release. I knew Mom's threats were very real and she would most definitely hurt me if she found out I'd told, but technically I wasn't telling. Jerri had already figured it out and I was just answering her questions. I could hear Jake's voice in my head encouraging me to tell the truth. Once I made my decision, I felt suddenly calm.

"I really did fall," I began, "but not on the stairs. I fell in the kitchen because I was pushed."

Jerri made a steeple with her fingers and touched her lips in thought. "Pushed by your mom?"

I pressed my eyes shut and nodded. There. It was out.

"Because she was angry?"

"Yes."

"Does this kind of thing happen often?"

"Well, I've never broken anything before." I looked at my wrist. "But she does...other things, like hitting me."

"What else?" Jerri opened her desk drawer and pulled out a blue Bic pen.

"What are you doing?" My forehead creased as I gestured to the pen.

"Taking notes," she replied. She opened another drawer and pulled out a piece of paper.

I leaned forward, perspiration dampening my face. "No, you can't. This stays between us."

Jerri studied my face for several seconds. The pause was nerve-wracking. "Why?"

"Because of her threats! If she finds out I told you, she'll...come after me...and hurt me even worse." I had trouble with the words, as if my mouth was full of peanut butter.

Jerri tilted her head and scrunched up her face. I think I'd had that same look when trying to solve a difficult math problem. Her next words surprised me.

"Your boyfriend, Jack, I think it is? He came by here on Sunday." Jerri placed her pen on the desk.

I felt a little off-kilter. What did that have to do with anything? "It's Jake, and we're just friends. What did he want?" I was almost afraid of her answer.

"I was walking through the store and bumped into him. We exchanged pleasantries and he mentioned your injury. Then he said something like he was tired of you getting hurt. I didn't understand what he meant, and he didn't elaborate."

I swallowed hard. I'd been with Jake yesterday and he'd said nothing about talking to Jerri. It sounded as if he wanted her to know.

Jerri interrupted my thoughts. "So, after your words today and your obvious fear when you talk about it, everything clicked and here we are." She spread her open hands out in front of her. The only sound was the ticking of the clock.

"What can I do to help you?" she asked.

"Ha! You can't do anything!" I said. "Believe me, I've tried."

I launched into my story – the history of abuse in my family, the way I protected my sisters from the worst of it, the fumbled plan to find Uncle Paul, my mom's current job loss. Jerri listened without interrupting. When I ran out of words, she asked, "What about your mom's ex-husband? Your sisters' father?"

"Trust me, I've thought about telling Nolan. But I don't have a phone number or address for him. He lives in Florida, and I never see him. My sisters fly there at Christmas and for a few weeks in the summer, that's it."

Jerri glanced at the clock and sighed. "My last suggestion would be to call the police, but since you haven't already done it, I'm assuming you don't want that, right?"

"No, that's my last resort. I can't take the chance my mom will act on her threats. And I absolutely believe it would happen."

Jerri rubbed her temples. "Okay, let's think on it some more. But right now, we both need to get back to work." After a pause, she asked, "Would you like me to try to find Nolan?"

I considered the question. "Yeah, I think I would."

Jerri handed me the pen and paper and had me write down Nolan's full name.

"Alright, I'll see what I can do. I'll be attending a funeral for my husband's uncle tomorrow up in Indianapolis, so I'll be back on Monday. Let's talk then." Jerri returned the pen and paper to their proper places and stood. I moved Linda's comfy chair back to her desk.

"Remember, Libby, you don't need to hide anything from me. I'll keep your secret, at least until we figure something out. But please be careful. I'm worried about you girls." Jerri pulled me in for a hug. Her arms around me felt comforting and made me tear up a little.

I just loved Jerri. She accepted me for me, and she cared enough to help, but in my way, not hers. I did trust her and just like when I told my story to Holly in the locker room, I already felt some relief. Sharing my problems with my friends felt so much better than keeping them locked inside. And maybe, just maybe, we could come up with something that wouldn't end in tragedy.

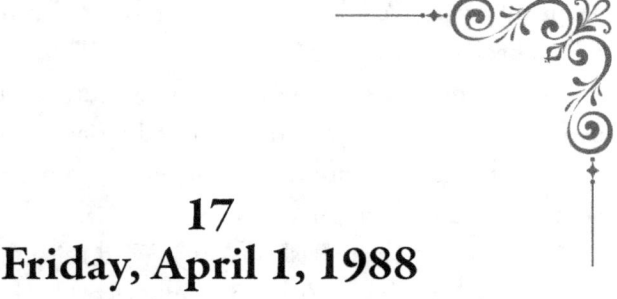

17
Friday, April 1, 1988

Wrapped in my grandma's green and tan crocheted blanket, I was sandwiched between my sisters on the couch, all of us still in our pajamas. The TV was tuned in to *The Price is Right* and Bob Barker was currently asking the contestants for their bids on a washer and dryer set. In unison, we called out our own guesses, and all overbid.

"Ha! You didn't get it this time, Libby!" Edie shoved my shoulder.

"Hey! Neither did you!" I tickled her ribs. She squealed and jumped onto the floor. Anna laughed.

"And neither did you!" I turned to my left and tickled Anna. She giggled and swatted my hand. Edie laughed and tried to tickle Anna's legs, but Anna squealed and pushed her back. Edie shrieked, then leaped on top of us. We were a big pile of wiggling bodies and laughter. Over the commotion, I heard the phone ring. I tried to get up, but we were all tangled together.

"Let me up. I've got to get the phone."

"Too bad!" Edie shouted and threw herself over my legs. I bucked my knees which sent her into another fit of giggles.

"Be quiet! I can't hear anything with your noise!" Mom roared from across the room. She held the phone receiver in one hand while covering the speaking end with her other hand. Her glare said she meant business. We fell silent and untangled our limbs while Mom walked back to the kitchen.

I patted down my mussed hair and we turned our attention back to the show. The surfer dude who had won the washer and dryer set was just wrapping up the Double Prizes game. His last guess was incorrect, and Edie groaned.

"What did he lose?" asked Anna. We'd missed the offered prize while we were tussling. Within a couple seconds, the prize flashed up – a new living room set.

"Well, he's probably glad he lost that," exclaimed Edie. "It's so ugly!"

Suddenly there was a loud bang from the kitchen. I flinched and Anna pressed herself into my side. Edie hopped up off the couch, tripped and stumbled into the kitchen, laughing. I heard her ask, "What's wrong?"

There was no response. Edie reappeared wearing a bewildered look and shrugged her shoulders.

Okay, something was going on. I left Anna on the couch and found Mom sitting at the table, her head in her hands. I glanced around, wondering what the bang had been. The coiled phone cord swung against the wall, and I realized Mom must have slammed the receiver. Whatever news she'd received, it wasn't good.

Chair legs scraped on the linoleum behind me. I turned to see Mom's jaw thrust in my direction.

"What happened?" I took a small step back. She was upset, and I didn't want it taken out on me.

Instead of answering, she spun around, snatched a glass off the table and flung it across the kitchen.

"Ahh!" she screamed.

The glass hit the dark upper cupboards and shattered into pieces. I gasped and backed further away. She screamed again, arms taut at her sides with her fists clenched.

"What's going on?" a small voice behind me asked. I spun around to see a wide-eyed Anna with Edie at her side. Edie looked like she'd caught someone red-handed and was delighted by it. A sharp shake of my head while pointing up silently directed the girls to leave the room. Thankfully even Edie scurried away. I turned to Mom, my initial fear now a spark of anger beginning to burn inside me.

"What is the problem?"

"Don't you talk to me like that!" Mom lunged forward and slapped my arm. "Do you hear me?!"

I gasped, the fire inside growing hotter than the sting of her slap. I returned her glare but clamped my mouth shut.

"I didn't get the job at the dentist's office," Mom said with clenched teeth. Then her volume increased. "I'm going to go there and demand to know why!"

I closed my eyes. What did she think that was going to do? It certainly wouldn't change anything.

"If they gave it to that fluffy-haired blonde in the high heels, I am going to lose my mind!"

My gaze drifted to the broken glass that sparkled in the morning sun as it lay scattered across the countertops and floor. Lose her mind? Hadn't she already lost it?

"Don't you still have other jobs you applied for? Maybe you'll get one of them."

"Well, this one was the one I wanted!" she screamed and stomped her foot.

"Sorry," I muttered. I actually was sorry but also ticked off at the way she took the news.

"Clean up this mess!" Mom waved her hand at the scattered glass, then turned and stomped to her bedroom. I bit my tongue to keep from saying what ran through my mind. *You made this mess. You clean it.*

The bedroom door slammed, rattling the windows in the kitchen and the back door. I sighed and rubbed my arm that still smarted from the blow. Bob Barker's voice carried in from the living room. I stalked to the TV and flipped it off. The house was deathly quiet. I assumed Mom was pouting in her bed and the girls were laying low in their room.

I ran upstairs to grab my Walkman and my INXS cassette. The Walkman was a gift from Nolan last Christmas and the tape was from Jake. I adored both gifts. If I had to pick up tiny bits of glass for a while, I might as well listen to something that made me happy. I poked my head in the girls' room and saw them dressing Barbie dolls. I whispered to them to get dressed and brush their hair and told them I was going to clean up the glass.

Anna whispered back, "What's wrong with Mom?"

"She didn't get the job at the dentist's office."

Anna made an "O" with her mouth, but Edie's face looked comical. Her eyes bulged and she stuck out her tongue, groaned and fell over. Anna swatted her.

"That's not nice. She needs a job."

I nodded my agreement and closed the door. My sisters always reacted in opposite but predictable ways. Anna was so much like the Nolan I remembered, and Edie was like Mom. I hoped she wouldn't grow up to be like her though. I was finding it more and more difficult to be around Mom. She was hard to like.

I pressed play on my Walkman and for the next 20 minutes bobbed my head to the music as I swept, wiped the countertops and the sink and even the top of the fridge. I had to make sure no glass remained. We didn't need any more injuries around here. On my hands and knees, I gave the floor one last inspection, then stood and stretched. The muscles in my back were tight and my knees were sore. My skin under the cast itched and I wished I could pull it off and give my arm a good scratch. I turned off the cassette and draped the headphones around my neck.

I nearly jumped out of my skin when I looked behind me. Anna and Edie sat at the table watching me. How long had they been there? "Geez, you scared me!"

They giggled. Edie lightly tapped the table. "We want food."

I'd forgotten we hadn't eaten breakfast yet. I looked at the clock. 10:02. That would explain my grumbling stomach. I pulled eggs out of the fridge and told the girls to get milk, butter, jam and bread. They must have been hungry, because there were no complaints from them. I noticed Edie had put on a pink jumper that was a hand-me-down of Anna's, and her hair had been styled in a crooked braid.

"Nice hair," I said, then smiled at Anna, the hair stylist.

She beamed. "Thanks, Libby."

Anna wore jeans and a tee shirt and had brushed her hair into a high ponytail. I looked down at my thin polka-dot pajamas. I still needed to get ready for work.

I put the girls in charge of the toast while I scrambled eggs. I checked the cupboard to make sure we had taco shells for dinner. I pulled hamburger out of the freezer and placed it in the fridge. It looked like I needed to pick up tomatoes and lettuce at the store when I went to work. No way was I bothering Mom with that today. I had some cash upstairs that I could use. I'd also had my eye on the new Bop magazine I'd seen in the magazine aisle last week when we stocked the new April issue. I'd flipped through it and found a few Kirk Cameron photos I wanted for my locker, so maybe I'd treat myself to it today. It was nice having my own money.

As we finished breakfast, Mom stormed out of her room. "How am I supposed to sleep with you all making so much noise?"

We'd actually been pretty quiet, but a little noise was to be expected. I looked at my plate to hide my scowl. Edie placed her plate in the sink, moving in slow-motion, probably so she didn't make a sound. Then she spun around and bowed at Mom.

"There you go, your Majesty!"

I gasped. What was she thinking? Anna looked at me, alarmed.

"What did you say?" Mom hissed.

I was glad to see that Edie had enough brains to say nothing. I felt a sudden sense of peril or doom or...something. Even with all that had occurred in this house, I'd never felt this feeling before and it scared me. I sat, paralyzed with fear.

In one rapid surge, Mom was across the kitchen. She yanked Edie's arm and pulled her toward her bedroom. Edie tried to dig in her heels, but it was fruitless on the smooth floor. Mom screamed at her. "You will not disrespect me, you little brat!"

Edie pried at Mom's hand with her free hand. Maybe she felt impending doom too, because the look on her face was pure panic. "No, no, no!"

I jumped up and followed them. "Hey, stop it!" I yelled, trying to be louder than both of them. "Stop!"

Mom turned and grabbed my arm too. I was a lot more weight to pull than Edie, so she released me. "Stay out of it," she spat, "or you're next!"

She pushed her bedroom door open with such force; it slammed into the wall with a bang. It was so loud, I almost didn't hear the crying behind me. I felt compelled to protect Edie, but I also needed to keep Anna safe.

"Go to the shed or to your room," I said.

"No," Anna sobbed. "I'm not leaving."

"Anna," I pleaded, "I need you to be safe."

Anna's eyes widened and she pointed toward Mom's bedroom. I had blocked out the sound of Mom's and Edie's screaming for a second and missed what was happening. Mom had pulled something from her closet while still holding onto Edie. In one swift movement,

Mom pushed Edie onto the bed and swung whatever it was she held in her hand. As the long slender strap descended across Edie's back, realization jolted me forward. My heart thudded painfully against my ribs, and I felt as if I might vomit. Edie's blood-curdling scream was like nothing I'd ever heard before.

"No! Stop! Please stop!" I begged as I ran into the room. Mom ignored me and brought the belt down on Edie again. Edie sobbed as she gripped the bedspread. She jerked and screamed when the belt struck her again. Mom's eyes bulged, her rage completely out of control. She looked insane, as if some deep trance had overcome her. I had to stop this madness.

My fury over the beating Edie was enduring propelled me forward, even though everything in me wanted to flee. Mom saw me jump toward her and raised the belt high once more. I dropped onto the bed and lay across Edie's small body. As the belt smacked down, a sharp stinging sensation spread like fire across my lower back and my right forearm.

"STOP!" I shrieked. Edie struggled to move beneath me, and I rolled off her, giving her a push so she fell off the far side of the bed onto the floor. Anna stood wailing in the doorway and Edie scrambled toward her, sobbing and gulping for air at the same time. The sound wrenched my heart.

"You think you're the big hero, don't you?" Mom sneered, her arm raised, ready to bring the belt down again. I shook my head and rolled away, self-preservation kicking in. I was almost across the bed when my right foot was suddenly trapped. I glanced back to see Mom gripping my ankle. I pulled, trying to keep the momentum I'd had, but the belt was whooshing down again, this time smacking just under my shoulder blades.

"Aahh!" I screamed and flinched at the intense burning sensation. Tears blurred my eyes, then fell in rivers down my face. My nose ran onto my lips, and I wiped my face against the bedcovers. I had to get away, but Mom still held my ankle with the strength of a vise. I had to force myself to focus on her words as she ranted about her horrible life, her good-for-nothing brats and how she wished we would all just die. As shocking as that seemed at first, it took me about two seconds to realize that I didn't care what she said. I just wanted to get away from her. I kicked my free foot back and up, not caring what I hit. I felt nothing but air and Mom laughed at my attempt to get loose.

She snapped the belt across my back three more times, in rapid succession before she released me. My back felt like pins were sticking into every inch of it and the image of Grandma's tomato pin cushion she used while sewing popped into my head. Tears and snot ran down my face as I scrambled away. I rubbed my face with my arm, forgetting about the cast underneath my sleeve that bumped hard against my nose. I crawled out of Mom's room and pushed myself to my feet. I stumbled and bumped one of Grandma's framed flower prints on the wall. It fell to the floor but didn't break. I left it and ran for the stairs. I had to find Edie and Anna. Were they upstairs or in the shed?

Ignoring the pain across my back I burst into the girls' room. Edie was curled up on the bed, crying softly into her pillow while Anna rubbed her hair, silent tears making streaks down her face. They both jumped when I entered. I leaned over, breathing heavily, relieved I didn't have to go outside to the shed to find them. I closed the door and pushed the tall dresser in front of it, moving fast in case Mom decided to follow me.

I sighed and leaned my head against the dresser. What had just happened? All hell had broken loose, and my brain needed time to process what we'd just been through. I rubbed my eyes and glanced at my sisters. Edie was partially sitting with her little arms wrapped around herself. Anna just stared at me and swiped her face with her hands.

I put my finger to my lips to keep them from talking. I climbed over the footboard with its chipping white paint and plopped onto the mattress. I beckoned both girls to me and they scooted close, still quietly crying.

"Edie, are you okay?" I whispered. She shook her head against my shoulder. I knew I should look at her back, but I was afraid to see the damage Mom had inflicted. I finally asked if I could take a peek, so I would know how to help. She unbuttoned the shoulder straps on the pink jumper and pushed it to her waist. She turned onto her belly, and I lifted the back of her shirt. There were distinct red marks crisscrossing her back like a giant X. Seeing them sent a hot poker of pain down my lungs. I closed my eyes and took a few deep breaths to steady myself. A little hand patted my arm. My eyes opened and flicked to Anna. Her comforting touch soothed me.

I gently touched one of the welts on Edie's back. She whimpered and my heart melted. I couldn't help it. I covered my face with both hands while hot tears squeezed from my eyes. All this time, Mom had mostly just gone after me, but now it seemed she was going after all of us. I could not let this happen to my sisters. I was an idiot not to have reported my mom before. There was no way I was letting this happen again.

"I'm sorry," I managed to say. "At least your back isn't bleeding."

I wracked my brain for how I could help her. Ice? A heating pad? A cream? I thought about my own stinging back. What would feel good? Probably a cream or Vaseline, but I didn't know much about first aid, especially for something like this. I glanced at the door. Mom hadn't tried to enter, so I had to assume she wouldn't, but I had to go across the hall to the bathroom to get the supplies.

Anna helped me move the dresser away from the door. I opened the door a crack and peeked out. No Mom. Just silence. I darted into the bathroom and opened the drawer where I kept the Vaseline, which I used to remove makeup. A few seconds later, I was back in the girls' room. Anna and I blocked the door with the dresser once again, then I sat on the bed next to Edie. I kissed her cheek, then once again lifted her shirt to expose her back. My own back felt like it had been ironed on the steam setting, but I focused on applying the jelly to Edie's wounds. She jerked at my touch but settled and relaxed after a few seconds. I knew she was hurting, but I had to bring up the sassiness that had set Mom off.

"Edie, why did you sass Mom? You know she doesn't put up with that kind of talk." I tilted my head so I could see her face. Her eyes were the saddest I'd ever seen, and a tear trickled onto the pillow.

"I don't know. She just makes me so mad!"

"I know, but you have to be careful what you say." I eased her shirt down over the welts and lifted her onto my lap. I hugged her gently.

"You scared me so bad, Edie." Anna's face reddened, then scrunched up and tears began to fall. Edie reached for her, and they held each other until they were cried out.

I peeked at my watch. I had to get ready for work, but there was no way I was taking a shower with fresh welts on my back. I asked the girls to put Vaseline on my back because I had to leave soon. Anna grabbed the salve and motioned for me to turn around, but Edie clutched my hand hard.

"You can't leave us here with Mom!"

I'd always thought my littlest sister wasn't afraid of anything, but now I knew differently. The panic in her dark eyes and the way her hand shook told me Mom had really gotten to her this time. I held up my hand to stop Anna while I responded to Edie. "I know. You can just come with me."

"But what if Mom won't let us go with you?"

"I'll think of something." I wanted to reassure her, but she'd asked a valid question. I didn't have long to figure it out.

Anna resumed her role as nurse. I got onto my belly, and she lifted the back of my shirt. All I heard was a sharp gasp. Even Edie breathed out an "oh!"

"Is it that bad?"

"It's so red!" Edie said.

"It's worse than Edie's." Anna said.

"Is it bleeding?"

"Just right here." Anna softly touched a spot in the middle of my back. I groaned, then tensed as she rubbed the cold salve on the welts. I buried my face in the pillow and gritted my teeth to keep from crying out. I wondered if my shirt moving over my back all afternoon while I worked was even going to be bearable. I was glad the girls remained silent. I needed time to think. By the time Anna had finished, I hadn't come up with any solution, other than to tell Mom I was taking Anna and Edie with me and hope she'd let me. I didn't want to threaten to call the police but that had suddenly become a possibility. I would not leave them here.

I knew Jerri wouldn't be in today, but I had to tell someone. I couldn't call from here though. I'd have to try from Pop's. Jake was my first choice. He was going to flip out. If I couldn't get him, I'd try Holly or Nicole. With that decided, and Anna declaring she was finished, I pushed myself up and let my shirt fall back down. My pajamas were softer and looser than my work polo. I dreaded putting it on, but I had no choice.

Once I'd changed my clothes and checked to make sure the girls were ready, I enlisted Anna's help to comb through my tangled hair. My back hurt too much to reach above my head. Anna was gentle and slow, and it made Edie impatient. She sat on the bathroom floor, asking if Anna was done yet until I shushed her and threatened to comb her hair out of its mussed-up braid if she didn't stop asking. Edie must have believed me because she didn't say another word. I looked at my splotchy face in the mirror, wishing I could apply some makeup, but I was out of time.

I wished Jerri hadn't left town for three days because I was unsure of my next steps. Mom had been so violent lately; I was more afraid of her than ever. I was scared to let the girls sleep in their own bedroom.

I said a silent prayer that Mom would get a job soon. That would help a lot. And Anna, Edie and I would have to be very careful around her. No sassing, no disagreements. Nothing. In fact, the less interaction the better. Hopefully, Jerri would find Nolan and if not, we'd move on to something else. But I had a deep sense that time was chasing us down.

I tiptoed downstairs first. Peeking around the banister into the living room, I saw nothing, so I waved the girls down. The silence in the house was almost eerie. We ever so slowly took our jackets from the coat rack and put them on. I winced at the abrasiveness of my shirt against my back. Then we hurried out the door.

"Walk fast!" I urged and the girls jogged to keep up. My thoughts raced as fast as my feet. Maybe Jerri would let us stay at her house when she got back in town? I pondered that over and decided she probably wouldn't, not without telling Mom anyway. Everything I came up with seemed to fall apart and I felt helpless. I heaved a huge sigh. Anna took my hand and squeezed. I wondered if she could read my mind.

When we got to Pop's, I left the girls in the breakroom with Edie lying on the floor on her stomach so she could color. I needed a phone and the only one I knew of besides the customer service desk was in the office. I crossed my fingers as I approached the office door. No one answered when I knocked. I glanced down the hall. Not a soul in sight.

Inside, I slid into Jerri's chair, picked up the clunky black receiver and dialed Jake's number. I stared at the door while I waited for someone to pick up. *Please stay closed! Please no one come in!*

"Hello?" the female voice could have been Jake's mom or his sister. I couldn't tell. I asked for Jake, only to be told he was working, and could she give him a message? Definitely his mom. Shoot! I hadn't thought about what message to leave.

"Um, this is Libby. It's really important I talk to him soon. Maybe he could stop by the store tomorrow when I'm working?" I tapped my fingers on the desk. The second hand on the clock above the door sped on. *Hurry, hurry, hurry!*

Mrs. Evans chuckled. "Well, what time do you work tomorrow, Libby?"

"Oh, um, twelve to four." I stood, ready to hang up and jet out of there.

"Is everything alright?"

"Yes, everything's fine, but I have to go now." I danced from foot to foot, anxious to end the call. I replaced the phone in the cradle and zipped out the door. I didn't stop moving until I stood in front of the restroom mirror. Taking a deep breath, I closed my eyes and counted to ten. Then I made my way to the back of the store to clock in, hoping Jake would get the message and more importantly, that he'd show up.

18
Saturday, April 2, 1988

I t was just past seven o'clock when I woke to the sound of birds chirping in the trees behind the shed. I moaned. My eyelids felt as if rocks were resting on them. I was still so tired. I'd gone to bed around ten but had such fitful sleep. I blamed it on my sore back. I lay there for several minutes, then because my mind began replaying scenes from yesterday, I knew I wouldn't fall back to sleep. Better just to get up and get going. I'd promised the girls if it was nice weather this morning, we would plant the flower seeds. They had seemed excited to help.

I slid off the bed and gingerly got to my feet. The skin on my back pulled at the welts and felt uncomfortably tight. In the bathroom, I lifted my pajama top and looked over my shoulder into the mirror. Yep. Still red but not bleeding. I needed Anna to doctor me up again. I wondered if it was too early to wake the girls. I was a little worried about fixing breakfast after Mom freaked out over the noise yesterday. But we still had to eat.

Last night, I'd made dinner as quietly as I could because I was afraid of a repeat scene. But Mom never came out of her room to eat, so I'd put the leftovers in the fridge and played games with Edie and Anna until bedtime.

I pulled on an old pair of jeans and a worn-out tee shirt, perfect for doing some gardening. I had to admit I was looking forward to the planting. For some reason, nurturing the plants sounded exciting to me and I hoped the girls would enjoy seeing the small green leaves of seedlings appear and become something beautiful. The front of our house really needed something to pep it up. The house was looking too rundown with its peeling paint and sagging porch.

I went downstairs and pulled out a box of oats and some brown sugar. I prepared the oatmeal on the stove, careful not to make a sound. As I turned to the cupboard by the sink for bowls to serve the oatmeal, I glanced toward Mom's room. At first, I thought the door was closed, but something seemed off, so I looked again. Mom's door was open just a crack. Uh-oh. I didn't want her to hear me and flip out.

I shuffled to her room and peeked in. No Mom. The bed was made but rumpled. The offending belt lay hanging off the footboard. I shuddered. Was she even home? I opened the back door and poked my head out. The air was crisp, but not too cold and the birds chirped in unison. At the side of the house, the gravel driveway was empty. So, either Mom had gone somewhere very early, or she'd left last night and slept somewhere else. At this point, I didn't even care. I just breathed a sigh of relief. No Mom meant no tiptoeing around.

I picked up the spoon I'd used to stir the oatmeal and purposely clanged it against the side of the pot, letting the oatmeal slide off. Just the sound made me smile. I added brown sugar, stirred again, and scooped the warm gooeyness into the bowls. I bounded up the stairs, feeling more like myself. I nudged both girls awake.

"Wake up, sleeping beauties!" I sang. "Breakfast is ready, and I have good news. Mom isn't here, so you can make as much noise as you want!"

Anna rubbed her sleepy eyes. "Where is she?"

"Well, I don't know. All I know is breakfast is ready and after we eat, we're planting the flower seeds."

Edie groaned. "My back hurts."

"I'm sorry, Edie." I pushed the hair from her face and caressed her cheek. "After we plant the seeds, I'll fix you up again."

She nodded, then stuck her feet out of the covers and slid off the bed. I kissed the top of her head, her soft hair tickling my nose. Anna followed and pulled the covers over the bed as she yawned.

"Come on, come on. Breakfast is waiting!"

The oatmeal was warm and comforting, and though no one spoke much, by the time we'd finished, the girls had perked up.

"Put on some old clothes and let's play in the dirt!" I said. I was determined to have some fun with my sisters, mostly to keep their minds off yesterday. I really didn't want to think about it either, at least not until I could discuss it with Jake. I said a silent prayer he would come to the store today.

Once the girls were dressed, we went to the shed, grabbed the flower seeds and the only small shovel we could find. The seed packet said it was a perennial mix meaning we could plant them and if they grew this year, they should return each year on their own. Our job would be to remember to water them.

I broke up the dirt with my shovel, while Anna waited her turn to try, and Edie dug right in with her hands. Once the soil had gone from hard and clumpy to loose and smooth, I handed the seed packet to Anna and let the girls take turns scattering seeds over the dirt. The biggest flower bed was in front of the porch, while a smaller one lay under my mom's bedroom window. We barely had enough seeds to cover the last bed, so I hoped it would fill enough to look pretty. We used a plastic water pitcher from the kitchen to wet the dirt. I told the girls we would take turns with the watering and that the reward would be worth it.

I gritted my teeth through my shower, the spray feeling like a hundred bee stings on my back. Relief came when Anna doctored my back with salve, her touch gentle. As she worked, I wondered again where Mom had gone. I wasn't worried, just curious since it was so out of the ordinary. It was so much easier to breathe with her gone. My thoughts again turned to Jake, and I hoped he'd gotten the message. He probably thought it was weird, but he would know enough to realize it was important.

Suddenly, I gasped. Tonight was the prom! How could I have forgotten? It had been on my mind a lot a few weeks ago, but with everything that had happened recently, I'd stopped worrying about Jake and Holly going together. But it was tonight. So, would Jake even come to the store at all? Or would he be too busy today?

I exhaled and something between a sigh and a moan escaped my mouth. First Jerri was gone and then Jake was probably unavailable right when it was critical. I needed both of them *now*, not a few days from now, but I realized that might not happen. Why couldn't we catch a break?

When it came time to leave for work, Mom had still not returned. The three of us walked to Pop's while we ate our bologna sandwiches. When my sandwich was gone, I pulled an apple out of my bag to munch on. The girls had one stashed in their backpacks for their afternoon snack. The day was warm, and the blue sky cloudless. The sun on my face lifted my spirits a bit.

I'd been working for over an hour stocking the paper products aisle when I felt a tap on my shoulder. I was standing at the top of a step ladder leaning over the shelf, carefully balancing packages of toilet paper in neat stacks. One bump would bring them all tumbling down, so even though the tap startled me, I took a moment to make sure all was still before I looked down.

Jake stood next to the ladder, his hands shoved into the pockets of his jeans. His electric blue tee shirt had rolled sleeves and was emblazoned with the words "Totally Tubular" in neon orange.

"Jake, you came!" I jumped to the floor.

"What's going on, Libby?" Jake's eyebrows pressed together, his expression intense. I couldn't tell if he was annoyed or concerned.

"I'm surprised you showed up. I'm sorry, I totally forgot about the prom tonight."

"That's all later." He waved his hands as if it didn't matter. "I've been worried since last night when my mom gave me your message. I figured it must be pretty important if you couldn't just talk to me at school."

I nodded my head, but before I could say anything, Portia came down the aisle to ask me about an order that hadn't been recorded properly. Her brown eyes shifted from me to Jake and back again. She wiggled her eyebrows up and down. I rolled my eyes and told her she'd have to talk to Jerri about the order.

When she left, Jake said, "I wasn't sure what to tell my mom when she asked why I couldn't just call you. I told her it had to do with a surprise for Holly for the prom."

"Yeah, sorry, I know it was weird."

"So, what's up?" Jake's words were casual, but his stance was rigid, as if he was bracing for bad news.

"Well, yesterday was horrible." I needed to do something with my hands while I spoke, so I sliced open the nearest box. "First, my mom found out that she didn't get the job she wanted, so she threw a glass across the kitchen, and it shattered everywhere. She made me clean it up. Then when we were making a late breakfast, she was trying to sleep and went berserk because we were too noisy."

Jake's scowl deepened and he leaned back against the shelf across the aisle. I paused as an elderly shopper came by, stopping to pick up a package of toilet paper. I smiled at her and waited until she'd shuffled off. I looked down the aisle, not wanting to be interrupted again. I lowered my voice to a loud whisper.

"Then Edie sassed Mom and she totally lost it."

"Lost it, how?"

"She dragged Edie to her room, pulled out a belt and whipped her back with it."

"She did what?!" Jake exploded. His pale face flooded scarlet, and his jaw clenched.

"Shh!" I glanced around, not wanting to attract attention from shoppers or Linda. I began emptying the large box and placed the toilet paper packages on the floor.

Jake stepped close and helped move the packages from the floor to the shelf. "You're telling me your mom beat her eight-year-old daughter with a *belt*?" Jake's voice was harsh, and fire danced in his eyes.

"Yeah, I was so shocked I couldn't even move at first. Then I followed them and threw myself over Edie to keep her from being hit. Mom hit me instead and kept right on going on my back." My voice quavered and I bit my lower lip.

Jake dropped the package he was holding and stuck his clenched fist to his mouth, sputtering. His other hand went to his hair, and he tightened his fingers through it. A guttural growl escaped his lips. Then he dropped his hands and stalked across the aisle. I stared, fascinated by the emotion that seemed to radiate off him. Just as quickly as he walked away, he returned to my side. "Are you okay? You and Edie?"

I dropped my head. "It was bad, Jake, the worst she's ever been. But we're okay."

Jake tilted my chin up so he could see my face. "That's it, Libby! I'm done standing by doing nothing."

"I know. I've had enough. She is not going to do this again."

"You can't be sure of that unless we act."

I sighed and climbed the step ladder so I could reach all the packages Jake had placed up high. I started stacking them carefully in front of the ones I'd finished earlier. I opted to change the subject. "I heard you ran into Jerri here the other day."

"Yeah, I did." Jake looked down the aisle. He rubbed his hand over the back of his neck. A slight flush crept over his face. That told me a lot. I'd been wondering if he had run into Jerri by chance or planned the encounter. He must have wanted to give Jerri a hint about what had happened to my arm, that it wasn't just a clumsy accident.

"And you told her about this," I held up my casted wrist, "and that you were sick of seeing me get hurt."

Jake sighed and flicked his eyes to mine. He looked away again, but not before I saw the guilt in his eyes along with a hint of something I couldn't quite put my finger on.

"I'm sorry, Libby. I just hoped maybe she could help you. Help us." He shrugged, looking like he just got caught stealing a cookie from the cookie jar.

"I'm not mad, Jake. Really." I told him about the conversation I had with Jerri. Everything from Jerri figuring out my secret, to the discussion about what to do, to the promise to chat again on Monday when she got back to work.

"So, now she knows. Good. Do you think she'll reach Nolan?"

"I don't have any idea. But we need a plan, one we all make together."

"I agree. But are you all going to be safe from your mom until then?"

"Let's put it this way. I *will not* let her do this again. If it gets to the point I can't keep my sisters safe, I *will* call the police."

"But what about keeping yourself safe?" Jake gazed at me, his blue eyes intense.

My heart thumped a quick beat, and my palms felt damp. "I'm not gonna raise a fuss about anything, and neither will Edie and Anna."

"You sure about that? I mean, Edie is feisty and when she gets fired up..."

Three customers came up the aisle and I focused on my job. I greeted them and followed with a "Have a good day!" as they walked away. I looked over my shoulder to find Jake staring at nothing, completely zoned out.

"Whatcha thinking about?" I asked. My back felt tight and itchy, and I wanted to get down from the ladder, but I continued filling the shelf as I waited for his response.

"I think you and your sisters should each have a bag packed, ready to go, in case you all need to leave your house fast," Jake said.

Okay, I hadn't expected him to say that. I twisted to face him. "And where would we go?"

"I'm gonna work on that. But I think you all need to be ready."

Well, it was something. Whatever it took to keep my sisters safe, I'd do it. I intended to keep my word on that. I was my sisters' only protector, but I hadn't done a great job of that lately. I sighed deeply, tired of this topic overtaking all my conversations lately. "Alright," I agreed. I attempted a lighter subject. "Did you pick up Holly's corsage yet?"

Jake shook his head with a wry grin. "Nah, I'm on my way to do that right now."

"Better go then. You don't want to be late." I hopped off the ladder and gave Jake a quick hug. "Thanks for coming, Jake."

As Jake walked away, I called after him. "Have fun! I want to hear about it on Monday."

He stopped and turned halfway around. He flashed a wide grin and a thumbs up. "Okay, but next year it's going to be you and me."

"Huh?"

"Prom. Next year. You and me, no matter what." Jake winked, waved, and continued down the aisle.

Had he really just said that? I smiled. For a few seconds, I let myself revel in that alternate reality. I imagined the dress – blue with a lot of sparkle and Jake in a black tux with a blue bow tie that matched his eyes. The two of us dancing a waltz in a large ballroom.

Wait, a waltz? I didn't know how to waltz. I giggled at my wild imagination. Just as suddenly I frowned. Unless circumstances in my life changed drastically over the next year, the whole idea was preposterous anyway. But there wasn't anything that said I couldn't hope.

19
Monday, April 4, 1988

I was irritated. Irritated and exhausted. Edie was cranky when I woke her for school, complaining that she was too tired to get up. I told her we were all tired, but we had to go back to school anyway. Anna forced herself to sit up. After I got ready, I found that Edie had fallen back to sleep. Anna was downstairs and unaware Edie was still in bed.

When I pulled Edie out of the bed, she moaned and whined, then stomped on my foot once she was upright. I wanted to yell, but knowing it would wake Mom, I settled for angry whispers. I said she couldn't stay home alone with Mom and that she was making me late. The momentary panic I saw flit across her face and her immediate compliance told me she understood. I left her in Anna's capable hands to make sure she had breakfast, then I bolted out the door.

Now I was running behind. I had hoped to talk with my friends about the prom before school, but it would have to wait. I also had more to tell Jake about the rest of my weekend. Only one thing kept me from worrying too much that I'd be tardy to my Spanish class and that was the fact that I was just happy to be back at school. No more being stuck at home most of the day with a bitter unemployed mother.

The first bell rang as I jogged through the courtyard. The sight of students lingering in the halls lifted my mood. The familiar sounds and safety I felt in these walls calmed me. Although I scooted through the classroom door fifteen seconds after the second bell rang, Señor Perez was in a good mood and didn't mark me late.

When I walked into second period biology and saw that the teacher's notes almost filled the entire chalkboard, I knew it was going to be difficult to talk to Jake this period. I pulled out my notebook while I waited for class to start. Jake barely made it into the room before the bell rang. I raised an eyebrow at him. He just shook his head and rolled his eyes.

Mrs. Zeigler took roll and began the lecture. Sometimes she talked so fast, it was hard to keep up on the notes. Today she spoke a little slower, but writing everything down gave me a good cover for writing notes to Jake in the margin of my paper.

You barely made it. What's up?

Donahue kept me after class.

Why?

He wants me to redo an assignment.

How was the prom?

Fun!

Details!

Jake smiled and kept taking notes. I drummed my fingers on the table and his grin broadened. Dork! He was such a tease.

Lunch on our bench?

Jake nodded.

Cool. Details then?

Another nod, then a grin. Mrs. Zeigler called on Jake to answer a question, so it took a minute before he wrote again.

Home okay?

There was no way I was writing down what had happened for anyone to see. I kept my eyes on my notes and shook my head slightly. Jake scribbled in his margin again.

Tell me at lunch?

Yep.

By the time class ended, my hand had cramped up from all the notetaking and I had to shake it out. Sometimes when Mrs. Zeigler lectured, it felt like she wanted to cover a year's worth of learning in one class period. Class was dismissed and chairs began scraping across the tile floor. I stood and stretched, the wounds on my back still tight. Jake poked me in the ribs while my arms were extended. I jerked them down again.

"Hey, stop it!"

Jake laughed and put his arm around me. He leaned in close and whispered, "You seem tired."

The two girls who sat directly in front of us stared as they pushed their chairs in and walked past. Tori, the brainy blonde, grimaced and tossed her big hair over her shoulder. Was she jealous or just being a brat? I nodded at Jake. Yes, I was very tired.

Jake and I parted ways in the hall. I saw Holly in math but didn't have a chance to talk to her either. Every teacher seemed gung-ho on keeping us especially busy. I guess they figured vacation time was over. By the time lunch rolled around, I was bursting to have a real out-loud conversation.

I grabbed my lunch from my locker and headed outside to the bench. As I passed the baseball field, I heard pounding steps behind me. Jake jogged up carrying a cardboard tray with a hamburger and fries. It smelled divine. Much better than my bologna and mayo sandwich.

"Ooh, trade you lunches," I said.

"Uh-uh, nope," Jake shook his head. "But you can have a fry."

I pulled out a piping hot fry and almost dropped it. Oh, it was delicious. I sighed. "Wish I could get school lunch every day."

As we neared our lunch spot, I peered around the equipment shed to see if our bench was unoccupied. It was. Before I took a big bite of my sandwich, I said, "Okay, spill it. I need details."

Jake chuckled. "Well, I picked Holly up around six. We went to Fritoli's over in Millsburg for dinner."

"Wait." I held up a hand and swallowed my food. "What did her dress look like?"

"Umm, just a dress, kind of frilly. It was dark green."

"That's it?"

Jake looked confused.

"Never mind. I'll ask Holly about the dress."

Jake went on with his story. After having the best pasta he'd ever eaten, they went to the dance in the school gym. It was crowded and hot and they had to stand in line for almost half an hour to get pictures taken. Then after the dance, they'd gone to Shawn's house to play games.

"That's it," he finished.

"Cool. Sounds awesome!"

"Like I said, next year will be you and me and it will be even better."

My face flamed with heat, so I looked at the baseball field instead of him. I appreciated he wanted to take me, but I had to keep his expectations realistic. "Hopefully."

"No, not hopefully," Jake argued. "Definitely."

Okay, I'd let it go for now. I had to tell him about my weekend before lunch was over. I took a moment to finish my banana while Jake took a huge bite of his burger. Mustard and ketchup smeared onto his upper lip. I watched, amused, then handed him one of the napkins he'd brought.

"My mom came home Saturday night around eight. She was out of it, and she tripped on the rug by the back door, then proceeded to cuss us out because it moved." I shook my head. "I'm so sick of her."

"Did she do anything to you?"

"Just a lot of yelling, swearing and scaring the girls. Anna didn't wait around to hear much of it before she went to the shed. Edie and

I joined her for an hour or so. When we snuck back in, Mom had passed out on her bed."

Jake rolled his eyes and muttered something. His mouth was full, so I couldn't understand what he said. When he was hungry, he ate so fast he barely took a breath.

"Then yesterday, she refused to give me any money to get groceries. She said she didn't have any because of not having a job."

Jake swallowed hard. "Do you need food?" His tone was serious. His eyebrows creased together. He chugged his milk and locked eyes with me.

I don't know why the question made me uncomfortable, but it did. I chuckled to cover my uneasiness. "No, I used my money from Pop's."

"Libby, that's so messed up. She shouldn't make you all pay for your own food."

"But I will if I have to. I didn't really have another choice."

"I know. I'm just sorry you had to do that."

We sat quietly watching a bunch of robins search for worms on the damp baseball diamond. I finished my sandwich and shoved the plastic wrap in my bag to throw away later. My hand brushed against Jake's arm and my heart flip-flopped. Suddenly, his arm was around me and he squeezed my shoulder.

"I wish you didn't have to go through this, Libby."

I nodded. What would I do without Jake as my friend? He'd been there through all of the difficult years, and he still stuck by me. We stood and Jake dropped his arm. My shoulder felt cold where his hand had rested.

"You'll talk to Jerri at work?" he asked.

"Yes, hopefully first thing."

"Good. After baseball practice, I'll head over and talk to her too."

In sixth period P.E., I updated Holly and Nicole. Unfortunately, it was a "body test" day, the day we recorded the number of sit-ups, push-ups, pull-ups and jumps with the jump rope we could do in one minute. I was lucky and got out of push-ups and pull-ups because of my cast, but I had to grit my teeth through the sit-ups. Even being on a mat, the wounds on my back stung. I felt the skin pulling and slowed down, so it wouldn't hurt as badly. I wasn't too concerned with my sit-ups score. If it was low, so be it.

The jump rope test was easiest for me since I jumped rope with my sisters at least once a week. I just had to wrap the rope around my thumb on my left hand before gripping it with my fingers. Trying to have a conversation during all of that was difficult, so my spring break saga was told in bits and pieces. Just before it was Holly's turn for sit-ups, I finished my story.

"I don't get what your mother's problem is," huffed Nicole. She folded her arms and scowled.

I shrugged. "Well, I'm no shrink, but I think she's been angry for so long, for a lot of reasons, that she doesn't know any other way. And drinking is her escape."

Holly grunted out her sit-ups while Nicole held her feet and I timed her with the timer Coach had given us. When the timer dinged, she lay on the mat breathing hard. "Your mom just sounds like a mean drunk to me." She propped up on her elbows, still trying to catch her breath. "The question is, though, what are we going to do about it?"

"I'm working on that." I was purposely vague. I wasn't sure we *all* had to be involved.

"Can't you just leave?" Nicole threw her hands out wide. "I mean you could come to my house!"

"Just move my sisters and me into your house? Just like that?" I snapped my fingers. I knew I sounded sarcastic. "Then when my mom figures out where we're hiding, with help from the police, of course, they'll all agree to let us stay there?"

Nicole's eyes widened, and she tugged on a lock of her hair.

I softened my voice. "I'm not trying to be rude. It's just not going to be that easy."

We lined up with the class to report our scores and huddled close so we wouldn't be overheard. Holly seemed lost in her own thoughts, so I nudged her shoulder. "What do you think?"

She blew some air up and out of her mouth, riffling her bangs. "I'm not sure yet. I still need to think some more." Once she had given her scores to Coach Barnes, she squeezed my arm. "You're so strong, Libby. I don't think I could deal with everything as well as you do."

I didn't get a chance to respond because Coach blew her whistle and told us to line up for ladders. Almost everyone in class groaned, but we obediently shuffled to our squads. I felt buoyed up by Holly's words, although I wasn't sure I believed them. I'd been so focused on me, I hadn't asked about the prom from Holly's perspective. I didn't get a chance until we were on our way to the locker room.

"Phew, I'm beat." I pulled the bottom of my shirt up slightly and leaned over to wipe my sweaty face. "How was the dance, by the way?"

"Fabulous!" Holly grinned, showing off her braces and her almost straight teeth. She pulled her long red hair out of the elastic band holding it back. Her hair swished back and forth looking like she'd just brushed it. Mine just looked limp when I took it out of a ponytail.

"My dress was gorgeous!" Holly gushed, "And the gym looked so fancy with all the balloons and decorations. The DJ was rad too. It was such a party!"

We stopped inside the locker room doors, forcing the other girls to wind around us as they came in. A couple of them called us some not very nice names, but we ignored them.

"Someday we'll all know what it feels like to go to the prom." Nicole fluttered her eyelashes and clasped her hands to her heart.

Holly laughed. She still hadn't told me what I really wanted to know. I didn't want to seem obvious, but I couldn't resist asking. "And how was Jake?"

Holly's lips rose in that perfect smile again. "He was fabulous too. He took me to Fritoli's for dinner."

I already knew that, but a twinge of jealousy pierced my heart. I hoped my face didn't give me away.

"But don't worry, Libby." Holly leaned close to my ear and held up her hand to block others from hearing. "Shawn actually planned it all. Jake's been a little preoccupied lately." She gave me an exaggerated wink.

I knew my face was bright red, but I smiled anyway.

As I came through the doors of Pop's after school, Jerri's voice rang out over the PA system, announcing one of the weekly specials. I headed to the restroom to change my shirt when I heard a soft voice on my right.

"Libby, is that you?"

An elderly woman with thin, white hair and sunken cheeks pushed her shopping cart next to me. "Oh, Mrs. Judd, how are you?" I couldn't recall the last time I'd seen my across the street neighbor. I was surprised at how much she'd aged. Her hand shook as she adjusted her tortoise-shell glasses and peered closely at me.

"You've grown up so beautifully."

"Thank you. I haven't seen you for a long time."

She nodded. "I've been staying with my son in Dayton, Ohio off and on for the past few years."

Past few years? Had it been that long since I'd seen her? This woman had helped take care of me when my mother couldn't cope after Grandma died. Then again after Nolan left. And I hadn't bothered to check up on her at all. I felt a little ashamed.

"I'm going to be putting my house up for sale next month so I can move close to him." Her eyes crinkled into a smile. "How is your mother?"

"Oh, she's okay," I lied.

"That's wonderful. If you need anything, you just come right over."

I hoped I wouldn't ever have to take her up on that. I thanked her and wished her luck with selling her house. It was kind of sad that I had forgotten about Mrs. Judd. Maybe the girls and I could help her box up her belongings or help her clean when she moved. I'd had a lot of practice with that.

As I walked out of the restroom after changing, my mind turned to other things. Jerri and Rosie walked out of the breakroom, deep in discussion. I didn't want to eavesdrop, so I jogged to the back of the store, punched my timecard and returned. Jerri had disappeared, so I knocked on her office door. I crossed my fingers that she'd reached Nolan. I bounced on my toes as I waited. I was surprised when Linda swung the door open.

"Hello, Libby! What can I do for you?" Linda's smile was radiant.

"Oh, I'm sorry. I was looking for Jerri. Do you know where I can find her?"

Linda pulled a pack of gum from her work apron, quickly unwrapping a fat piece of Hubba Bubba and popping it into her mouth. She held up the gum with raised eyebrows. "Would you like one?"

I was never one to turn down gum, especially the fruit flavored kind. I took a piece from the pack.

"Jerri is at the customer service desk today. We have a product recall on some baby food, so she's dealing with refunds and exchanges. I believe she has you working in the cereal aisle. Let me check."

She disappeared into the office, where a Beach Boys tune played softly, and returned with a blue clipboard. She skimmed over the schedule with her finger. "Yes, cereal it is." She flipped through the papers and pulled out my assignment sheet. As anxious as I was to talk to Jerri, I still had to work, so I headed to the back to get started.

About halfway through my shift, long after my sisters had arrived, I finally saw Jerri coming my way. I crossed my fingers and the Raisin Bran box I'd been holding fell to the ground. Jerri's limp was more apparent when I watched her walk from a distance and today was no exception. Her hair was in its typical braid, the end of it swinging in and out of my view.

"Yay, you're back!"

Jerri's eyes twinkled. "Yes, I survived Reed's family for four days. I'm happy to be back!"

"How was the funeral?" I wanted to be polite although I really wanted to talk about my problem. I slowly chewed my still-soft gum.

"Long." Jerri shrugged, then laughed. "He was very old, so it was his time."

"So, were you able to reach Nolan?" I knew it was an abrupt change of subject, but I was antsy to know.

Jerri's smile disappeared, replaced by a perplexed expression. She shook her head. "I found a number for him in the town you said he lives, but I've called it several times and still no answer."

My stomach dropped like when I soared high in the swings at the park, then swung back toward the ground. That was always a thrill, but this felt more like pain. Would anything ever go right? Jerri must have seen my disappointment.

"Right now, it doesn't matter if we reach him," she said.

I was confused. How would we get away from my mom otherwise? I swiped my bangs back from my forehead with both hands and held them on top of my head, my cast resting on my hair. "Why not?"

"There are other ways to go about this." Jerri gently pulled my arms back down, then glanced at her watch. "Sorry, my break is almost over and duty calls." She grasped my hands and gave them a squeeze. "I spoke with my husband, and I know your friend, Jake, is coming later to talk with me. We'll figure out some things and let you know. Just get a bag packed and be ready to leave at a moment's notice." She dropped my hands and hurried up the aisle to the customer service desk.

Packed and ready. Basically, the same thing Jake had mentioned. And Jerri had told her husband about me. For a second, shame burned through my chest. Everyone would know what went on in my home once we left. What would people think of me? Would they praise me for getting us out of a bad situation or would they judge me for betraying my mom? These thoughts shrieked through my brain like a runaway train, assaulting my mind with guilt, embarrassment, and fear.

I put my hand on the shelf to steady myself, closed my eyes and took a deep breath. *Stop it! Just stop! I am doing nothing wrong. I'm doing it for my sisters.* Edie and Anna were the two people I loved most in the world, and they were too young to protect themselves. I *had* to do this. My mom created this problem, and she would have to live with the consequences. The shrieking train quieted and rolled to a slow stop. *No more, Libby! No more embarrassment and no more fear!* I had to rein in my emotions and not forget the reason I was doing this. I wanted Anna and Edie to have a normal, happy upbringing without feeling unsafe in their own home. I couldn't back down now.

I don't know how long I stood there with my eyes closed. I was startled by a tap on my shoulder.

"Libby, are you okay?"

My eyes flew open. Portia leaned in close as if she had a secret. I stared into her dark eyes. All I saw there was concern. That's it. No judgment.

"Oh yeah, I'm fine." I shook out my arms and smiled. "Just tired today."

"Do you need a break?" Portia backed away from the shelf as a shopper drew near.

"I think I'm okay." I pulled more Raisin Bran packages from the large box. "Thanks."

"Sure thing." Portia walked away, her thick dark hair swinging as she went.

When I finished my shift, I gathered my sisters and our backpacks and headed for home. My stomach rumbled loudly enough for them to hear, and they giggled. "Yeah, I'm starving. I think I'll make spaghetti tonight."

As usual, Edie dominated the conversation. She told us about a new game she and her friends had created at recess. It sounded like a combination of kickball and Red Rover but really made no sense to me. I smirked at Anna. She shrugged, as bewildered as me.

When Edie finally took a breath, I asked Anna about her day. She seemed stressed over a book report that was due soon. The genre was general non-fiction and somehow, she'd ended up with a book about aviation which she didn't really understand. She claimed the class had to choose out of the books her teacher had on the shelves in her classroom. Anna was slow in getting in line to choose and ended up last. When it was her turn, there were two options left, one about aviation and one about presidential elections. They both sounded terrible to me too. Anna normally enjoyed reading but was worried about this topic. I promised my help, even though I had a load of homework myself. Anna smiled and squeezed my hand.

"Thanks Libby. You're the best."

Her sincere gratitude touched me. I wrapped my arm around her shoulders and squeezed her back.

The closer we got to home, the more knotted my gut felt. I hated not knowing what to expect. I'd been hoping Mom would be gone, but her Buick was parked by the house in its usual spot.

"Mom's home, so be quiet going in. Anna, please water the flower beds and I'll get dinner going. Edie, you can help me."

Edie started to grumble but I shot her a "don't you start that" look and she settled for a frown.

I turned the doorknob as quietly as I could and pushed the door open. I was surprised by the aroma of something delicious wafting through the house. The three of us exchanged a puzzled look and silently left our things near the door. With me in the lead, we peeked into the kitchen. Mom stood at the stove, her back to us, stirring something in a pot. Then she reached for a spatula and flipped a sandwich over in the pan. Grilled cheese.

"Hi," I said, hesitant to break the silence.

Mom spun around, holding a hand to her chest. "Oh, you scared me!"

She didn't seem upset, but I just stared at her, confused. Why was she cooking? She never cooked anymore. And she looked different today too. Her hair had been curled and half of it was pulled back, giving it a fuller appearance. She was dressed in black slacks and a pink blouse that brought out the rosy blush on her cheeks. Anna and I exchanged a look. *Weird.*

"Well, are you just going to stand there or are you going to set the table?"

I was so happy dinner was already made, setting the table was nothing. We sprang into action and between the three of us it took about one minute. Then I filled a pitcher with water so Anna could play gardener. While she was outside, Mom put sandwiches on plates, and I dished soup into bowls.

"Where is Anna?" Mom asked.

"She's watering our flower seeds," Edie replied.

Mom sat down, a small smile lingering on her lips. "Well, go get her. I have something to tell you."

Since she was smiling, it was likely something good for a change. I went for Anna. After she placed the pitcher in the sink, we plopped into our chairs, eager to eat. The food smelled yummy, and my stomach rumbled again. I picked up my spoon to dig in.

"Wait!" Mom said. "First, my news." Suddenly, her mouth stretched into a full smile, something I hadn't seen in a long time. "I got a job at an insurance company. I start tomorrow."

Oh, thank goodness! I released the breath I hadn't realized I'd been holding. A weight seemed to lift off my shoulders. There would be money for food and bills, and Mom wouldn't be home all the time, growing more upset over being unemployed. Maybe this would be a peaceful night after all.

The girls chattered happily, while I listened and filled my stomach with firsts, then seconds. As we were finishing up, Mom announced that she had more news for us. I froze, immediately on guard. Good news twice in one day? Not likely.

"I want you to meet the man I'm dating. He's coming over later."

Wait, what? I tried to keep my expression neutral, but I was not expecting that at all, and my eyes widened before I could stop them. I gazed at the girls. Edie's face was scrunched up in disgust and Anna's eyes roved all over the place as if she didn't understand. This explained Mom's appearance but why was this the first time we'd heard about it?

"Um, we didn't know you were dating anyone." I said.

Mom set down her glass. "Well, you do now, don't you? You girls clean this place up. He'll be here soon."

With that, she got up and walked down the hall towards her bedroom. I stared at my sisters with a sinking feeling. This might just be another complication to my plans. I willed myself to stay calm. There was no sense panicking until I'd at least met the guy, but I did not have a good feeling about this.

THE DOORBELL RANG AND Mom hopped off the couch to answer the door. She seemed eager to see her mystery man. The rest of us, not as much. The anticipation of his arrival had given me indigestion, and I was wishing we had some antacid in the medicine cabinet.

A stocky man, not much taller than Mom, strutted in. He had stringy black hair that he wore in a mullet and beady dark eyes that flicked from Mom to us girls. His jeans were dirty, and his worn AC/DC shirt was snug on his shoulders. His arms were muscular, but filthy-looking and his hands even more so. Yuck!

"Girls, this is Roy." Mom didn't take her eyes off him.

"Yo," Roy said, tilting his head up in a reverse nod.

Edie looked like she'd swallowed something gross. "Why are you so dirty?"

"Edie!" Mom scolded.

Roy flashed a cocky grin. "Bein' a mechanic, you get a little stained up, you know." He slipped his arm around Mom and pulled her down on the couch next to him. She giggled and I mentally gagged.

Anna looked a little green. I wondered if her stomach felt like mine. This guy made me want to throw up. To make matters worse, Roy propped his dirty sneakers on the coffee table and squeezed Mom close to his side. Mom realized we were staring at them and said, "Okay girls, time to do your homework."

"I don't have any," Edie said.

Mom's jaw tightened, and the sweetness left her voice. "Then go find something to do!"

Roy laughed and shooed us away with a wave. "Yeah, little brats, off with you."

Anna didn't wait for another invitation. She ran like she was trying to escape a haunted house. Edie glared at Mom and Roy and slowly thumped up the stairs. I couldn't believe Mom liked this guy. In the two minutes he'd been in the house, I could tell he was a total jerk. I bit my tongue hard, until the pressure in my head fell to a simmer. I was curious to know one thing.

"So, where'd you guys meet?" I directed my gaze at Roy.

Roy looked at me like I was a bug to be squashed. "The shop."

Well, that made sense. Mom had taken her car to the shop for repairs a few weeks ago, but the way they were cuddled together made it seem like they'd known each other longer than that. I wondered why Mom kept him a secret until now. I kind of liked being kept in the dark about Roy. Now I wouldn't be able to erase him from my mind. Even though I'd been dismissed, there was no way I was leaving the room, no matter what they said. I didn't trust either of them.

Roy got up and switched on the TV and asked Mom for a beer. When Mom left the room, Roy fixed his gaze on me, his black eyes narrowing in a challenge. Mom walked back in with their drinks, and he smoothed his face into a neutral expression.

"Aren't you gonna make that one go away?" he whined as Mom wrapped a strand of his hair around her finger.

"Take a hike, Libby," Mom said without taking her eyes off Roy.

Roy's cocky grin returned.

I didn't like this nasty dude coming into our house acting like he could take over. "No."

Mom immediately went from lovey-dovey to spewing swear words. She stood and ordered me to leave, pointing at the stairs. I ignored her and focused on breathing evenly while I stared at the law drama on the TV. Roy stood and reached his hand toward me.

I ducked away, not wanting his grimy hand to touch me, but also a little afraid of what he might do.

"Listen to your mother, you little brat!" Roy's voice was hard as steel.

Mom picked up her beer. "Let's just go to your place, Roy."

Roy sneered at me. "You sure weren't wrong about this one."

My legs quivered as I scowled back at him. Mom looped her purse over her shoulder. Once Roy sauntered out, she turned to me with daggers shooting from her eyes. "I know what you're doing, Libby. You always think you're so smart, but you won't run him off that easily."

She slammed the door behind her, and I sank to my knees, my entire body trembling. Roy was most definitely another complication I did not need right now.

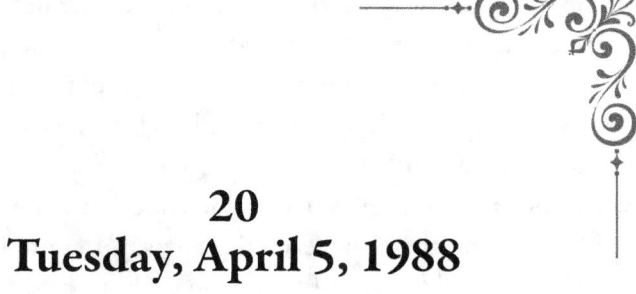

20
Tuesday, April 5, 1988

I smeared some peanut butter over three pieces of bread, then plopped a glob of grape jelly on each. I spread it quickly, not bothering to cover the slices evenly, and slapped the three remaining slices of bread on top. I pulled plastic wrap from the roll and cut three squares, accidentally rubbing the sharp cutting edge against my knuckles. "Ouch!"

I expected blood but saw only redness. I wrapped my sandwich and shoved it in a paper sack along with a banana and two graham crackers. Anna wrapped the remaining sandwiches and opened two more lunch sacks.

A short, but loud honk made me jump. I glanced at my watch. "He's here."

I rolled the top of my lunch bag down and slid it into my backpack as Anna looked on. Edie barely looked up from her cereal bowl. If she hadn't been moving the spoon to her mouth, I would've thought she was still asleep. I slid my arms into my jacket.

"Edie, be good for Anna. I'm sorry I had to get you up early, but I have to go." As if to reinforce that statement, the car honked again, just a short beep. "I'll see you this afternoon at Pop's."

Anna leaned against me for a quick hug. She seemed anxious.

"Don't worry, sweetie. Just leave twenty minutes earlier and you'll have extra time on the playground. Mom doesn't work until nine. She won't be up by the time you leave."

She opened the door for me, and I kissed her head as I went by. I ran to the street where Jake waited in his sister's white sedan.

It had been go, go, go, since I'd fallen out of bed this morning. I'd gotten up early so I'd have time to talk to Jake. Last night, I'd written a note telling Mom I had to be to school early and placed it on her bed where she wouldn't miss it when she came home. Since Anna and Edie left on their own each day anyway, I figured they'd be fine. Plus, Mom would be too focused on making it to her new job on time to worry about them.

Jake waved as I rounded the front of the car to the passenger side. The morning sun blinded me as I plopped into the seat, so I pulled the visor down to stop the assault on my eyes.

"I'm glad you called last night," Jake said, as he checked his mirrors and pulled into the road.

"Yeah, when Mom left with Roy, I took the chance. I was scared she was going to come back, so I wanted to talk in person instead of staying on the phone."

Jake's forehead creased as he narrowed his eyes. "Should I know who Roy is?"

"Apparently, he's my mom's new boyfriend." I cringed as I said the words, still unable to accept the idea, along with the grungy loser who had made himself at home in our living room last night.

Jake's jaw dropped. He looked as shocked as I felt last night. "She has a boyfriend? Since when?"

"I think it's been a few weeks now. But we first heard about him last night."

Jake shook his head as he pulled into the school parking lot. It was empty except for a handful of cars bunched in the closest parking spots. Getting there early meant Jake could also snag a front row space. Once he turned off the ignition, he said, "Start at the beginning."

"When the girls and I walked home from Pop's yesterday, we saw Mom's car was home. Of course, we never know what we might find when we open the door. We were surprised to find Mom cooking dinner for us. I mean, I was happy to have a night off, but it was weird, you know?" I finger-combed my damp hair as I spoke. Jake watched my hands move down and up, over and over.

"Yes, definitely weird," Jake agreed.

"Then she broke the news that she got a job."

"Oh, well, that's awesome. Where's the job?"

"Some insurance company. I didn't even ask which one."

"At least now you can stop worrying about that. So, she cooked dinner to celebrate?"

"I guess so." I shrugged. "But then when we were finishing up, she said she had another announcement. That's when she dropped the bomb about Roy."

Jake's hair lost its battle with gravity and fell forward over his eyes. He pushed it back. "Yeah. Didn't see that coming."

"Right? Anna and Edie just looked at her like a tree sprouted from her head."

Jake was quiet as I told him about being introduced to Roy. When I got to the part about Roy reaching for me, he interrupted. "But he never touched you, right?" His lips pressed together in a white line.

"No, never!" I shuddered. "But he'll be back. And now Mom is going to be after me too."

"I don't think you'll have to worry about her much longer." Jake tapped his fingers on the steering wheel.

I whipped my head around so fast, I felt the pull in my neck. "You worked something out?" I was eager for some news, some kind of plan. I was beginning to feel desperate and after last night, afraid that Mom's icky boyfriend would be landing blows to my ribs right along with her.

Jake turned toward me and as he did, his arm bumped the horn on the steering wheel. The short honk made me jump, along with a few girls who were walking by. They fell into each other, giggling. They glanced at the car, then recognizing Jake, two of them ran to the car and slapped the hood, yelling halfhearted threats. Jake rolled down the window and yelled, "Sorry!"

As he rolled the window back up, the bell rang. "Already?" I glanced at my watch. Apparently, I'd been talking for most of the last half hour, not even noticing all the students arriving at school.

"Guess we gotta go." Jake held out his hands. "That went fast."

I growled, frustrated. I wanted to know the plan. How? When? What did I need to do? Did Jake think it would work? I needed answers so my stomach would stop feeling so twisted up.

Jake locked the car and pocketed the keys. We fell in with the throng of students making their way inside. Jake leaned over my shoulder and said, "It's going to be on Friday."

I stopped dead, and Jake stumbled into my back. "Libby, keep moving. I can't be late again."

"Friday?" In the commons, we parted ways and Jake responded with a thumbs up that left me with more questions I had to wait to get answered.

The day flew by. I didn't chat with Jake at all in science because we had a test. The multiple-choice section wasn't too hard, but the essay questions were a little tougher. I was relieved when it was over. On the upside, Jake winked at me before I left class and my stomach felt full of butterflies, a much better feeling than the tight knot that had been the norm recently.

In English class, I realized the group project I was assigned to work on with three others was due in two weeks and we hadn't even started it yet. I scrambled for a piece of paper to write down everyone's phone numbers. Samantha wanted to stay after school to use the school library which stayed open until 4:30. Rich and PJ agreed to stay, but I explained that I had to work. I felt uneasy as I considered how much work we needed to complete. I told the trio I would call the store and ask if I could take the afternoon off. If so, I'd meet them in the library at three o'clock.

I was a little mad at myself for not being more on top of my homework. Falling behind just wasn't me, and I chided myself for letting it happen. I had good reasons, and my job wasn't to blame. It was home—all home—and the stress that came with everything there.

After class was over, I hurried to the office to call Pop's. I asked to talk to Jerri, but Portia explained that she was tied up, so did I want to talk to Linda? When I explained my problem, Linda said it would be okay for me to miss, and she would inform Jerri. She said she understood group projects because her kids had them too, but asked us to schedule our meetings after work time from now on. I barely listened after she agreed. I was about to leave the office when I realized I needed to call the elementary school. I asked the secretary to look up the number, which she did with a huff. She blinked at me while I called the school and left a message for the girls to meet me at the high school library after school instead of at Pop's.

My stomach was practically eating itself, so after stashing my books in my locker, I headed to the cafeteria with my sack lunch. I squeezed in next to Holly and Shawn. I felt Holly watching me as I pulled my sandwich from the bag. Did she know the plan? What about Nicole? I'd have to ask them in P.E.

Lunch was relaxing. Shawn entertained us with his near-perfect imitations of the "Church Lady" and "Hans and Franz" from *Saturday Night Live*. I nearly choked on my sandwich when he did an impression of our school principal, Mr. Goff. I coughed and sputtered while tears ran down my face. Shawn's eyes crinkled, amused at my reaction. He patted my back a couple times which sent everyone else into more gales of laughter. I thought I was going to pee my pants when Mr. Goff himself walked by and told us to quiet down.

In P.E., Holly told me she knew the plan was to get me and my sisters out on Friday. She didn't know any of the details yet either. We were outside playing baseball, which I was self-conscious about, because, well, it wasn't basketball. I was a terrible catch and was worried I'd be even worse having to wear a mitt on my right hand because of my cast. I proved why I shouldn't have been placed in left field when one of the jocks hit a pop fly straight to me. I panicked as I squinted into the sun and lost track of the ball. It landed with a thud about two feet in front of me. I heard the mixture of cheers from the opposing team and the groans from mine. Embarrassed, I yanked off my glove, then scrambled to pick up the ball and throw it to second base. My throw was short, but I was glad when the spotlight was off me. Naturally, all eyes were on Mr. Pop Fly as he headed home. I shrugged off my mistake, but I knew I'd get razzed about it later.

I caught sight of Jake in the hallway after school. He extended his hands in question as I walked away from the commons area and the exit I usually took. I yelled past a group of rowdy freshmen that I wasn't going to work because of a group project. He pushed past a rail-thin, preppy boy who was blocking his way.

"What time are you going home?" he asked.

"I'm not sure. No later than 4:30."

"Can I stop by your house after practice if your mom's not home? I can tell you about Friday."

"Sure, I guess." I was nervous to agree, but I'd waited all day to hear the plan, and I was anxious to find out.

"K, see you later!" Jake raced toward the gym, and I entered the library right behind Samantha.

For the next hour, my group worked on our project, breaking it into four sections, one for each of us. I scoured the shelves for books relating to our topic of comparing the literary styles of the 20th

century to those of the 19th century. I found three books that seemed relevant. The only problem we ran into was having Edie there. She and Anna entered quietly enough, then sat at a table nearby. Anna worked on homework, but Edie was bored and kept interrupting our group discussion. I told her to find a book to read. She got lost in the shelves for a while, then returned with a grumpy face and no book in hand.

"None of the books have pictures," she whined.

I knew that wasn't completely true, but there probably were zero books that would interest an eight-year-old. I told her to find something to do, which she took to mean as bother the librarian. Mrs. Duncan put her to work sorting returned books. I had to give her credit; she was more patient than I had been.

Around 4:15, the girls and I headed home. It was a longer walk home from the school than from Pop's and Edie dragged her feet. I wanted to get dinner started so I'd have time to talk to Jake if he stopped by. Edie moped along and ended up falling behind by half a block, forcing Anna and me to wait. She ignored my pleading to pick up the pace, until I promised she could watch TV when we got home.

It was around a quarter after five when Jake stopped by. He pounded loudly on the front door, which made me jump and burn my finger on a hot pan. I'd just finished making dinner and was pretty sure I had about 45 minutes before Mom got home, so I invited him in instead of visiting on the porch. Jake's hair was wet, so it looked darker than normal, and he looked beat. Edie was excited to have a visitor and asked Jake to sit by her while she watched cartoons, but I opted to go to the kitchen where we could have a private conversation.

"Tell me," I said, as soon as Jake fell into a seat at the table. My leg bounced under the table, so I pressed my hand on my knee to still it.

Jake ran his hand through his hair, causing it to stand out like porcupine quills. I giggled and he hurried to push down the pokies.

"Alright, so Jerri wanted to wait until Friday so she'd have a few more days to try to reach Nolan. I'll come pick you and your sisters up after I get done with baseball practice. You should bring whatever you need with you – clothes, schoolbooks, whatever." He lifted his palm. "Hopefully, it will be before your mom gets home from work, so we don't have to argue with her. Then I'll take you to Jerri's house. You'll call Nolan and tell him everything, assuming Jerri can reach him," Jake said.

I exhaled loudly and tried to relax the tension in my muscles. Everything was tight. I wanted to do this, but at the same time, I dreaded it. If I was scared now, I knew I'd be ten times more afraid on Friday. A sudden wave of nausea hit me, and I swallowed hard.

"You okay?" Jake gave me a quizzical look.

I took a shuddery breath. "Yeah, just nervous."

From the living room, I heard the cartoon's catchy theme song followed by a commercial for a popular hot dog brand. Edie appeared a second later and pulled on Jake's arm. "Come on, come watch the show with me."

Jake tousled Edie's already untidy hair. "Sorry, champ, I really just need to talk with Libby. Then I have to go."

Edie frowned and trudged back to the front room.

"Once you talk to Nolan, he and Jerri will both call the police," Jake said.

My heart pounded painfully hard. I blew a puff of air up at my bangs. "What if Jerri doesn't reach Nolan?"

"Maybe the cops will be able to reach him."

"Will Jerri get in trouble if we go to her house?"

"I doubt it. I'll tell the cops I've been worried about you, and I thought the best place you could go to be safe is your boss's house."

I nodded, but my mind raced. There were several things that could go wrong, but so had everything else up to this point, so we may as well try. Eventually something would succeed. Right?

I was so focused on the plan; I didn't hear the back door open. Jake flinched and I looked up, confused. His eyes were fixed on something behind me, so I turned in my chair to see what he was staring at. Mom stood there holding a six-pack of beer. Her eyes flicked back and forth between me and Jake.

"Well, well, who's this you've invited over without permission?" Her jaw tightened into a deep frown. I clasped my hands together to stop them from shaking. I was in big trouble now.

"You gonna move so I can come in?" a nasally voice whined behind Mom. Mom set her beer on the counter and Roy pushed his way past her, dropping his own six-pack, a different brand, next to Mom's.

"Ooh, looks like Libby's got a boyfriend," Roy drawled as he looked me up and down. I shivered. Roy's leer made my skin crawl.

"Not my boyfriend, just a friend." I squeezed my arms to my sides as I snuck a quick glance at Jake. He stayed silent, his gaze wary.

Roy opened his mouth to respond, but Mom beat him to it. "So, what do you think you're doing?"

"Just talking."

"Uh-huh, right." Mom's eyes shifted to Jake, then she narrowed her eyes at me. "Did I say you could have a *friend* over?"

"No, he just came by for a minute."

"Really? How would this boy know where you live if you didn't invite him?" Mom challenged.

Jake spoke before I could. "I've been here before when I was younger."

Mom looked startled for a second. Roy leaned back against the counter, crossed one foot over the other, then folded his arms. His stance was cocky, and he raised his eyebrows at me, clearly enjoying himself.

"Well, it's time to leave now," Mom clapped her hands once and pointed at the door.

Jake glanced at me, apology in his gaze. It wasn't his fault. I'd told him he could come.

Jake's eyes were filled with worry as he pulled the door closed behind him. "See you tomorrow, Libby."

As soon as the latch clicked, Mom lost it. Anger flooded her red face.

"You broke the rules, so you're going to pay for that!"

"What rules?" I shot back. There went my vow not to do anything to upset Mom.

She must not have liked my tone because she marched up to me and slapped my face. I gasped and placed my hand over the flaming heat.

"Ooh-wee, we got ourselves a cat fight," Roy cackled.

"Shut up, Roy! You stay out of this!" Mom ordered.

Roy threw his hands up and shook his head. He sauntered to the living room.

Mom leaned close to my face, her nose almost touching mine. Her breath tickled my chin. Her hair smelled like cigarette smoke, and I grimaced. If a jolt of fear hadn't just buzzed through my brain, I would've said something about the smell. My chest was tight, and I tried to control my breathing.

Mom grabbed the back of my neck, digging her fingernails into my skin. She pushed me to the living room, steering me forward until I stood facing the corner near the TV.

"You will stand right here until I say you can move!"

Stand in the corner? What was I, three years old? This was a punishment I'd never seen from her. She probably had to think of something besides her fists since Roy was watching.

I sighed and placed my right hand on the wall.

"Hands have to stay by your side!" Mom barked. "No leaning on the wall!"

I dropped my hand.

Edie asked why I had to stand in the corner. Roy told her I was a rule-breaker. When I tried to explain, Mom said, "No talking!" Then the lecture began, all about what happened to rule-breakers. Roy's staccato bursts of laughter sent my temper soaring.

Mom called for Anna to come downstairs for dinner. I was starving, but Mom didn't allow me to eat. She and Roy ushered my sisters to the kitchen, and I heard Anna ask why I couldn't eat with them.

For the next three hours, I stood facing the corner. My legs were tired, my back ached, and my left hip felt numb. I was so hungry, my stomach twisted and growled. My emotions swung from anger and exasperation to wanting to weep from exhaustion. This was just cruel. And what purpose did it serve? I had so much homework to do and wasting this much time was stressing me out.

At one point during my three-hour sentence, while Mom and Roy enjoyed their beers and watched TV, Roy threw Edie's bouncy ball and pelted me on the back of my head.

"Knock it off!" I yelled.

Roy laughed and threw it again, this time hitting my shoulder. I glared at him with all the energy I had, which made him laugh even harder. Mom told me to stop complaining, so I turned my face to the corner and gritted my teeth. I guess it became a game because I got smacked with that ball probably twenty times before Roy grew bored of it. Each time I was hit, my blood boiled. Edie giggled at first, then grew silent. After about ten hits, Anna stood up for me.

"Leave her alone!"

"Nope. Can't. Too tempting," Roy said.

I shuddered. I wanted this slimy snake out of our house, but here I was stuck in a corner for breaking a nonexistent rule. Inviting a friend over was something I did know could likely land me in hot water, but it still was *not* a rule. I fumed inside.

Anna advocated for me and asked a few times if I could be finished standing in the corner. Finally, Mom told me to leave the room. At first, I didn't dare leave for fear she was tricking me. I believed her once she screamed my name. My legs felt like jelly as I walked straight to the kitchen for food. Just as I suspected, dinner was all gone, so I filled a bowl with Cheerios and milk. I didn't care that it was breakfast food. I took the bowl upstairs with me. Edie and Anna followed and closed my door behind them.

"I don't like that guy," Anna said.

"You and me both."

Anna hugged me while Edie piped up, "Yeah, he's mean."

So is Mom, I wanted to say, but I clamped my mouth shut.

I gently sat on my bed, careful not to spill milk all over my quilt. I shoveled the cereal into my mouth, leaving a trail of milk dripping down my chin. I brushed it away with my sleeve.

"Why does Mom like Roy?" Edie asked. "I think he's a jerk. And he needs to wash his hands!"

Through a mouthful of cereal, I explained that Roy's mechanic work had permanently stained his skin, although I had no reason to defend the guy.

Anna's eyes were sad. "Does your head hurt from the ball?"

"I do have a little headache," I admitted. I cautioned the girls against making Roy angry. "We don't know what he'll do if he gets mad, so let's not find out."

I gulped the last of my milk, then yanked my books from my backpack and tossed them onto the bed. There wasn't enough room for the three of us and my homework, so I sent the girls to their room to get ready for bed. I wanted to help them pack a bag, but since I was hours behind on my homework, it was my first priority. For a moment I let the weight of my responsibilities press down on me. I pounded my pillow with my fist. Once, twice, three times, then I took a deep breath and picked up my pencil.

21
Wednesday, April 6, 1988

I yawned for probably the sixth time in ten minutes. Señor Flores directed his pinched stare at me. Beside me, that brown-noser Kyle, with the freckles and old-fashioned horn-rimmed glasses, snickered. He leaned across the aisle and whispered loudly, "How about another one?"

My cheeks felt hot, and I ducked my head, letting my long hair fall like a screen between us. What a dweeb! I wasn't yawning on purpose. I'd stayed up until one in the morning catching up on my assignments and making a huge dent in the English group project.

Señor Flores passed our assignment papers down the rows, but instead of walking back to his desk like he normally did, I was surprised to find him standing next to me. I gazed up at him, wide-eyed.

"Señorita Curtis, me gustaria hablar con usted un momento."

Ugh. He wanted to speak with me. Was this about the yawning? I sighed and followed him to his desk at the back of the room. He sat in his cushioned chair over which was draped a brightly colored woven blanket. The red, green and yellow stripes clashed with Señor Flores' pink button-up dress shirt. I waited while he opened a dark green spiral notebook that had 'Grades' written on the front cover. He found my name and followed a line with his finger across a row of boxes filled with scores. He pointed to the last four boxes, which sat empty.

"Señorita Curtis, you are missing several assignments." He spoke in English this time, probably to ensure I understood everything he was telling me. He leaned back and folded his arms. "Then you sit here in class obviously very tired. This isn't like you. What's going on?"

A lot. A whole lot is going on, I wanted to say. *My mom drinks every night. She lost her job. Then she got a new job. I'm the Cinderella of the family – cooking, cleaning, taking care of everyone. On top of that, I have an after-school job and still have to keep up on my homework. That's what's going on.* But that wasn't what I said.

"I've just been really busy lately. I'm tired because I stayed up until one o'clock finishing homework."

Señor Flores's stiff smile relaxed. "That's it?"

"Yes." I nodded and pointed to the first period in-box that sat along the side cabinets. "I turned in those four missing assignments when I got here this morning."

"Please try to get more sleep tonight," he said.

As if I hadn't already planned on it. If I closed my eyes, I could easily be asleep within seconds, even standing up. I forced myself to focus on the assignment and breezed through most of it but got stuck on two questions. I wanted to turn this assignment in before class was over so I wouldn't have to take it home to finish. I knew Kyle would have the correct answers, so I took a chance and asked him. He seemed reluctant to help at first, waving his hand at me as if trying to swat a fly, but when I stifled yet another yawn, he dropped his attitude and told me the answers. I thanked him with a small smile, then closed my eyes for a couple minutes until the bell rang.

Each class brought much of the same—me handing in assignments and then trying to stay awake. I resorted to pinching my arms in English class to stay alert. Finally, it was lunch time.

In the cafeteria, Nicole waved and patted the chair beside her. As I fell into the seat, a low groan escaped my lips. What I wanted more than anything was to curl up in my bed for a two-hour nap, but instead I was in the noisiest place on earth, eating the same crappy lunch I had every single day.

"How's it going, Libby?" Nicole leaned her head close to mine, whispering the words only I could hear.

I opened my mouth to respond, but all that came out was a yawn. I shook my head sharply and reached up to my neck to massage it. I rolled my eyes at Nic as she watched me try to revive myself. Across from me, Jake gave me a funny look, then pushed back his chair. He took off in the crowd of students still pushing their way into the lunchroom.

"Where's he going?"

"Probably forgot something." Nicole shrugged and her dangly turquoise spiral earrings twirled. She had on matching turquoise eyeshadow which clashed a bit with her deep blue eyes. Her hair sported a matching scrunchie in her high ponytail.

"How many of those do you own?" I pointed at the scrunchie.

"Oh, probably around twenty-five or thirty." She scooped mashed potatoes covered in brown gravy onto her fork and took a bite. I had to settle for the large red apple in my bag and a cheese sandwich.

After a minute, I was surprised to see an arm appear over my shoulder. A can of cola was placed on the table with a loud thunk. I glanced up to see Jake smiling down at me.

"Maybe that will help you stay awake."

My mouth was so full I couldn't open it to thank him. Jake made his way around to his seat. I finally swallowed and caught his eye. I mouthed the words, "Thank you." He acknowledged me with a wink and jumped into conversation with Shawn about the baseball team's stats.

"So, are you ready for Friday?" Nicole leaned over to me again.

"Ha! Nope. Not even close." I took another bite of my apple.

Nicole looked alarmed. "You're not? Don't you want this nightmare to be over with?"

"Oh, yeah, I do." I'd misunderstood her meaning of ready. I nodded and held her eyes. "Definitely ready for that. I thought you meant physically ready, like having our bags packed."

"Haven't had time?"

"No, plus I need to do all the laundry first."

"Do your sisters know what's happening?"

"Nope. I'm debating whether I should tell them or not. I think I'll wait 'til the last minute."

"Anything I can do to help?"

I shook my head and gave her a grateful smile.

"Holly and I get to help out on Friday." Nicole's eyes gleamed behind her thick lenses. I couldn't tell if she was excited to help me, to witness some drama, or to play an important role.

"I do know that much." I took a huge bite of my sandwich, squishing the bread flat under my fingers. A dab of mayo squeezed onto my mouth and chin, and I swiped it away with a napkin.

"We're going to come to your house around five. We can help with any last-minute stuff if you need us to come earlier though." Her voice was hopeful.

"I'll let you know," was my non-committal reply.

Through the fog in which my brain seemed to be encased, I had a sudden thought. "Wait, five o'clock? I don't get off work until six on Friday."

Nicole shook her head, and her earrings spun again. "Maybe I have the time wrong then, but I swore Jake said five."

I stared at Jake across the table, waiting to see if I could snag his attention. He and Shawn kept right on talking, oblivious to anyone else in the room. Shawn laughed at something Jake said, and it seemed to break the spell they were under. Jake relaxed his shoulders and stretched back in his chair, shoving the rest of his burger in his mouth. I waved my hand in his direction. His eyes flicked to me, and he leaned his elbows on the table and slid forward in his chair.

"What's up?"

"What time on Friday?" I kept my question vague on purpose. I didn't figure anyone could hear amid all the chatter, but I wasn't taking chances. As far as I knew, Shawn didn't know about any of this.

Jake flashed me a five sign with his hand. I held out my empty, upturned hands. "I work until six."

"Um, talk to Jerri about that, okay?" Jake said.

Huh. Maybe I wasn't working until six. Jake seemed sure of the time.

At that moment, Holly's long red hair swung into my peripheral vision before she plopped into the empty seat to my left. "What's up, peeps?" Her smile was brilliant...and pearly-white.

I gasped and my jaw dropped. "You got your braces off!" Why didn't I know this was happening?

Nicole squealed and jumped around me to hug Holly and inspect her perfect smile. "You look so good!"

"Whoa!" Across the table, both Jake and Shawn had a similar reaction. "You didn't tell us you were getting those off today."

Holly's eyes crinkled as she reveled in the attention. "I wanted it to be a surprise. Only Nic knew it was happening."

Lunchroom hubbub continued to swirl around me. Talk about retainers and being allowed to eat popcorn and hard candy became the topic of conversation. I heard more baseball talk and speculation over what Misty Zeman's student council election skit was going to be this year. Shawn said it would be hilarious, and Misty was a shoo-in for junior class president next year. I really didn't care who won the election. If only that was all I had to worry about.

I finished my lunch, followed by the last half of the cola. Finally, I began to feel alert, even peppy. I'd have to remember a caffeine jolt the next time I was overly tired.

Gym class came with more baseball. So again, not much time to chat. Holly said if I forgot anything at the house on Friday, she would be happy to lend me things. I thanked her and hugged both Holly and Nicole in a group hug, glad to have friends who were aware of my life even if they didn't completely understand it. The fact that they were willing to help me gave me motivation to do what I could to get my sisters out of our volatile situation.

When I got to Pop's, I hunted for Jerri but discovered she was in a meeting. As I stocked shelves, I kept an eye out for her. The store was extremely busy for a Wednesday afternoon. It seemed every mother there had a screaming infant or toddler. At times the crying drowned out the Top 40 songs playing over the speakers. Whoever had set the radio today would have to be thanked since I liked most of these songs, but I felt irritated when I couldn't hear them over the wailing. Everyone seemed frazzled today. The shoppers' stress increased mine and for the first time since I'd gotten the job, I wished I didn't have to work.

A short, balding man approached with a scowl. His oversized belly jiggled as he walked. "Excuse me, I'm trying to find anchovies. Where would they be?" His words were polite, but he had an air of superiority that turned me off.

"They'd probably be next to the cans of tuna on aisle five," I replied. I'd never seen anchovies when stocking that aisle, but that's what made sense.

"Probably? You mean you don't know?" Baldy-with-the-Belly asked. "I don't want to look all over the store." I was surprised his frown lines hadn't cut his face they were so deep.

"I've never seen anchovies here before, but that would be my guess." I tried to answer with patience, but I was fatigued, and I could hear the edge in my voice.

"Fine!" Baldy blustered and strode away on his stubby legs.

I shook my head and yawned as I watched him leave. I jumped as Jerri appeared by my side.

"What's wrong with that guy?" she asked, nodding toward the retreating figure.

I sighed. "He wants anchovies and got mad because I said they'd *probably* be by the tuna cans."

Jerri chuckled. "He'll be even more upset when he finds we don't carry those here. I mean, who likes anchovies?"

Jerri's matter-of-fact response made me laugh, easing some of my tension.

"How's everything at home? You look worn out."

"I am, and I have so much to tell you."

Jerri's eyebrows scrunched together. "Let's go chat in the office."

"Sounds great." I yawned again and stretched my back before following Jerri. We passed by the soda aisle and the cola called my name. I desperately wanted to snag one as I walked by. The energy rush from earlier had worn off.

Jerri opened her office door, then pushed a pile of papers aside with her foot. "My garbage can is full. I need to take it to the dumpster." She motioned for me to take Linda's seat. "I heard you took yesterday off."

"Yeah, there were last minute plans to meet for a group project."

Jerri got right to the point. "So, what's going on?"

"We got introduced to my mom's new boyfriend on Monday." My voice held zero enthusiasm. "He's a real winner."

Jerri's eyes popped open. "Seriously? That came out of nowhere."

"No kidding. He gives me the creeps."

"Oh no. That bad?"

I nodded. "I just want to steer clear of him, but last night I got in trouble, so I was in the same room as him for a few hours."

"In trouble for what?" Jerri leaned forward, our knees almost touching.

"Jake came by to tell me about Friday. My mom came home earlier than normal and Roy—that's her boyfriend's name–was with her. My mom claimed I broke a rule by having Jake over and she wasn't happy."

"Oh boy," Jerri sighed. "And then?" She rolled a pen back and forth over her desk calendar.

"First, she made Jake leave. Then she hit me, but it was like she was trying to keep it together in front of Roy, so she came up with a new punishment. She made me stand in a corner for three hours."

Jerri's hand hit the table. "Three hours?"

"Yep." I tried to stifle a yawn, but it came anyway, so I covered my mouth, then rubbed my face hard, trying to regain some energy.

Jerri looked away and rubbed the back of her neck.

"And Roy kept throwing a ball at me while I stood there." I leaned back in my chair and stretched again. My back was healing and stretching didn't hurt nearly as much anymore.

"Oh, my word." Jerri's eyes hardened. "You're right, he sounds like a real winner. And your mom just let him do that?"

"Yeah. She finally made him stop after, like, twenty times. But I wasn't allowed to leave the corner, so I just had to stand there and take it."

Jerri sighed again and pinched the bridge of her nose. "I'm sorry, Libby." She reached across her desk, and I took her hand. She squeezed it and said, "Jake told you what's happening on Friday?"

"Yeah, but said he was coming to pick us up around five. I'm supposed to work until six."

"Normally, yes, but not this Friday. I'm taking you off the schedule for Friday and Saturday. I want you and your sisters ready to leave when Jake comes, which hopefully will be before your mom gets home from work." She held up crossed fingers.

"Why can't I work on Saturday?"

"We have no idea how this is going to go, Libby. You'll likely be dealing with police and social workers this weekend...and beyond."

I must have looked confused because Jerri jumped in again. "I'm sure it's more complicated than either of us realize." She ran her hands down her long braid, smoothing the fly-aways.

I swallowed hard. I hadn't thought past the plan, assuming it was the most important part, the crowning event where we would be victorious and live happily ever after. My lungs felt like they were being squeezed, and my feet bounced, stimulated by fear of the unknown.

"What about Nolan?"

Jerri's lips pressed into a firm line, and she shook her head. "Still nothing. I just don't know if I have the wrong number or what." She shrugged. "But Libby, I don't want you to worry. You just let Reed and me worry about it. It will all work out as it should."

I wanted to believe her, but doubt filled my mind. There were too many "what-ifs?" Too many variables. I was jumping off a cliff without knowing if my landing would be in water or on rocks.

"I appreciate all you're doing for me, Jerri," I said. "I really do."

Jerri hopped up and pulled me into an embrace. Her arms around me calmed me, and I inhaled deeply the peachy scent of her perfume.

Jerri pulled back and placed her hands on my shoulders. "I could never live with myself if I didn't help you."

We silently stared at each other for several seconds.

"Okay, girlie! Time to get back to work!" Jerri's eyes crinkled in that way I'd come to love. She swatted my arm lightly.

I smiled. "Alright, I'm going." I mimicked a marching soldier and we both laughed.

Later, as the girls and I walked home, I debated telling them about Friday. I wavered between their need to know and thinking if they did know, the plan might backfire. So, I kept my mouth shut.

When we arrived home, I had Anna gather all the dirty laundry so it could be washed while I cooked dinner. Edie gathered ingredients for chili. She happily jabbered away, filling my ears with a tale of two boys fighting at recess. She even acted out their altercation, much to my amusement. Edie possessed a flair for the dramatic and not for the first time, I told her she should take a drama class when she got to high school.

Mom didn't show up until a little after six, which gave me hope we would be long gone when she arrived home on Friday. Roy didn't accompany her today, which was a relief.

"Where's your boyfriend?" Anna asked.

Mom fixed her with a glare. "Not your business."

Anna's cheeks colored and she hung her head. "Sorry."

"Did you get in a fight?" Edie teased, but before Mom could answer, she exclaimed, "I saw a fight today!"

I was glad she rattled off details of the fight because it kept Mom from engaging in any talk with us. I secretly hoped Mom and Roy *had* gotten in a fight. I could do without seeing him again.

Once I folded the laundry, I had to decide what to use to pack everything. Edie and Anna both had small suitcases that they used to go to Nolan's house every year, but I didn't have one. I wondered if Grandma had one stowed away in the attic or the shed, so I went on a search.

I spent about an hour going through boxes while everyone else watched TV. Twice Mom asked what I was doing. I told her I was looking for something for a school project. I knew she wouldn't get up from the couch to check on me, especially once she got started on her beer. I never found a suitcase, but I found a gym bag that was folded and stored in a box of old toys in the shed. When I unfolded the gray nylon square, it was much bigger than its original size indicated. I refolded it as best I could, then stuffed it under my shirt just in case Mom was watching me when I came back into the house. But she was engrossed in a show and didn't look my way. I stuffed the bag under my mattress for tomorrow. Finally, I started on my homework in hopes of finishing my part of the group project before the bomb dropped on Friday.

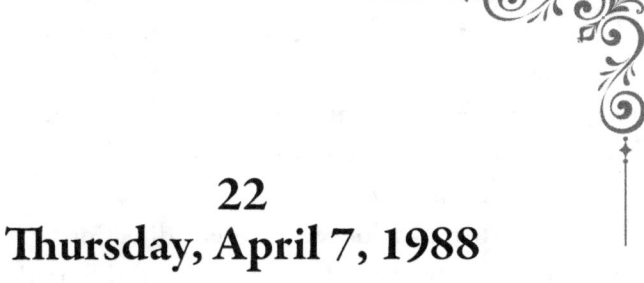

22
Thursday, April 7, 1988

I tossed and turned, becoming more agitated. I'd fallen asleep early and hard, but now it was four in the morning, and my brain wouldn't turn off. Neither would my stress. All my thoughts were on leaving Friday. I started to drift off to sleep a few times, but then I thought of more things that could go wrong. It was killing me.

I tried again to clear my mind, imagining I was walking through a garden with multicolored flowers of every variety surrounding me, their fragrance tickling my nose. I sucked in a breath trying to smell all of them at once. Deep breaths in, then slowly out. I relaxed my shoulders and loosened my jaw and concentrated only on breathing. Nothing else. Slowly, I felt the tension in my muscles ease.

I was surrounded by trees, tall, full, and vibrant green. The sky was an azure backdrop against which the leaves danced in the soft breeze. A fruity scent of pollen hung in the air. I wasn't sure where I was, but I wasn't complaining. A feeling of peace encompassed me.

As I followed the path that led through the woods, I realized I did know this place. This was the path that led from the pond to the bus stop and library on the other side of Buckley. I briefly wondered if I was supposed to meet Jake here. I looked back to see if Edie and Anna were nearby but saw no one. When I turned back around, I caught a glimpse of an older woman about thirty feet ahead of me. Her hair was gray, but full and thick and it hung halfway down her back. She walked quickly and I was fine giving her space. I was in no hurry to leave this place, so I strolled along, content. I hadn't felt this calm in ages. And I certainly didn't want to go home, but...why?

A sharp pain shot through my left wrist, and I raised my arm, surprised to see a cast there. I considered the cast as I continued down the path. Maybe I fell playing basketball.

"Libby!" a female voice called.

"Who's there?" I looked in every direction, but only saw the woods: brambly bushes, majestic trees and soft, dark dirt along the path. And shoes. I jerked my head up. The older woman who'd been ahead of me now faced me from a few feet away. She beckoned me to follow her.

I did as she requested, curious to know what she wanted. I studied her as I went. There was something familiar about the way she moved. And that tilt of her head. Shock ricocheted through me. I sucked in a breath.

"Grandma?"

I ran forward, eager to see, to find out if my grandma was really here. I hadn't seen her in so long and I missed her terribly. I caught up to the woman and placed my hand on her shoulder. She paused, then turned around.

"Grandma? Where have you been?"

I extended my arms, ready to wrap them around her. She was smaller than I remembered, but her smile was the same.

"Libby girl, I've missed you!" she said, her voice soft and sad.

She enveloped me in her arms and squeezed. I'd forgotten what Grandma's hugs felt like, but I was transported back. I felt so safe and happy, I wanted to sing with the chorus of chirping birds overhead.

Grandma pulled away. Her smile dwindled and worry created a sagging around her mouth.

"What's wrong?" I stepped back and mirrored her expression.

Grandma leaned over and rummaged around under the bush to her left. She gave a hard yank and pulled on something hidden there.

I gasped and stepped away. It looked like a snake!

"Do you recognize this?"

My eyes narrowed. It wasn't a snake after all. But where did Grandma get that? Surely it wasn't really hidden in the bushes.

"It looks like the belt that Mom..." my voice trailed off. I stared at Grandma, not wanting to say the words.

"Hit you girls with?" Grandma finished for me.

I nodded. I didn't have any clue what was happening. I asked the only question that came to mind.

"Where did you get it?"

"It doesn't matter. What matters is that you follow through with your plan to leave. I wanted to warn you that you may run into...difficulties, but do not give up."

"O-Okay."

"Libby, your mother is not the daughter I used to know. When your grandpa left us, your mom was just a child, and she became quiet and withdrawn. She wasn't the same spunky girl I'd known. I thought she would heal and be happy since our home life was more stable with him gone. I didn't realize I should have gotten help for her. As she became a teenager, she became sullen and angry. I thought it was just adolescent moodiness. She never coped with her feelings; she just buried them under these layers of rage. She drove people away with her abrasive attitude and then was furious when they walked away. People like your father. Your mom's been living this vicious cycle her entire life. She turned to alcohol as a solution and things went from bad to worse. And the worst part of all is that you girls have had to pay the price." Grandma's lips trembled and tears threatened to fall from her green eyes. "It pains me that you've had to endure such awful treatment, but you are so brave, and you've protected your sisters as best you could. You've had to be the adult, and I admire you so much."

Grandma wrapped her arms around me again. I didn't want to let her go but she pulled back and placed the belt in my hands. Weird that the leather felt soft against my skin, when the last time it touched me, it stung like fire.

"This is a weapon, Libby. You must hide all the weapons."

I stared down at the belt. It *had* been a weapon and could be again. When I looked up again, Grandma was gone.

"Grandma?" I spun in a circle. Where had she gone?

"GRANDMA?!" I lurched forward on the path, running over the bumpy terrain, screaming her name.

"Grandma!" I jerked upright, panting, and disoriented. Where was Grandma? I tossed the quilt aside, then slowly it dawned on me. I was home, in bed. It had all been a dream. Grandma wasn't with me. Tears welled up, then rolled down my face. It had felt so real. *She* had felt so real, so alive. I ached to have her here. I flopped back on my pillow, flustered and frustrated. How was that only a dream?

I closed my eyes, remembering what Grandma had said. Her explanation about Mom made sense and I felt a little sorry for her. But then she'd said to follow through with the plan. There might be trouble. Hide all the weapons.

That last part sounded ominous and made me even more nervous about Friday. But it was also confusing. Anything could be a weapon. And I needed to hide all of them? The more I thought about it, the more daunting it felt. Grandma's visit no longer felt calming. It was a yellow danger sign, flashing at me from every direction.

"JAKE, I'M SO STRESSED out!"

It was lunchtime and we were sitting on our bench. I'd just related the dream about Grandma that I couldn't get out of my mind.

"Alright, just chill for a second." Jake took a sip of his chocolate milk.

Chill? Easy for him to say. He didn't have to look at everything in his house as if it could potentially become a weapon.

"How am I supposed to figure out what I should hide?"

"Well, what are some 'normal' weapons?" Jake seemed distracted as he popped a French fry in his mouth.

"Well, sharp objects, like knives, scissors, broken glass. Even nails or screwdrivers. Hard objects like bricks, rocks, bats, hammers, rolling pins, beer bottles. Anything else?"

Jake quirked a grin.

"What? What's so funny?" Did he not care how anxious I was? I frowned and turned my back to him. I didn't care if it was childish. I didn't understand why he couldn't take this seriously. I took a huge bite of my peanut butter sandwich.

"Hey, I'm sorry. But don't you think this dream might just be a dream?"

I whipped my head around, chewing furiously. The peanut butter made my mouth feel as if it was glued shut. I gave Jake my fiercest glare.

"Okay, okay!" Jake threw up his hands in surrender. "I just meant you should consider that too."

I took a couple swallows of my Capri-Sun, trying to clear the stickiness from my mouth.

"It was so real though."

Jake sighed. "Then hide everything you just named. But if we're taking this dream seriously..."

I growled.

"...then the part I'm more worried about is that she said we might run into trouble." Finally, his eyes registered concern and not amusement.

"I guess I just have to be prepared in any way I can. But, yeah, that worries me too."

We sat in silence, each engrossed in our own thoughts. I'd hoped telling Jake my concerns would relieve my stress, but for some reason, it had only seemed to intensify it. And there was something else that had been weighing on my mind all morning.

"I don't want you, or Holly, or Nicole, or Jerri, or anyone, to get hurt because of what we're doing."

"Yeah," Jake agreed. He looked everywhere except me, then stared at his milk carton. "About that."

"What is it?" A dull pain rolled around my head like an ocean wave. I rubbed my forehead and gently pressed my cold fingers to my eyes.

"I want to tell my parents what we're doing." Jake's blue eyes were soft and pleading.

At once, the pain in my head became more like a violent sea storm. I hadn't seen that one coming. "But what if they try to stop you?"

"They might," Jake admitted. "That's why I haven't said anything yet. But I feel like they should know."

I knew Jake's relationship with his parents was completely different from mine. I talked to Jerri more than I did my own mother. But until Jerri came along, I kept everything to myself. It surprised me how much I'd shared lately, and not just with Jake and Jerri.

I blew a puff of air at my bangs and felt them flutter. I couldn't really say no, could I? Did it scare me? Yes. But Jake had to make this decision on his own. I shrugged my shoulders. "Could you maybe wait until tomorrow though?"

Jake thought for a bit before he said, "Yeah, I guess I can do that. I even thought about writing a letter and leaving it for my brother to give to my mom at dinner tomorrow night. Then she won't be able to stop me, but she'll still know where I am and what's going on. You know, in case something happens and we need more help."

I nodded. Having Jake's parents on backup was probably a good thing. It was all just so hard to predict. Anything could happen. But I had to stay positive because Grandma had warned me that we had to follow through. That meant no chickening out.

"JERRI'S LOOKING FOR you," Keith said as soon as I walked through the automatic door at Pop's after school. I was pulling my headphones from my ears and removing my backpack to place my Walkman inside. I'd started listening to my three cassettes on rotation on my walk to the store every afternoon.

"What did you say?"

Keith turned around but continued in the direction of the restrooms, walking backwards.

"Jerri wants to see you. You in trouble or something?" He grinned, then spun around and moved out of sight.

"Something like that," I mumbled, heading in the same direction. I changed into my black polo and placed two barrettes in my hair to keep it out of my face. I glanced at my cast and briefly wondered when my next appointment with the doctor was scheduled. I needed to find that out before tomorrow in case someone else had to take me to it. I picked up a lock of hair and inspected the ends. It was also time for a haircut.

Jerri found me five minutes later as I was pulling my work assignment from the back wall. The first thing I noticed was that her hair hung loose and fell past her shoulders in waves. I'd never seen it down. It was always in a braid or ponytail.

"Whoa, your hair!" I couldn't stop staring. "I love it like that."

"Well, you know, I thought I'd try it today, but I have to say that for work, it's better pulled back." Jerri's smile was wide, and her eyes twinkled with even more sparkle today.

"Keith said you wanted to see me."

"Well, I do have some good news." Jerri practically sang the words.

I slid a boxcutter into my pocket. "What is it?"

"Nolan finally called me back."

I sucked in a squeaky breath. "No way! Really?" My heart fluttered, excited and hopeful.

Jerri's smile was so big, I thought her face would crack in two. I grasped her arms and jumped up and down.

"You're for real, right?"

"Yes, completely for real." Jerri bounced a little with me, then stopped as Mick walked by looking annoyed. "Let's get your boxes out to the floor and then I'll fill you in."

I picked up my list. Together we located the boxes and loaded them onto two dollies. I was a little shaky over Jerri's news. It was such weird timing. I mean, right before we were planning to leave? And what the heck took him so long to call back? How much did Jerri tell him? Was he upset? I shook my head. Stupid question. If Nolan was still the same man, then yes, he'd be upset that his ex-wife was beating his girls.

I bumped into Jerri when we stopped near the end of the candy aisle. She quirked an eyebrow at me, then winked.

"So enthusiastic about work today! Just what I love to see."

Although I wanted to run to Jerri's office to chat, I forced myself to be calm and walk like a normal human. Keith passed by, jostling a set of keys. He paused, put his hands on his hips, his face smug. "I see you found her, Boss."

I rolled my eyes and stifled a snicker. *Well, duh. Thanks, Keith.*

Jerri was kinder than me. "Yes, thanks. Keep up the good work."

Keith beamed. Nodding at me, he strutted off.

Jerri's office door was ajar, meaning Linda was probably in there. Jerri popped her head around the door and as it opened, I heard Linda talking on the phone. Jerri scooted back out and gestured toward the breakroom. Finding it clear, she waited until I entered before locking it behind her, giving us a few minutes of guaranteed privacy.

I was too keyed up to sit down. "Tell me everything."

"I was just about to get in bed last night when the phone rang. Reed was already snoring, so it woke him up and he started ranting. I answered, ready to give the caller a piece of my mind about calling so late. It wasn't a voice I recognized, so I was about to hang up until I heard him say his name. I almost dropped the phone, I was so surprised."

"Why did it take him so long to call you back?"

"Nolan said he's been gone for a month working on construction of a resort hotel over in one of the islands near Florida. Bahamas, maybe? Apparently, his wife works for the same company, so she's been there with him."

"What did you tell him?" I crossed my fingers behind my back.

"I told him I work with you and that you're having some problems at home that are bad enough that we need to get you girls out of there. He had a lot of questions, and we talked for probably twenty minutes."

I leaned forward, anxious. "How did he react?"

Jerri sighed. "I actually tried to downplay it a bit. I want you to have the chance to tell him, not have it come from some stranger. He said he was exhausted and happy to be home, so I decided he should have a couple days to settle in before his life gets turned completely upside down. He sounded like a very nice man."

"Yeah, that's how I remember him. The girls love being with him every summer. I've always been jealous they got to go spend time with him." Talking about it brought back some of those feelings: the yearning to go with Anna and Edie, the loneliness of staying behind with a mom who didn't engage with me, the tears I shed because I wasn't allowed to do much with friends.

"I told Nolan you would call him tomorrow. I warned him not to call Donna or our plan could backfire. He seemed unsure, but I asked him to trust me. I told him that you trust me, so that seemed to convince him. I was so relieved he finally called."

"Yeah, it's awesome," I agreed. I twisted my hands together. I had a couple questions I'd been mulling over for a while, waiting for the right time to ask. I wasn't sure I was ready for the answers, but tomorrow was the big day, so it was now or never.

"Um, Jerri? What do you think will happen to us after we report to the police? I mean, to me, Edie, and Anna?" My voice was low, and I stared at the worn, industrial, maroon carpet. It was covered in stains left from years of employees spilling food or drink on the floor. There were several small areas worn down by table and chair legs being pushed back and forth. "And to my mom?"

"Libby, look at me," Jerri demanded.

I jerked my head up, surprised to see Jerri's jaw set and her eyes stern. "You have to remember you are doing the right thing. Above anything else, you remember that. You are providing a way for your sisters to experience a good home life–most likely with their father. You may end up there too. Who knows? Either way, you'll graduate in two years and then be on your own, so whatever happens, remember you're making life better for all of you. You can do this. I know you can."

Jerri folded her arms against her stomach, her forearms tight. She looked almost angry. "As for your mother, well, I can't really say because it isn't up to me. But she has broken the law, and she needs help. Hopefully, she will come to realize that and want to change. But, if not..." She shrugged.

"I just don't want her to hate me for it," I whispered, "or for the girls to hate me."

"I understand. I really do. You are all going to benefit from counseling. I have no idea how your mom will feel, but your sisters? You're their hero and I don't think that will change."

Jerri's words unleashed tears I couldn't contain. I hoped with all my heart her words were true. Those little girls were my whole reason for doing this scary, dreadful thing. I swiped at the tears as Jerri plucked a paper towel from the roll near the sink.

"Here you go, sweetie." Jerri squeezed my shoulder, then lifted my chin, and gazed into my eyes. "You are the bravest person I know, Libby. Now, tonight, you go home and prepare for tomorrow. I'll be praying for you." She waited until I'd finished dabbing at my face and we walked out of the breakroom together, each going in separate directions. It wasn't until I was placing bags of gummy bears on the rack that I realized I hadn't told her about my dream.

I'D BEEN THINKING THAT I should make a nice dinner because if all went well, it would be our last in this house together. But reality hit as I searched through the fridge and cupboards. We had random items that really didn't go together for a meal. I found an unopened bag of rice and a can of cream of chicken soup, an onion that was beginning to soften, and a few carrots. There was a small pack of chicken in the freezer, so we'd end up with a decent meal at least, even if Roy showed up for dinner today. I told the girls to clean their room and organize their dresser drawers in the hopes I could easily find the items that needed to be packed tonight.

I defrosted the chicken, then chopped it and the onion and placed them in a pot with the soup. I mixed in a cup of water and placed it on the stove. I got the rice going in another pot and peeled the carrots before cooking them in the microwave. As I cleaned the dishes I had used, I stared at the knives lying in the bottom of the porcelain sink. Weapons.

"Oh no." Instead of focusing on preparing dinner, I should have been hiding the weapons before my mom got home. I quickly washed and dried the knives, then gathered all I could find in the kitchen. But where was I going to hide them? There weren't many options in this small house. I yanked open another drawer and removed the kitchen towels and washcloths, shoved the knives in, then covered them with the towels.

I could hear the girls thumping around upstairs, their voices just a buzz. They wouldn't see me search Mom's room and the rest of the main floor for anything that could be used to hurt us. I was worried Mom might walk in early again, so I locked the back door, then realizing she would go around to the front door if she couldn't get in, I ran through the living room to lock that door too. Mom would be irritated if she couldn't get in without using her key, so my search had to be quick. I ran back through the kitchen and down the short hall to Mom's bedroom door. The cheap brass knob felt cold in my hand. The room was dark with the rust-colored drapes closed, so I flipped on the light to see a rumpled bed. If Mom didn't make her bed tight and neat, it usually meant she was running late.

"Great way to start a new job," I muttered. I crossed the room to the closet and slid the golden-paneled door back in its track. I pushed metal hangers draped with various articles of clothing aside, searching for the belt. Where did she keep it? I thought back to the recent episode in her room and shuddered. Where had she placed it? Had I even noticed? I closed my eyes and forced my mind to focus. I replayed the aftermath of that event but came up empty. I dropped to the ground, pushing aside her shoes. Nothing. Could it be under the bed? I peeked underneath but had no luck there either. My pulse picked up as panic began to press in on me. I glanced up into the closet and noticed the belt curled against a cardboard box on the shelf above the clothing.

I sprang to my feet and pulled it down. I would have to hide it in my bedroom, but before I went upstairs, I had other things to hide. I stalked back to the kitchen and opened the junk drawer. The scissors with the bright yellow hand grips were easy to spot. I yanked them out and shoved them in my back pocket. I rummaged through pens, pencils, paper clips, rubber bands, a pencil sharpener, a ruler, a flashlight, and a bottle of old prescription medication of Anna's from an earlier ear infection. Gosh, potential weapons everywhere. I placed the belt on the counter and made a sack with my shirt, holding it up with my casted hand. I grabbed everything except the flashlight and threw it in my shirt-bag. I gently lay the flashlight and belt on top and gathered the hem of the shirt to my chest so nothing would fall out. I went up the stairs as fast as my awkward load would allow. I knew exactly where to put it.

Nothing fell out of my shirt until I knelt next to my bed. Half the load spilled when I reached blindly under the bed for an empty shoe box. Crap. Mom could come home any minute. I scrambled around on all fours, retrieving the items and tossing them into the box. I slammed the lid on and shoved it under the bed, all the way to the wall. Now for the bathrooms.

I couldn't see many weapons, but I snagged my curling iron and placed it under my bed to pack later.

"Whatcha doing?"

"Ah!" I nearly jumped out of my skin. Anna was watching me as I smoothed the long quilt down over the gap from the bed frame to the floor.

"Sheesh, Anna! You scared me to death!" I stood and wiped my hand across my sweaty forehead. I ignored her question and asked one of my own. "Did you two finish in your room?"

"I'm done, but Edie doesn't want to finish. She's looking at a comic book her friend let her borrow."

I groaned. Getting Edie to work for more than twenty minutes at a time was harder than playing a concert piano piece without having one lesson. I marched to the girls' room. Sure enough, Edie was splayed across the bed on her belly with the comics propped in front of her face.

"Edie!"

Edie looked over her shoulder at me, her face blank. "Huh?"

"Get up and finish the job I gave you. You don't get dinner until it's done. Anna is going to supervise."

Anna's mouth popped open. "But..."

"Sorry, Anna. We have to get this done now." I felt bad making it her responsibility, but I needed her help. I'd explain later when we packed.

"But why?" Anna crossed her arms and huffed a big breath.

"We just do. I'm sorry." I kept my tone stern.

Edie ignored us and continued to read the comic book. I walked over and snatched the distraction from her hands. "This is mine until you finish."

"Hey!" she yelled and rolled off the bed, following me out of the room. "Give that back!"

I held the book high above my head as Edie jumped and scratched at my arms, screeching at me to return it. "You'll get it back after you're finished. Now stop it!"

"Come on Edie," Anna moaned. "Just do it. I'm hungry."

I stared at Edie, whose face had turned a splotchy red. "Finish, then come down for dinner and I promise you'll get it back."

Edie threw her hands in the air and shrieked, "Fine!"

I ran down the stairs to the slamming of the bedroom door. I was going so fast, I stumbled a few steps from the bottom. I grabbed for the handrail to steady myself, my breath coming in rapid puffs.

I unlocked the front door, then the back, and plopped down at the table to catch my breath. Okay. Weapons were taken care of.

I finished making dinner, then rested at the table. I was on page three of the comic book, reading about the adventures of Archie and Veronica when Mom walked in the door. I quickly closed the book and scrambled to my feet.

"Mom, hi."

Mom's eyes narrowed as she looked me over. She held her embroidered purse in one hand and a brown sack in the other. She set the sack on the counter with a clunk. Food or alcohol? I'd bet the second. I placed the comic book on top of the fridge while Mom headed tos her room with her purse. My heart sped up, hoping I hadn't left any evidence I'd been in there. While she had no reason to look for the belt now, I still worried she might see it was missing.

I realized Mom had left the back door open wide, so I reached out to close it when Roy appeared. *Ugh!* I was so hoping he had gone somewhere far, far away.

"Well, if it isn't the beautiful Libby," Roy drawled and raised his eyebrows at me. His eyes took on a suggestive look and I tried not to gag. His blackened hands carried another sack. I stepped back to let him in, but as he passed, Roy reached his hand to my face and trailed a finger down my cheek.

I flinched, twisted my head away and stepped back. A wave of nausea rolled through my gut. I didn't want this creep anywhere near me. Mom could force me to serve him dinner, but he was not going to touch me again. It took all my willpower not to shudder.

"Isn't dinner ready?" Mom reappeared in the kitchen.

"It's ready. I just need to set it on the table."

Roy thunked his sack on the counter beside Mom's and flopped into the closest chair. Mom took the seat next to him and sighed. They engaged in quiet conversation about their day, completely ignoring me. I was fine with that. But I was irritated at having to cook for this bum. Even though it would be my last day to do it, knock on wood, I was itching to speak my mind.

I carried the plates and forks to the table, then stared at the forks in sudden realization. Oh, no! I forgot that forks could be weapons too. I'd have to hide them after I did the dishes. But no, I couldn't do that. What if someone needed one? I couldn't exactly say, "Oh, you need a fork? Let me go get one from under my bed." I'd have to take my chances with the forks.

"Is he going to be eating here every night?" I kept my tone neutral as I nodded at Roy.

"Excuse me?" Mom snapped. She grabbed my wrist and dug her nails in. I kept a stone face, not wanting to let on that she was hurting me.

"I just need to know so I can make enough food."

Mom glared but released my wrist. "Plan on him every night."

Well, wasn't that just peachy? Mom smiled at Roy, and he grinned. His smile reminded me of the wolf in *Little Red Riding Hood*, smug and devious.

"If he's going to be here every night, then you need to buy more food because we're almost out."

Mom groaned. "Fine. We'll go to the store after dinner."

I felt a twinge of guilt knowing they'd be buying extra food for no reason, since three of us would be gone. I carried the food to the table and yelled for the girls to come downstairs.

A flash of annoyance crossed Mom's face. "Do you have to be so loud?"

I pressed my lips together. *Patience, Libby*. Anna and Edie pounded down the stairs, sounding more like ten people than two. The hanging light above the table swung slightly. I set the rice on the table and eased the light to a stop. I looked at Edie.

"Did you finish cleaning your room?"

She nodded. "Uh-huh."

I glanced at Anna with a quirked eyebrow.

"Yep, she did." Anna scooped some rice on her plate. "I helped her finish."

"Edie, did you thank Anna?"

"You think you're the boss, Libby?" Roy smirked and took a huge helping of rice. There wasn't going to be much left for the rest of us.

I clenched my jaw. "Kind of."

I didn't look at Roy or Mom. I didn't care what they thought of my response. I had too many other things to worry about tonight. I dished what was left of the food and took a bite. I only half-listened to the conversation and ate as fast as I could. Mom asked why I was in a hurry and reprimanded me for having appalling manners.

"What's appalling mean?" Roy asked.

Mom furrowed her brow. Her eyes shifted around, looking at everyone except Roy.

I looked at my lap and tightened my lips so the laugh that was trying hard to escape would stay inside.

"Yeah. What's 'palling mean?" Edie mimicked Roy.

Mom rolled her eyes. "It just means terrible."

"Well, why don't you just say terrible?" Roy asked. "Why you gotta use such big smarty-pants words?"

I couldn't stop the laugh this time. I covered my mouth and coughed a couple of times to hide my grin. I had to get away from this idiot. I picked up my dishes and took them to the sink. Anna followed with her dishes, then stayed to help wash them.

I looked over my shoulder to see if anyone else was coming near. I whispered in Anna's ear, "I have something to talk to you about after Mom and Roy leave."

"Okay." Anna nodded and took the wet plate I handed to her. I wished Mom and Roy would hurry. I had things to do.

I ENDED UP HAVING TO make the grocery list for Mom because according to her, she was too busy talking to Roy. I didn't want her to buy too much food, but I had to make the list look real, so I wrote down the basics plus some dinner and lunch foods for a week's worth of meals. As they started out the door, Roy noticed the items in the brown sacks they'd brought home still sat on the counter.

"Hey, Libby," he called, "come put these drinks in the fridge."

Curious, I peeked in the sacks and found more than I expected. Beer, some other kind of liquor, but also a couple six packs of root beer and orange soda. I wondered if those were for me, Anna, and Edie. I shoved them in the nearly empty fridge above the fruit and vegetable drawers.

I asked Edie to water the flower beds outside and then to take a shower. I needed her to be occupied while I explained tomorrow's plan to Anna and got her help in packing their bags. I wasted precious minutes arguing with Edie, who didn't want to do either task.

"Come on, Edie, just cooperate," I pleaded. "If you do, I'll buy you a candy bar from Pop's." I wasn't typically one to make deals, but I was in a hurry and desperate.

Edie popped off the couch. "Can I have a Whatchamacallit?"

"Whatever kind you want."

Her eyes gleamed and she went to the kitchen for the bright orange water pitcher we used for the job.

"Come on, let's go, Anna."

Anna followed me upstairs and into her room, which did look neat and organized. I knelt next to the bed and stretched my arm under as far as I could reach. I barely touched the suitcase handle.

"What are you doing?" Anna asked.

I flattened myself to the floor and pulled out suitcase number one, followed by suitcase number two. They were small and boring black with silver latches.

"Anna, I have to tell you something and I don't want you to be frightened or sad." I paused to let the words sink in. Anna just looked bewildered.

"Tomorrow, you, Edie, and I are leaving. Hopefully for good."

Anna's eyes widened and I saw the panic in them. "What are you talking about?" She stood rigid, her eyes glued on the suitcases.

I placed my hands on her shoulders. "I know this is difficult, but I've been trying to come up with a plan to get us away from Mom because of how she treats us. You know what I mean, right?" I gently tilted her chin up, so I could see into her eyes.

"But..." Her eyes filled with tears. "I don't want to leave our house." Her chin shuddered and the tears flowed fast, like a dam had burst.

I pulled her to me and squeezed her tight. "Shh, it will be okay." In all my planning, this was something I had not foreseen. I thought the girls would be as happy as I was to escape. I ran my hand down Anna's hair and waited for her to settle. "Anna, listen to me. You know what Mom does to me, right?" She looked away and nodded.

"And you know she's been hurting you and Edie too." It wasn't a question, just a statement of fact. She nodded again. She looked at me and more tears welled up. I snuck a look at my watch.

"Can you just help me pack some clothes and favorite things and we'll talk about it later? We have to do this while Mom is gone."

She swiped at the tears, looking resigned.

"Thank you," I whispered. "I'll explain it all, I promise." I pulled on a dresser drawer. "Socks, underwear, pajamas, plus four or five outfits and anything else you might need. You'll also need your backpack, but we'll get to that after school tomorrow."

Anna mechanically placed clothing in her case while I worked on filling Edie's. Anna grabbed Mr. Muffin, her stuffed rabbit, off the bed and gently pressed him into her case.

I smiled. "Do you think Edie wants Kitty-Poo?" I motioned toward the scruffy stuffed cat that sat on Edie's pillow. She nodded and I grabbed the animal that looked more mean than friendly and jammed him into Edie's case.

"Anything else?"

Anna looked around the room. "Can I take my books?" She had ten or twelve books stacked on the dresser.

"As many as you can fit," I agreed. "What about Edie?"

"Can she take the TV?"

"Huh?" I glanced at Anna. Her small smile told me she was joking. I was proud of her for being brave in the face of something so overwhelming. I nudged her shoulder. "That *is* what she likes," I agreed. The front door slammed, so I ran across the hall with the suitcases and shoved them under my bed. Anna followed me.

"Are you going to tell Edie?" Anna's brow rose.

"Not tonight." I kept my voice low.

"I'm getting in the shower now!" Edie shouted. "You owe me a candy bar!"

"Yeah, thanks Edie!" I yelled.

"But you'll tell her tomorrow?" Anna asked.

"Yes, I promise. But I need you to promise that you won't tell her before I do."

"Why?"

"Because what if Edie slips and says something that Mom overhears? What do you think would happen then?" I wanted Anna to put it together on her own. I needed her to realize the abuse really was a problem. I understood it was a huge upheaval to leave the only home she'd ever known–and Edie too. But even if she could see the problem, this was still our mom we were talking about. I hoped someday she would understand. Maybe if she had a home where she didn't have to tiptoe around for fear of setting someone off, she could look back and be relieved not to live that way anymore. But we just had to get there first.

"Mom would be so mad." Anna's eyes flickered with fear.

"Yeah, exactly." I gave her shoulders a squeeze. "Thanks for being brave."

Anna buried her face in my side and shuddered. I held her for several minutes, each of us pulling strength from the other.

A DOOR SLAMMED DOWNSTAIRS.

"Libby," Mom called, "come put these groceries away!"

Ugh. I'd just opened the duffel bag to start packing my things. "Coming!" I called back. *Whether I want to or not.*

Mom and Roy were already vegging on the couch when I got downstairs. "You'll have to bring them in from the car," Mom said, without looking away from the TV. "Oh, and bring us some drinks."

Rolling my eyes, I grabbed one of each brand from the fridge and set them on the coffee table. The tabs popped before I was even back in the kitchen. This seemed to be a nightly ritual. *So lame.*

When the job was complete, I escaped back to my room to pack my belongings. I struggled with what to take and finally decided the basics would do for now. Once I packed those, I shoved the remaining space with as many other items as would fit. Mom must have sent the girls outside to play because I could hear them in the yard, their squeals drawing me to the window to see what fun they were having. One of them had managed to throw a jump rope over a high branch of the elm tree and Edie was using it as a swing to catapult herself toward Anna, who stood about ten feet away. Their giggles were contagious; I couldn't help smiling. The dimming daylight left much of the yard in shade and prompted me to switch on my overhead light.

As I flipped the switch, it was as if I'd electrified the mood downstairs. Mom and Roy both began shouting. I shoved the duffel under my bed and the eased the door open to hear the argument. It only took a moment to get the gist of their disagreement. It was about a TV show. *Oh brother*. Talk about immature. The only good thing about Roy being here was that Mom was distracted. I'd been able to pack, so I guess I owed him for that. I didn't want to venture downstairs, but Anna still needed to shower before bedtime, and I knew from past experience the girls wouldn't come inside without being called in.

Mom and Roy were so involved in their spat, I was able to sneak past them into the kitchen. I went out the back door and let it close softly behind me.

"Anna, Edie! It's time to come inside."

The girls paused in their play, then both groaned in unison. I expected Edie to complain and stomp around, but she pulled the jump rope off the branch without a word. Anna flashed me a disappointed look but scooped her jump rope from the grass.

"I'll put those away," I said, reaching out for the ropes. "Anna, you need to shower. Edie, just go upstairs to your room. Stay away from Mom and Roy. They're arguing."

"About what?" Edie asked.

"Something stupid," I replied.

Once the girls had closed the back door behind them, I opened the shed door. It was always unlocked. No one in this town worried much about things like locking up a shed. Besides, there wasn't much to steal in this one except an old push mower and a few tools. I scanned the dark corners and saw the metal baseball bat Edie had gotten as a birthday present from Nolan when she expressed an interest in playing ball with the boys at the park. Not that she used it often.

I placed the bat and jump ropes under the stack of blankets in the back corner. It was really the only place in the shed to hide anything. The blankets were already hidden behind a stack of boxes, so I figured they'd stay hidden there. On the opposite end of the shed, a wooden ledge extended about a foot down the entire side. The ledge was dusty and covered in an array of items: a toolbox, string, sprinklers and a worn-out, patched garden hose, a rusty gas can and many of the girls' toys. A bottle of bubbles, sidewalk chalk, a baseball, jacks and two blue and green water guns were jumbled together close to the door, some dustier than others. The shed could really use a good cleaning.

The toolbox was open. Two screwdrivers with neon orange heads lay on the ledge next to it. I put them in the box and snapped it closed, the metal latches pinging off the rusted box. But wait. Where was the hammer? I moved things around on the ledge and squinted around in the dim light. If it was here, I couldn't see it. Maybe I could look tomorrow afternoon. I placed the toolbox under the blanket pile. I didn't see anything else that could be used as a weapon, so I shut the door behind me. *I did it Grandma. I've hidden everything I could find.*

I paused with my hand on the peeling paint of the back door, my skin tingling. Goosebumps raised the hair on my arms as I listened to the raised voices in the house. Were they still arguing over a show? I closed my eyes and shook my head, weary of it already. *Sure hope I'm not this annoying when I'm an adult.*

As I stepped into the living room, something hard thumped my head and pain seared over my eyebrow. For a second, everything in the room looked kind of wavy. What had just happened? Mom and Roy stopped yelling obscenities at each other, and the room grew silent.

"Ow!" I felt dizzy, so I dropped to my knees and clapped my right hand over the pain. My palm was wet when I pulled my hand away. There was blood smeared there, a lot of blood.

"Oh, crap!" I fought the unsteady feeling in my limbs and pushed upright, using the wall for support. Roy and Mom sat silent, their eyes wide. My head throbbed, but I was so sick of crying, I refused to allow tears to come. Instead, my anger flared like a bonfire. What had hit me? A quick glance at the worn carpet revealed a brown ceramic coaster lying a few feet away.

"What was that for?" I cried.

Mom and Roy stared at each other, still wide-eyed. Then Mom snickered.

"You're laughing? I'm bleeding and you're laughing?" I should have known. Mom had never been sorry for hurting me before, so why start now?

Mom's snicker turned into a full-blown, guttural laugh that had her bent over her knees. Roy took that as permission to laugh too, his chuckles growing to side-splitting laughter.

"You got her good!" Mom said, grabbing her stomach.

I spun around and ran to the first-floor bathroom, slamming the door and pressing the lock button with a resounding click. My breathing came in angry pants. The mirror reflected the anger that radiated off me. I pulled my hand from the wound. The cut was bleeding heavily and without pressure on it, the blood began to spill over my brow. A few drops fell into the sink, leaving harsh red splatters against the tan basin. I slapped my hand to my brow again. Did I need stitches?

With my free hand, I rummaged through the drawer that held Band-Aids in search of something that would work better. It was awkward with my cast and produced nothing.

"Well, this is just great," I growled.

I pulled several squares of toilet paper from the roll and folded them as best I could to make a bandage. I quickly slapped the bandage in place. Holding the bandage with my cast, I washed the blood off my right hand and out of the sink. Then I slumped to the floor. The olive-green bath rug I'd plopped onto had matted clumps and was fraying at the edges. It was way beyond needing to be replaced. I kicked the bathtub in frustration.

Roy and Mom were still laughing. I didn't know what was worse, the arguing or the laughing at my expense. I initially thought Mom had thrown the coaster, but apparently it had been Roy. I wondered if he was trying to hit the wall or just randomly threw it because he was angry. Either way, I just happened to be in the wrong place at the wrong time.

After ten minutes of sitting on the floor holding the bandage in place, I decided to take a peek. When I pulled the bandage away, it stuck to my head in a couple of places, but blood still oozed from the middle of the cut although more slowly now. I made another small toilet paper bandage and used my mouth to pull the tabs off several Band-Aids that I used to hold the TP in place. The Band-Aids crisscrossed my forehead in such a haphazard way, I looked ridiculous. The dark glare in my eyes caught my attention in the mirror. I'd always thought my hazel eyes had a soft openness to them, but the ones staring back at me were fierce and determined. And so very angry.

23
Friday, April 8, 1988

"Anna, Edie, I need you to come straight home after school today." I threw my lunch into my backpack while the girls ate their cereal. I set their lunches on the table next to them.

"But why?" Edie wanted to know. "I want the candy bar you promised me."

"I won't forget. But I'm not working this afternoon."

Edie stuck her bottom lip out, pouting.

I stared at Anna, who had barely said two words to me all morning. She'd kept her eyes and head down since she'd climbed out of bed, and I worried she might tell Edie what was happening after school. She must have felt my gaze on her because she lifted her eyes to mine. I shook my head almost imperceptibly. Her face flushed and she dropped her eyes back to her bowl. Her whole countenance was just...sad.

Before I left for school, I gave each girl a huge hug. As I whispered a good-bye in Anna's ear, she mumbled softly against my shoulder, "I'm scared."

I squeezed her for several seconds more. "I know. It will be okay." I hated making a promise when I couldn't be sure of the outcome. I had no guarantees the plan would work. So much could go wrong, but I couldn't send Anna off to school while it gnawed at her insides all day. No ten-year-old should have to deal with anything this heavy.

Walking to school, I focused solely on my anger. I wanted to feel it. Seizing that fury was the only way I could chase away my fear. My right hand folded into a fist, and I allowed my blood to boil as I recalled finally leaving the bathroom last night with my head bandaged. Neither Mom nor Roy apologized as I walked through the living room. They didn't even acknowledge me at all.

By the time I pushed my way through the throng of students in the courtyard at school, I felt determined and ready. Jake found me at my locker, took one look at the two Band-Aids I had plastered under my bangs and asked, "What happened?"

"Wrong place, wrong time." I gave a condensed version of the story, then waved away his concerned stare. "Just more fuel for the fire."

He looked like he had something on his mind but checked his hair in my mirror before he spoke. "You ready for this afternoon?"

"Absolutely," I replied, grinning like a crazed clown.

"Are you sure you're alright? You're acting weird." Jake peered into my eyes.

"Never been better!" I lied.

It wasn't until gym class that Holly and Nicole told me they were coming home with me after school. They wanted to be there when Jake showed up to take us to Jerri's house after practice. I appreciated their desire to help. Having more people to back us up couldn't hurt, right? At the very least, they could distract my sisters from being scared.

I DRUMMED MY FINGERS on the desk as I stared at the clock above the blackboard. As the day wore on, I became more anxious and fidgety. Mr. Wilkes had assigned a chapter in our Ancient Civilizations textbook, then given us the last twenty minutes of class to read it. I skimmed over the words, no patience for it today. When

I finished, I couldn't remember a single thing I'd read, so I began again, this time taking notes to help keep my attention.

When the bell finally rang to signal the end of the day, I bolted. First out of the classroom, I had a clear hallway for only twenty feet or so before teens poured out of other rooms like water spilling over a dam. The raised decibel levels that came with crowded halls both rattled and soothed me. Rattled me because of all the what-ifs playing through my brain; soothed me because I felt safe at school. Before I started my job at Pop's, I'd always lingered after school, just to stay away from home a little longer. Now, though, there was pressing business to take care of.

A cute, wavy-haired boy leaned against my locker. He was doing his best to capture the attention of the gregarious cowgirl whose locker was two down from mine. She tended to draw a lot of attention from the boys with her collection of colorful cowgirl boots and awards as a barrel racer. Wavy-hair's attention was only on her, so I gave him a little nudge. I wanted to get my things and be on my way. A look of annoyance crossed his face before he gave me some space.

I filled my backpack with binders and textbooks, zipped it and slung it onto my back. I grabbed my small gym bag that held my stinky P. E. clothes, briefly wondering where I could wash them this weekend. I gave the door a satisfying slam and stood tapping my foot as I waited for my friends to show up. I heard Nicole's squeal before I saw her. Her height, or lack thereof, could keep her well-hidden if she chose, but her voice would give her away every time.

Nicole's laughter died out when she sidled up to me. Holly didn't say a word, just gave me a serious nod. The task at hand seemed to weigh down the air between us. I could see they felt it too. Jake showed up about ten seconds later. He pulled me into a one-armed hug and whispered, "I left a letter for my mom. Tyler will give it to her at dinner."

Before I could respond, he kissed my cheek and dashed away, promising to see us a little after five. My face felt hot, and I knew it was as red as a stop sign. At least the heavy mood had lifted but I didn't dare look at Holly or Nicole.

"Woo-hoo!" Holly giggled and squeezed my arm.

I blushed harder. I knew the teasing was coming, so I hid my face with my hands. Nicole laughed and I stole a glance at her. She raised her eyebrows, her eyes crinkling as she grinned big. Oh boy.

At the house, my friends busied themselves with math homework, but I couldn't concentrate on mine. I paced around the house, checking on I-don't-even-know-what, just going from room to room until Anna and Edie walked in from school.

Anna's face was a blank mask, but Edie was riled up. "I want my candy bar real bad," she whined as soon as she came in. When she saw my friends sitting at the kitchen table, she dropped her backpack on the floor and rushed to greet them. Holly and Nicole must have decided that was all they'd be able to get done on the math assignment, so they put it away and gave Edie their full attention. It gave me a moment to talk to Anna, who was hanging back by the door.

"How are you doing?"

She shrugged, her eyes downcast.

"Do you want to talk about it?"

She didn't look at me, just shook her head.

I put my arm around her and pulled her into a hug. "Why don't you go talk to my friends? I need to tell Edie what's going on."

Anna stared at the floor for a few seconds. Finally, she nodded and walked to the table where Nicole complimented her hair.

I grabbed Edie's hand and pulled her away with me.

"What do you want, Libby? I want to talk to your friends." Edie tried to wriggle her hand out of my grasp.

"I know. I'll try to make it quick."

Edie grumbled all the way upstairs to my room. I patted the bed, so she'd sit with me. She rolled her eyes and perched on the edge of the mattress. "Am I in trouble?"

"Nope, I just need to tell you why my friends are here today."

"Okay, why?" Edie's tone was impatient. She wanted to get back to having fun instead of listening to her boring sister jabber on.

"Nicole and Holly are helping us," I explained. "And Jake will be here later to help too."

Edie's eyes narrowed. "Helping us do what?"

"Leave."

"Huh? Leave where?"

I stared at Edie's bewildered expression and let out the breath I'd been holding and inhaled deeply. "We're going to my boss's house. We're trying to get away from Mom because of how she treats us."

"Oh. Because she whips us and beats you up?" Edie's accurate perception made her simple question sound so much more grown-up.

"Yes, exactly."

"Then she'll have to stop it, right?" the child's voice was back.

"Yes, she will."

"Okay." Edie shrugged and slid off the mattress. "Can I go back down now?"

"Sure." I was glad to have the conversation over with, but worried Edie didn't really understand the gravity of the situation.

"Hey, Edie." I trotted after her. "You have to listen and do everything I tell you, okay?"

Her back was to me, but she nodded and started down the stairs.

"Go give Anna a hug. She's having a hard time."

"Does Anna know?" Edie stopped her downward descent and glanced up at me.

"Yeah, she does." Once again, my sisters responded in completely different ways.

For the next hour, we watched TV and ate some of the snacks Mom had bought, washing them down with cold root beer and orange soda. But no matter my friend's efforts to distract us, I found myself nervously watching the clock. The closer it got to five o'clock, the sweatier my hands became, and the faster my heart pounded. I noticed Anna was also watching the time tick on. A chill ran down my arms and I shivered. I had a nagging feeling I'd forgotten something.

We were in the middle of a rowdy game of Uno when Mom and Roy walked in. I sucked in a sharp breath. *No, no, no, no!* They weren't supposed to come home until we'd gone! Mom's face turned to stone, her eyes piercing mine. Roy's grin became a smirk. I could see "Gotcha!" written all over his face. My heart went into overdrive and my breaths were short and quick. My friend's faces mirrored mine. Wide, fear-filled eyes, and dropped jaws clearly expressed our shock and panic. For me, fear so real, I thought I might even wet my pants. *Oh, what have I done? And what do I do now?* Anna pushed herself against the wall where Mom couldn't see her, her body visibly shaking. Edie scrambled to her side.

"What is going on here?" Mom asked, her voice low and hard.

I stood abruptly, scattering some of my cards on the carpet. This was all my fault. I couldn't let Mom hurt the other girls. I had to draw her attention away from them. "We were just playing a game."

"So, you're having friends over again without my permission." This time Mom's voice doubled in volume. Nicole shuddered. Mom folded her arms and glared at me. This was a standoff, and I knew I couldn't back down, no matter the cost to me.

I walked into the kitchen, my legs shaking, and leaned against the sink. Mom and Roy followed me just as I hoped. "Well, it's Friday." *That's lame, Libby.* My tongue felt tied in knots. If I sounded stupid to myself, I certainly sounded that way to Mom. My brain was too addled to come up with a better reason to be playing games with friends without having asked if they could come over.

Roy smirked harder if that was possible. He kept turning his head to look between me and Mom.

"Oh, really?" Mom drawled, sarcasm stretching the words out.

Roy must have been ready for the action to start. He came closer, reminding me of a cat sneaking up on an unsuspecting bird. He rested his hands on his hips, and his expression was more menacing than I'd seen yet. Holly and Nicole peeked into the kitchen behind Mom, momentarily distracting me from Roy's approach. Holly pointed upstairs and then they disappeared. I heard them on the stairs, presumably going up to get our bags. We hadn't even brought them down yet because we were waiting for Jake to come. Dumb move on my part.

"I thought you were supposed to be at work," Mom went on. "Instead, I find you throwing a party." A party? That was an exaggeration. And wasn't she supposed to be at work, too?

Mom stepped up next to Roy, effectively trapping me in place. There was no way I could get around either of them. I hoped Anna and Edie had sense enough to leave the house, but I was worried Anna might be frozen with fear.

"I wasn't scheduled to work today. I thought *you* were supposed to be at work."

"Of course you did. That's why you thought you could throw a party." Another step closer. Roy mimicked Mom, down to the cocky glare. It was easy to be cocky when they held all the power. Roy's hands clenched into fists, itching to hit something. Someone. Me.

"Besides, I don't answer to you, Libby. But you do answer to me." Quick as a snake, Mom darted forward. Her fingers dug into my right arm, and she yanked my hair back with her other hand, pushing her body against mine. The edge of the countertop bit into my lower back.

"You will pay for disobeying me!" She spat the words in my face through clenched teeth. Her breath was hot on my cheek. I tried to turn away, but she yanked my hair again. A small smile appeared on her face when I shrieked. She enjoyed this, the confrontation, the violence, the power over someone younger. It was how she dealt with situations she didn't like. Add alcohol to that and everything blew to pieces.

"Go find my belt, Roy. It's in my closet."

I heard Grandma's warning in my head, grateful I had listened. But how was I supposed to get out of this? *Grandma, if you can hear me, I need help!*

I knew what was coming. I tried to focus on my breathing, but Mom dug her fingers into my bicep even harder. Every muscle in my body tensed. Suddenly, she released my arm and swung her fist at my face. I ducked to the right, and her left hand loosened its grip on my hair. Mom's knuckles hit the side of my neck. I groaned.

"I can't find it!" Roy yelled.

Mom tightened her grip in my hair and muttered, "That imbecile."

She yanked my arm and threw me off balance. Then she pulled me towards her bedroom. What would she do when she couldn't find the belt?

"It should be on the shelf, Roy! Find it now!"

"It ain't here! That's what I'm telling you!"

Mom pulled me into the room. For a split second, she looked unsure of her next move. To get near the closet to search for the belt, she would have to release me. The belt must have been more important than hanging on to me because she let go of my arm. I took off running, slamming the bedroom door behind me.

"Grab her, Roy!" Mom screamed.

As I passed by the back door, I thought I saw movement. I paused. Should I go out that way? No, I couldn't leave Edie and

Anna. The door moved again, and Jake popped his head in. Seeing me, his eyes widened. "What's going on? I heard screaming."

I must have looked like a crazed lunatic, but Jake didn't hesitate to enter. Roy threw Mom's door open, and it slammed into the wall. He lumbered toward us, the tendons in his neck popping out. Jake pushed me toward the living room.

"The girls," I said, breathless. But Jake wasn't looking at me. He was watching Roy.

"Anna, Edie!" I scanned the living room. No one. I didn't know if they'd left the house or were still upstairs.

"Libby!" Edie's voice rang down the stairway. Why hadn't they left yet?

I felt bad leaving Jake to fend for himself, but I had to get my sisters out of the house. I pounded up the stairs. Edie ran to my room and a few seconds later, I burst in after her. The bags we'd packed were sitting by my bed. Nicole was consoling a sobbing Anna on the bed. Holly had pulled back a panel of flimsy curtain and was peeking out the window. She jumped and turned, startled by my entrance.

"What are you guys doing? Why didn't you leave?" My words made Anna cry harder. I felt more frantic than I'd ever felt in my life. Everything was going wrong.

From downstairs, the sounds of a fight pulled my attention away. Yelling, accompanied by banging, and the crash of something breaking drew me back to the top of the stairs. "Jake!"

No response. Just more grunts and groans and Mom screaming profanities.

"Jake!" I screamed again from the hall. I hated not knowing what was happening down there. My heart hammered in my chest, fear threatening to crush me.

Mom screamed, "You're gonna pay for that!"

Pounding footsteps followed by Jake hurtling himself up the stairs sent my nerves through the roof.

"Oh my gosh! Jake!" He had blood on his upper lip and his eye was puffy and red. What had Roy done to him?

"Go, Libby, go!" Jake panted. I shot back into my room, and he bounded through the door a second later. The yelling from Mom and Roy got louder, closer.

"They're coming up here!"

I slammed the door behind us. Jake was already pushing my dresser in front of the door. I hopped out of his way, stubbing my toe on the wood. Thank goodness for Grandma's heavy oak furniture. I thought we were safe until I saw the door open an inch. Oh, man, Roy was sure strong.

Jake threw his body against the dresser. "Help me!"

I hadn't noticed what my friends and sisters were doing while we barricaded the door, but I whipped around, frantic. "Come on, guys! We can't let them get in!"

There was a jumble of movement as Holly, Nicole and Edie jumped forward to reinforce our blockade. Anna stayed on the bed, shaking her head back and forth. Then she clapped her hands over her eyes. My sister was traumatized, but I couldn't comfort her until we got out of this mess. Out of this room. But I had no idea how that was going to happen.

"Open this door!" Mom shrieked. Fists pounding on the door were followed by resounding bangs that could have only been Roy throwing his body against it. Jake gritted his teeth and pushed harder. His red face accentuated the vein throbbing near his hairline. Holly leaned on the dresser and pushed with her back and legs. I turned to check on Anna.

Anna was using her feet to scoot herself closer to the wall. She had uncovered her eyes, only to clamp her hands over her ears. I didn't blame her one bit. The screaming and cursing from the other side of the door was harsh and unnerving. Mom sounded like a madwoman.

I wanted to console Anna but didn't dare leave my position. The four of us crammed together against the dresser. Edie had one hand against the dresser as she had managed only to squeeze her arm in between me and Nicole. Still, she pushed with all her might.

"Hey, Nic, could you go to Anna? Edie can take your place. I think we'll be okay." I nodded toward the bed.

Nicole jumped onto the bed and wrapped her arms around my sister. I should have been doing that, but I couldn't do two things at once. And keeping the crazies out took precedence right now.

"Shh, it's okay," Nicole said as she rocked Anna back and forth. Her worried eyes met mine and communicated what we both knew. We were not okay. Roy was bound to break through the door soon. He seemed as determined to get in as we were to keep him out.

"We have to get out of here," Holly muttered. "This is nuts."

A stab of guilt pierced my gut. "I'm sorry I dragged you into this."

Holly shook her head but didn't meet my gaze, so I focused on Jake. He had more injuries than I'd first realized. His arm sported a few raised welts and some scratches that were bleeding a bit. The blood on his upper lip seemed to have come from his nose.

"Jake, are you hurt bad? What did they do to you?" I felt those pangs of guilt again. He had bravely placed himself between me and danger and was injured because of it. I felt a surge of love and appreciation for this boy.

"I'm fine, Libby," he grunted.

Boom! Boom! Boom! The pounding continued, and my head began to pound right along with it. I prayed Mom would lose her voice soon. Her screams frayed my fragile nerves. I wished there was a way to get to a phone.

"What are we going to do, guys? The only way out of here is through the window."

"Then we'll go through the window," Jake replied.

Anna heard Jake's solution and squeaked out a protest. Edie, on the other hand, liked the idea. "I want to go out the window!"

Holly, Nicole and I exchanged a look. Sudden silence on the other side of the door drew our attention back to it. No one spoke. No one moved. And, as if our muscles were in-sync with our thoughts, everyone relaxed. If no one was out there, we could stop pushing.

"Do you think we could get out the window?" Jake asked.

I stepped over to the glass and peeked out, trying to picture dropping two stories to the sidewalk or small patch of grass below. We'd probably break all our bones.

"We'll need some way to lower us down or we're gonna get hurt."

"Let's tie the sheets together," Holly suggested.

"Do it," Jake said.

A sudden movement outside drew my attention back to the window. Roy was entering the shed. Where was Mom?

"Roy's going into the shed," I announced.

Nicole scooted off the bed and joined me at the window.

"You can't stay in there forever!" Mom screamed from outside the door. We all jumped, and I scrambled back to Jake's side. Mom must have been waiting to see if we'd open the door to leave the room. A few loud thumps followed her outburst. My pulse ratcheted up again. Jake's biceps tightened as he resumed pushing against the dresser.

"What is he doing in there?" Nicole leaned toward the window, peering out the glass.

"Hey, I'll need help with the sheets," Holly said. She helped Anna off the bed and gathered the quilt from the top, handing the bunched fabric to her. Anna huddled in the corner with her face pressed into the quilt while Holly and Edie made quick work of stripping the sheets off the mattress. Nicole helped Holly tie the sheets together. They were so quick about it; I wondered if they'd done it before.

I motioned Anna to come to me. She threw herself into my arms as I pressed my back against the dresser, employing Holly's technique. I hugged her tight but said nothing.

Nicole must have heard a noise from outside because she looked out the window again. "Hey, guys, he's got a hammer." She jerked around with a petrified stare.

A hammer? Where had he found that? I thought back to the toolbox I'd hidden yesterday. I had looked for the hammer but forgotten to go back to the shed this afternoon to look in the bright light of day. My gut clenched tight, and I felt as if I might vomit. There could be only one reason he wanted the hammer.

My panicked eyes sought out Jake's. His gaze flashed with fury, but underneath I saw the uncertainty.

"We have to hurry!" I kept my voice low. We couldn't alert Mom and Roy to what we were doing.

"Who's going first?" Holly asked. She and Nicole carried the sheet rope to the windowsill. Nicole cranked open the window and pushed the screen out. It fell to the sidewalk with a clatter.

"Drop the bags, too," I reminded them. "Anna, hand them to Nic."

Anna dropped the quilt and took two suitcases to Nicole, who flung them down onto the grass. I was happy they didn't bust open or break. My duffel bag followed.

Bang! The slam of the hammer against the door elicited a scream from all five girls. Jake's face turned almost purple. The rage and determination on his face seemed to radiate through his body as he used all his strength to push against the dresser.

"We're coming in, you little brats!" Roy yelled. Bang! Bang!

"Edie, you go first," I instructed. "Hold tight and don't let go until you're close to the ground." Worried for her safety, but knowing speed was imperative, I asked Jake if I could help at the window.

"Go," he said. He wiped the sheen from his brow, causing his damp hair to stand on end.

"When you get down, run to Mrs. Judd's house and tell her to call the police," I instructed Edie.

Bang! Bang! The hammer thudded into the wood again. I knew Roy wouldn't stop until he broke through.

"Open this door!" Mom screamed.

I glanced at Jake. We had left him to the wolves.

Edie bounced, her eyes excited. To her this was all one big adventure. The pounding at the door paused, then resumed.

"Wrap this around your hands." Holly handed Edie the sheet rope.

Edie wrapped the sheet around one arm, then gripped with both hands. I hoisted her onto the sill. I held my breath as her legs dropped over the ledge. If she fell, I'd never forgive myself. "Please hold on tight!" I said. Holly leaned her head out the window to watch Edie's descent and I braced my feet against the wall to counter Edie's weight.

"I need a little help here," I grunted. Holly wrapped her hands around the sheets, relieving me of some of the burden. I heard Anna's sniffle and Nicole's soothing tones in between the hammer blows to the door.

"Oh no!" Jake gasped.

"We've got you now!" Roy yelled. He sounded closer. Had he broken through? I felt Anna leaning against my back. I couldn't turn to her until Edie touched the ground.

"She's a couple feet above the sidewalk," Holly informed me. Then she called out the window, "Jump down! Hurry. Go to your neighbor's and call 911!"

The sudden slack in the sheets made me lose my balance. I quickly righted myself and gazed out the window. Edie was on her knees on the pavement. She sprang up, waved wildly at us and took off running around the side of the house.

"Someone help me!" Jake yelled.

Holly and I jumped to either side of him. All the muscles in Jake's arms strained with the effort of pushing against the dresser. I gasped when I saw that Roy had made a jagged hole in the door and was reaching his arm through it, right toward Jake's neck. Jake twisted away. Roy's grasping fingers instead caught a lock of Holly's long red hair, and he yanked hard. Holly shrieked, lost her balance and fell into the dresser on her ribs as she was pulled forward. Her hand flew to her scalp, and she pulled back on the tresses Roy had gripped in his fist. Roy's laugh must have lit a fire in Holly. With her free arm, she reached up and dug her manicured nails all the way down his arm. Roy yelped and released her hair, pulling his arm back through the hole. He directed his verbal tirade at her, and she smirked. "Serves you right, you ugly creep!"

Roy slammed his body against the door, and it opened a bit, scooting us back a couple of inches.

"Libby, get Anna out," Jake said. "We'll be alright."

I was reluctant to leave his side, knowing it would make it easier for Mom and Roy to get in. But he was right. The girls' safety was the most important thing right now.

I pulled Anna to the window while she protested.

"Anna." I gave her a little shake.

She looked at me with watery, red eyes.

"Go to Mrs. Judd's."

She nodded and swiped at her eyes. Nicole took the sheets in hand and shoved them at Anna. She barely took hold of them.

"Anna, please stop crying! You have to hold on tight. Are you ready?"

There was a commotion behind me. Jake, Mom and Roy were all yelling. I glanced over my shoulder at the dresser that was rocking back and forth.

"Hurry, Anna!"

She shook her head, but I insisted. "We have to get you out now!"

I boosted her onto the sill. Nicole wrapped the sheets around her arms. I planted a quick kiss on her head. It hurt my heart to see her so afraid. "You can do this! You are so brave."

She seemed resigned to her fate and tightened her grip. As she went over the ledge, she cried out. Her weight, more than that of Edie's, pulled against me. I had to crouch in a squat under the sill to keep from being pulled out the window. Nicole crouched behind me, her breaths coming in quick puffs on the back of my head. I was already perspiring, but new beads of sweat broke out on my face as I strained to release the sheet a little at a time without dropping my sister.

"I can't see how close she is," I panted.

Nicole edged up and peeked over the sill. "Uh, about four more feet, I think."

We continued to lower Anna, then as we felt the release, I heard the most welcome sound. Sirens. Police sirens!

I jumped up and peeked out the window. Anna was running away from the house, her legs wobbling like a new colt's.

Nicole and I flung ourselves back against the dresser. Mom caught sight of me through the much bigger hole and spouted profanity-laced insults. When she took a breath, I heard the sirens again. It sounded like two of them. Buckley wasn't a huge town, and we probably didn't have more than six cop cars for our entire law enforcement.

"Hear that?" I asked my friends.

A smile broke out on Nic's face. "Edie did it!"

Edie would be so glad to know she was a hero. A wish come true for her, I'm sure. I could just hear her during show-and-tell at school.

Roy stuck the hammer through the hole and aimed his blow at Jake. Holly and I yelped out warning cries and Jake jumped back, releasing the power he'd been applying to the dresser. The hammer came down hard on the oak where Jake's fingers had been moments before. Roy's maniacal laugh sent a chill down my spine.

Out of nowhere, my mind lit up with an idea. I whispered it to Jake and Holly, and we all ducked below the smaller drawer at the top of the dresser. I pulled the horseshoe-shaped handle and eased the drawer completely out. I dumped the socks on the floor and picked the drawer up with both hands. Roy was pounding away at the top of the dresser, trying in vain to reach fingers or arms, whatever he could find. I stood and swung the drawer down onto his arm. He screamed, then pulled his arm back through the hole.

"You little witch! I'll get you for that!"

Mom asked Roy what happened, then peered through the hole, the rage in her eyes burning bright. They were so caught up in their anger, in their quest, I didn't know if they hadn't heard the blare of sirens approaching or if they just didn't care.

"Libby!" Mom screamed. "I will kill you when I get my hands on you! You won't live to see another day!"

She disappeared and a moment later, the hammer flew through the hole. Grateful I was still holding the drawer, I used it as a shield and blocked the blow. The hammer bounced off the top of the dresser and fell to the floor.

Outside, shrill sirens announced the arrival of the police. I heard car doors slam and male voices yelling.

"Ah, they're here," Nicole whispered, her voice laced with relief. Jake exhaled a big "whoosh" and wiped his face on his shirt. It was already dirtied with his blood, and maybe Roy's too. I didn't know. It became eerily silent on the other side of the door. I hoped Mom and

Roy weren't sneaking out of the house through her bedroom window or the back door.

Bam! Bam! A cop pounded hard at the front door.

"Police! Open up!"

The four of us stared at each other. I could see the question on their faces. Should we leave the room and go to the door? Would the cops leave if we didn't come down? And where were Roy and Mom?

"I'll go," I whispered.

Jake shook his head. "No, I will."

"You've done more than enough," I argued. Jake's eye had swollen so much, his eye was just a slit. I couldn't risk him being injured more.

"We'll go together then. Holly and Nic can wait until we get down there and we'll let the cop know they're here."

Holly scowled and folded her arms but said nothing. Nicole seemed relieved not to go with us and busied herself by picking up my socks and placing them back in the little drawer. Not that it mattered.

The four of us scooted the dresser ever so slowly over the worn carpet, away from the door. There was more pounding on the front door. "Police," the same guy bellowed again.

Jake motioned for me to let him go first, in case Mom and Roy were still there waiting for us to come out. I clung to Jake's shoulder so he could be my guide while I kept a lookout for Mom and Roy. I figured they were hiding somewhere since the police were still at the door. We tiptoed out of the room and to the stairs, my senses on high alert.

Jake made it about two stairs down, when a flash of movement registered to my right. Mom, her expression crazed, shot toward me from my sisters' room. Her fist was raised, and in her eyes, I saw pure rage.

"Ahhh!" I screamed at the top of my lungs. "Help! Help!"

Jake picked up his speed down the staircase and I stumbled forward as Mom's fist landed on my back. My face hit the wall as momentum and gravity took over. I tumbled down, headfirst. Jake somehow caught hold of my shoulders and held them tight.

"Put your hands up! Now!"

I glanced from my upside-down position at the policeman. His hair was a sunny yellow blond. He wore a dark blue City of Buckley uniform, his gun belt empty. The gun was in his hands, and it was pointed at my mother.

I couldn't see if she obeyed his orders, but she tossed back her own. "Shut up! I haven't done anything!"

"Hands up! Now!"

I dared not breathe or move a muscle, even as uncomfortable as I was in my position. Blood was rushing to my head and my back ached from Mom's blow and hitting the stairs. At least there was carpet to soften my fall. The cop came halfway up the steps and motioned for Jake and me to move to the side. It took a few seconds to get my hands under me to rotate my body out of his path. Jake pressed himself flat against the wall and the cop stomped by.

I hazarded a glance at Mom. She was wringing her hands together but as the policeman moved closer and again commanded her to raise her hands, she slowly put them up, a defiant glare frozen on her face.

I scooted on my butt down the stairs, not daring to rise. My hands were shaking, and I didn't trust that my legs were steady either. I wasn't sure where we should go. Outside? Or just sit on the couch and wait? I shrugged at Jake, and he reached down to help me stand.

From the direction of Mom's bedroom came a scuffling sound. Another male, this one with a deep gruff voice, yelled, "Drop the knife and put your hands up!"

It had to be Roy he was talking to. I stared at Jake. Now Roy had a knife?

I jumped and squealed as a third cop, this one younger, with reddish hair, kicked open the back door and rushed inside with his gun raised. How many cops were there? He made eye contact with me, and I pointed toward Mom's room. He disappeared just as a crash of breaking glass came from Mom's room. Someone must have broken the window or the overhead light. There was more scuffling, some cursing and a loud bang. Jake nudged me toward the front door. He had the right idea. It would be less dangerous outside the house at this point.

I paused to look up the stairs. Blond Cop had placed handcuffs on Mom and held her arm, keeping her right at his side as they began their descent.

"Move it," he ordered.

Mom's eye fixed on me. I don't know what I expected to see, maybe a little remorse or some sense of responsibility or humility. Instead, her gaze was filled with hatred. Her lower jaw thrust forward defiantly.

"You'll pay for this!" she seethed.

"Quiet!" Blond Cop barked. He marched Mom down the stairs and jerked her toward the kitchen. He hooked his foot around a chair leg and pulled it away from the table. He ordered Mom to sit and pulled his gun out of his holster as he called out to the other cops in Mom's room.

Gruff cop responded that they were bringing the other suspect out. "Get up!" he bellowed. There was a slam and then shuffling as Roy appeared, disheveled and defiant, his hands also cuffed behind his back. Gruff Cop appeared behind Roy. His salt-and-pepper hair was thick and perfectly combed. He had huge caterpillar eyebrows which hooded his eyes. His scowl said it all.

Young Cop followed and opened the back door. It all felt so surreal. It was like watching a scene from a movie. I couldn't tear my eyes away.

Jake nudged me again. "Let's go outside."

But I couldn't move. My heart felt heavy. It didn't matter that my mom was angry and unrepentant. I felt guilty for widening the breach between us, but also scared to death of what she might do now. I stood in a trance. Jake must have read something in my expression, because he patted my shoulder and waited.

It's my fault. I did this. Our family would never be the same again. And I was to blame.

"Libby," Jake whispered, "you did it." He smiled down at me.

It was enough to snap me out of my spell. Of course it wasn't my fault things had ended this way. It was because of Mom's actions it had come to this. No matter what she said or wanted me to believe, this had never been and would never be *my* fault.

Mom and Roy were escorted out the back door and Jake and I hurried through the front. The first thing I saw was a fourth policeman standing straight down the walk, away from the house. Next to him, waiting on the grass, stood Edie, Anna, and Mrs. Judd. Off to the right, across the street, Jerri stood by her white Pontiac, her hands clasped under her chin. Jake's parents, Gary and Colleen, waited beside her. Gary had his arm around Colleen's shoulders. Upon seeing Jake emerge from the house, Colleen cried out and covered her mouth with her hands. Several small groups of bystanders gathered across the street, but other than seeing them there, I paid no attention to them.

I sprinted forward, eager to reach my sisters, and they ran to greet me. Tears threatened as I hugged them both. I felt so drained, I dropped onto my knees and held them tight. Sidewalk Cop came to us and asked us to move away from the house until they were sure no one else was coming out.

"Oh, my friends..." I began.

At the same time, Jake said, "Our friends are still in there."

The sound of slamming car doors drew our attention to the side of the house. Gruff Cop appeared and told Sidewalk Cop they had the suspects and were taking them to the police station. Sidewalk Cop was to begin taking statements and someone would return to help him.

As the police cars crunched over the gravel drive, Anna looked away. Edie and I watched as they turned out in front of us. There was no glare from Mom this time. She kept her head faced forward. I briefly wondered if Mom had ever been in a police car before or if it was her first time. I wondered what was going through her mind. Roy, on the other hand, even went so far as to bare his teeth at us. I flipped my head away. I hoped I would never see him again. My musings were interrupted by a soft hand resting on my arm.

I stood upright again, feeling sore and weary. Mrs. Judd looked so fragile. I took her aged hand in mine, recognizing how frail she was by the softness of her grip. Small veins crisscrossed her prominent bones and splotchy skin. I gazed into her eyes, which were as full of tears as mine were. Hers were filled with sympathy. I hoped she could see the gratitude in mine.

"Thank you."

"For what, dear? I didn't do anything except listen to your sister and call the po-lice." She emphasized the first syllable of the word.

"Well, you saved us once. And now you've helped do it again."

Mrs. Judd bowed her head and gave it a slow shake. "No, actually, I failed you. I stopped keeping a close eye on you all those years ago, thinking I'd done my part. Maybe if I'd been paying attention, you all wouldn't be in this mess."

"It isn't your fault," I insisted, wrapping my arms around her.

Sidewalk Cop interrupted. "Alright, I'm sorry, but we need to start taking statements." I took a good look at him now. He looked like a 1970's transplant: long dark sideburns, longish hair, a bushy mustache. He had a no-nonsense attitude.

Nicole and Holly called out to us as they ran out the front door. Jake and I had gotten distracted by the police cars driving by and hadn't gone back for them, but in reality, probably only two minutes had passed since we'd gotten outside ourselves.

Sidewalk Cop sighed. "There *are* more. This is going to be a long night."

"Is everyone okay?" Holly called. Her long legs covered the ground between us faster than Nic's shorter ones. Her hair was the messiest I'd ever seen it. It didn't even look that bad after gym class. Nicole still looked put together. I had no idea how she'd done that. I didn't even want to look in the mirror to see how I had fared.

"We're alright." I heard the emotion in my voice as I hugged Holly, then Nicole. Anna stood next to Mrs. Judd, looking sad and lost while Edie asked the officer if she could see his gun. I shivered as I thought of the guns I'd seen pulled earlier. I spotted Jake across the street with his parents. He was talking fast and gesturing with his hands. Colleen held her hands to her cheeks, her eyes wide and her mouth open in an expression of disbelief. Gary had his hand on his hip, his stance a bit aggressive, as if he wanted to bolt into action. His mouth was pursed, his brows angled down. From the looks of it, Jake was in some trouble, no matter his injuries or his heroics.

I sighed. Not ten feet from the Evans family, Jerri waited alone, her arms wrapped around herself in a hug. She leaned against the hood of her car, staring at the ground.

"Jerri," I called.

She jerked her head up and when our eyes connected, I saw relief in hers. I waved her over. Nicole and Holly still had hold of me, but I focused just on Jerri for a moment. She checked for traffic, then rushed across the street, arms extended.

As her arms embraced me, I finally relaxed. This all felt like some crazy dream. Actually, nightmare was a better word for it. And yet, as much as I wanted not to believe it, I knew it was real, and my tears spilled over.

"You're okay, Libby," Jerri said as she rocked me back and forth. "You're safe now."

Little arms wrapped around my waist and Jerri chuckled. I wiped my eyes to see Anna's arms around me and Edie's wrapped around Jerri's waist from behind. Although Jerri also had tears in her eyes, they twinkled behind the moisture.

"I'm sorry, ma'am," Sidewalk Cop interrupted our reunion. "Everyone is going to have to make a statement, so we need to get going."

"Jake!" I yelled. His mom was inspecting his face, fretting over the purple welts and bruises that were going to look a lot worse tomorrow. His dad was gazing at the clouds above, hand still on his hip. I couldn't tell if he was angry or upset, or both. I owed them an apology for dragging their son into a dangerous situation.

"We have to give statements," I called.

He nodded, then hugged Colleen. Before he could run across the street, Gary caught his arm and pulled him back in an embrace. It lasted so long, the cop had to call Jake over. I felt a twinge of jealousy, wishing I had grown up with that kind of love.

Sidewalk Cop began barking instructions. We were to wait on the lawn to be questioned either by him or any other officers who showed up.

"Can they come with us?" I gestured to Jake's parents.

"Why not?" he smirked. "The more the merrier." He herded us up to the porch.

Jake's parents came to the lawn and stood in conversation with Jerri. We moved near the house and plopped onto the grass. I wanted to lay back and close my eyes. Jake took longer to sit down. He had to be exhausted.

"Thank you," I whispered, searching his face for some emotion. "You've been my best friend for so long and I couldn't have...no, *wouldn't* have been able to do it without you. You saved us up there."

Jake's head dropped, his face flushing red. I smiled, his blush secretly delighted me. He didn't say anything until the redness disappeared.

"You're my best friend too, you know. There was no way I was going to let anything happen to you."

He gave me a hug, and I giggled as he released me. "Your hair is crazy!"

Jake looked horrified and ran his fingers through his wild locks. It did nothing to tame it, and I shook my head. He shrugged and let his hand drop, right on top of mine. I glanced down at our hands and back up at Jake. His smile was mimicked by Nicole, who'd seen the entire exchange.

I heaved a cleansing sigh and rested my head on Jake's shoulder. Life had been difficult for a long time and today's events had been terrifying and stressful. I was glad it was over, at least that part of it. *Grandma, we did it. We got away.* I didn't expect a response, but a light breeze tickled my hair and nose. I briefly caught a whiff of roses, just like the scent Grandma used to wear. Of course, I couldn't see her, but she was near. I think she'd been here watching over us all along.

24
Friday, April 8, 1988
Later that day

A few policemen returned to the house to take care of business. They took pictures and went in and out of the house with bags and notebooks. The yellow "Do Not Cross" tape I'd only seen on TV was placed over the doors until the investigation concluded. Two reporters from our local newspaper, the *Millsburg Monitor*, appeared out of the growing crowd and began asking questions. Sidewalk Cop, who I learned was named Officer Shane, put a stop to that real quick. He told them to leave and if they wanted a statement, they'd have to contact the police chief. The nerdy, young guy with Clark Kent glasses and the lady with graying hair and sagging nylons split up and milled about the bystanders, occasionally writing in their pocket-sized notebooks.

Instead of the crowd diminishing like I'd first thought, it grew. I wondered if people had been listening to police scanners and decided to come check out the show for themselves. I saw several people from school, and I suddenly felt self-conscious. Jake waved at a few people and seemed relatively unfazed by the attention. Holly could see the attention was unsettling to me and suggested I turn my back and ignore them.

Officer Shane must have decided there were too many distractions, so we relocated to the police station downtown. Jake rode with his parents. Edie wanted to ride in Officer Shane's car, so

Holly gamely went along with her. Nicole, Anna and I rode with Jerri.

At the station, Holly and Nic called their parents to explain what had happened. From the high-pitched response I heard coming from the phone receiver, Nicole's mom was very upset. She had to leave work early to come to the station to be with her daughter. Holly's parents were worried, but calm, like Jake's parents. The girls were able to leave quickly, but they were the only ones.

A petite woman wearing a flowy, turquoise skirt and a pale-yellow blouse and yellow flats marched into the police station. Her flaxen hair was twisted into a bun and her face looked pinched. She looked to be all-business, and her voice held a commanding tone. She introduced herself as Rita Manning and explained she would be our case worker. She interviewed my sisters separately, talking to Edie first. I spent almost an hour answering her questions and asking a few of my own. She wanted to know everything about life at home, when the abuse started and why I never told anyone. When I told her my father's name and that he'd died in a military accident, she wrote on her notepad with furious speed. Something about that made me nervous, so I hurried to add that Nolan Rigby was my sister's father and I wanted to call him. She agreed that I could once she and the police spoke with him. After dismissing me, she asked Jerri to come into the small room she'd taken over to speak with her.

Jake got called back to talk with Sgt. Killpack while I was with Miss Manning, so I didn't have any opportunity to talk to him. I sat back down in the hard plastic chair that was welded to a metal support, leaving no way to scoot to a different spot. Jake's parents watched me from across the waiting area. Their faces looked serious and although I wanted to apologize to them, I couldn't bring myself to do it.

Finally, I was taken to another small room with Detective Sealy. The room was also bare except for a desk and two chairs, which were of the same hard plastic as the others in the waiting area, except they could be moved. Detective Sealy must have been trained to put people at ease, because once he started talking, I felt my heart calm. His sharp eyes seemed to soften as he introduced himself and told me he'd be recording the conversation. He asked about my family, how and when the abuse began, what made me want to get help now. It wasn't easy. I definitely got emotional. It was difficult to admit what went on in our home, because honestly, it was embarrassing. Detective Sealy assured me Mom's actions weren't my fault and commended me on my courage, but deep down, I was worried about Mom. I asked Detective Sealy where she was, because I'd fully expected to see her at the station but hadn't. He said she'd been taken to Millsburg for questioning. When I asked what was going to happen to her, he said the judge would have to decide. Back in the waiting room, I discovered Jake and his parents had gone. Jerri must have sensed my disappointment. "You can call him tomorrow, Libby," she'd said with a pat on my back.

Jerri said that while I was being questioned, the girls complained they were hungry, so she ran to Pop's for some food. She returned a short time later with grapes and pretzels, and cinnamon rolls from the bakery. I was glad they'd saved me some, because I was famished. As soon as I finished eating, Anna curled up in the hard chair next to me and fell asleep using my lap as her pillow.

When Miss Manning finished talking to Nolan on the phone, she crooked her finger at me. I had to wake Anna so I could get out of my seat. My body ached from sitting on the hard chairs all night and my heart hammered behind my ribs. I don't know why I was as nervous to talk to Nolan as I'd been to talk to the cops and Miss Manning. I wondered if he would blame me or would be angry that I hadn't found a way to tell him sooner, before it had really gotten out of control. But from the first word, he was so kind. Just like I remembered him being when I was young.

"Libby, are you alright?"

I heard the stress in his voice and imagined him pacing as we spoke.

"Yes, I'm okay. So are Edie and Anna."

Nolan blew a loud breath into the receiver. "I'm so glad. I..." He paused and cleared his throat. When he spoke again, his voice shook. "I'm so sorry. If I had known, I would have gotten you girls out of there so fast."

"I didn't know how to reach you. Mom didn't want me talking to you, so she kept all your contact information hidden from me."

"I realize that now. I always asked to speak to you when I called the girls, but she wouldn't allow it. I'm sure she wanted to make sure you didn't rat her out." There was a hard edge in his tone.

"You wanted to talk to me?" This was news to me.

"Of course! But Donna always said you weren't my 'real' child, so it wasn't going to happen. I think she got annoyed that I kept asking."

My chest tightened. Nolan called every Sunday night to talk to my sisters, but I was usually sent from the room or put to work, so I rarely heard any of the conversation. I did know Mom sat right next to the girls as they talked, because Anna had told me. It was exactly why I'd never asked one of them to tattle on Mom.

"Listen, Libby, I'm catching a flight out there tomorrow. I've spoken with the police and Miss Manning, so they know I'm coming. I understand your boss, Jerri, wants you girls to stay at her house tonight and I've agreed. So, you go get some rest and I'll see you tomorrow, okay?"

I handed the receiver back to Miss Manning, who leaned forward as if she wanted to tell me a secret. "Just so you know, Libby, I think you are very brave." She gave me the first smile I'd seen from her all night, then she called my sisters in to talk to Nolan.

Edie jumped up and down when she heard Nolan was coming, but Anna cried. At first, I thought it was from relief. Turns out, she thought she was in trouble. At that point, I knew she was too tired to deal with anything more. I hugged her, explained that Nolan was coming to take care of us, and we joined Jerri, who loaded us in her Pontiac.

Jerri chattered the entire drive to her house. She seemed determined to take our minds off the ordeal we'd just survived and distract us with what we could look forward to at her house. She seemed excited and even after spending a draining evening at the police station, was as bubbly and energetic as ever. I was surprised though, when instead of staying in the main part of town, she steered the vehicle out toward the pond.

I had imagined she and Reed lived in a small, older home like mine. Most of the town was filled with homes like mine, except for a few new neighborhoods that had been popping up in the new part of town, so it was a fair assumption. The new neighborhoods included larger homes, some split-levels, some two-story, and most with brick facades and large garages. Jake's house was in one of those neighborhoods. His family had built a home there when their large, growing family outgrew their older home a few years back. But when Jerri bypassed the new neighborhoods, I was confused.

"Where exactly do you live?"

"Just a bit further. Now, when we get there, you younger girls will have the guest room to sleep in. Libby, you'll have the couch. I do have one more room, but since Nolan and his wife are coming tomorrow, I've invited them to stay with us, and they'll need that room."

I nodded. I didn't care where I slept. I just wanted to crash. Even the floor sounded fine to me. I knew I'd be out as soon as I closed my eyes.

Whatever my expectations had been for Jerri's house, the real thing was not it at all. I still had no idea where we were going, but soon Jerri slowed and turned down a narrow lane that was surrounded by large trees. There were no streetlights, so I couldn't see anything except darkness. A gentle curve in the lane put us directly in front of an oversized, white farmhouse with a picket fence that wrapped around the yard. Every light in the house seemed to be on and it looked so welcoming, it made me want to cry.

"Is this a castle?" Edie squealed.

Jerri laughed. "No, no. Just home sweet home."

We spilled out of the car and Jerri opened the trunk so we could retrieve our bags. The front door opened, and a large figure filled the doorway. Although I knew it was Reed, I couldn't make out any of his features with the light shining behind him.

"About time you made it home!" his baritone voice boomed.

Jerri laughed as we filed up the steps behind her to the wraparound porch. I was with Edie on this one. This house did have a dreamy, castle-like feel. Reed hugged Jerri and stepped back, "Glad you're home, woman!" he said.

Reed greeted my sisters, then turned to me. He wrapped his large hand around mine and gave it a firm shake, his dark eyes searching mine. He had thick, almost-black hair and the beginnings of a beard. He wore jeans that were held up by a belt with an oversized buckle.

"How do you do, Libby?" Reed's deep voice was full of warmth. His eyes seemed to scrutinize my face. I felt exposed somehow but couldn't figure out why he looked at me so closely.

Jerri moved beside him. "You see it too, don't you?" she asked.

His nod was solemn. "I do."

"See what?" Whatever it was, I just needed the staring to stop. I felt caught in the spotlight and it made me uncomfortable.

"Your eyes are just like my mother's eyes," Reed replied.

Okay, that was a tiny bit weird, but I was too tired to analyze his response. I'd think about it tomorrow.

Jerri must have seen my weariness. She gave us a little push past the front room. "Let's get you girls to bed."

When I tucked Anna and Edie into the cozy guest room bed, Anna hugged me tightly and didn't want to let go. I assured her I wasn't going anywhere, and we could talk in the morning. The last thing I remember was falling onto the plush green couch in the same clothes I'd worn all day, too tired to change into my pajamas.

25
Saturday, April 9, 1988

Jerri woke me around seven o'clock. My body wanted to rebel, but she reminded me I had to return to the police station. A hot shower helped perk me up. In the car, Jerri handed me a leftover cinnamon roll to eat on the way back to town. She dropped me off and promised to come back for me later.

Detective Willis and Sgt. Killpack were kind and thorough. They took me back to the house and had me walk them through recent events. Two more policemen were also there, finishing with their pictures and evidence-gathering. When we returned to the police department, Sgt. Killpack took me to his office. The room was small with stark white paint and a bulletin board covered in random papers. At least this room had a window. Sgt. Killpack asked why I'd never told anyone about my mom's abuse. I knew it was his job to ask, but I turned it around on him.

"Well, if you were threatened regularly with your life if you told, would you have wanted to say anything?"

Sgt. Kilpack ran a hand over his face and was silent for a moment. He glanced at the photo on his desk of a short-haired brunette who had her arms wrapped around twin boys with big blue eyes and curly hair. They were probably a bit younger than Edie. I wondered if she knew them from school. Sgt Killpack seemed emotional, but blinked a few times, cleared his throat and continued. I hated rehashing everything, but I knew he was just doing his job.

Rita Manning also showed up, wearing black slacks and another neon-colored blouse, this one hot pink. She joined us for a while, then stayed to talk to Sgt. Killpack after I left the room. I felt completely gutted with the admissions I'd offered up over the two days and although I knew I was doing the right thing for my sisters and for me, I couldn't help but feel that guilty twinge again for turning on Mom. Detective Willis let me call Jerri, then bought me a soda and some Peanut M&M's from the vending machine in the lobby, which I snacked on while I waited for my ride.

When Jerri showed up, my sisters accompanied her. The girls looked surprisingly happy and were excited to tell me about their morning.

"Uncle Reed made pancakes for us, and we got to make faces on them with fruit and chocolate chips! I even gave mine hair and a beard with the whipped cream." Edie said, her eyes sparkling.

"Wow, that's great!" I wondered if Reed had told the girls to call him 'Uncle.' It seemed so much more personal than Mr. Argus, or even just Reed.

"And we got to feed the chickens. And pet the bunnies and the goats," Anna added. "I want a bunny, Libby. They're so soft and cuddly."

"Don't forget the dog, Anna!" Edie said. "His name is Ranger."

Jerri flashed a squinty smile at me. "I told the girls they can come see the animals any time they want."

"I had no idea you had all those animals."

"Reed loves all things nature. His "farm" is his hobby. We also have an enormous garden that takes a lot of work, but he does most of it, so I can live with that." She went on to tell me that Reed's regular job was as an administrator at the community college in Millsburg.

Thinking about Reed, I wanted to ask the question that had been burning in my mind all morning. Why was there such a weird exchange between him and Jerri when he'd said my eyes were like his mother's? But before I could ask, Jerri changed the subject.

"Nolan and Rachel's flight lands in two hours. Reed drove to the city to pick them up."

The girls jumped on the topic of Nolan and took turns telling Jerri and me what they wanted to show him at Jerri's house. I tilted my head back and closed my eyes, letting their chatter lull me to sleep.

Back at Jerri's, I busied myself with homework while the girls played outside. Jerri's home was idyllic, and I felt myself relax and focus on my work. I felt grateful to be in such a peaceful setting. Honestly, it was a little strange not feeling on edge.

I heard Reed's truck before I saw it because he tooted the horn all the way down the lane. I abandoned my reading and ran outside, calling the girls to join me on the porch.

"It's Daddy!" they shrieked.

Jerri walked out of the house behind me, drying her hands on a kitchen towel. She'd been cooking and baking up a storm.

Nolan didn't wait for the truck to come to a complete stop before he jumped out the passenger side door. His dark, wavy hair had grown longer in the back since I'd last seen him. He still had the beard, although it was trimmed short. He ran straight for us and scooped the three of us into a giant bear hug. Edie wrapped herself around his leg, squealing. Anna got the middle, and I got his opposite side. I was surprised to discover that I was just as tall as Nolan now. He seemed startled by the height similarity too. Otherwise, he still looked the same, except for a few wrinkles near his eyes and a little gray hair at his temples.

Nolan held Edie at arm's length, his eyes flicking over every inch of her. She giggled and threw herself around his legs while he gave Anna the same inspection. When he was satisfied the girls were okay, he gazed at me.

"Libby, you're so grown up!" He placed his hands on my shoulders and pulled me in for another hug. "I am truly sorry about all of this. You've been carrying a huge burden for so long. I'm so sorry I wasn't here for you."

"Daddy, pick me up!" Edie whined.

He did so, then said, "I have a ton of questions for you. Maybe we can chat later tonight."

Nolan introduced me to his wife, Rachel, who was very obviously pregnant. Rachel had a feathery fullness to her auburn hair. Her green eyes were friendly, and she had the whitest teeth I'd ever seen. She hugged us, then Edie jumped out of Nolan's arms and pulled her toward the animal pens in the backyard.

In the middle of our happy reunion, Jake called. When Jerri told me it was him on the phone, I tensed up, not because I didn't want to talk to him, but because for years I wasn't *allowed* to talk to friends on the phone. But Jerri just handed me the phone and left the room.

"Jake?"

"Libby! How are you? How did the meeting with the police go? How are your sisters?" Jake's questions burst rapid-fire through the phone.

"Whoa, slow down. Better to just tell you from the beginning." I launched into a replay of my chats with Miss Manning and Detective Sealy and Sgt. Killpack. Jake said his interview was fairly straightforward. It was the talk with his parents that was harder for him.

"Were they mad at you? Are they upset at me? Do you still get to play baseball?" I asked.

"Hey, now who needs to slow down?" Jake said with a laugh. "Yes, they were a little mad at me for not coming to them myself. No, they aren't mad at you. They know none of it is your fault. And my baseball playing days are safe. They never even brought it up."

Jake let me express some of my feelings about the whole situation. How I found myself feeling guilty over Mom and how uncertain I was about what the future held. I got a little teary, but Jake reassured me, "Whatever is coming is better than what you had before."

I wished I could hug him through the phone for that comment. Just before I ended the call, I remembered how Reed compared my eyes to his mother's, and I told Jake.

"It probably doesn't mean anything," he said. "Best way to know is to ask." He promised he'd see me tomorrow and hung up.

The rest of the day was a whirlwind of activity, lots of talking and even more food. Jerri's pork chops with mashed potatoes and homemade gravy were to die for. We followed that with strawberry pie, and I managed to eat the whole piece despite my already full stomach.

After the girls had been tucked in to bed by both Nolan and me, he asked if we could chat privately. I spilled my guts about how scared I'd been living with Mom's abusiveness, how helpless and trapped I'd felt and how hurt I'd been when Mom told me she hadn't wanted to raise me, how it all made sense and yet made no sense at all. Nolan expressed his sorrow for the trauma we'd been through. He mentioned counseling for the three of us, which I'd already discussed with Miss Manning.

"You know, I went to counseling after Donna and I divorced," he admitted. "It helped me a lot. But Libby, I want you to know that when your mom and I were married, she only ever became violent with me, never you girls, so, I never thought she'd hurt you." That's when his tears began falling. "I'm so angry with her," he confessed, "but she obviously needs help, and I hope she'll be able to get it."

"What's going to happen now?" I had asked Jerri this question before we got away, but since we'd left, I'd hesitated to ask it again, preferring to live in my bubble of peace.

"That's a good question. The short answer is I'm not exactly sure. The long answer is that Donna and her boyfriend will have charges brought against them very soon and will have to stand trial. I'm going to file for sole custody of Anna and Edie. I'm also going to see how I can become your guardian, if that's what you want."

I so rarely got asked my opinion, but the truth was, I wasn't sure what I wanted. "So, you'll take us all to Florida? How does Rachel feel about that? I mean, you all are having a baby soon, plus with us there, that makes a lot of kids to take care of. Wouldn't I just be in the way?" I knew I was rambling.

Nolan reached out and placed his hand over mine. "I don't want you worrying about that. Rachel is happy to have you. And yes, Florida."

Florida was so far away, and my friends were here in Buckley. Then again, my sisters would be in Florida, and I always missed them when they spent time away with Nolan. Not knowing what to say, I just nodded. Nolan seemed to accept that response as a yes, but I couldn't bring myself to say the words.

Once everyone had gone to bed, I cocooned myself in blankets on the couch and thought about Nolan's offer. What did I want? I made a list in my head. 1. A safe home. 2. For my sisters to grow up in a safe home with loving parents. 3. My friends. 4. Buckley.

The problem was I couldn't have them all.

26
Sunday, April 10, 1988

J ake pulled up to the house and I stepped off the porch to greet
him. He hopped out of his sister's car and looked around. He was
wearing a new Billabong tee shirt and peach-colored shorts. His hair
had even been trimmed. "Wow! This is nice. I never knew this was
here."

I smiled. "Neither did I."

"Are you doing alright?" Jake leaned down for a hug. "I've been
worried about you."

I exhaled deeply. "I'm okay."

He looked skeptical, but didn't say anything, which I
appreciated. We'd already hashed out my feelings enough on the
phone. I didn't want to talk about it anymore.

"Let's go out back. Jerri and Reed are out there watching my
sisters, so maybe we can talk now."

There had been no opportunity to talk to Reed about his cryptic
remarks from Friday night. Now was probably a great time. Nolan
was on the phone with his brother, working out something with
their construction business and Rachel was taking a nap, because in
her words, "this pregnancy is wearing me out." My sisters were busy
with the animals. They were going to have a hard time leaving them
behind to move to Florida. Jerri was reveling in being "Aunt Jerri"
and had spent the morning preparing more delicious food for her
guests. Not having to do all that work myself was a relief. I rested and

finished my homework and tried not to think too much about my situation, or my stress ramped up. I didn't want to think about Mom or the testifying I'd have to do. It was too painful and downright frightening. I was more curious to ask Reed what his mother's eyes had to do with me.

As we walked, Jake casually placed his arm around my shoulders and my heart did a little flip. I smiled at him and he winked. Ooh, a double flip this time.

An arbor separated the front yard from the back. The vines covering it were turning green and Jerri said it would have pink flowers trailing over the wooden posts by June. "It's like something out of a fairy tale," I said. Jake just laughed.

We found Reed and Jerri rocking on the red porch swing. Jerri hopped up to hug Jake and I introduced him to Reed. As Jerri scooted herself back onto the swing, I asked, "Can I ask you a question?"

They answered in unison. "Of course."

I settled into a wicker chair, and Jake sat in an identical one across from me. "Reed, you said my eyes look just like your mother's eyes, then you both looked at me like I was a puzzle you couldn't solve. What was that all about?"

Jerri snuck a quick peek at Reed, and he nodded. I loved how they could communicate with just a look. She pushed her bangs out of her eyes and leaned forward, hands on her knees.

"When I first saw you, when you applied for the job, I was startled by how similar you look to Reed's mom. Looking into your eyes feels just like it did to look into hers."

"So that's all?" I asked. "It's just a coincidence then." I shrugged at Jake and started to rise from my chair. Jerri held out her hand to stop me.

"I'll show you what I mean." She patted Reed's leg. "Go get that picture of your mom."

Reed stood, and the swing bounced slightly and swayed. He walked into the house, letting the screen door slam behind him. Edie and Anna squealed as the bunnies in the pen reacted to the sudden noise and darted from their laps into the hutch. Edie dragged a gray bunny out of the hutch and handed it to Anna, then pulled a white rabbit out for herself. They were going to love the animals to death.

"I'm sorry about them." I apologized.

"Psh. Don't be sorry. I love having them here. Having children around my house is something I've only ever dreamed about."

"Haven't you had to work this weekend?" I knew Jerri worked at least one weekend day, but she'd been home the whole time we'd been here.

"I took this week off. I'm thinking it might be a bit chaotic for all of us."

I swallowed hard and stared at Jake. I didn't want to think about court or school or making plans. I just wanted to live in the moment.

Reed reappeared, letting the door slam again. The bang elicited more shrieks from my sisters. I shook my head, amused. At least they seemed happy.

Reed handed me a black and white photograph. "This is my mother, Kathryn."

The young woman in the picture had large curls rolled up around her face and head. When I focused on her face, I almost dropped the photo.

"See what I mean?" Jerri's voice was soft.

The young woman, Kathryn, had brown hair and large eyes that were a bit wide set, just like mine. Her smile revealed a dimple in her left cheek, also just like me. Her nose was more upturned, but other than that and the old-fashioned hairdo, she could have been my twin.

"Whoa. I didn't realize you meant I look exactly like her! How is that possible?"

Jake must have been anxious to see the photo because he unfolded himself from his chair and stood behind me. I heard his sharp inhale, then he placed his hand on my shoulder.

Reed rubbed his stubbly jaw. "We're wondering if you might be related to me through your father."

I gasped and Jake squeezed my shoulder.

"Seriously?" I squeaked out the question. Was he for real?

Reed chuckled. "Got your attention now?"

"But Jerri, you said you knew my father. You said he was your friend, and you hung out with him before he left town. Wouldn't you have known if he was related to Reed?" I didn't see a connection.

"Oh, no. I didn't meet Reed for several years after I last saw your dad. If their last names were the same, I might have wondered, but not necessarily, because Reed is from Ohio, not from around here."

"So why do you think it's a possibility now?" I was still confused. I saw Jake slide back into his chair, while the girls giggled and squealed behind me.

Reed jumped in. "Well, there's a whole line of family I've never known. In fact, I don't even know their names."

Okay, this was getting weird. I pinched my arm to make sure I wasn't dreaming. I tried to catch Jake's eye, but his eyes were glued on Reed. He leaned forward, eager to hear more.

"From the family stories I've heard, my mother's dad and his brother had an argument over some land. Who was entitled to it, which portion each would receive, something like that. It caused a huge rift in the family and split them into 'sides.' Mom's father chose to move away to avoid his brother, and they never reconciled. That's how my mom and I both grew up in Dayton." Reed picked up his glass of ice water and took a long swallow.

"The brother and his family stayed on the family land which is over near Millsburg. As far as I can tell, they raised their family there, and then the next generation stayed in the area, meaning that my mom would have cousins in this area. I think your dad might be related to them." Reed peered at me, waiting for my reaction.

My jaw hung open and I snapped it closed. Jake stared at me, his hands extended palms up. My mind flew into overdrive, trying to connect the dots

Jerri broke the silence. "When I first saw your resemblance to Kathryn, I did think it was a coincidence. I saw your name on the job application, and I immediately knew who you were because I knew your mom and dad, so I thought nothing more of it. I happened to mention the resemblance to Reed a few weeks ago and we've been discussing the possibility."

"So, you don't know anything for sure? It's just a guess?" I felt my spirits deflate a little.

"We're going to get his family puzzle pieced together and we'll know soon enough. Reed's already been making phone calls."

We chatted for a few minutes more, then Rachel and Nolan joined us on the porch. Reed popped a couple of lawn chairs open, then he and Jerri took the open seats, giving the swing to Nolan and Rachel. I introduced them to Jake, a tickle of nerves in my belly. It was important to me that they like him. Nolan thanked Jake for his part in rescuing us and then he and Rachel had what felt like a hundred questions for him. When Jake realized he might be conversing with them for a while, he settled back into his seat. After the fifth question, I asked Jerri if Nolan knew about their theory that I might be related to Reed. Nolan's eyebrows shot up and his eyes shifted around the group. I guess that meant no.

Reed filled them in, and Nolan shook his head back and forth the entire time. "No kidding?"

"Wow! Wouldn't that be something?" Rachel's smile was wide.

I handed Nolan the photograph of Kathryn.

"Holy smokes!" he whispered. Then to me he said, "You do look like her!"

Rachel seemed just as surprised. "Wow, Libby, it's you dressed up for the forties. Or maybe thirties? I'm not sure." Her hands rested on top of her protruding belly, while her short legs barely skimmed the ground as she and Nolan gently swung.

For the next few minutes, we discussed the possibility. What if I found my dad's family? What would that mean to my situation now? I didn't want to get my hopes up, but I couldn't help myself. I could see in the way Jerri looked at me that her heart soared with hope too. No wonder she'd shown me so much care and concern. Every time she looked at me, I reminded her of someone she loved, and she had showered me with that same love. I choked back the emotion I felt in my heart, but my body took over and I reached for Jerri, holding her tightly as my tears gushed. Whatever happened from here on out, at least I knew I had people on my side, people who were rooting for me, people who loved me. It was the best feeling in the world.

I'd gone through a lot of garbage, but this felt like a true turning point for me. I had Jerri, Jake, Holly and Nicole to thank for bringing me to this point. Without them, I wouldn't be looking forward to a brighter future. A future that included everyone who surrounded me on the back porch and maybe even a family I'd never met that was a part of me too.

Epilogue
April 23, 1989
One year later

I watched in the mirror as Jerri wrapped the final section of my hair around the curling iron. She caught my eye and smiled. "You're going to knock his socks off!"

I blushed under my makeup but said nothing. I checked my watch. Jake would be here in half an hour, plenty of time to change into my sparkly royal blue dress with matching heels.

Jerri released my hair, and it fell into a perfect coil. She set it in place with hairspray, then gave my shoulders a squeeze. "I'll let you change now." She softly shut the door behind her as she left the room.

Finally, this night was here! Last year when Jake said he would take me to the Prom this year, I had hoped it would happen, but my life had been so different then. It had been difficult to hope for a better future. Now, it was really happening.

When I first went back to school after Mom and Roy were arrested, I spent my days wishing I could run away and hide. Everyone was watching me, whispering about me, or asking questions I couldn't answer. Surprisingly, I did make some new friends. They were the ones who were genuinely concerned about my welfare, and I was glad to have them rally around me.

My mother was convicted on felony child abuse charges last May and sentenced to eight years in prison. Roy had lesser charges and was sentenced to two years. Mom gave up her parental rights to Nolan without much of a fight, so that was a lot less stress on everyone. We thought she'd fight it just for the sake of a fight, but that didn't happen. Mom had recently started writing letters to us girls and although I wanted to rip the first letter to shreds without even reading it, I was also curious about what she had to say. She apologized for the way she'd treated me, for her alcohol problem, for never giving me information about my father and for holding her anger with him against me. I think looking at me often elicited feelings of hate and revenge because I look so much like my father. I know because I've seen pictures of him. Mom told me the drinking made it worse, and she never could "get her head on straight." She asked for forgiveness whenever I could bring myself to give that to her, even if it took years.

I wrinkled the letter from gripping it so tightly and after I finished it, I cried all over it too. Then I smoothed it out and carefully folded it back into the envelope for safekeeping. Mom mentioned the counseling she was receiving and asked if we were seeing a counselor too. Of course we were. And still are. Edie and Anna were proving to be very resilient, probably because of the stable home life they now had. My weekly appointment with a counselor in Millsburg was helping with my feelings of anger and guilt. She was helping me realize the abuse wasn't my fault and my sessions with her gave me an outlet for my emotions. I was working on forgiveness, but I knew it would take a while. Maybe even years like Mom said.

Nolan took me and my sisters to Florida once things were settled with the court. We enjoyed swimming in his pool and adapting to a new home life. Because I'd been unsure about moving to Florida, I told Nolan and Rachel I'd at least go for the remainder of the summer. Jerri had been eager for me to live with her and Reed, but I decided I should stay with my sisters at least for a while. Then I wavered on that almost every day. When Nolan and Rachel saw me struggling to make the choice, they let me know they would support me either way. Nolan said I could go back to Buckley and live with Jerri and Reed for my last two years of high school, then come to Florida during the summers and Christmastime.

Jake and I talked on the phone a few times a week and I talked with Holly and Nicole just as much. Our friendships were cemented together because of the experience we'd gone through. Jerri also called quite often. Even she and Rachel talked a lot. I think it helped Rachel as she adjusted to becoming a full-time mom before she even had her own baby.

Rachel had her baby at the end of July and that changed my feelings about staying in Florida. Little Kevin was smothered in love from his parents and especially Edie and Anna. What surprised me was how much I enjoyed caring for him. Holding him, rocking him, admiring his tiny features mesmerized me and filled a hole in my soul. And so, I decided to stay for school, at least for the first term. Jake was sad to hear I wasn't coming back right away but I promised to return soon.

Jerri couldn't have been more excited when I told her I was coming back to Buckley after the first term. You'd have thought Ed McMahon had shown up on her doorstep to award her millions in the Publisher's Clearing House Sweepstakes. My friends threw me a surprise welcome home party, and it *was* a surprise to see how many of my schoolmates showed up.

The transition back was easy. Reed and Jerri relished the chance to help "raise me right," an opportunity I knew they'd wished for but never gotten. I was finally allowed to be involved in extracurricular activities, and it opened a whole new world for me. I made the girls' basketball team, just as Holly had predicted. I also discovered classes that let me explore my love of music. I decided to learn how to play the piano and I turned my habit of constantly tapping on every surface into learning to play the drums. I learned notes, tone, pitch and rhythm. And even though my recitals included much younger children who far exceeded my abilities, I was okay with it. Some of us start things later than others, but that's alright. Nolan was paying for the lessons, and I practiced at the school every morning. Reed and Jerri had also found a clunker for me to drive. I finally felt like the real Libby.

Reed and Jerri also investigated the possibility of me and Reed's mother, Kathryn, being related. With the help of the county records clerk, they found that my father's parents are Ron and Sophia Fletcher. Just as they suspected, Kathryn and my Grandma Sophia are cousins, meaning so are Reed and my dad, Dennis.

The best part about their discovery is that my dad's parents are still alive, plus he has two sisters and a brother, which means I have grandparents and aunts, uncles and cousins. I felt a little overwhelmed by sudden, instant family, but they welcomed me with open arms. When I first met Sophia, she cried, overcome by how much I resembled my dad. The thrill of finding my new family hasn't worn off and I visit them at least once a week. I feel a sense of belonging there, just like I do with Nolan and with Jerri. They are all my home.

I glanced at my watch again and chided myself for dawdling. I slipped the silky blue gown with the sequined and beaded bodice over my body and remembered my daydream of wearing a royal blue dress to the prom with Jake. That's why when I saw the dress, I knew it was the one. I slid my pearl stud earrings in and checked my makeup one last time. Stepping into my heels I did a little spin in the mirror. The girl staring back at me looked so different from the Libby I used to know.

The doorbell chimed and I froze, my heart catching in my throat. Jake's voice floated upstairs, and I couldn't help but smile. I descended the stairs, watching Jake's face for his reaction. His blue eyes sparkled as much as the gown and his grin stretched from ear to ear. This is where I want to be, surrounded by those I love and who love me in return. I wouldn't have it any other way.

My journey has not been easy and if I could change anything from the past, it would be to have trusted more in those around me. If they'd known what kind of life we lived, we could have gotten help sooner and avoided some of the trauma we endured. But that life is in the past, and for now I just want to enjoy what I've got. Jake takes my hand, and we walk out the door. Together.

THE END

K. D. Capener is a graduate of Weber State University. She has always been an avid book enthusiast. Her favorite genres are mystery and historical fiction, but she's wanted to be a children's book author since she was young. She has too many hobbies and wishes there was enough time for all of them each day. She loves puzzles of all kinds, game nights, genealogy and traveling. She lives in beautiful Utah with her family. *Hidden by These Walls* is her debut novel.

FIND OUT MORE AT KDCAPENER.com and connect with her on Facebook or Instagram.

Acknowledgments

The dream of writing a book has been with me for years, but making the decision to finally take the leap was both exciting and nerve-wracking. I wasn't sure if I could bring my vision to life or find the right words to fill the pages. But without the support, guidance, and encouragement of many wonderful people, this book would never have become a reality.

I'm deeply grateful to author Kaylynn Flanders for patiently answering my many questions about the writing industry and for being my biggest cheerleader along the way. Her encouragement helped me believe in myself and gave me the confidence to reach this goal.

A huge thank you to the amazing ladies who read my very rough draft and gave me such helpful, honest feedback that made this story so much better. Carly Zemcik, Kelly Hammack, Jodie Allen, and Brenda Burton—thank you, thank you, thank you!

A heartfelt thank you to Madison Taylor for pointing me in the right direction when I felt a little lost. I'm also incredibly grateful to both Madison and Wendy Swensen for their careful editing and proofreading, which helped polish the final manuscript.

Thank you to author Richard Paul Evans and the AuthorReady team for offering such valuable opportunities and a clear roadmap to publication. The monthly Zoom calls and online courses have been an incredible learning experience.

Since I'm one who always judges a book by its cover, I must thank Getcovers.com for their amazing cover design.

And last—but most importantly—my deepest thanks go to my family for their unwavering enthusiasm, encouragement, and support. To my husband, Danny: your technical know-how (and patience with my lack of it) made this entire journey possible. We truly make a great team! To my amazing children and their wonderful spouses—Carly, Jace, Preston, Kimber, and Spencer—thank you for being proud of your mama. Your love and belief in me means the world. I love you all so much!

Resources

Call 911 if you are in immediate danger.

Childhelp National Child Abuse Hotline: 1-800-4-A-CHILD (1-800-422-4453) or childhlep.org

National Domestic Violence Hotline: 1-800-799-SAFE (7233) or text START to 88788 or TheHotline.org

National Coalition Against Domestic Violence: ncadv.org

Individual states also have hotline numbers that can be found online.